(1896-1970) was born Elsa Yureyevna Kagan in Moscow, the daughter of Jewish intellectuals. Her older sister, Lili Brik, was Mayakovsky's lover, and Elsa and Lili were closely involved with the Russian Futurist movement. In 1918 Elsa married a French naval officer, André Triolet, with whom she lived in Tahiti for the two years of their marriage. Elsa then went to Berlin and, encouraged by Maxim Gorky, she published her first book in the Soviet Union, *Na Taiti* (1925).

That year she moved to Paris, where, in 1928, she met Louis Aragon, the Surrealist poet. They lived together, marrying in 1939, and through him she knew the major writers and artists of this century, including Matisse and Picasso. During the thirties, together with Salvador Dali, Giacometti, Leonor Fini and Meret Oppenheim, she produced jewellery and accessories for the fashion house of Schiaparelli. She published three further books in the Soviet Union, but the increasing censorship there prompted her to turn to the French language. In 1938 her first french novel, *Bonsoir Thérèse*, was published. By this time Aragon and Triolet had become affiliated to the Communist party, although she never became a party member. In 1939 Triolet's book on Mayakovsky was seized and destroyed by the government, and when France surrendered to the Nazis, she and Aragon fled to the unoccupied zone. In 1942 they were forced underground. Important figures of the French Resistance, they edited and contributed to *Les Lettres Françaises* and Elsa wrote stories of Occupied France, published illegally by Underground presses. Three of these interlinking stories, later published in book form as *Le Premier accroc coûte deux cents francs* (A Fine of Two Hundred Francs, 1945), were awarded the *Prix Goncourt*.

Following the war, Elsa Triolet was decorated as a heroine of the French Resistance. She became a leader of the National Council of Writers and the Union of French Women, and a delegate to various peace conferences. She was awarded the *Prix de la Fraternité* for her novel on the subject of anti-semitism and refugees, *Le Rendez-vous des étrangers* (1956), but her most controversial work, *Le Monument* (1957), was denounced by the Communist party. She published twenty-seven books in all, the last, *Le Rossignol se tait à l'aube*, appeared in 1970, the year she died from heart disease.

ELSA TRIOLET

A FINE OF
TWO HUNDRED
FRANCS

With a new Introduction by
HELENA LEWIS

PENGUIN BOOKS – VIRAGO PRESS

PENGUIN BOOKS
Viking Penguin Inc., 40 West 23rd Street,
New York, New York 10010, U.S.A.
Penguin Books Ltd, Harmondsworth,
Middlesex, England
Penguin Books Australia Ltd, Ringwood,
Victoria, Australia
Penguin Books Canada Limited, 2801 John Street,
Markham, Ontario, Canada L3R 1B4
Penguin Books (N.Z.) Ltd, 182–190 Wairau Road,
Auckland 10, New Zealand

First published by Editions Denoel, Paris, 1945 under the title
Le premier accroc coute deux cents francs
First published in the United States of America by Reynal & Hitchcock 1947
First published in Great Britain by Hutchinson International Authors Ltd. 1949
This edition first published in Great Britain by Virago Press Limited 1986
Published by arrangement with Harcourt Brace Jovanovich, Inc.
Published in Penguin Books 1986

Printed in Great Britain by
Anchor Brendon Ltd. of Tiptree, Essex

Set in Garamond

CONTENTS

INTRODUCTION

ELSA TRIOLET was a major literary and political figure on the left in Europe. The first woman to win the Prix Goncourt, she was also decorated for her heroic role in the French Resistance and was a peace activist in the post-war era. Author of twenty-seven books, she was an essayist, a journalist, a biographer, a theatre critic and a translator of Russian prose and poetry. It was she who introduced French readers to the work of Marina Tsvetaeva, Anna Akhmatova, Osip Mandelstamm, Velimir Khlebnikov and Vladimir Mayakovsky, and she also translated classic nineteenth-century writers such as Chekhov and Gogol. But most important, she was a novelist whose fiction is a unique blend of political *engagement* and fantasy. Although she was internationally known in the 1940s and 1950s, she is now unfairly neglected except in France. And even there she does not have the literary reputation she deserves. She was a woman and a foreigner and therefore not part of the French literary establishment. She was married to Louis Aragon, a more famous writer, so inevitably she was "Mme Aragon who also writes". Although never a Party member she was identified as a Communist and so was not seriously regarded by non-Communist critics. But she was never sufficiently orthodox for the Communists since her novels are not works of socialist realism. They lack the "correct" style, the necessary optimism and the idealized working-class heroes. Her love of the bizarre owes more to Gogol, E.T.A. Hoffmann and Edgar Allen Poe than to the proletarian literature movement. She was also influenced by the existentialist fiction of Camus and Sartre and was one of the pioneers of the *engagé* novel of the Second World War. Clearly, political considerations have prevented a valid assessment of this controversial figure.

Triolet was born Elsa Yureyevna Kagan in 1896, the younger daughter of intellectual Russian Jews privileged to live beyond the Jewish Pale in Moscow. Swept up in the excitement of the years before the Bolshevik Revolution, she and her older sister, Lili, became part of the Russian Futurist avant-garde. Through Lili's husband, Osip Brik, and Lili's lover, Mayakovsky, with whom the Briks lived in a *ménage à trois*, the two beautiful sisters were at the centre of the movement. The group published *LEF (Left Front of Art)*, the most important Futurist journal. But it lasted only until the mid 1920s when restrictive government policies put an end to the cultural freedom of the earlier period. In 1917, André Triolet, a young French naval officer, came to Moscow as part of a diplomatic mission sent to persuade the Bolshevik leaders not to sign a separate peace treaty with Germany. Like many in the delegation, he came to sympathize with the Soviet cause and frequented Futurist gatherings at which he met Elsa. They married in 1918 and went to Tahiti where they lived for two years. André was a rich man interested only in horses and in beautiful women; not surprisingly, the marriage failed.

Elsa, who kept the name Triolet from then on, went alone to Berlin where there was a large Russian colony. There she met another Futurist, the formalist critic and writer, Viktor Shklovsky, who fell in love with her. She did not return his affections but agreed that they could write to each other provided he promised never to speak of love. Using their correspondence, Shklovksy published an epistolary novel called *Zoo or Letters Not About Love*, subtitled *The Third Heloise*, an anagram on the name Elsa. Without her knowledge, he had included some of Triolet's letters in his book and, as was customary, he presented a copy to Maxim Gorky, then in Berlin. But Gorky hated it. The only good things in the book, he said, were the letters signed by a woman, and when Shklovsky confessed that a woman friend had actually written them, Gorky insisted on meeting her. Later, Triolet said that without Gorky's encouragment she would never have become a writer. It was at his suggestion that she wrote her first book, *Na Taiti*, recollections of her life in Tahiti, and it was published in the Soviet Union in 1925.

As Gorky's protegé, Triolet published two more books, *Zemlianitchka (Wild Strawberries, 1926)*, a sketch based on childhood diaries, and *Zachtchitni Tsvet (Camouflage, 1928)*, also largely autobiographical, about an unhappy Russian woman living alone in Paris. Both books were attacked by Soviet critics for their pessimism and despair, which were a reflection of Triolet's own feelings during this period. She was now in Paris, having divorced her husband, and like her fictional heroine she was an object of suspicion. As a foreign woman with no job and no visible means of support, she was rumoured to be either a spy or a prostitute. She was actually living on money André had given her and, discouraged by the hostile reception of her work, she was unable to go on writing and could not decide whether to stay in Paris or return to the Soviet Union. But in 1928 she met the French Surrealist poet, Louis Aragon, whose work she admired because it reminded her of Mayakovsky's poetry. They began living together but did not marry until 1939. Aragon was gifted and charming but rather unstable and seemed destined to be dominated by strong personalities such as Nancy Cunard, who was his lover before he met Triolet, and André Breton, the leader of the Surrealists, who was his close friend. He was an illegitimate child whose family had brought him up to believe that his grandmother was his mother and his mother his older sister. Only as an adult did he learn the truth about his parentage. He was genuinely devoted to Triolet and they remained together for almost forty years. On the surface, they appeared to have an ideal marriage of intellectual equals. Yet much of their well-publicized intimacy must have been a facade, probably forced upon them by Communist Party morality, because Aragon had homosexual leanings.

Through Aragon, Triolet became part of the Surrealist movement in Paris. Her convictions about literature and politics had been formed by the Futurists, and at first she admired the Surrealists because they too professed to be revolutionaries and were nominally members of the French Communist Party. But she was exceptionally politically astute and soon realized that their art, with its blatant sexuality and its ludicrous games and jokes, could never reach the masses. She saw that, like the Futurists, the Surrealists had become politically isolated. They were being attacked by the French Communists in ways that were similar to the Soviet campaigns against Mayakovsky which had ended with his suicide. She also hated Breton for his extremely conventional attitudes towards women, and Triolet, author of three books, was unwilling to play the subordinate role of muse and inspiration expected of women among the Surrealists. She wanted Aragon to break with the Surrealists so that together they could join the mainstream of the left, and it was she who persuaded him to become a militant Communist.

The couple were invited to the Soviet Union to attend the International Congress of Revolutionary Writers in 1930 and she used her influence to have Aragon appointed a delegate from France. He was charged by Breton with securing a favourable resolution on Surrealism, which he failed to do. Instead, he became so carried away by his new enthusiasm for proletarian literature that he wrote his first socialist realist poem, *Front Rouge*. The violence of the poem, which calls for the shooting of various politicians, so alarmed the French government that Aragon was accused of inciting treason. The Surrealists rallied loyally to his defence and charges were eventually dropped. But Aragon broke with them in 1932, never again spoke to Breton, and soon became the leading intellectual of the French Communist Party. He ruthlessly put his past behind him and moulded himself into a socialist realist writer. The more he succeeded, however, the worse his fiction became. His five-volume novel, *Les Communistes*, is virtually unreadable and, indeed, Aragon must have agreed because it was never finished.

Interestingly, Triolet never joined the Party, and unlike Aragon she ignored the dictates of socialist realism, or rather, she redefined it to suit herself. In her definition, it is merely a perspective which "imposes neither content nor form, leaving to the artist complete liberty of creation. At least," she added, "that is how I understand socialist realism."[1] Her fiction combined political themes with elements of fantasy and humour and, while she asserted that "the novel is the intermediary between man and history", she also said, "I delight in the dimension of the fantastic found at the heart of reality."

In the 1930s, because they desperately needed money, Triolet began to make jewellery for the *haute couture* houses. Her creations of metal, plastic and even horsehair sold very well but she hated the wealthy, reactionary clientele and wanted to return to writing. She wrote a book about these experiences in 1934, later translated into French as *Colliers*. But it was rejected by her Soviet publishers even though her contempt for that bourgeois milieu was clear and the political "slant" would seem to have been correct. With the Kirov assassination trials beginning in 1934, censorship became increasingly severe, and with the death of her mentor Gorky in 1936 it became even more difficult to publish. Triolet's solution to this dilemma was one which very few writers have attempted: she changed languages and in 1938 her first fiction in French, a book of short stories called *Bonsoir Thérèse*, appeared. Her style in French, as in Russian, is spare, and many of the stories are funny and whimsical. But they also reveal her feelings of loneliness and her consciousness of being a foreigner in France. Her sense of exile was all the more deeply felt because while she often visited the Soviet Union the Russia of her childhood no longer existed. The heroines of these early stories seem to drift helplessly through life and contrast sharply with the strong, independent women she created later.

1.   Elsa Triolet, *La Lutte avec l'ange* in *Le Monument*, Paris: Gallimard (1957) 1965, 220.

When Germany invaded France, Aragon was drafted into a special punishment battalion for political unreliables while Triolet had to endure repeated police interrogations and searches of their apartment. Even before the fall of France, many Communist leaders were jailed or forced into exile. Party newspapers were shut down and Triolet was again a victim of censorship. A book she had just published, *Maïakovski poète russe: souvenirs* (1939), was seized by the government and destroyed. Hardly a threat to the Republic, the book contained selections of Mayakovsky's poetry, Triolet's reminiscences of him and comments of Soviet critics. But it was one of many titles destroyed in the government's anti-Communist campaign merely because they had been issued by a Party press. After France surrendered, Triolet and Aragon fled south to the Unoccupied Zone and stayed with various friends. At first, unless writers were willing to work for the pro-German Vichy press, they could not publish at all. German censors had issued a *Liste Otto* of forbidden works by or about Jews, Communists or well-known anti-Fascists, thus effectively silencing the left. There were many pro-Nazi collaborators such as Aragon's former friend, Drieu La Rochelle, who denounced Triolet as a Jew and a Communist in his Fascist journal, *Je suis partout*. But there were others, like Vercors, author of the first Resistance novel, *Le Silence de la mer* who founded the clandestine *Editions de minuit* as an outlet for Resistance writers. His press illegally published more than twenty-five books and it became a mark of distinction to have been published by him.

In November 1942, when the whole of France was occupied, Triolet and Aragon were warned they were to be arrested and were forced to go underground for the rest of the war. They became major figures in the intellectual Resistance and Triolet's record was outstanding. Camus and Sartre, whom Triolet met in the Resistance, maintained that it is wrong to make a distinction between writing and activism because writing is really a political act. This was never more true than in the Resistance when writing was activism of the most dangerous kind, when simply being caught with illegal weapons in one's possession could mean deportation and death. Triolet, Aragon, Camus and Sartre all wrote for *Les Lettres françaises*, the most important literary journal of the Underground published in Paris by the Conseil national des écrivains, the organization of Resistance writers. The founders, who included Jacques Decour, François Mauriac and Jean Paulhan, proudly declared that the journal was to be "the writers' arm of combat in the struggle to the death of the French nation to free itself from its oppressors". The danger was great and Decour, arrested with the copy for the first issue, was executed. But others took his place and Triolet and Aragon both later served as editors. This meant they had to make frequent illegal trips to Paris, and once, as they were crossing the Demarcation Line, they were arrested. They spent several weeks in jail but their false papers held up and they were released. On another occasion, Triolet was on a train to Paris with an underground manuscript when a German soldier came through the compartments searching the passengers' luggage. There was no time to hide her notebooks and she was sure she would be arrested. But as the soldier leafed through the papers, it became clear that he could not read French. He simply returned the notebooks to her and left. She was also editor of another underground journal, *Le Drôme en armes*, and she was a leader and courier for another Resistance group, Les Etoiles. She made trips to the mountains to report on the *maquis*, those who had taken to the hills to evade forced labour in German factories, and she served as liaison for escaped Russian prisoners of war.

Of the fiction she wrote during the war, Triolet said, "to write is my freedom, my defiance and my luxury", and her work clearly reveals her commitment. Her stories vividly evoke daily life under the Occupation; the mass exodus of panic-stricken Parisians fleeing south while the Germans bombarded them from the air; the newspaper columns on "how to find your loved ones"; the ration cards; the lack of heat, electricity and water; the black-marketeering, and the accidental deaths caused by rationing the gas supply. The plot of one of her best novellas, *Mille regrets* (1942), turns on this last point. The aging and destitute mistress of a man whom she believes was killed in action dies by asphyxiation, and the ending is deliberately ambiguous because the reader cannot be sure whether her death was an accident or suicide. Surprisingly, the novel *Le Cheval blanc* (1943), translated as *The White Charger* (1946) and as *The White Horse* (1951) was legally published in Vichy France. Its hero Michel, an aimless playboy, secretly longs to be a knight on a white horse, a doer of brave deeds. Only when the war begins does he find his cause and he dies at the Front, a hero at last. The last lines of the book, deleted by the censors, said that Beilinky, a Jew who had been Michel's closest friend, never knew Michel was dead because he had been deported and "they don't forward your mail to the concentration camps". But readers understood. The French became adept at reading between the lines and grasping the veiled allusions made by anti-Nazi writers.

A Fine of Two Hundred Francs is the book for which Triolet won the Prix Goncourt. The title comes from the code used to signal the Allied landings in Normandy, and in 1945 its meaning was clear. It also evoked memories of pre-war France as the phrase was often seen in provincial cafés above the billiard table, warning customers against tearing the expensive felt. The stories were originally published illegally and the "Epilogue" was based on a true account of a parachute drop that resulted in severe German reprisals against a small village. The "Epilogue" was unusual in that Triolet rarely recounted atrocities or even details of the clandestine activities of Resistance workers. She usually preferred to explore the ways in which people contrived to live under such extreme conditions, as she did in these three stories. The magical city of Avignon where Petrarch met Laura, is the setting for the first story, *The Lovers of Avignon*, but the German occupation leaves no time for love. It was originally published in book form by Vercors' Editions de minuit in 1943 under the pseudonym, Laurent Daniel. Triolet chose the name to honour the Resistance heroine Danièle Casanova, founder of the Communist women's organization the Union des femmes françaises, and her husband Laurent. The couple had been deported to Auschwitz where Danièle died, but Laurent survived to become an important post-war Communist official. An interesting passage has been left out of the translation in which the hero praises the role of the Party in the Resistance and calls it "the Party of those who've been shot". After the liberation, this became a popular slogan and, to Triolet's astonishment, Communist posters all over France asked everyone to "join the Party of those who've been shot, as a writer of the Resistance has called it".

Also clandestine was *The Private Life of Alexis Slavsky*. The artist hero is, in part, a fictional portrayal of Matisse who was said to have complained bitterly because the war was interrupting his work. Triolet and Aragon knew Matisse and saw him in Nice where he was living during the war with his mistress. His attitude was very different from that of their good friend Picasso, who was very much *engagé* and, like many others, Triolet was critical of Matisse for not being involved even though his wife and daughter were Resistance workers imprisoned by the Gestapo. Slavsky was the first of many artist heroes in Triolet's novels for she was fascinated by the theme of art and the artist's function in society and her fictional characters were often painters, actresses, singers or writers. *Notebooks Buried Under a Peachtree* is a sequel to the previous story and it is the most autobiographical of the three. The notebooks of the title are a personal journal written by Louise as a way to pass the time while in hiding from the Gestapo. Although she is French, she reminisces about her childhood in Russia, and her recollections of sleigh rides in Moscow, of her nursemaid, and of a beautiful older sister whom she envies, are actually Triolet's memories. When Louise speaks of writing articles about the *maquis*, of driving around with them in a stolen Gestapo staff car and of working with the Communists in the Resistance, these were, in fact, Triolet's experiences. And like Louise, Triolet had hidden her manuscripts by burying them in the garden. It is possible that Triolet was happier during the war than at any other time for it was then that she discovered her own strength and courage, and in the comradeship of the Resistance she could escape from her loneliness and sense of exile. She said later that only in the Resistance did she come to feel that France was her country.

In a lighter vein, Triolet's love of fantasy literature was apparent even during the war years. She was interested in existentialist theory and she especially admired the absurdist fiction of Camus. In 1944, she wrote a comic story about an elderly woman who dies then inexplicably comes back to life, begins to grow younger every day and lives her life in reverse. The title *Quel est cet étranger qui n'est pas d'ici, ou le mythe de la baronne Mélanie*, deliberately incorporated elements from the titles of Camus' *The Stranger* and *The Myth of Sisyphus* as a homage to his work. While Triolet had good relations with Camus during the war, they later became bitter enemies. She and Aragon also knew Simone de Beauvoir and Sartre but after the war their paths diverged politically and France's two most famous literary couples had no contact with each other.

After the brief euphoria of the Liberation, the ideals of the Resistance were shattered, and no one has written more movingly than Triolet of the *révolution manquée*, the disillusionment of the left with conservative Cold War politics. In the novel *Les Fantômes armés* (1947) she incorporates actual incidents of former heroes of the Resistance who, now being treated as criminals, are in jail for having stolen from collaborators during the war. She often uses characters from previous books, showing them in a different light, and in *Les fantômes armés*

Celestin, hero of *The Lovers of Avignon*, reappears. But now he is a general involved in a sinister military plot against the Fourth Republic that originates in Algeria. Remarkably, it was just such an attempted *coup d'état* that toppled the government and brought De Gaulle to power in 1958. A disturbing book, *L'Inspecteur des ruines* (1948), translated as *The Inspector of Ruins* (1953) and seemingly not at all *engagé*, is also a pessimistic reflection on the post-war mentality of France from the perspective of the left. The hero, Antonin, returns after the war from a German prison camp only to find that his village has been destroyed and his family killed. In despair, he goes to Paris and meets a black marketeer who proposes to hire him as "inspector of ruins". His idea is that Antonin should go to Germany and sift through the rubble of bombed-out cities looking for valuables. At the end, Antonin dies a senseless death, and with no papers and no one to identify him, he remains the "unknown man", a casualty of the war like the "unknown soldier".

Triolet's bitterness earned her many enemies after the war. She vehemently denounced former collaborators whose books had become popular and she supported the campaign to blacklist them conducted by *Les Lettres françaises*, now a Communist journal. She argued angrily with such former friends as Camus, Mauriac and Paulhan who opposed the black-list, and she organized a "Battle of the Books" to encourage sales of left-wing writers' works. Alarmed by the intensity of post-war anti-Communism, Triolet worked closely with the Party and she and Aragon, dubbed "the royal couple of the Communist Party", became leaders of the international peace movement. They marched at the head of protest demonstrations against the atom bomb, NATO, the Korean War and the execution of the Rosenbergs. Triolet also served as vice-president of the Conseil national des écrivains, which continued in existence but was increasingly dominated by the Party, and she was active in the Union des femmes françaises. The Cold War inspired her book *Le Cheval roux* (1953), about the aftermath of a nuclear holocaust, but despite its apocalyptic theme it has some comic elements. She called this novel her "anticipated autobiography" because the heroine, Elsa, is a Communist writer in France. She has lived through an atomic war but is hideously disfigured, and the first survivor she meets, equally disfigured, is a conservative American preacher. This grotesque Adam and Eve join forces and go in search of others and they are appalled to encounter several settlements ruled over by petty dictators. Everyone is sure that the Americans will come to rescue them and they refuse to believe that there are no more Americans. Elsa and the preacher leave in disgust to found their own egalitarian society even though the threat of lethal radiation hangs over them.

In *Le Rendez-vous des étrangers* (1956), Triolet explores the fate of the victims of history: refugees, stateless persons and poverty-stricken immigrants. There is no real plot. Aragon called this experimental fiction a "collage", and Triolet called it her "proletarian novel" because it describes the plight of such groups as Polish miners, Algerian workers and Spanish exiles, all badly treated by the French. It could also be called her "Jewish novel" since several of the main characters are Jews. The heroine, Olga, is a beautiful Russian woman who has changed her last name because she is ashamed of her traitor father; she has chosen the name Heller because it sounds Jewish. This is the only book in which Triolet deals with anti-semitism. She did not indentify as a Jew, but as she grew older she expressed an interest in Israel, despite the Party's view of Zionism as racist and of Israel as a tool of American imperialism. The book won the Prix de la fraternité, awarded by Le Mouvement contre le racisme, l'anti-Sémitisme et pour la paix, an organization founded during the Resistance.

In 1957 Triolet's most controversial novel, *Le Monument*, was published. It appeared during the prolonged crisis caused by Khrushchev's anti-Stalin speech at the Twentieth Party Congress of 1956 and the book was denounced by French Communist leaders for its attack on socialist realism. Lewka, the hero, is an artist in an East European country who is commissioned to sculpt an enormous statue of Stalin. As a good Communist, he agrees to do it. But he is so horrified at the result—the hideous statue dominates the medieval section of the city and spoils the vista—that he commits suicide in despair. The plot was based on an actual incident in which a Czech sculptor killed himself after completing a huge statue of Stalin in Prague, and in the 1960s the statue was torn down. Triolet's growing disenchantment with party politics is readily apparent in this book. *Le Monument* was a clear challenge and it created such a furore that a special meeting was called to debate the issues it raised. Many Communist intellectuals were pleased with the opportunity to discuss the problems of art in socialist countries and, rather than criticize Triolet, most speakers praised her courage. Aragon also publicly defended her, calling *Le Monument* her masterpiece. But from then on, Triolet's work was largely ignored by the left and reviews of her books rarely appeared in Party journals except for the two of which Aragon was editor. That same year, she resigned as vice-president of the Conseil national des écrivains and was no longer active in any Party organisations. She was not overtly attacked because Aragon was still an important figure in the Party; moreover, although French Party leaders remained sceptical of de-Stalinization, a more liberal tendency in the arts had begun. Ironically, she came to be more widely read in Eastern Europe, where numerous translations of her work appeared, than on the left in France.

After the hostile reception of *Le Monument*, the content of Triolet's fiction changed dramatically. She wrote a very popular trilogy, *L'Age de Nylon*, in which elements of the supernatural were interspersed with such contemporary issues as consumerism, space travel and cybernetics. The trilogy consists of *Roses à Crédit* (1959), *Luna Park* (1959), and *L'Ame* (1963). But even in these ostensibly apolitical novels many characters are identified as either former resistance fighters or as collaborators, and the plots of the three novels unfold against a background of violent demonstrations provoked by the Algerian war for independence.

In her last major work, *Le Grand Jamais* (1965), Triolet continued to assert her intellectual independence. The heroine, Madeleine, a young widow and former student of Régis, a famous historian, tries to uncover the truth about her husband's past to write his biography. She struggles against the distortions of both his critics and his supporters who want to appropriate his ideas for their own purposes. Triolet said that the theme of the book came from her sister's untiring efforts of over thirty years to rehabilitate Mayakovsky's reputation in the Soviet Union. In a comic episode, Régis, whose brilliant book on Catherine the Great had made his reputation, confesses that it was really a hoax based on his wife's student memories of his lectures. He declares that he does not believe in the possibility of historical truth and Madeleine, angry at Régis's many deceptions, insists that historians only tell lies for profit. This novel's pessimistic perspective on history was hardly in accord with the Party line but was a further indication of her bitter disillusionment. She grew more and more outspoken and scornful of those who still conformed. In an essay of 1969, she proudly said that, unlike other left-wing writers faced with the task of accommodating themselves to the post-1956 thaw, "I have never had to rewrite my books."[2] She had protested against the invasion of Hungary in 1956, against the trial and conviction of Daniel and Sinyafsky in 1966, against the invasion of Czechoslovakia in 1968 and she defended the Soviet dissidents, Sakharov and Solzhenitsyn. But her intellectual independence was achieved at great personal cost. Her last book, *Le Rossignol se tait à l'aube* (1970), is almost entirely an interior monologue. An unhappy old woman, formerly a famous actress, muses on her past, and at dawn she dies. This bleak meditation on loneliness, old age and death was published just weeks before Triolet's own death from heart disease.

Helena Lewis, Cambridge, Mass., 1986

2. Elsa Triolet, *La Mise en mots*. Geneva: Skira 1969, 28.

THE LOVERS OF AVIGNON

I'VE always been fond of Juliette Noël. I find her extremely charming and attractive. People tell me that I am too easily pleased by women, that I think them all pretty, or at least see something pretty in all of them. I admit I can be captivated by a nice skin, shining hair, rosy fingers, a mole or a dimple. But this time you can believe me: it's impossible not to find Juliette as alluring as a typist in a film. She has silken hair, long lashes, and a kind of natural elegance in her close-fitting pullover, her very short skirt, and very high heels. She really is a typist, but one of the best. So much so that after being one of the twenty typists in the aircraft factory she became secretary to M. Martin, the engineer, and later private secretary to the Director. Her career was pretty much like that of an understudy who is suddenly called on to take the place of the star, and turns out to be a big success. When the stenographer to the board of directors didn't turn up, she was called in at the last minute to take her place, and made such a good transcript of all their reports, and even of their controversies, that the Director annexed her for himself. Martin, the engineer, was inconsolable.

Combined with a very ingenuous face Juliette has a kind of dignified reserve that keeps people at a distance. When she had been at the aircraft factory for two years they didn't even suspect her of sleeping with the Director (a retired cavalry general with a good figure, a black coat decorated with the commander's rosette, and striped trousers)—in spite of the *marrons glacés* he brought her on New Year's Day, and the flowers for her birthday. But then everybody knew the old gentleman's gallantry. What people didn't know was that he did ask her, with elaborate discretion, to become his mistress; this was the best he could do, since he was married already. Neither did they know that M. Martin had asked her to marry him. She refused them both so charmingly and with so much finesse that she was able to go on working there. Her boss credited her with the strength of mind and sense of duty of a Clarissa Harlowe or a Princesse de Clèves, and he didn't know how right he was, because already at that time she

7

had met her Lovelace. But in general everybody agreed that she was charming, although a little cold, and some even thought secretive, which only made her more attractive.

She really hadn't any secrets in her life. She was born and raised in Paris, and later her father, a civil servant, was transferred to Algiers. She had three younger sisters and an older brother. After her mother's death she was sent back to Paris because money was short, and her Aunt Aline, her mother's sister, had asked that Juliette be sent to her. Juliette didn't remain as a charge on her aunt for long. When she was eighteen she got a job as typist in a Parisian lawyer's office. She stayed there a year and then left. Her Aunt Aline had to believe her when she said she was ill, she looked so thin and pale.

Aunt Aline was neither inquisitive nor censorious. She wasn't in the habit of asking questions like "Why are your eyes red?" or "Why don't you eat?" She sat by the fire, and without raising her marvellous white head from her knitting (it was she who knitted Juliette's sweaters), she would say:

"I've put your supper on the stove. There's a little custard. . ."

Behind her the grandfather clock rose straight up like an elongated violin, the bureau gleamed with all its little drawers, and Juliette's place was laid on a round table with many little doylies . . . Everything suggested calm and repose. Juliette herself grew calm and recovered her fresh complexion. She wasn't twenty yet.

The day she told Aunt Aline that she wanted to adopt a child, her aunt stopped knitting, snatched off her glasses, and said quickly: "Not a bad idea. I have a feeling you'll be an old maid like me, so you might just as well adopt a child now."

Juliette came home with a little one-year-old Spanish boy who had been found, in his swaddling clothes, inside a burning Spanish train and brought to Paris. Without troubling to rack their brains for a name, they called him José.

Juliette was already working at the aircraft factory. She was in more of a hurry than ever to get home; she and her aunt no longer went to the pictures, because they didn't want to leave the child alone. Juliette appeared content and didn't seem to want to see people, except of course her family—especially her older brother, a reckless lad of whom she was very fond.

Then the war came, and the exodus ... Juliette, Aunt Aline, and the child found themselves in Lyons; Juliette worked as a shorthand-typist for a newspaper.

2

ALL night the rats did an infernal dance. It sounded as though they were taking the house by storm, but actually they were well inside. Things fell over, rolled along the floor, bumped against the wall; the creatures could be heard scurrying and gnawing quite close by. ...

And yet when dawn broke the house became silent and still. Soon, the window appeared, sparkling with the snow that had silently fallen overnight. As far as you could see through the window the surface stretched smooth as a freshly ironed tablecloth, unspotted by footstep of man or beast. It took courage for a woman to sleep alone in this desolate house in the mountains. She got down off the table where she had spread her straw mattress, and, still shivering in the overcoat which she wore over her night-gown, she squatted in front of the fireplace. Fortunately the fire kindled rapidly. There were still some live coals left from the night before. Her teeth were chattering, but she felt better now that she could warm her fingers round the cup. "All the same," she thought, "they had some nerve to send me to a place like this."

A big, low-ceilinged room with old rafters of hard, dark chest-nut wood, walls that had once been whitewashed, one little window in an embrasure a yard deep, and a floor of disjointed planks through which a gale swept ... The table she had slept on, a few ramshackle stools ... It was an abandoned farm, and in this part of the country, where even the inhabited farms seem to belong to the Stone Age, an abandoned farm looks like a robbers' den.

She almost had to get inside the fireplace to dress. Six inches away from the fire the cold was intolerable. She combed her hair as best she could, at the little pocket mirror in her handbag. Ashes covered her hair, and she laughed as she caught sight of a spot of soot on her nose. She put on her beret and overcoat ...

When she had shut the door and hidden the key in the baking oven, which was attached to the house and full of broken bottles, old shoes, and leaky pots, and when she had left the snow-covered courtyard, paved with big flat stones, with its rivulet running into a stone basin patterned with ice crystals, she noticed the landscape and was dazzled by it. The big, low house, embracing the hill for protection against the wind and mankind, roofed with old rose-coloured tiles blown into undulations by the wind, formed the foreground of a vast landscape.

The cone-shaped mountains, ranged one behind the other, changed their places as she walked along. She climbed the slope, leaving behind her in the immaculate snow footsteps no larger than a child's. Her complexion, too, was like a child's now that last night's weariness had been washed away by the air against her face as she walked; but her eyes were those of a woman. At the top of the slope there was a road. She followed it as far as the copse, where she left it for a path that led through the trees.

The snow smelled good in the woods, like a closet full of fresh linen. It wasn't cold at all, and if the sun had been a little warmer it could have made all this whiteness, fragile as beautiful lacework, slide to the ground. With extraordinary perfection the snow edged each naked branch, each pine needle. . . . As she came out of the copse she found herself on the other side of the hill. It might have been a different country: a valley closed in by mountains, but mountains of a different character, more bleak and bare. Here not all the slopes were snow-covered, some of them looked like badly shaven cheeks, dark and wrinkled. There were a few farms. . . . She crossed a field where there was a hut and came to another road. The sun shed a glow on to the rocky peaks and the white folds of the snow. On the slopes a herd of sheep nibbled colourless grass, moving together as a body. Shepherdesses all in black, wrapped in shawls and scarves and wearing round black hats, stood upright in the sun and knitted, staring at the passer-by. Sheepdogs barked gaily and bounded after her and then went back calmly to their tasks.

Again she left the road, clambering down a steep bank to meet another road that levelled off and seemed to continue round the mountain across the valley. Beside this road a house appeared; it was greyish white like the smoke rising from its chimney.

The road turned to mud. On either side, as far as the gate, stood
tall haystacks. There was no wall, but there was a gate. In the
courtyard the mud was mixed with straw. Faggots lay strewn
beside a woodpile that reached to the tiles of the roof. Two big
black pots were filled with swill. Chickens roamed at large, and
some turkeys kept aloof in a separate flock. Dogs howled
frantically but didn't approach the intruder; they seemed to want
to announce that there was a stranger near the house. At last a
large woman in a black beret, wearing a woollen shawl crossed
over her broad bosom, came from behind the house. This must
be the place.

"Good morning," she said. "Are you Mme Bourgeois? I've
been sent by Dominique. My name is Rose Toussaint."

Juliette Noël knew how to lie.

The peasant woman got busy at once.

The husband came home about eleven o'clock, and like
his wife, was tall, round-faced, and clear-eyed. The five children
round the table would grow up to look like their parents. They
ate bacon soup and white cheese, and drank red wine, with
barley coffee and a glass of brandy. . . . That same day Juliette
visited two more farms which the Bourgeois had told her about.
The Bourgeois were intelligent people, and she had felt quite at
home with them. She had never thought that she and the peasants
could meet on common ground. Whenever she had had dealings
with them before, which hadn't been often (during summer
holidays, or when she had had to ask her way in the country),
they had always seemed to speak a strange language, or to be
deaf, so that she could make herself understood only with
difficulty. But the Bourgeois understood her very well; they
spoke the same language: they both talked *French*. On the other
two farms she was received with the same hospitality. Once
again Juliette ate bacon soup and white cheese and drank red
wine and brandy. Later they sat round the fire and discussed
the same matters. . . .

Fortunately there was a moon. Flushed with alcohol and
hope, Juliette took what she hoped was the right road. The mild-
ness of this winter of 1942 was like a good omen. The white
countryside, shimmering in the moonlight, didn't make her
afraid. Impossible to be afraid when everything was so beautiful.

She didn't feel like going home; you don't go home on nights like these. . . . Others might need company to be happy—not she! The memory of her old love affair sent a shudder through her. . . . As she skirted the copse she heard a sudden movement, like a heavy body falling, followed by a grunt. . . . Wild animals. She had heard that there were wolves in this part of the country. Wolves! In this calm landscape. Such weather was incredible on the eve of Christmas. God had sent this soft weather in order that Mary might be delivered amidst a springlike warmth. The mountain peaks rose one above the other, white under the high moon, which had a great golden ring round it. She saw the three poplars —three sentinels—guarding the house behind the slope, and here was the house itself. It was a dark mass against the moon, but when Juliette had gone round it she stopped and stood alert: someone had turned on the electric light in the courtyard. No, how stupid of her! It was only the moonlight gleaming on the stones, the old shoe, the potsherds, and the tiles of the roof. The drip of the cistern could be heard, thin as the trickle of water falling into the basin.

That night Juliette didn't hear the rats. She fell asleep in her clothes on the straw mattress. She had walked about fifteen miles. The sun's first weak rays were unable to wake her; she barely woke up when the alarm clock shouted itself hoarse in her ear. She opened her eyes and realized that she was aching all over, that the house was terribly cold, that she would have loved a hot bath, coffee, butter, and jam. All this great, empty, sombre room had to offer her was the little white square of the window and the cold fireplace. There was rat dung on the table close to her head. . . .

Yet outside it was even milder than it had been the night before. A light mist suffused the landscape, and the snow had melted a little everywhere. Juliette faced the mud and the puddles.

The day turned out to be less successful than the preceding one. She got a poor reception at the first farm. The second was so evidently a mistake that she said nothing. It was a dark house, and even though there was bright sunlight outside, it seemed as though the day didn't wish to come inside, but preferred to remain on the other side of the pale window. A few live coals in the

fireplace sent out a fitful glow. One girl sat on the floor, another
on a stool in front of the fire. Juliette could make out a table and
an oil lamp, and she could see that the girls were young, about
sixteen. A youth with a beret on his head and wearing a sweater
torn at the elbows stood behind the table. The girls were under-
sized and ragged. They were peeling chestnuts; the husks littered
the floor and crunched underfoot.

Juliette asked the way to the village of B——: she had to
explain her presence in some fashion.

"My dear lady, this isn't the right road. This road doesn't lead
anywhere . . ."

Both girls started talking at once, trying to tell her how to get
there. The one sitting on the floor had a shrill, rasping voice.
Every time she said anything she jerked forward as though she
were about to jump in your face. While they talked they didn't
stop peeling chestnuts, the girl on the floor working with
almost frantic haste.

"Do you peel them before you boil them?" Juliette asked.
"I've always done it the other way round."

"It's quicker this way," said the blonde who sat on the
stool.

You could see her bare thighs, spread apart to catch the
peeled chestnuts in her skirt, and the big, white holes in her black
wool stockings. Two short pigtails were pinned round her head.
The youth behind the table fiddled with his knife without touching the few chestnuts in front of him.

"You're staying at B——?" snapped the girl who sat on the
floor, jerking her shoulders at Juliette like a wildcat.

No, I'm only passing through."

"Why not come to the café tomorrow? We're celebrating
my brother's engagement to her." She pointed to the little
blonde.

"Oh, well, in that case I may stay. But now I must try to find
my way."

Juliette shook hands with the three children and walked out
into the misty countryside, which seemed quite radiant after the
dark house.

At the third farm she found sensible people. When she
mentioned that she had come from a farm where there was an

engaged couple, the white-haired, pink-skinned old peasant woman shook her head.

"The old man died mad," she said. "And the young one would be locked up too, if she hadn't taken him, he was so set on it. If she ever plays tricks on him he'll go mad or die. Poor orphans, with nobody to look after them. . . . They've eaten everything they could get their hands on, and there was plenty! How many times have I said to her: 'Renée, go and wash yourself. Sew up the rip in your dress. . . .' But she won't. . . . Who told you to go there?"

In honour of her visitor, the old woman put a juniper bough on the fire, which crackled like July tbe Fourteenth fireworks. The old peasant, with his pendulous moustache and his sabots lined with straw, muttered, staring into the fire:

"It might be done . . . I'd like to have kept my gun—what's going to happen in the spring with the foxes coming to steal my chickens? Still, there's always somebody to give you away . . ."

The old woman poured cordial into small glasses on a tray.

"The police say, 'Give an old nail away, and keep the good one'," the peasant went on. "But where am I supposed to find the old nail? They say, 'Kill the pig; they'll take it away from you, anyway'. How do I know? Those policemen, they come up here to forage for themselves. That may be why they tell you to kill the pig. . . . You have some education, mademoiselle. What do you think?"

The old woman handed round the small glasses on a tray.

"I can't tell about the pig," Juliette confessed. "It's just as you say. Policemen are policemen, but they're Frenchmen too. . . . If I were you I wouldn't give up the gun; when you need it— for the fox or no matter what—you won't find another one. Don't take your gun to the town hall."

"My son says the same thing. But there's always someone to give you away."

No, it hadn't been a good day. Juliette was very tired. It was three or four miles between farms, and the peasants weren't all like the Bourgeois. The mist had lifted, there was a beautiful moon, and the night was fair like the night before. But Juliette was in no mood to admire the beauties of nature. . . . Her house behind the slope held no meaning for her. The yard was lighted up the way it had been last night. Juliette's legs buckled under her with fatigue. She rummaged a long time in the baking oven before she found the cursed key . . .

It was much colder inside than out, and Juliette was too tired to go to sleep right away. It was better to make a fire and sit up than to lie waiting for a rat-haunted sleep. The wood was stacked in the stable adjoining the room. Roused by the electric light, a huge chestnut-coloured rat ran along a half-rotted trough. Juliette let out a shriek and then walked calmly towards the wood-pile. The light played fitfully among the ceiling beams and the raised shafts of a carriage. The floor of beaten earth, littered with straw, hay, and wood chips, was as cold as ice. There was a pile of broken dishes, wash basins, glasses, and bottles by the wall, and a heap of manure. . . . These balks of wood were tree-trunks, not logs. It was all she could do to drag them to the fireplace. The faggots were entangled like barbed wire. Juliette felt hot before the fire was even started. The flames leaped from the wood, crackling, like strips of glittering fabric. Fire keeps you company; its sound and movement enliven solitude. . . . You can see it alive and active; its caprices, its sudden outbursts, then slyly dwindling down behind a log as though it were dying, and then flashing forth once more its wanton gaiety, its boundless appetite, and the calm glow of the embers. . . .

Small black andirons supported the flames. They were delicately wrought to represent the head and torso of a woman, her hair prettily done up in a bandeau, a scarf crossed over her naked breasts. These elegant little drawing-room sphinxes, undergoing the ordeal by fire, seemed to have been put in this house merely to keep Juliette company. They were as much out of place as she was, put there God knows why or how, a grotesque joke. . . . Juliette took off her shoes, drew close to the fire, and fell to dreaming. . . .

Dreams were her familiar companions. But when a dream becomes part of life it seems natural. Even walking on water becomes natural. . . . "That's perfectly normal," as the red-headed doctor said when told the most outrageous, most monstrous stories: of a daring escape, prices on the black market, or the unimaginable horror of the execution of hostages. . . . Perfectly normal. . . . And yet it was only in dreams that Juliette Noël, typist, could walk alone over the snowy roads, instead of working for the paper, and going home at night to Aunt Aline and José. Only in a dream could she stay alone in this house surrounded by a white expanse and listen to the scurrying of the rats. . . . This dream she must now live couldn't be the right one: it must be someone else's dream, because Juliette's dreams, in the secret places of her heart, were simply dreams of love. Not the kind of love she had experienced, which was only shame and contempt. . . . A man who doesn't measure up to love should be banished from its kingdom, lest love become a sacrilege. Love should be total, like war.

What times are these, that Juliette Noël has no leisure to dream of love, but must hasten along snowy roads?

The flames sank and turned bluish, and the logs, though they still retained their shape, looked like transparent tubes full of liquid fire. Juliette poked them hard, till they crackled and sparked like fireworks. Once she had been afraid to stay alone at night in a big apartment house in the very heart of Paris; she would have fainted at the sight of a mouse! She was like that: when faced with a decision she felt fearful, cold, tired. If there was no choice . . . Was there a decision in 1942? The fire had turned to a mass of gold. She had better go to bed before she started to shiver again.

Yes, dreams were her companions. Sometimes the man looked like Gary Cooper, sometimes like Charles Boyer. . . . But how can you dream of love, lying on a straw mattress with the rats dancing about and shadows flickering across the black-and-white striped ceiling, whose beams seem to be sinking lower and lower over your head? Juliette left the light burning; perhaps it would keep the rats away. Electric light in this house was an anomaly. It burned unsteadily, as though it felt out of place. The bulb, at the end of a wire hooked up over the table, reddened, almost expired, and then burned intensely. . . . There were a great many hooks and nails in the black beams and in the white gaps between them, which were encircled with smoke and dirt. It was not pleasant to think of the loft above her where the rats galloped about. . . .

Towards morning the roar of an aeroplane engine filled the

countryside. It passed over again and again, while down below, in the houses belonging to the Stone Age, people were getting up to feed the animals and light the fires, and the children were leaving for school in the early morning, craning their necks to see the German 'planes fly over. Juliette thought of the boy yesterday, with his beret and torn sweater, who would have gone mad if the girl had refused him. Two short, blonde pigtails round her head, and holes in her black stockings. . . . It couldn't be easy to love a girl like that! Juliette would have liked to fall in love with someone handsome. . . . There would be music, singing. . . .

She got up. The fire had to be set again. Peasant life must be horrible. She looked at her hands, encrusted with soot. To have to live only for one's body, to feed it and keep it warm. . . . The song of the lark! The peasants didn't have a chance to listen to it often. They would need tractors to give them the leisure for such enjoyments, she thought, and was surprised at her solemn thoughts. . . . Her hands stiff with cold, Juliette gathered her belongings together and put them in a little suitcase. The few provisions which the Bourgeois had given her were already in the knapsack. Among them was a rabbit. The most important items she shoved down into the knapsack, under the rabbit: you never can tell.

It was a good six miles to the village of B——. Juliette took the narrow path through the copse and reached the other slope, beyond which rose the bare mountains. Luckily it was downhill. After her sleepless night Juliette dreaded the long road, despite the fine morning and the display of whiteness all round her: it had snowed again during the night. There was nobody on the road, and the solitary farm she passed seemed deserted, with no smoke coming from its chimney. But road-menders had been working here; the roadway had been dug up, the turned earth mixed with coarse, sharp gravel. Juliette was bothered by her shoes, which were the only solid ones she owned, though they were still not stout enough for roads like these. . . . The suitcase and the knapsack with the rabbit began to drag her arms down. She had to stop several times; she had almost reached the limit of her strength. At last she could see the highway; the village in the valley below must be B——. A smooth, wide road, edged with neat white stones picked out in red. . . . But here more trouble began; the road had frozen to a smooth, icy surface. Juliette continued slowly, putting her load down more and more often.

At the outskirts of the village she came upon drab ruins, with only one wall of the buildings standing. A cemetery, small houses with tiny gardens, a little bridge, the road . . . the post office . . . a haberdashery . . . a café . . . the church . . . a small square . . . And here was the café where the bus stopped.

A café with a fine, open stove that gave off heat! Juliette laid her things on the bench and sat down close to the stove, suppressing a sigh because her arms ached so. She was much too early for the bus: the café was empty except for a great many parcels, and two workmen having a snack in a corner. A lean dog came up to sniff Juliette's hand. The proprietress asked her pleasantly what she would like, but only from force of habit, because there was nothing to eat or drink except some lemonade with saccharine. The poor woman seemed very embarrassed. "If it weren't for the parcels we'd be closed . . ." The workmen put the rest of their lunch and the empty wine bottle back in their knapsack. Fortunately good Mme Bourgeois had given her, besides the rabbit, a hunk of bread, and some cheese and hard-boiled eggs. Juliette set out her food. Presently the proprietress came from the rear of the café to bring her a glass of wine. "This is our own," she said. "After all, we can't let you eat without having a drop to drink. . . ." Juliette thanked her with a characteristic touch of dignity, and the dimple that accompanied her smile added charm to her thanks.

The ugly, grey little bus arrived an hour late and was crammed. In the beautiful, immaculate Christmas season in the mountains you forgot what holidays were like. A policeman appeared at the same time as the bus. Looking very important, he asked for the papers of all the men who got on or off. In spite of everything, Juliette got a seat in front, right behind the heap of parcels. The young man beside her drew in his long legs so that Juliette could put down her little suitcase. Then he offered his seat to a lady carrying a screaming child, thus securing a better position for discreetly admiring Juliette. The child hated travelling, to judge by his screams and the explanations of his grandmother—the woman was his grandmother. All the passengers smiled and made faces at him, and asked the grandmother for news of her daughter and her other grandchildren. . . . At every stop more people got in, and more parcels were handed to the driver. The bus overflowed with them. Enjoyment of the countryside was impossible. An old woman, well wrapped up in black garments, with her back to Juliette, leaned her weight against the girl's knees, in order to counter-balance the weight of three baskets. In one was a live turkey, in another two live turkeys, in the third a large number of packages. When she got on a stench filled the bus. The red heads of the crazed turkeys peered from the baskets. Two or three times her neighbour gave the old woman a shove when she was just about to sit down on Juliette's knees. The passengers cracked jokes; the turkeys made messes on Juliette's shoes and stockings. At last they arrived. The bus stopped in front of the post office to deliver its parcels. There was the length of the little town to go before they would reach the railway station.

The passengers waited patiently, but there seemed to be no end to the Christmas parcels. The bus completely blocked the main street, and from behind came furious honkings. When the parcels had all been unloaded the engine gave out, and the bus wouldn't budge. The driver began tinkering with the motor, the disgusted passengers got off one by one. . . . A soldier in field grey stepped in front of the radiator and waved his arms. Now that the bus was almost empty Juliette could see a German lorry through the rear window: that was where the wild honking came from. Suddenly the bus started to move. The German jumped out of the way, and the driver got behind the wheel. "All right!" he shouted. "They seem to be in a hurry. Want to finish up the war, I suppose." The woman behind Juliette leaned forward to say: "That would be all right. We'd be glad to see them go. When will it all be over? . . ."

"I wonder," Juliette sighed.

She left her suitcase at the baggage room, bought a ticket, and set out to look for a room. If she found one she would sleep here; if not, she would take the evening train and spend the night somewhere else.

The main street was very gay. Looking at the shop windows, you would have thought there were really things to buy in the stores. They'd brought out everything they had for the holidays. The rationed shoes and boxes of scouring powder were decorated with tinsel, and there were tiny mangers with the Magi and their gifts. The columned church, where the street widened, looked like a grown-up among children, so tall, large, and imposing beside the houses of the main street. It wasn't far to the hotel. They had a room but no sheets: that is, there were sheets, but they weren't dry because they had frozen on the line. "If you care to wait, mademoiselle, until they dry . . . The room isn't heated, but you can sit in the dining-room."

The dining-room, where people no longer dined, was heated after a fashion. Juliette sat down on a chair close to the stove. An old spinster dressed in many layers of woollens came in, followed by a dog. She walked as though her feet hurt and she couldn't decide which foot to limp on. The Pekingese trotted behind her. She held her gnarled hands to the stove, while the dog climbed on to a chair and began sneezing. "He has a cold," she said, smiling at Juliette. She spoke with a strong English accent. Juliette had already heard English spoken in the street. This must be a place where foreigners were interned. The old lady drew out a pair a stockings from a shopping-bag and put them on the stove to dry. There was no danger of their burning. "It's so damp in the room nothing gets dry. . . . Oh, Millie, don't cough like that!" The dog went on gurgling.

The sun was shining outside, and snow was falling in a whirl of diamond flakes. "Can't you make it stop?" The old lady pointed to the snow, addressing her question to the proprietress, who appeared in the aperture where formerly they had handed in the dishes. The proprietress smiled at the joke: "I'm afraid not. I'd like to, but at Christmas snow is seasonable. . . ." She disappeared. A girl of fifteen or sixteen came into the room. "Mama," she called, "where are we going to have tea, here or in the back room?" She gave Juliette a cool look. Evidently Juliette was encumbering the dining-room to such an extent that they might have to have tea in the back room. . . . The girl had a pretty figure; she had not quite finished dressing her hair. "So you can't make it stop," the English lady went on joking. "No, mademoiselle, it has to snow for Christmas." She opened the door wide and moved a table out. Apparently they were going to eat in the back room. Juliette felt like an intruder in this hotel, where it seemed visitors were not popular. She took up the knapsack containing her rabbit, and left, hearing the girl cry out to somebody, "Come into the back room, there's a fire. Mama, bring the bread and butter!"

It was snowing against a grey background. The day drew to its close. Juliette walked towards the station. She stopped again before the hairdressers' windows to admire the bottles of so-called eau de Cologne, and looked at the buttons in the windows of the drapers' shops. . . . She went into a shoe store, tempted by unrationed children's espadrilles. But they didn't have José's size. He had big feet for a child of six. A young couple were buying a pair of shoes with wooden soles and leather uppers. They were probably engaged. Juliette also went into a pharmacy to try to buy a thermometer. José had broken theirs, and sometimes it was easier to find things in small towns than in the cities. But there weren't any thermometers. Shopkeepers apologized for not having what one asked for. They seemed to feel humiliated.

In the little train, with its broken windows, a pursy police officer, his thighs bursting his blue breeches, kept talking all during the trip to a respectful young man, who, to judge from his fragrant smell, had just come from the barber. It appeared from their conversation that the policeman was on his way south to bury his mother-in-law. The young man tried to make up his mind whether or not condolences were in order. He said, "That's a sad business, though it isn't always so. . . ." The policeman didn't make things any easier; he kept still, and the condolences ended in a timid smile. After a while conversation grew livelier; they talked about the mountains, and the ski championships. These were being held on the Italian border, where nothing mattered but a good run. Yet from time to time the war reared its head. "Yes, indeed," said the young man. "I knew him very well. He was a dark-haired fellow. He was killed right beside me in June, 1940. We were the same age. . . ."

The train was exasperatingly slow. The conversation, about ski-ing, growing more and more animated, became interspersed with names of women, which were accompanied by little side-glances at Juliette. Finally they reached the junction.

It was almost dark. In the station, lighted only by a night light, were *gardes mobiles*, blacker than the night, and masses of travellers on the platform waiting for a train to pull out so they could cross the lines. The train was a goods train, which presently started to move. The people watched it pass in silence: motor-cars, machine-guns, tanks mounted on open trolleys, upright German soldiers, standing guard . . . then sealed box-cars. . . . A phantom train which seemed to glide interminably on and on, only the noise of wheels attesting its reality. Now and then a helmeted head peered from a vehicle mounted on a trolley. . . . "They must be running out of petrol if they ship them around on trains," someone behind Juliette said in a low voice. Nobody answered. "They're going back towards Paris . . ." a woman's voice said. It was the woman from the bus. "Yes," said Juliette. "And I thought they were going towards the coast." "I just don't understand . . . they've taken everything, but if we go into the country for a few provisions we take a terrible risk . . ." said the woman. The train stopped with a screeching of brakes and then backed up. . . . Voices shouted in German and a soldier ran along the tracks. The train shuttled backwards and forwards. "It's cold," said the woman from the bus. "If it doesn't leave pretty soon we'll miss our connection. . . ." Finally the train got under way and the cars filed past. It went on and on . . .

They had to wait a long time for their connection. Juliette waited with her back against a pillar. "What did you pay for that rabbit, mademoiselle?" This woman was beginning to annoy her. She stuck like a burr. The air grew colder and colder. ". . . but wait and see, they'll get out quicker than they came . . ." People stamped their feet and looked along the tracks, hoping to see the train. At last they saw it coming, almost alarming in its speed and power. Juliette hoisted her suitcase on to the train and climbed aboard with her knapsack, the woman right behind her. . . . Every seat was taken. Here was one! Juliette entered the compartment. "There's only one seat," said the woman, still behind her. "Never mind. . . . " But her face was bitter, as though her best friend had let her down. Without searching any farther, she stationed herself in the corridor near Juliette's compartment, her squalid black suitcase at her feet. Juliette saw that she squinted and that her hair resembled her black fur collar, which was wet with snow.

In the third-class compartment were a small man, sickly and

pale, his wife, and their attractive little girl; in the corner a young woman with an ageless face, dressed in black, perhaps in mourning; opposite Juliette a man who had just come back from dinner, colourless, with grey-blond hair, and a jacket that hung loosely on him. It was a pleasant, friendly group: the sickly little man, father of the girl, took in through the window a lady's red handbag and suitcase, and also a brief-case of yellow leather. "How about a tip?" he said. "How about a tip?" The handbag belonged to a hatted lady who must have been attractive not so very long ago. . . . At this late date she seemed to think of her appearance only somewhat absent-mindedly, from force of habit, her hair being henna'd and her face made up rather carelessly. The brief-case of yellow leather was followed by a youth of rather Levantine appearance, handsome, his hair rather long, in a well-cut overcoat. People exchanged places so that the family could sit together for their meal.

"Excuse me," Juliette addressed the person opposite her, the colourless man in the loose clothes. "Is there any room in the dining-car?"

"Sure, you can go there. Potatoes for thirty-five francs. And that's about all. Oh, I forgot the celery. . . . Celery makes you amorous. But as far as meat goes, nothing doing!"

A smile flitted through the compartment.

"A while back I went to a black market restaurant in Marseilles. I got my bit of sausage and waited for the next course. . . . At the table next to me were some fellows eating like me—what am I talking about: like kings! I'd hardly finished my sausage when they got up and came over. 'Monsieur, you've been eating sausage. Where are your papers?' I told them that after eating the way they did they oughtn't to pester anybody about a slice of sausage and ask for their papers. . . . I refused to show them my papers, so there was a big fuss. They called the cops, and there I was! Next thing I found myself in the police court. . . ."

' We're all out on licence, so to speak," said the father of the little girl.

"And I lost my virginity, too. . . ."

Everybody laughed, including the young woman in black. The lady with the hat asked:

"Whatever do you mean?"

"I no longer have a virgin police record." He seemed very annoyed. "I've lost nine pounds in weight over this celery business. Look, madame"—he took his identification papers out of his wallet and showed her the photo—"look at what I was and what I am now!"

"To be sure," said the lady.

"However long it lasts," went on the man in baggy clothes, "and it will last another two years at least——"

"Oh no!" the whole compartment cried out.

"They're very strong yet," the man affirmed. "Look at their uniforms and supplies. You should see them in Paris."

"You've come from Paris?"

"I go back and forth——"

"I do, too," said his neighbour, the lady in the hat. "I must have crossed the line illegally at least twenty times."

"No, sir," said the father of the little girl. "I'm a railway man. I come from Paris. And that's where you can see they're through. . . . Doriot has already been eliminated. . . ."

"Is that story true?"

"Yes, indeed! That is, I'm not positive that he's dead, but I know the attempt was made."

"My son is a prisoner," said the lady in the hat. "He writes me that the day the prisoners come back. . . . They don't understand how we can come to terms with their jailors. It's beastly! To think that those are Frenchmen who act that way. . . . All these anti-Jewish measures. It's enough to make you die of shame . . . Frenchmen!"

"Good Aryans," said the man deprived of his virginity. "Good-for-nothings! As for forced labour, I don't know what you think of it, but my grandfather hasn't got much use for it."

The whole compartment, including the girl in black, rocked with laughter. A German of about seventeen appeared in the corridor, carrying a box. He was followed by other soldiers in field grey. . . . Leaning against the door of Juliette's compartment a man in a slouch hat stood reading a spread-out newspaper, blocking the passage of the box and the whole file of Germans. There was a tussle. The Germans kept smiling, while the Frenchman shouted loud enough to be heard, through the closed door,

inside the compartment. "Don't push me, you dirty bastards!"
he thundered, but the Germans passed on with the box, still
smiling.

"There's a brother," cried the hatted lady. "There's a brother!
Did you hear him? Let's ask him to come in. We'll all move
over!" She opened the door.

"Come in, monsieur. That's the way to talk. You're a real
brother. We're going to make room for you here."

Visibly embarrassed by his unlooked-for success, the man
came in. Everybody moved over so that he could sit down, and
he immediately started telling a long story about a German who
had pushed a woman with a child, in the presence of a friend of
his. He related what his friend had said and done on that
occasion.

"I hear the British have bombed an airport near Paris,"
ventured the Levantine youth, who had taken no part in the
conversation.

"Ah!"

The interest became general, for they were all Parisians,
refugees or not. Everyone speculated which airport it could
have been.

"True," said the humorist in baggy garments sitting opposite
Juliette. "But I still say they're very strong——"

"They'll hold out until spring if we're lucky, until autumn if
we're not," said Juliette. The fellow annoyed her.

"What's the source of your information, mademoiselle?
Nostradamus?"

Juliette gave him a pretty, dimpled smile.

"The general situation," she said, taking out the rest of her
provisions; she wasn't going to pay thirty-five francs for
potatoes.

"If the British had opened a second front in '42, the Germans
would be beaten by now," said the railway man, giving
Juliette an approving look. "It's the British who have saved
them."

Juliette's *vis-à-vis* said nothing, but watched her eat.

"Quite right," the man in the slouch hat confirmed. "The
British are putting up a poor show. You'd almost think they did
it on purpose. . . . But the Russians are going to win in the spring.

We've been hearing lies all along," he continued, with a violence that seemed natural to him. "The Russians have no army, the Russians have no generals, the Russians have no supplies, and so on. Haven't they just ! . . ."

"Do you know what the different countries think of the army in general?" interrupted the humorist. "To the English it's a profession, to the Germans a necessity, to the Italians it's a pretty uniform, and to Frenchman it acts as—a purgative."

The whole compartment roared, including the young woman in black. The hatted lady, who a minute ago had closed her eyes to try to sleep, smiled.

"You sleep with one eye open, if I may say so," he went on, and began whispering in her ear, since she sat next to him.

Juliette closed her eyes too. The Levantine youth joined in the conversation. He talked about Turkey, the Turkish anti-Nazi movement, and the interest of the Turks in ranging themselves on the side of the British and Russians. He had a timid, cultured voice, and his accent might well have been a Turkish accent. . . . The compartment grew very hot.

"In any event," said the previous speaker, "the British aren't making much progress. By the time they reach Tunisia across the desert——"

There was a general outcry. Either he didn't listen to the radio, or he didn't understand the map. And they started explaining to him in great detail, citing names and distances, that the British would be there very soon. . . .

"There aren't any highways in the desert, it's all sand," said the other defensively.

Then there was a lull. Outside, the night was black; it was raining. The window-panes were spotted as though by smallpox. As a defence measure the curtains were drawn, and the compartment was faintly lighted.

"Have you got a room in Lyons?" he continued, addressing Juliette.

"Yes, indeed, monsieur."

"Because I can always find a room (I don't suggest we should share it—far be it from me), but I thought if you didn't have one I could get one for you. . . . In the hotel where I always stay I've told the cashier once and for all that I'll sleep with her if she doesn't give me a room. Sanctions, you understand. . . . That lipstick of yours, is it black market?"

He looked at Juliette roguishly. . . .

As she tried to make her way through the crowd on the platform, Juliette thought that the man on the train was a bit suspicious. She looked back several times, but she was well ahead of the other passengers in her car. Besides, if she were to be upset by every suspicious person . . . The woman with the squint, for example: was it natural for anyone to hang on like that? She was probably bringing back supplies from the country and thought that Juliette was doing the same thing, and in her anxiety wanted company . . . Juliette left the station. The black, muddy town closed around her.

Her appointment wasn't until the next morning. She had been given the address of an hotel where she would be sure to find a room in case her train arrived too late for her to go home. She got there half dead with fatigue. She had reached the limit of her strength. The hotel lay back in a courtyard. Two huge, sleek wolf-hounds stood shuffling beside the rather sly-looking land-lord. Without asking Juliette to register, he conducted her up a narrow staircase into a very hot room. That was all she knew. She undressed with her eyes closed, lay down, and was just dropping off to sleep, when she suddenly leaped up, put on her overcoat over her nightgown, got on her slippers, and went out into the corridor. She had left the knapsack with the rabbit in the office.

The corridor was oppressive with silence, and she could smell the central heating. She groped her way to the staircase and was just about to descend, when she saw the front door opening: men . . . three . . . five . . . eight . . . slouch hats, overcoats, fat backs, ugly faces. . . . Juliette pressed herself against the wall, hoping to be taken for the design of the wallpaper. It didn't occur to her that the staircase wasn't lighted, and that there was little chance of her being seen from below.

"Here's the hideout," said one of the men, rubbing his hands together.

"Yes," said another, surveying the landlord, who had come out of his office, and the huge dogs who followed him and began circling and sniffing among the men like wolves. "Yes, to have to walk six miles for this! . . ."

They filed through the office one by one . . . Juliette waited in the dark at the head of the stairs; she had to get her knapsack back at all costs! To have the knapsack lying about with men like that in the house—gangsters, black marketeers, white slavers! Once again there was utter silence. Juliette waited another minute and then dashed down. The office was completely dark, but she didn't need a light, because she remembered exactly where she had put it. . . . If it was still there . . . It was there! Praise God! . . . She took the stairs four at a time.

She lay down without switching off the light, her heart beating wildly. How could she sleep now? She had been too frightened. She began to notice the details of the room. Once again, as in the farm-house, she thought: "They had a nerve to send me to a place like this. . . ." One needn't be familiar with places like this to know what they are like. She fell asleep at once.

3

THE copper plate on the door read: *Dr. Arnold, Gynaecologist*. The house was very new and white, a white handkerchief dropped among the squalor of Lyons. Juliette climbed a staircase that smelled of varnish and plaster, and rang at the mahogany door. The copper plate and the bell-button gleamed like sunlight. A maid let her in. "You have an appointment, mademoiselle?" She led Juliette into a very hygienic waiting-room, with cane chairs, a waxed uncarpeted floor, a glass-topped table strewn with books and magazines, two cabinets with glass doors filled surprisingly with Chinese bric-à-brac instead of steel instruments. Framed water-colours hung on the walls, and in a corner a stand with a glass top held a big bouquet of mimosa. Three women waited sleepily in a typical waiting-room silence. Juliette picked up a copy of *Dimanche Illustré* and tried to read. . . . The other women weren't even trying to read, they just waited. Time passed, and nothing moved behind the doors. The silence began to hum in Juliette's ears like a big black fly. She was just about to doze off when the door opened and the red-headed doctor appeared.

One of the women jumped up, and the doctor drew back to let her pass. Juliette resigned herself to waiting. This time it wasn't long before the door opened, and the doctor said to her, "Will you come in, mademoiselle," at the same time motioning to another woman, who had already risen, to sit down again, with a typical surgeon's brusqueness.

"So," he said, closing the door and seating himself in the arm-chair behind the desk. Juliette sat down opposite him. The examination table behind her looked like an enamelled torture instrument. And it wasn't Chinese bric-à-brac that gleamed in the cabinet.

"You can send ten at the most. . . . Of course in almost all the farms they expect help with the work. But the men will be well fed, even without ration cards. Not only men called up for forced labour, but also politicals could be hidden there."

"Good. I have two sleeping on the floor in the waiting-room at night I'd like to be rid of." The doctor rubbed his hands, all pink from being washed a hundred times a day.

"I've brought you this . . ." Juliette rummaged in her knap-sack, lifted up the rabbit, and took out a roll of bills. "There's a hundred thousand."

"You carry that round in an open knapsack? At least you're careful, I hope." He counted the money. "And how is Dominique?"

"He seems to be doing all right. He sends you his regards."

"By the way, I've just learned that they are about to arrest six railway men in Avignon. Marvellous fellows. I think we have time to warn them—at least there's a chance. . . . I've absolutely nobody to send, and I can't possibly go there myself. . . . Could you go there at once? Six men——"

"Right," said Juliette. "Is there time for me to go home? If I could get a wash and something to eat . . ."

"There's a train a little after four. . . . Excellent! And look here; since you're going to Avignon you may as well take along some blank ration cards: if the men want to join the *maquis* they'll find them useful. Anyway, I promised them to Celestin. . . . It's a man called Celestin you're going to see in Avignon. On your way back stop at Valence. It's absolutely necessary to get some of these cards to our men there. You'll be careful, won't you?"

"I'm very careful," said Julette. "If you could get me something hot to drink . . . I don't feel too well. I don't know what's the matter. I didn't have any breakfast this morning."

"Forgive me, I'm a brute."

The doctor rang. "She'll bring it to you. Also a glass of brandy. . . . My wife and the children have left for the holidays, but you may as well lie down in the bedroom. Madeleine, show Mademoiselle to the bedroom, and bring her something hot to drink, and some toast. She must rest before she goes. I'll get rid of these women in no time, and then I'll be at your service."

Juliette looked so pale that the maid, full of sympathy for this young woman who was probably pregnant, saw nothing out of the way in these orders. Quickly she removed the silken counterpane, and Juliette stretched out on the doctor's large, conjugal bed. She was fast aleep when he came in.

"Something else," said the doctor, sitting down on the bed. "It's noon. If you want to look in at your place . . . When you get back from Avignon——"

"Remember, when I get back from Avignon, the holidays will be over and I'll only have my mornings free. . . . And there's the Letter Box. . . . Did I hear you say something about a glass of brandy?"

"I'm a brute . . ." The doctor ran his pink hands through his hair. "I'll get it for you." Instead he took Juliette's hand and kissed it: "Poor child, this is no life! I have a pretty girl in my bed, and instead of making love to her I send her off on a ghastly job for which she's quite unfitted. . . . You're going to tell me this is normal——"

"No, you're the one who says that."

"All right, make fun of me. You can't tell me that in times like these it isn't normal for everything to be abnormal! Not that it isn't possible to amuse myself with a woman if need be, but where am I to find leisure and ease of mind to talk about love to a charming girl like you? One barely has time to get children . . ."

"I'll let you off," said Juliette, and the doctor blushed like a young girl. He got up.

"I'll fetch you that brandy," he said, and went out.

Juliette put on her shoes and avidly drank the cold tea on the tray by the bed.

"I hope you appreciate this . . ." The doctor returned with a bottle of cognac and two glasses. "You know it's unprocurable now. . . . And here are the ration cards. Where are you going to put them?"

"Under the rabbit."

"Does it taste good? Excellent. Now quickly, give me the details of the hideouts with the peasants."

"The best thing for them to do is to go first to the Bourgeois. . . ."

Juliette started explaining minutely what to do. As for the landing field, Dominique had told her to say that nothing was certain, but it would be very odd if, in that deserted country, where the people were reliable, they couldn't find a likely spot. In that district, if you can call it a district, considering the distances between farms, they had all voted communist in '36. . . . That showed you how much they liked the Boche! It was the Bourgeois who had told her that. Odd to be named Bourgeois, and be communist! . . . The old landing field was functioning very well; Dominique had sent people there to receive parachuted packages . . .

"Perfect. . . . Your train leaves at four-fifty. All you have to do when you arrive is 'phone. Here's the number. And here is the list of the railway men. They must get away at once, without taking time to collect their belongings or kiss their wives. It may be a question of minutes—a matter of life and death. . . . You understand? You'll call M. Celestin on the 'phone. He'll make an appointment with you, and you'll hand him the list. Get going, child. It's a question of life and death, don't forget . . ."

"I won't forget."

"Good. . . . You'll be careful?"

"I'll be careful."

"Come and see me when you get back."

When Aunt Aline and José learned that she was going away again they were distressed. To be away on Christmas Eve! Aunt Aline had stood in a queue for three hours to get oysters, and there was sauerkraut, with real sausage, to take the place of turkey. . . .

The rabbit which Juliette had brought was received with little enthusiasm, because it would have to be eaten without her. And Santa Claus surely wouldn't come if he heard that Juliette wasn't going to be there. José threw himself on the bed in the bedroom. His sobs were heartbreaking to hear.

"Aunt Aline, I tell you it's a question of life and death. . . ."

Aunt Aline, still erect, though hollow-chested, her white head swaying a little, said nothing and busied herself among the pots on the stove. The electric light was burning at midday, because the kitchen opened on to the courtyard. However, since it was the only heated room, they stayed there. Two places had been laid on the peeling oil-cloth: they hadn't expected her for lunch, and there were only potatoes and, by chance, a piece of cheese. Did she want a glass of wine? Actually the wine was to have been saved for Christmas Eve. Oh, it didn't matter. José lay on his stomach crying, his head in Juliette's pillow, in the long, narrow bedroom, with its deep alcove from which Juliette had moved the beds because she didn't like to sleep in corners, and because it was such a good place to keep the potatoes. There were two narrow iron beds in the room, and José's little bed at their foot. José always went to sleep on Juliette's bed.

"My little darling, my sweetheart," Juliette said, covering him with kisses, "be a man. You know very well the Germans are a bad lot, and that we have to drive them out of our country . . ."

"I don't want you to drive them out at Christmas! You can drive them out some other day."

"You'll get your horse, even though I'm gone, I promise you. And you must learn to ride it, so you'll be a real horseman when I come back, day after tomorrow. Right? Save some sauerkraut for me. It keeps very well, you know——"

"And oysters?"

"And some oysters. . . . We'll buy some more. Perhaps I'll even bring some. All right? You'll have a big piece of rabbit. You like rabbit, don't you? My little sweetheart . . ."

She didn't scold him for putting his shoes on the knitted counterpane which they had brought from Paris. She held him in her arms, little José hot with tears and anguish, with his eyes like black diamonds, his hair in tendrils, his chunky little body, and the gallant little head of a pure-bred Catalan peasant.

"Aunt Aline says that you know how to tell the time. Do you?"

José ran to the table between the two beds. On the table there was a large photograph of Juliette's brother, who had been killed in Libya, in a silver frame adorned with crêpe, a carafe, a glass in which Aunt Aline kept her false teeth at night, and a precious little nickel clock, brought from Paris. . . . Aunt Aline couldn't have borne the dreariness of this furnished apartment without these few objects which made her forget the miserable rickety furniture (no matter how often she cleaned it, it looked tarnished and dirty), the dented pots, the chipped crockery, the corridor, the dark staircase. . . . To think they paid seven hundred francs a month for this hole, and had to consider themselves lucky to have found it, after living one whole year in an hotel, with the child. . . . At least there was a basin with running water in the bedroom. Juliette undressed and washed herself, with José pulling at her skirts. Aunt Aline presented her with a sweater which she had just finished knitting: it was her Christmas present. Juliette put it on right away. It was so pretty! What if she did soil it during the trip? Navy blue, with a close neckline, all done in a complicated stitch invented by Aunt Aline. Lunch was almost gay. They drank coffee. . . . Juliette soaked her hands in hot water, but she couldn't get them clean after the days in the country and that horrid wood fire. Aunt Aline brushed her navy-blue coat. Every time she took it up she remarked that Juliette had got a bargain the day she bought it at a big sale. It would wear forever, and sports coats never went out of fashion. "I wonder if your shoes will last out the winter. . . ." Aunt Aline turned them this way and that, cleaning them with a strong-smelling paste. All these creams smell very strong nowadays, but they don't clean anything. . . . Só the peasants had been nice to her? It seemed the country's state of mind was improving. Perhaps they'd end up by understanding. You'll have a cup of tea before you leave, won't you?

Juliette put on her beret, kissed José and Aunt Aline. She mustn't miss her train. Yes, she would be careful, very careful. . . .

4

FIERY butterflies danced before Juliette's closed eyes. They were still there when she opened her eyes. A Christmas tree held up fingers of fire, sombre and silvery, in a corner, its star touching the vaulted arch of the ceiling. Candles burned on the cleared table, and there was a fire in the fireplace. All these flames, as they flickered to and fro, revealed between the furniture the rugs, the draperies, the pictures, glimpses of pearl-grey stone. Above the doors stone cupids held up heavy, sculptured garlands. There were other stone cupids above the fireplace, but the narrow Gothic bays, with delicately carved ogives, hidden now behind the curtains, might have belonged to a church. So might the furniture: there were chairs with high, straight backs, and others insidiously vast and soft.

"*L'aria, l'acqua, la terra è d'amor piena.* . . . Love hold you within the walls of my city. . . . 'Avignon-la-Folle!', holy, satanic town, dedicated to miracles and sorcery, to the Virgin, to Venus, to demons, enflamed by the smoke of pyres and by night festivals. . . . Sinful, heedless city, renowned for beautiful and amorous women, and for gallant men. . . . Here, when love grows wings, it is sacred love, eternal love. Convent doors close over women leaving the world. You'll find out what it is, this magic of Avignon. In what other town will you find an inscription like this on a wall, celebrating the birth of a great man's love, 'Here Petrarch conceived for Laura a sublime love which made them both immortal'? But don't think that Avignon bows under the weight of history; this town, a network of legends, each day adds a new strand to it; here every man is Petrarch, every woman Laura. . . . How many immortal couples have roamed its streets dedicated to love, mystical and amorous city! . . . Now they have taken everything away from us, even our dreams of love. . . . There are only parted lovers in this world, only rent and rending love. . . . Their flags are on our walls, their conquering soldiers flock here."

He stared at the fire through the red wine in his glass. Riding breeches, boots, a braidless tunic, unbuttoned. . . . A large body, whose movements were so abrupt one would expect him to overturn things. But he wasn't like that at all. He had the grace of a horse who takes an obstacle cleanly. The head of an archangel, sombre, fallen, with burning, prominent eyes beneath bold eyebrows. . . . The tropical heat in the room seemed to emanate from him.

"What with hunger, pistols, and prison, where shall we lodge love? It avenges itself, escapes us, we have lost it. You or I would walk barefoot in the snow to save an unknown comrade from death. We have learned to kill . . . the traitors. There's not the smallest crevice in our hearts where any love but that of the partisan can hide. Men are worn out by an unspectacular heroism, devoid of any outward glories, by privation, disillusionment, the hideousness of the enemy and of the traitors . . ."

Juliette followed the flight of the fiery butterflies. She felt the fire invade her until she was a receptacle brimful of fire like the live embers in front of her.

"My little friend," he said. "Today we were able to save six of our men. . . . You came neither on a comet nor a curvetting horse. You took the train and braved the policemen. You ate a sandwich made of sawdust, and I mounted my bicycle to warn our friends. . . . I've seen wretched, half-crazed men, leaving their wives and children to hide themselves. We do whatever we can. We rescue, we attack. But sometimes I think we are about as effective as a mosquito on an elephant's hide. . . . Rose, you are so quiet. . . ."

"My name is Juliette, not Rose. . . . Fill up my glass. I want to suggest a game. . . . Let's pretend we're lovers . . ."

"How do you play it?"

"The way we used to play at visiting, or going to the doctor. Everything is *as if*, you know——"

"I'm not quite sure I know how it goes. . . ."

"Oh yes, you'll know how, very well. And try, for my sake."

"You're the soul of courage and womanhood! Now that you are my love, Juliette, I'm going to tell you something . . . because I love you and am a little drunk: I killed a man day before yesterday . . ."

"Oh," said Juliette, "I love you . . ."

"He was a torturer, a killer. . . . We decided to eliminate him. He's in the Rhone."

"That's war."

"He had to be followed and watched for days. . . . A man needs much hatred and a belief in his cause if he is to keep on and not collapse."

"I hope no one suspects you. I love you, I don't want to lose you . . ."

"Juliette . . ."

Celestin slid to his knees and kissed Juliette's little bare feet. "I'm going to bed," she said.

She leaned on his arm, in her trailing house-coat with its puffed sleeves, its skirt with so many flounces that they made her waist look thin enough to break in two. Her bare feet were thrust into slippers with gilded heels.

Three lights flamed in the lamp. The bed was turned down, and a nightgown lay on the cover, its lace sleeves outspread. The poster bed faced a mirror in a gilded frame; on either side of the mirror was a beautiful carved door. The windows were concealed behind portières of white silk embroidered in white. The dressing-table between the windows, its mirror-lined lid raised, held flasks and boxes of all shapes and colours. Ornaments on the mantelpiece, a fire in the fireplace, cushions on all the chairs and on the floor. . . . On the wall above the toilet table hung a life-sized photograph of a woman sitting upright, looking away from the beholder, her arms crossed lightly on a table but not leaning on it. She wore a high-collared dark dress. "I want her to live in this room, even when she is away," Celestin said, looking Juliette straight in the eyes.

"Good night, my love," said Juliette serenely, embracing him. "Until tomorrow."

"Until tomorrow you are going to rest, sleep . . ." He began to sing quietly:

> "There's a river in the bed,
> And it is so deep
> That we can plunge in it
> And go to sleep.

A pretty song for you . . ."

Celestin pressed her against him. He was floating in a black, starred Christmas sky. The sweetness that enveloped him was so intense that he barely had strength to say:

"I love you . . ."

"Good night," Juliette repeated. Celestin was gone.

Christmas, Christmas, Christmas. . .

I like to talk about a town after I have left it, when I can no longer photograph it with my eyes, or fill in the gaps of memory on the spot. I like to be able to speak of it freely and to paint it as it appears across time and space, reflected in the distorting mirror of memory. Avignon, high-walled city, reaching towards heaven. . . . In my heart and before my eyes appears an immense harp, its top touching the sky, its base resting on a pedestal of clear grey stone. The terrible wind of Avignon swoops through these walls, and I think I have heard some of those discords trapped there. . . .

But the next morning when Juliette, after a dreamless night in the poster-bed, walked arm in arm with Celestin along the Rhone, they did not see the countryside, the vast curved Rhone flowing with its ancient turbulence. They gazed absently at the trees and the sky, concerned only to stay together, and not be separated an inch. The people hurrying along with swinging arms seemed to be performing a ritual. Like a sound of bells around them, Christmas, white and starry in broad daylight.

They had Christmas dinner in a restaurant. The whole country had made a desperate effort to dine well, or merely dine, this Christmas. They ate turkey with chestnuts. The waitress wore a starched apron. There were carnations on the table, bits of mistletoe overhead, and a little Christmas tree in the corner. The room was heated, and the garden behind the windows was celebrating Christmas. When they had finished their coffee they went up to Fort Saint-André.

It was grey and solitary against a formidable sky, an eagle on a rock. The two frontal towers, huge binoculars made for a giant astronomer, kept growing larger as they approached. They passed beneath the arch between the two towers: the old fort, disarmed, did not bar their way. . . . They were alone (this was no time for sightseeing tourists) ; perhaps there was no one else at all inside these walls. . . . On a pebbly road they passed ruined houses with interiors laid bare, fragments of arches still intact, steps that still held together, at times even a whole staircase, crumbling walls, with a window, a door . . . debris of clear, dry, pearl-grey stone. The path went up, cut across the enclosure, and stopped before a low wall without crenellations: from here they could see far out over the country. A country lofty and austere as a monk's cell, calling up visions of miracles. . . . Leaning on the wall, shoulder to shoulder, they drank in the heady air. . . . Then they followed the great crenellated wall of the fort, which seemed to sustain all this debris, this crumbling mass. Sitting close to each other in a deep embrasure, they beheld secretly through the chink of a loophole, as through a keyhole, all the luminous country. Here they were sheltered from the wind which rose now and again, wildly tossing the dishevelled bushes and sombre foliage. . . . When they had climbed as far as the chapel, the country opened wide arms and they saw the magic town of Avignon. The vast harp shone in the sky, all its long strings taut and gleaming, set on a pedestal of houses merged with the light grey stone. The sun warmed the wind which carried the odours of aromatic plants crushed underfoot. Christmas rime glittered in the narrow band of shade at the foot of the chapel wall, suggesting the cause of all this brilliance in the air. . . . Christmas, Christmas, Christmas. . . . The wall about them was huge, luminous, its towers affirming their strength like fist-blows. The air, the stone, the sun, the grass underfoot, the wind, didn't even try to appear innocuous. They asserted their magic power, which caught and held these two.

The steps took them close to the wall again. Heads raised, they admired the rectangles of the crenellations, whose edges cut into the living sky. A door opened before them and they entered a great room of stone, pierced by beautiful Gothic windows. The staircase of the tower went up and up in a spiral to a small platform with door ajar. A small stone room, almost a prison cell, with a window high in its wall. When they had grown used to the dimness they were able to see big, uneven stones, an iron ring clamped into the wall, slabs underfoot. . . . Celestin closed the door. In the stony silence children's voices rose abruptly, very clear and distinct. The tower was high, the earth remote. Celestin took Juliette in his arms. He could kiss that lovely face for ever! Love it is that flings a man beyond mortal limitations. . . . Juliette, who had grown pale, steadied herself against the wall. It was cold, cold.

"Look," she said. "Lovers have written on the walls. . . ."

The wall was completely covered with pencilled or carved inscriptions: *Alain and Marguerite, July 7, 1938* . . . *Raynaud de Sainte-Cécile, 1799.* . . . Four concentric hearts, one within the other: *Suzanne, Lucie, Félicien, Robert.* . . . Other names and dates. . . . Down the edge of the door-jamb was a long column written in capital letters. It started at the top with: 5–6–26—SHE HAS COME.

They turned away from the wall and began reading the legends on the slabs underfoot. There, engraved in the stone, they saw what looked like a big obelisk in a Phrygian bonnet; the square pedestal bore a half-obliterated inscription. One could still read TO THE MARTYRS—OF . . . On another slab was a crucifix flanked by two candlesticks bearing candles as tall as the crucifix . . . elsewhere the following inscription: LONG LIVE . . . WHO . . . Many hearts, many horseshoes, also life-sized hands, with fingers spread apart. . . . *Laurent Derlys, 1815.* . . . In the corners it was too dark to make out anything. They returned to the inscriptions on the walls, the one beside the door opposite the window, at which the sun now pointed a pale finger:

5–6–26—SHE HAS COME

Underneath in the same handwriting, the same capital letters, written in blue-marking crayon:

1–6–29—SHE HAS COME 1929

24–7–31—THEY HAVE RETURNED
HIS HEART IS STILL
BEATING FOR HER

Juliette, on Celestin's arm, leaned against him more heavily. "Are there any more of them?" she asked. There were more . . .

THEY HAVE COME
FAITHFUL TO THAT PILGRIMAGE
HE LOVES HER   WHAT COURAGE
7 YEARS 1932

23–8–33—HE HAS GROWN OLD
BUT HIS HEART IS FAITHFUL
8 YEARS

The inscriptions went lower and lower, so that they had to bend double to decipher them. Perhaps there were no more. Yes:

ONLY HIS HEART IS FAITHFUL
HE IS OLD   SHE IS BEAUTIFUL
LORD MAKE HIS LOVE FOR HER ETERNAL
9 YEARS 1934

"Juliette, why are you crying? . . . We love each other. . . . Tell me that you are weeping for love. . . ." Juliette, on her knees before the wall, read:

HE IS OLD
SHE IS ALWAYS BEAUTIFUL
IF ONLY HE MAY DIE
NEAR HER
19 JULY 1936

They searched a long time on their knees: that was all. But standing up, they read above the door:

1937 AUGUST 30—HE IS OLD
SHE IS BEAUTIFUL
THEY HAVE COME

"Juliette, if I were chained to this ring I wouldn't feel my chains, because you exist, because your name exists! I would like to say to you all the old words of love, the stale words which are true once in a man's lifetime. . . . When I tell you that I love you madly, it's the truth. I'm mad with love!"

The blue-and-white air, driving the sun before it and crying *Christmas*, gathered them up and carried them into Avignon, where they were caught in the spider-web of streets. In the centre of the web lay the papal palace like a fat spider with a cross on its back. Without letting go of each other for a moment, they strayed through the narrow streets, which were twisted like branches between these walls, where France, Italy, and Spain met in watchful intercourse. Here the stone found expression for its glory and decay in the Gothic menace and in the luxuriant folly of the Baroque, or shaped in dough-like curves grimacing like a gargoyle. Here were decayed ramparts, churches, concealed mansions, enclosed courts, high-walled gardens from which a green branch escaped. . . . Nowhere could silence be more complete than in the chapel in the Rue des Teinturiers. The flood that had swept the chapel (how many centuries ago?), the waves which had parted here in a miracle, seemed to cradle the obscure silence, with its red stars as the vigil lights of perpetual adoration. Tearing themselves from the silence, they followed the sea-green canal, with the huge, motionless wheels of the dye works soaking in its brackish water. The streets swallowed them again, and they walked for a long time. . . . "Here's the prison," said Celestin. "But they shan't get me, because you love me, because I must help rid our country of the blight . . ."

The sun began to go down before the great walls of the prison, and Juliette felt the chill of December. A motionless crowd of men and women, loaded with packages, waited before the closed gate. The chapel of the Black Penitents of Mercy, built against the long, blank wall of the prison, stood at some distance from the crowd of people. The front of the chapel, with its exquisite, columns and elegant bays *à la française*, might have belonged to a a small private residence had it not been for the top-heavy aureola in the middle of the first storey, with the head of St. John the Baptist carried by angels in the centre. The interior might have served as a ballroom: gilded wainscoting, marble, pictures looking quite profane in large, gilded frames, a gilt ceiling. . . . "Here," explained the caretaker, "those condemned to death could attend Mass . . ." Condemned to death. . . . It wasn't simply a legend; perhaps the man beside her was a condemned man. He would lie chained in this prison; he would feel the burden

of his chains. . . . Juliette imagined herself standing in the crowd
before the big gates. She saw *Peter Ibbetson* again, as she had been
doing all day long. At that picture, though everyone around her
had laughed, she had cried so hard that she had had to wait before
going home, so Aunt Aline wouldn't see her tear-ravaged face.
Peter Ibbetson, in chains, being tortured, yet smiling at the angels
through his torment because he loved and could feel nothing
but his love. Love, the need of a certain presence, has been told
and retold, wept and sung. . . . "To have the certainty at dawn—
of seeing you before the night . . ." And lacking this certainty, or
the desolation that pervades the world, in every possible gesture,
every possible word, in all we see or hear! The ignorance of
how to come to terms with this life, with time that will not pass.
The desolation that would destroy us amidst futility, ashes,
waste. . . . To be like Peter Ibbetson, to triumph over absence!
Nothing could separate them. She lived in him, here and now,
fingering his chains, smiling at him, loving him. . . . He had killed
for Her, but it wasn't for Juliette that Celestin had killed! . . .
"Come," she said to him.

They climbed towards the capital of A of Avignon, the papal
palace. Their eyes sought the tops of the magnificent pinnacles,
lost in the sky. Fortress, cathedral, palace, heel set against the rock,
head high. . . . In the long, paved courtyard loomed a black
equestrian statue of Crillon. They went down again into the
narrow streets, into the huddled quarter that clings to the foot of
the colossus. Grass grew between the uneven stones underfoot.
. . . The little square was as quiet and deserted as a school play-
ground when classes are in session. A latrine, pasted with
advertisements, occupied the middle of the square, as might a
fountain or an equestrian statue. The women knitting on the
doorsteps, with their overcoats thrown over their shoulders, had
nothing aggressive about them. There were pretty legends on
the house-fronts: "*Au petit Chabanais*" . . . "*Chez Margot*". . . .
The street led them direct into the gipsy quarter. It grew so
narrow that they pressed even closer together. A chord was
struck somewhere; it faded away and was repeated. . . . They saw
a group of gipsies, dressed in dirty rags, sitting on the pavement.
Their fingers plucked from the guitar strings tunes that scattered
the air into a thousand fragments. . . . "How I love that disturb-

ing instrument!" said Celestin. "Don't you? Listen to those chords! Try as they may, though the sounds linger, they never dissolve into one another; each one is a hole into which your heart plunges. The song has ended. No, it's starting again. . . . Listen! Some of them are singing. . . ." The voices and guitars followed them as they lost themselves in the narrow lanes. They were well prepared for the sight that met their eyes. . . .

She was tall and slim, and wore a low, square neckline as though it were midsummer. She was embracing the fountain with her round, bare arms, pressing herself against it. The tall pitcher stood on the far rim, beneath the jet of water. She was magnificent, like a painting in a museum, like the papal palace, like a cloistered garden. . . . They stopped in their tracks, dazzled. The sound of the gipsy guitars faded away, and only the gurgling of the water was audible. A man came up to the fountain. He lifted the full pitcher and put his free arm around the girl's shoulders. They went away, leaving behind them a trail of water drops. Juliette and Celestin saw only the man's back. He was wearing a bowler hat, and his overcoat was darker than the dusk.

Later they found themselves seated face to face in a very small *bistro*. It looked like one of those miniatures which astonish us by imitating life-sized objects so well: chairs, curtains, crockery. . . . The pink walls were almost completely covered with advertisements, gay as flags. There were five or six sticky marble tables. The high zinc counter had an embossed pattern at the rim, and behind it bloomed bottles of all colours. The girl behind the counter was so young that she seemed to be playing at serving the customers.

Holding hands, looking into each other's eyes, they rested, after their long walk, on either side of the narrow table. Imagine someone you had seen only from a distance, or only in dreams (Madame Bovary, Anna Karenina, Werther, Gary Cooper, Charles Boyer), sitting at the same table with you! Imagine such a being, familiar and yet remote, suddenly endowed with a particular texture of skin and hair, fingernails, a shape of ear, all those details one would never think of imagining. They looked at each other, surprised and curious, as though through magnifying glasses. The little mirror that Juliette drew from her worn handbag, the lipstick in its worn gold case, and the wool gloves carefully darned at the thumb. . . . Her way of setting her beret on her hair, which was as blonde and fine as a child's; the way she put her finger behind her small, perfect ear; the chain round her neck—with a locket at the end of it, no doubt; the mauve circles beneath her eyes; the astonishing mother-of-pearl of her teeth. As for him, he had hard, well-shaped hands, the index fingers stained with tobacco, a signet ring. . . . There was a button missing on his raincoat. . . . A few wrinkles beneath oval eyes, an unsteady gaze, rather tousled hair . . . an occasional smile. . . . The brandy glasses were ridiculously small—mere thimbles. The pile of saucers mounted.

They dined at Celestin's, in the arched room filled with living fire. Celestin had ordered his servant to bring out his most treasured stores; the tin of sardines, the pineapple preserves, the remains of yesterday's goose. The dinner was first-rate. . . . The radio played dinner music, just suited to their mood. As for the wine, Celestin could still be proud of his cellar. They were madly, foolishly gay. They were just starting to dance when the servant knocked at the door. . . .

"Captain," said the servant, "it's the same man again. He won't go away. . . ."

Celestin went out at once. Juliette remained in her armchair. She moved her shoulders as though she were dancing, turning, reversing. The radio swept her off her feet. . . . But Celestin didn't come back. How long it took him! The Christmas tree at the back of the room seemed like the edge of a dark forest, the candles on the table wept their last tears, the radio was silent, and here she was, useless as a squeezed lemon . . .

Celestin returned to the opening strains of "Maréchal nous voilà". . . . He switched off the radio and said: "I have to go. I'm terribly sorry to desert you like this. . . . If you want to spend the night here you're perfectly welcome. Unless you'd rather go on tonight . . . François could take you to the station . . ."

"I hope it's nothing serious?"

"No, not at all. . . . Simply a job. Another job, an urgent one. Will you go straight to Lyons?"

"I'm going to stop off at Valence."

"Well, then, Juliette, I'll say good-bye. . . . You'll get a train in about an hour. Give your instructions to François. . . ."

"Celestin!"

Celestin straddled a chair, and then dropped on to a low stool before the fire. His curious glance, which sometimes seemed to leap from his face and sometimes became immobile, was fixed straight before him on the fire.

"Juliette, you said 'Let's pretend . . .'"

"Oh!" she cried faintly.

"It's a terrible game. . . . You have given me a taste of everything that I don't possess, that I'll never possess, wonderful Juliette! I feel more miserable now than I ever did before, because I know that there's nothing left beneath the ashes. For a moment I was able to *believe*, but it's no use. If you couldn't work the miracle, no one else ever will. Juliette, don't cry. We're not masters of our hearts. I'm a blunt man. . . ."

"I'm not crying," said Juliette, snatching up her beret and putting it on. "I've always known that love is counterfeit, and that nothing is genuine but illusion. People don't love each other. No one loves anyone. . . . I'm not in love with you. Where's my coat?"

"So you're going to leave tonight?" Celestin had risen; he was stooping a little, his hand at the level of his heart.

"Yes, I'll spend the night in Valence. What's the matter? Is anything wrong?"

"No. Good-bye, Juliette."

"Why good-bye? *Au revoir* would be better, wouldn't it?"

"Well, then, *au revoir*. . . ."

They shook hands.

Celestin's servant walked behind Juliette, carrying her suitcase. The streets were dark, but you didn't need to see, you could hear them. *They* alone could make such a noise with their boots, as though they were made of lead or cast iron. Avignon was a German town. . . .

5

So Juliette Noël, typist, found herself once more in a train. A packed train, like all of them. She sat on her little suitcase, in the corridor packed with people and luggage, although four com-

partments in this car were empty and locked. At each stop new-
comers tried the doors, which were labelled *für die Wehrmacht*.
They tried them all the same, cursed, and went on, since there
was no longer even standing room in the corridor. An old
gentleman in an elegant overcoat, who wore a pearl tie-pin and
had only two teeth, said loudly that if there were a German here
he would be only too pleased to open the doors and let people sit
down, because the Germans were so glad to oblige, and so
polite. When the corridor heard the words "so polite" they
echoed them in a Greek chorus: "So very polite!" A young
boy fiddled with the lock of one of the *für die Wehrmacht* compartments with his pocket-knife, his neighbours encouraging
him. . . ."They shoot you, too, so politely," Juliette said sadly.
The young man next to her, travelling sedately with his mother,
who had said a moment ago "so very polite", suddenly looked
like someone who has missed the step on a ladder. He whispered
to Juliette, "Have they shot very many in Valence?" "In Valence,
and other places," Juliette replied coolly. The window wouldn't
stay shut. Every two minutes somebody closed it, but it promptly
started sliding down again, and an icy blast pierced the travellers
in the corridor.

"Can't you open these empty compartments for us?" Juliette
asked the collector as he passed through, pressing the people
against the walls of the corridor.

"Can't you read? They're for the occupying forces."

"I don't understand dialect," Juliette answered, and the
whole corridor roared. The collector shrugged his shoulders
and passed on.

At the stations people boarded the train, dragging suitcases
and children after them. The passages looked absolutely jammed,
but still they came and went. They tried the doors of the empty
compartments, as if they wouldn't have been opened long ago
had it been possible. There was plenty of comment:

"What's all this—are these for the mail?"

"Can't you read—that's for the Fritzes."

"Damn the Fritzes!"

They moved on, somehow. Or else they stood on other
people's feet.

The handle and lock of the suitcase cut into Juliette's flesh.

She was sick of travelling. She was very, very tired, unnerved, and she felt like giving her opinion in a loud voice on all sorts of subjects. But she had to hold her tongue. She'd already attracted too much notice; the old man with two teeth was looking at her askance. "Have you seen their uniforms and equipment? And what discipline!" said the old creature in a pompous voice.

"I'd like to spit in his face," Juliette mused, while the corridor chorus echoed, "What discipline!" The open window let in the damp night wind. The young man travelling with his mother must be beckoning to *her*. He had moved away. Trying to get near her, he shoved the others aside. "Mademoiselle," he said, "there's a seat for you back there. My mother's holding it for you——"

"Thanks. But this is Valence. I get off here."

The hotel room at Valence was unheated for a change. . . . Juliette spent an uneasy night, sleeping with one eye open. She had registered at the hotel as Rose Toussaint (the doctor had expressly instructed her to do this, as she had valuable papers on her), but her forged identification card wasn't ready yet. When she had that she would no longer be running a risk. She dreamed of stone catacombs from which she was unable to escape. Their walls were gloomy and rough, and grey shadows floated about her, whispering that she could never, never leave! They needn't tell her that; she knew it well enough; it was simply a refinement of torture. On the wall of this nightmare prison, in huge capital letters, she read: THEY HAVE COME. She couldn't tell whether the despair she felt was the result of this legend or of the knowledge that she must remain here for ever. "Blessed lovers of Avignon, who are in heaven, have mercy on me, help me . . ." prayed Juliette in her dream.

The next morning, while she waited until she would be sure to find someone at the meeting-place, she roamed the streets. Valence is a big town. . . . A large railway station, large cafés, large stores, large cinemas. There were Germans, and also Italians . . . The latter have such an air! But they're really only funny. You can't take people seriously who dress themselves up in cock feathers. Juliette's feet were so cold she could have cried. Fortunately it was almost time for her to look for her people. She could go there any time after eleven.

It was one of those cafés near the station, filled with packages which people had deposited. "No, I don't want any saccharine lemonade. It's so cold. I want hot coffee . . ." "Would you like a hot brick for your feet, mademoiselle?" Yes, indeed. While she waited for her coffee Juliette surveyed the man behind the zinc counter; he must be the one. But there was a policeman standing up drinking his coffee, and two more seated at a table. . . . They were getting up to leave. What a lot of space they occupied! They were well fed in this region. Almost as plump as the *gardes mobiles*. Opposite Juliette a German officer drank his coffee, with a little glass of yellow liqueur. He had a thin, haggard face, and bony hands. . . . Not much of a warrior. Juliette rose and went over to the counter.

"Could you give me a drink like the one that German has?" she asked. "Dr. Arnold sends his regards . . ."

"That drink isn't so good," said the proprietor. "Would you mind putting your suitcase back there, near the toilet?"

Juliette went back and picked up her suitcase and carried it where he had indicated. . . . The proprietress followed her. "Hurry," she said. "Sometimes people come in unexpectedly." Juliette took the ration cards from her knapsack, and the proprietress shot them into her blouse. "Now, little lady," she said, "I'm going to give you hot coffee and a liqueur—a real one."

Both the German officer and the policeman standing by the counter were still there. Two men were playing cards. The magohany tables, the yellow walls, the brown benches, the men's leather jackets, one man's necktie, the other's yellow scarf, provided just a touch of yellow to enliven the master's painting called "The Card Players".

There was an afternoon train. Juliette had lunch in a cheap eating-place, greasy and crowded. She had a cup of coffee at another place. Outside it was cold. The snow was beginning to melt underfoot, and everything had an after-the-holiday air, as unpleasant as going home at dawn after a wild party, or as a table strewn with the debris of a meal. Juliette stopped in front of a cinema. The afternoon show was about to begin. . . . She went in.

The house was an attractive one, almost as nice as the Paramount in Paris. It was empty, completely empty, and heated. Juliette chose a seat in the middle, at the right distance from the screen. The plush seat was comfortable. She had no neighbours, nobody to pay any attention to her. At this moment Juliette was glad to have no one notice her. . . . A solitary young man, looking like a student, sat behind her reading a newspaper. Usherettes leaned against the walls. Three youngsters came in noisily, but quieted down after a moment in the churchlike silence. How nice and warm it was! The boys sat down close to the screen. Here in this gilded silence she could forget the house in the mountains, her muddy shoes, the dawn, barley coffee, and the grey vermin in the streets. Juliette began to feel hot, cosy, and sleepy. She was just about to doze off when she was roused by a clicking sound. . . . She started, sensing danger. From the direction of the screen confused sounds came, took shape, and became music. The familiar voice of Edith Piaff began singing:

> "He was big and he was handsome,
> And the hot sand smelled good . . ."

It was as though the heat of this room had thawed Juliette's heart, and the water streamed from her eyes. . . . How it hurts when the blood begins to flow in a frozen limb! Have you ever had the tips of your ears or a finger frozen on a skiing trip? So long as they are frozen, white and bloodless, you don't feel anything, but when they start coming to life they hurt very badly, as though a thousand needles were sticking into them . . . God, how her heart ached! How alone she was in this big, gilded cinema, as though she were buried alive in a huge sarcophagus! Blessed lovers of Avignon, pray for her!

Throughout the newsreel the cinema remained in semi-darkness. Perhaps they thought that Juliette would cause a disturbance at the sight of those model soldiers, in their nice white overalls, repairing a telephone wire in a blinding snowstorm, while nasty, invisible Russians fired on them from behind. Afterwards she watched the main feature, which was so bad that she could doze and think of nothing at all. . . . She almost missed her train.

6

"Juliette, are you ill?"

"I?" What makes you think so?"

"The way you look! Has anything happened? Is anything wrong?"

Aunt Aline took off her coat, while José clung with both arms about her knees. He was jubilant.

"Juliette has come back! Juliette has come back!"

"Will you please tell me whether everything is all right?"

"Yes, yes, Aunt Aline. If you only realized what travelling is like nowadays. . . . José, my little darling, you're suffocating me! Have you been a good boy?"

"Let Juliette rest. Lay the table, like a big boy. Quick, now."

Aunt Aline followed Juliette into the bedroom. "My child," she said, while Juliette was taking off her clothes and putting on her old wrap and slippers. "God knows I approve of everything you do. But I'm an old woman. . . . It's getting to be too much for me. If I could go with you—but this waiting! Whenever I hear a step on the stair I think it's the police. I think you'll never come back, that you've been caught. . . . Can't you stop for a while, long enough to get a breathing space? Think of José. What would become of him without you?"

Juliette washed her hands and brushed her teeth. The beaded fringe round the lampshade prevented her from seeing herself in the cheap little mirror, and she smoothed her hair by touch. . . .

"I can't stop. . . . There are so few people to do the work. . . . You always hear that everybody's in this together, but when it comes to doing anything . . . Did José like his horse? Did you have a nice Christmas? How did you cook the rabbit? You mustn't worry, Auntie, I'm very careful. In any case I'll go back to the newspaper now. That means I won't travel any more."

"If I could only believe you! I wish you could see yourself. You're so pale, you worry me; you're going to be ill . . ."

"Nonsense! I'm perfectly all right. Just tired, of course. How good it is to be back!"

"Juliette!" José shouted. "Juliette, come on!"

"You look very tired, Mademoiselle Noël. Why don't you take a day or two off?" asked the editor-in-chief, who was dictating to her. Juliette always made men feel protective.

"But why, monsieur? I feel very well, thanks. It's only that I don't like Lyons."

"Neither do I . . ." said the editor-in-chief with a sigh.

Her nostalgia for Paris, which from the beginning of her exile had made her find fault with every place because it wasn't Paris, had increased at Lyons. Lyons was a close, heavy town, like a secret, persistent pain, ill-made for consolation. Her dislike went so far that she had acquired a prejudice against people who pretended to like Lyons, as though they are abnormal and found a kind of morose satisfaction in their misfortune. What could anybody possibly find to like in this town? Houses like cubes, without colour or relief? Streets of such houses? This petty-bourgeois air that made you think of the outer boulevards of Paris? Staircases like service stairs? Rows of little mail boxes on muddy red-brown walls? Balustrades that looked as though they were made from prison bars? Or perhaps the apartments, with their alcoves, and alcoves within alcoves, and alcoves of alcoves within alcoves, progressively darker and more hidden? This mania for the narrow, the hidden, the scrubbed step. . . . Juliette had never read *La Girl Prisoner de Poitiers*, but the feeling she had for Lyons and the people who liked Lyons might be compared, I imagine, to what she would have felt towards "the little grotto", where the victim in the story slept. Or was she supposed to like the climate of Lyons, the fog, the mud, the melting snow? In Paris one never noticed the weather except to decide that it was too nice to go home, that it would be a pity to lose the least bit of it.

To go into the street in Paris was to enter a marvellous adventure. To walk in the streets of Lyons was to wade in cold slush, past grey barracks with a swastika flag over the gate, two field-grey sentinels helmeted and armed to the teeth, striding smartly along the pavement. . . . The little sailors strolling through the streets of Lyons (why on earth should there be sailors in Lyons? Was it just they managed to get round everywhere? But *she* saw them at Lyons). . . . The little sailors no longer wore their pretty red pompons. They were no longer smart and trim.

They were adrift. . . . And the army, stripped of its braids and insignia, broken, like an officer cashiered, wore the angry look of defeat, of those from whom everything has been taken. 1918, 1918, 1918 was written on all the walls. The same as in Paris, no doubt! The same as everywhere . . . 1918. . . . Running after tramcars, or else waiting for them interminably, feeling the cold pierce your bones, standing on the lowest step, your hands frozen and almost ready to let go. . . . Oh, the wonderful warmth of the Paris Métro! Well-dressed women, men who get up to offer you their seats, compared with the tramcars in Lyons. . . . The Rhone is pale and tragic as the empty sleeve of an amputated arm. . . . But the Seine is full of charm, and never makes you shudder. Small comfort to remember that once upon a time Lyons was a paradise of good living, that these wretched *bistros*, these wineshops where people sat in huddled discomfort over a mouldy dumpling, were once upon a time temples of gastronomical culture.

God knows it wasn't Lyons that made Juliette pale and gave her those rings round her eyes, arousing the compassion of the editor-in-chief. But Lyons was a handy scapegoat. . . . Mlle Gérard, another typist at the paper, a swarthy girl whom Juliette had become friendly with, said: "Juliette, can't I do the Letter Box? Go and rest for a while. I'll manage. . . . You look awful." "I tell you, Marie, I feel perfectly well. I'm not ill, I just fret. The nearer the end seems, the more I fret. It's horrible to think of men dying on the eve of victory!" "They've caught Pierrot," Marie Gérard whispered. "The little typesetter, you know, the communist. The Gestapo raided the *bistro* where he lives . . . they gave him a beating right in the *bistro* in front of everybody, and then took him away. Just a child. . . . Yesterday they searched Benoît's house. . . . Luckily he wasn't at home, but they picked up a chap who was waiting for him."

Mlle Gérard had been the first to talk to Juliette about the Resistance. Very cautiously at first, not knowing what was in the mind of that charming but reserved and distant girl. But on the day the news came that Juliette's brother had been killed in Libya, Marie Gérard, overcome by rage and pity, suggested to her point-blank that she should work for them. Her brother's blood was sufficient guarantee for Juliette. After that, with one thing leading to another for over a year, Juliette had become deeply involved in the organization. They used her more and more: she was discreet, steady, and efficient, and never refused a job. And there were plenty of jobs. The information which had to be circulated daily among the Resistance members (passwords, news of arrests, incidents concerning forced labour, acts of sabotage completed or planned, the discovery of informers, Gestapo raids, secret literature) was amassed and distributed through the Letter Boxes. The Resistance grew, armed with secret weapons gathered from everywhere, stolen from arsenals, hidden away in 1940 at the time of the Armistice, or parachuted from British 'planes. . . . The country's heart was beating, and Juliette Noël, typist, was helping to keep the blood flowing into it. A national front rose against the usurpers, a Maginot Line that was alive, bleeding, painful, yet gathering strength day by day.

Juliette had Lyons at her finger-tips: Fourvière, the Croix-Rousse, Saint-Jean, Villeurbanne no longer held any secrets for her. She knew all the tramcar lines, the little blue train, the cafés, the *bistros*, the benches in the squares, and the *traboules*, narrow tunnels threading the old blocks of houses in every direction, which were first-rate short cuts (some of them have as many as six or seven exits on all sides: imagine a game of hide-and-seek there . . .). Juliette kept saying "I don't like Lyons", but perhaps this wasn't strictly true any more.

Lyons had become the accomplice of her life and her work: its taciturn houses, the dark refuge of the *traboules*, the great leprous walls devoid of grace or lightness, the fine stuffs woven behind those walls, the treasures amassed, the schemes plotted in under-tones . . . On this mild February day she climbed to the top of the Croix-Rousse, and leaning against a wall above the cable of the funicular she looked down on the city. Not without emotion, she watched the sun redden the face of Lyons, a face pale and dark with poverty when not sicklied by the greedy and selfish process of digestion. In front of her were the straight, serried ranks of windows, aligned on walls which offer nothing to the eye but this array of black rectangles. She saw them across a forest of black, smokeless chimneys, a tragic forest wasted as though by a great fire. Far below, the Rhone was bordered by large buildings which, in the proximity of the river, looked rather majestic and

impressive, even beautiful. . . . In the distance the skyscrapers of
Villeurbanne drank in the light. . . . Juliette dreamed, holding the
package tightly under her arm. The air was so lovely and mild. . . .
What was going on behind her placid brow? Dreams were her
old companions. . . . Juliette put a finger behind her ear and
turned her back on the scene. It was getting late. She had almost
forgotten the time.

The sounds of activity were like live houses breathing—the
great silk factories, just rows of windows and the pulsations of
those breaths. Juliette followed one street, then another, until a
stairway opened before her, large, bare, interminable, solemn,
like a stone cloak falling from the shoulders of a giant. She
descended the stairs. There were a great many of them. A balus-
trade of straight black bars, like prison bars, ran down alongside
the houses. . . . At the bottom of the stairs Juliette went on a few
steps and then plunged into a *traboule*.

Like all the *traboules*, this one commenced with a display of
small letter-boxes against the decaying wall. Each little box bore
a name on a copper plate, a calling card, or a scrap of paper.
Each had a little lock, and the number of these little boxes
indicated the congestion in each house. Each tenant carried a little
key to the secret of his correspondence. One of the journalists
on the paper was being persecuted by a woman who wrote him
several letters a day. The crazy creature enclosed each of these
love letters in several layers of envelopes, which was rather
symptomatic of her character, not so much of the Lyonese themselves, as of the dwelling. The *traboule* which Juliette had entered seemed to emerge from its mystery into a large, square
courtyard on two levels, with a stairway in the middle. The stairway, the wrought-iron gate at its foot, surmounted by a lantern,
and another staircase zigzagging up to the top storey of the
building, gave the courtyard a rather prison-like effect. Passing
the staircase in the middle of the court, Juliette entered the base-
ment of the house, went down a few greasy steps which seemed
to lead to a cellar, and entered another passageway, which ended
in turn with another row of letter-boxes giving on to a different
street. She crossed the street (high walls with rectangular windows, nothing else) and entered an even narrower, darker,
dirtier *traboule*, with angles, steps, complicated turns, and two

courts as narrow and dark as the inside of a chimney, decorated with staircases whose landings formed balconies railed in with prison bars at each floor. She came out finally at the Place des Terreaux, where she took a tramcar.

She rang at the lodge on the ground floor (this was a handsome modern house, with a caretaker); the concierge came out. The woman looked completely distraught. "Mademoiselle," she said in a breathless voice, "*they're* here. . . . I don't know why you've come. . . . Maybe you shouldn't go in. There are five, Germans, I think. . . ." Steps could be heard behind the door. When the door opened the vestibule was empty, the heavy outside door shut.

Juliette ran along the street, or rather she didn't run but walked very fast, like a horse about to break into a gallop. She felt a pain in her side. Here was the tramcar that would take her to the Rue des Cordeliers. . . . The streets were already dark, crushed beneath the weight of the blackout. What if nobody was there? She must run, whatever the consequences.

The small courtyard was illuminated dimly by the light from the windows all around; round café tables had been stacked one on top of the other in a corner. Boxes were piled at the entrance to the staircase, above which, in the orange light coming from within, could be read *Bar: Service Entrance*. Juliette stumbled over a dustbin, groped her way up the stairs, and gave the prescribed number of rings. . . . Dominique himself opened the door.

"What's the matter?" he asked, grabbing her arm.

"They're raiding Rue——"

"Come in. . . ."

At the back of the room, which was like a prison, a man, fully dressed, lay on a mattress on the floor. . . . He jumped up and ran his hands through his tangled hair. His eyes had red circles round them, and his cheeks were dreadfully hollow.

"I didn't have time to deliver the Box. I was late, thank God. Here are the pamphlets."

She put the parcel which she had been carrying under her arm on the table.

"We'll have to change all the addresses . . ."

Dominique put on his leather jacket. His trousers were

clamped with bicycle clips. He'd need more than his looks to get by on. "Juliette," he went on, "go and tell the doctor that I'm sending M. George—no, there are too many Georges: M. Amadéé—for tomorrow's conference. Go on, now. You haven't been followed, have you?"

"No, I don't think so. I came as fast as I could. . . ."

Dr. Arnold banged his fist on the desk. "The bastards!" he shouted. "They'll have got him!" He banged his fist again. "There's no doubt about it now, that dirty Jacques gave him away. The same thing happened with Lafont. . . . He'll pay for it, the filthy brute!" He left the room. Juliette heard him telephoning. Then the door opened gently and the doctor's wife came in, silent and furtive. She must have been ten years older than her husband. . . . "What a calamity!" she said. "Poor Mlle Noël; there doesn't seem to be any end to it . . ." She began to cry quietly, and was gone before the doctor came back.

"Juliette, my child," he said, "you were lucky not to get caught. . . . Would it be asking too much of you to reserve a room for a friend who is coming the day after tomorrow? A fellow named Celestin—but of course you know him. I'd forgotten all about that. You met him in Avignon, remember? That will work out fine. You can pick him up at the station, that is, if you are free . . ."

"I'll be free," said Juliette.

"Right. He'll have to put up at that nasty hole where you spent the night . . ."

Juliette rang up the newspaper and told them she had the flu. She was actually very tired. The business of the raid had shaken her up.

7

SHE caught sight of him from a distance. He was much taller than the other travellers. When she touched his sleeve Celestin's eyes gave a characteristic quiver. He hadn't expected to see her. . . . But he gave no sign of surprise, and no smile of recognition added warmth to his handshake.

"Did you come for me?"

"Yes. The doctor asked me to reserve a room and go to the station to fetch a fellow named Celestin. . . . You're going to sleep in a low-down hotel. . . . You'll be all right there. I spent a night there myself. They don't ask you to register."

"Do we take a tramcar?"

"No, it's just a few steps . . ."

"All the advantages. . . . But how is everything with you . . . Juliette?"

"Have you forgotten my name? I'm very well. And you?"

"No, I haven't forgotten your name. . . . But I'm not sure I'm permitted to call you so familiarly by your Christian name."

"You are. . . . It will sound more natural at the hotel. I'll have to go up with you. I have a letter for you. Are there still as many Germans in Avignon?"

"More, if possible." He began enumerating the hotels that had been taken over by the Germans; a German library had been installed in the Rue de la République . . .

"Here's the hotel," said Juliette. "Look: there are three exits, or entrances, if you prefer. One into the court, that's the main one . . . the others are impossible to find unless one knows them. See, there's one here, by the cinema; the other opens on to the street at the back . . ."

Neither the hotel-keeper nor his dogs appeared. A dozing servant watched Juliette indifferently as she took the key from the rack. The curtains were drawn in the room. Curtains of flowered blue sateen, a divan covered with the same material, even the rug on the floor was blue. . . . Mirrors reflected all this blossoming azure, the shaded light fixtures. . . . It was delightfully warm, the warmth of paradise. A person could have lived here as the Lord created him.

"Do you like it?" Juliette asked.

"No fairy-tale palace could suit me better than this hotel . . ."

A smile passed across his face—the sombre face of a fallen archangel.

"Will you give me the message, Juliette?"

She handed him a letter which she drew from the lining of her coat.

"The doctor said to tell you that he got this from the radio this morning. He thought you would be on your way already. This is the text. That's all I know . . ."

Celestin tore open the envelope and went to the window, but the window opened on to a blank wall. He had to resort to one of the dim lamps, of pink ground glass. It took him a long time to read the two small pages. From time to time he gave Juliette an absent look. Then he burned the note over the washstand, and let the tap run until the ashes had disappeared. He still wore his raincoat.

"I'll go out first," he said. "Wait five or ten minutes. . . . *Au revoir*, Juliette, since you don't like saying good-bye. Many thanks."

He was gone. Juliette sank down on to the blue coverlet of the divan. The room, with its immense sateen bed, the mirrors, reeked of a case-house. Juliette began to laugh hysterically. . . . Beautiful indeed, her lost paradise! Beautiful enough for laughter, and then tears. How my heart aches for her, for all women. . . . Juliette! A little dignity, please, even if nobody sees you. Blessed lovers of Avignon, for the love of love forgive her. . . . Stay, she must not be profane! . . . "They have come!" she cried. "They have come!" No, I'd rather not hear, not know. . . . It must have been the fatigue of the last months, a nervous exhaustion.

When Juliette Noël left the hotel she became vaguely aware of a man in a long, light overcoat watching her from the pavement opposite the main gate of the courtyard. She had reached the Place Bellecour before she thought of it again and turned round: sure enough, there he was, with another man. . . . But perhaps it didn't mean anything. . . . She looked back furtively once or twice: they were crossing the square behind her. All right, she would take the tramcar. The two men stopped right beside her. Why were they following her? Celestin? The Letter Box? This wasn't the first time she had had the sensation of being followed. But always before it had turned out to be sheer imagination, or men wanting to pick her up. It was impossible to tell whether these were police or the other sort. . . . Here came the tramcar. . . . Juliette darted forward, letting herself be jostled. Would they get on too? Apparently not. . . . The tramcar started to move.

. . . Juliette leaped on to the step, but a hand dragged her back.

"Don't make a scene," said the man in the light overcoat. "We won't hurt you."

He spoke French very well, with the merest suspicion of an accent. The two men flanked her solidly, hemming her in without letting it appear that they did. The second man had a long nose, and disorderly blond hair that pushed his hat up. He spoke a few words in German. . . .

"I'm done," said Juliette to herself. "What have I got on me? . . . Nothing compromising; no, nothing. . . . I have my forged identification card: my name is Rose Toussaint. . . . At least I think so. . . . Yes, of course, I took it because of Celestin. Oh, God! Aunt Aline gave me her ration card so I could get some coffee at last, since I was going to town. . . . Poor Aunt Aline, once she gets a bee in her bonnet . . . you'd think nothing else in the world mattered but coffee. Poor Aunt Aline, how she has aged! She didn't use to be like that. . . . Poor Aunt Aline won't get her coffee. . . . If only I didn't have that card! I'll tell them it isn't mine. It belongs to Juliette Noël, a friend of mine. It's very simple. . . . I'll never get out of this, never. . . . I'll tell them I'm a tart . . ."

"Just tell us when and where you are going to meet your boy-friend. That's all we ask. After that you may go."

They walked up the Rue de la République, Juliette still between the two men.

"Which boy-friend?"

"My dear girl, don't be silly. The one you went to meet at the station and took to the hotel."

"What if I don't tell you?"

"Have you ever heard of the Terminus Hotel?"

"What do you mean?"

"The Gestapo, mademoiselle, the Gestapo. Does that mean anything to you? They question you very thoroughly there. . . . Will you kindly tell us at once where and when you are to meet this man?"

My God, thought Juliette. This is why I shouldn't have seen him again. . . . Who knows, under torture . . . I needn't worry. I won't say anything. I'm just not meeting anyone.

"Why don't you go to the hotel after him? You know this is no fun for me . . ."

"Because he won't go back there. . . . That's enough arguing. Understand? Hurry up and tell us what we want to know."

"But I haven't got a date! He doesn't want me any longer. . . . He took me to the hotel and dropped me there. . . ."

The blond fellow with the big nose again said something in German, while the other watched Juliette sceptically.

"Go on, that's a story. Nobody drops a pretty girl like you. The captain is a man of good taste, like all his kind. That is, if you know your stuff."

They both laughed loudly, and the German nudged Juliette in the waist with his elbow, as though it were a good joke.

"But I don't," said Juliette.

"Oh, don't you? If you insist, we'll take you to the hotel and give you a lesson. Well, are you going to talk now?"

"You're hurting me," moaned Juliette, and turned her tear-filled eyes to him. Tears brimmed in her eyes without falling, like the glycerine tears in a film. . . . He was confused. Juliette had a type of beauty that would have touched any man.

"You needn't cry," he said. "It's not your fault that you picked up a bird like Celestin. Next time you'll be more careful, won't you?"

"Yes, indeed," said Juliette. "And yet I'm usually so careful. . . . What on earth can he have done? Is it very serious?"

"No, not at all. Take us to him and we'll come to an understanding very quickly. Come now, we won't hurt your man . . ."

"Oh," sighed Juliette, "this is awful . . . I had a date with him at . . . But you know he's never on time. We may have to wait. . . . He promised to meet me under the arcades of the Opera in half an hour, perhaps an hour . . ."

The tables of the shops in the thoroughfare, the people stopping in front of shop windows, the movement to and fro, recalled the arcades of the Odéon in Paris. Only here they sold a little of everything: postcards, spectacles, underwear. . . . And the whole place had the rather secret, shady air so characteristic of Lyons.

"Let her walk by herself. There's no chance of her getting

away," said the man in the light overcoat. They had been jostled from all sides because they continued to walk three abreast under the arcades of the theatre. The open arches between the pillars were barred half-way up by iron railings. The German released Juliette's arm with visible reluctance: he had been pressing her closer and closer. "*Voran* . . . walk ahead," he said. Juliette walked on ahead of them, the two men at her heels. She had no idea why she had chosen to come to the arcades, except that one had to give the miracle time to work . . .

She stopped in front of an optician's window and scrutinized the eyeglasses. Continuing to the other end of the arcades, where sheet music was pinned on a display board, she began reading the titles: "Silk Workers' March" . . . "Marvellous Tango" . . . "Margot in the Village" . . . "This Cursed War" (Big Hit). . . . The covers, long exposed to the dust, were yellow and spotted, the thin leaves wilted as though they had been rained on. She read on, a pang in her heart: "Little Quinquin" . . . "The Street of Our Love" . . . here was "My Legionnaire" with a picture of little Piaff on the cover . . . "Flowers are the Words of Love". . . . What was she to do?—she hadn't a straw to cling to. . . . The two men behind her were as compact and implacable as a prison door. . . . Should she whisper to a passer-by, or scream? . . . This crowd was suffocating. . . . "The Violin in the Night" . . . "My Heart is with You" . . . "Lorraine March" . . . "My Sweetest Song". . . . By now she was so cold that she thought she would never be warm again. She had to keep moving, lest despair should grip her by the throat. As long as there's life . . . She turned back, the two men still behind her. Back and forward, back and forward . . . "Wait a minute," said the German, stopping in front of a stationer's. He tilted his long nose, and the hat perched on his thick hair, over a glass case set out on a table. The man in the light overcoat asked the shopman, who wore gold-rimmed glasses, if he had any postcards. Yes, there were some inside. The German walked in. The old shopman looked decent. She felt certain that he would have helped her if he had known. Provided he had been able, because, even when you know, you can't always help . . .

"I'm tired," Juliette said, sitting astride the iron railing of the arch. She saw the street, with its dirty houses, trucks, cyclists, and crowds of pedestrians. This quarter, with its wholesale houses (Silk Goods . . . Silk Goods, said the signs), reminded her of the Sentier in Paris, minus the Paris goods. In this filthy district are located business houses that have tentacles in every part of the world. They would think it beneath their dignity to yield to the luxury of fine buildings; instead, they overflow their premises, encumbering the narrow streets which reek of peddlers and hucksters with bales and boxes of merchandise. . . . Here there are complicated *traboules* with stairs going in every direction, embedded into stone and iron, dips, passageways, openings on well-like courtyards, doors bearing the signs: Silk Goods . . . Silk Goods . . . Letter Boxes. . . . *Traboules* where you climb dark stairs, turn, descend, retrace your own steps to find the exit from the maze. Many of them are reinforced by high iron gates with narrow openings, one or two bars having been removed, so that a man can pass through sideways, but not a crate nor a bale can pass. . . . Precautionary measures, they say, on the part of the silk merchants.

"Your young man certainly keeps you waiting," said Juliette's jailor.

On the other side of the railing were stone steps leading down to the street: the arcades were some distance above the street level. The German had come out of the shop and stood writing postcards against the wall.

"Let's walk a little further," said Juliette. Once again they started pacing the arcades, she and the man in the light overcoat. There were fountain-pens, articles made of raffia, ration-card cases . . . *Bridge in Ten Lessons* . . . *Games of Chance* . . . *The Violin in the Night* . . . eyeglasses. The German finished writing his postcards and rejoined them. The two whispered together. God only knew what they were up to . . .

"Mademoiselle, my friend wants me to ask you if you'll accept a little souvenir?" The fellow in the light overcoat sniggered softly.

"A souvenir? What do you mean?" Juliette gathered herself inwardly. What was this new danger?

"Don't be frightened. He only wants to give you a little present. . . . You needn't feel embarrassed. His pockets are full of marks."

"I really don't know. . . . What kind of a little present? Let him choose it, if it's supposed to be a surprise . . ."

The German went back inside the stationer's shop, and Juliette sat down again on the railing.

"I think your friend needs your help," she said. Inside the shop the German could be seen conversing at length with the merchant. The man in the light coat cast a glance that way.

"He'll manage," he said, still jokingly.

Juliette flung both legs over the railing and jumped from the top of the steps into the street . . .

". . . I can't leave you here alone, you might try to make a get-away . . ."

Juliette ran like a shot into the *traboule* of the house facing her.

When she reached the court she stopped, half crazed, not understanding what had happened, barely knowing where she was, whether to walk up or down this staircase, or whether this was part of the passageway or simply a courtyard. She stood still, as people sometimes stand in the middle of a crossing with cars coming from all directions. A man appeared carrying a bale.

"Excuse me, how do you get out of this *traboule*? This way?"

The man explained the complicated exit.

Traboules within *traboules*. . . . Streets to cross in between. She dived into the maze. But now she was sure of her escape. Even if they had tried to follow her the network of the *traboules* would baffle them.

A *bistro*, a telephone . . .

"I want to speak to Dr. Arnold. . . . Doctor, this is Madame Rose Toussaint. . . . Will you please tell my husband that after I left the hotel I began to feel queer. I think it's starting . . . it's very bad. . . . Please get hold of him."

"Yes, of course," the doctor shouted. "Are you still able to come here? Are you sure there's no danger? Shall someone fetch you?"

"No, I'll come . . ."

8

THE servant took her straight into the doctor's office. When they saw her come in, her cheeks and lips pale, her eyes like mauve anemones, all three of them jumped up, the doctor, the doctor's wife, Celestin; they almost carried her to an armchair . . .

She told the whole story. ". . . I said to myself here goes, and jumped! Like Douglas Fairbanks! If I'd had high heels on I'd have fallen on my face. Thank God it started to drizzle this morning when I was putting on my new shoes, so I had to wear these old things with flat heels . . . I said to myself, if I can only get as far as the *traboule* they can run till they drop and never find me— they're not Lyons people, they're Germans. That's all . . ."

"All quite normal," said the doctor. "Suzanne, will you make her a hot drink? She's shivering. Come now, my dear child, you're going to stretch out for a moment under a warm blanket with a hot-water bottle and drink a grog. . . ."

"No, I'd rather stay with you . . ."

"We'll keep you company in the bedroom. We won't leave you. . . . Never . . ."

"And Celestin? Isn't he in danger here?" Juliette could barely speak, her teeth chattered so.

"I'm in no danger. SHE HAS COME. I'm in no danger now . . ."

Juliette lay beneath the blanket in the bedroom listening to voices which seemed to come from a great distance. Yet when she opened her eyes she could see the doctor and Celestin close to her bed. She felt wonderfully warm, and her head swam with weariness and alcohol.

". . . They've taken Dominique. The first time, he slipped away and hid in a room in the suburbs. The odd thing is that he had a loaded Colt and a tommy-gun and didn't use either of them. He must have seen someone he thought was a friend. . . . A traitor. . . . There were five people who knew his hideout. He must have fought. There was blood on the walls. . . . They took him away in a Gestapo car that was waiting downstairs. All quite normal . . ."

"I want to stay, if only to expose the traitor . . ."

"You will clear out and not argue. Everything is ready. You have your route. . . . The 'plane will land at——"

"I don't want to leave . . . SHE HAS COME . . ."

"But you must. If necessary I'll use force. Isn't Dominique enough? And all the landing fields burned. . . . As for the man, blast him! . . . What shall we do with Juliette?"

"Do you think she's in danger?"

"I wonder. They might recognize her in the street. . . . The trouble is she's too pretty for this work. She attracts attention. . . . Lyons is a small place. People run across each other all the time. . . ."

"Don't you think she could leave with me? SHE HAS COME."

"What?" asked the doctor. . . .

There was a long silence.

"No," the doctor spoke again. "There's only one seat available."

Again there was a long silence.

". . . The best thing would be to hide Juliette for a while," said the doctor's voice. "It may be only a matter of months now."

"And Aunt Aline?" said Juliette from beneath her covers. "And José?"

"So you weren't asleep? We'll take care of them, don't you worry. . . . Tonight you could sleep at . . . let's see, at Adrinopoli's . . . or what's her name, that good woman . . . it's a very safe place."

"I won't allow it," the doctor's wife said abruptly. So she was in the room too. "You can't send this child to lodgings where there are nothing but men—a dormitory! . . . Only a man would think of such a thing . . ."

The doctor looked at her in embarrassment.

"I'll take her to my cousin Marthe," continued the doctor's wife.

"Your cousin Marthe? The wife of the silk merchant? Come now, Suzanne, what are you saying? . . ."

"Certainly. She'll be all right there. . . . There's a big garden, and she can have the pink bedroom. I'll tell Marthe to give her the pink room. It was her room as a girl. I've slept there often myself, before my marriage. . . . There are trees outside the windows. It's funny, and the furniture is white, and there's a frieze of birds under the ceiling. My cousin always had good taste. There's a pretty dressing-table and sweet little armchairs. . . . It's so nice to dream there. There's no place like it for dreaming. The servants are well trained. . . . The food's as good as before the war. . . ."

She spoke volubly, her cheeks faintly flushed.

"What about the silk merchant?" asked the doctor timidly.

"Her husband?" She shrugged her shoulders superbly, as though that were no concern of hers! "Marthe is mistress in her own house. She does as she pleases. And the house is big enough."

"All right, have it your own way, Suzanne." The doctor gave in. "Perhaps it's the best solution after all. If you really think your cousin will agree . . ."

"Come, my child," said Suzanne. "Get up . . . I'm anxious to see you settled there, away from all these horrors . . ."

She bent down, picked up Juliette's shoes, and began putting them on her.

"Madame!"

Juliette jumped out of bed. . . . The floor swayed dangerously under her feet, but she made a desperate effort and managed to say in a natural voice, slipping on her coat and pulling the beret on to her hair:

"Doctor, I rely on you to notify my aunt. Right away, this evening, will you? Tell her I'm safe, that everything is all right, perfectly all right. You'll tell her, won't you?"

"Absolutely."

"Good-bye, Doctor; good-bye, Celestin . . ."

"Good-bye, Juliette. May I kiss you good-bye?"

The doctor took her in his arms and kissed her. Celestin seized her hands, the left one gloved, the right bare.

"The thumb is still darned," he said, and kissed her left hand with the darned thumb. He laid her right hand against his cheek, gazing at her half crazily. "LORD MAKE HIS LOVE FOR HER ETERNAL," he said.

She drew her two hands away and went to the door. The doctor's wife had already opened the door for her, so eager was she to take Juliette to the bedroom with the bird frieze beneath the ceiling and the trees outside the window, the room where one could lie and dream. . . .

And dreams were Juliette's familiar companions.

Written in February, 1943. Let History continue my tale.

The Lovers of Avignon was published illegally by the *Editions de Minuit* in October, 1943, at Paris, under the pseudonym of *Laurent Daniel*, a name that served as the author's dedication to Laurent and Danièle Casanova. At the time this story was written Laurent Casanova had escaped from Germany, and was working for the Resistance movement in France; his wife had just been deported to Silesia, where she was to die in the concentration camp at Auschwitz.

THE PRIVATE LIFE OF
ALEXIS SLAVSKY, PAINTER

I would like to tell about the rose and the nightingale, about lovely night, about a fair day and a beautiful life, happiness, and fragile, floating, vaporous dramas. . . . Let the woman be beautiful, the man great and generous, the air around them pure and free from danger, the waters blue and tepid as the skies. Let the earth blossom beneath their light footsteps, and let destiny grant them the leisure to perceive each leaf on the trees, each insect on its grass blade, each movement of the heart and of the mind. . . . But life holds me by the wrist and I fall, as though there were a millstone round my neck, down to the very bottom of reality.

THE PRIVATE LIFE OF
ALEXIS SLAVSKY, PAINTER

ONE of his grandmothers had not been quite orthodox, and even though he was French by birth and heart and education, and on his identification card, he bore a Polish name. Consequently he fulfilled all the necessary conditions for getting into trouble, and wisely he had chosen to live south of the demarcation line, in the zone of lesser evil. He had had the perspicacity to have himself demobilized there, just as previously he had taken to his heels to avoid being captured, while his friends had preferred to trust the generosity of the conqueror and let themselves be caught, thereby curtailing, as they thought, the annoyances of war. Alexis Slavsky showed good judgment for one who had never done anything but paint. Perhaps his conception of human nature helped him. . . .

Alexis Slavsky, painter, was second-generation French, the product of the blue blood of a petty Polish nobleman and the red blood of a beautiful Russian Jewess. These two had come to Paris about a century ago to squander their joint fortunes, derived respectively from land and finance. They had oscillated resplendently between the great world, the *demi-monde*, and the world of the theatre and the arts. After the death of Alexis' grand-parents, his father's means had vanished. When the private house in the Faubourg Saint-Honoré had been sold at auction, nothing was left him of their fortunes except the life-sized portrait of the beautiful Esther, Alexis' grandmother, painted by her husband. It was this beautiful grandmother, with her elaborate coiffure, her eyes like gold louis, her slender body, so lovely in its voluminous gown of green velvet, who was the cause of Alexis' misfortunes. . . . Yet all he had actually inherited from her were the reddish reflections in his hair, and his golden eyes. His excessive slender-ness, his long, hollow cheeks, the distinction of his feet and hands, his small, decadent ears with their lobes pressed close against the head, came from his father and grandfather, while from his mother, a typical Parisian, a dressmaker by trade, he had inherited his liking for manual work, his quickness, and his love for Paris. And when his father, who began as a sculptor for a firm making funeral monuments, finally established his own business, it was the angels of *Slavsky & Co.*, *Funeral Monuments*, who be-queathed to Alexis his resilient grace and airy attitudes. . . .

Alexis had been painting since childhood. The more he painted the more painting possessed him. All his spare time dur-ing high school he spent working in a corner of the shop, which was like a garage, among great and small angels of bronze, plaster, and marble. After graduation, when he could spend all his time painting, he went to the studio in the *Grande-Chaumière*, where there were living models. His parents respected painting, and were happy to give Alexis the opportunity of doing what his father had never been able to do—devote himself to art. He had had no teacher but his father, the paintings of the great masters, and his own zeal. Painting with him was one of those all-consum-ing passions under the influence of which, in the pursuit of his inmost thought, the scientist gets run over, the poet puts two stockings on one foot, and the lover talks and sings to himself. . . . Alexis painted with the *naïveté* of a factory girl, the fervour of an artisan, a touch of Slavic folly, and then gradually, with the conscientiousness and knowledge of a professional drawing on his own experiences.

He had met Henriette in Montparnasse, where she had been in circulation for a while, thin, fierce, whimsical, and promiscuous.

She had come from Toulouse with a young student, got rid of him in a hurry, and exchanged Saint-Michel for Montparnasse. Her parents, who were farmers near Toulouse, had dropped her. It was a big family, four boys and eight girls, and if they had had to disown each daughter who went wrong ... Henriette became a model, set up housekeeping with one artist and another, and became before long one of the attractions of Montparnasse. Her fiery body, her spontaneity, a character at once forceful and disarming, made her seem like a force of nature, enchanting to her circle. But the career of this Montparnasse celebrity came to an end on the day she met Alexis. "Oh," she exclaimed, when she saw him at the Rotonde, "I love that vicious schoolboy!" Alexis was past twenty, but as soon as Henriette said it everyone could see that he was the typical youth with inkstained fingers, who smoked cigarettes in lavatories, and lived in terror of women. ... Henriette fell in love with Alexis on the first day, resolved to love no one but him, to live for no one but him, with indomitable energy and all her unappeased maternal instinct. It was doubtful whether such a devotion was the right thing for Alexis, but at any rate he accepted and exploited it. How remote all this seemed now! ... Alexis was now over thirty, his parents were dead, his paintings sold well. He had his own dealer, a profitable contract, an apartment, in addition to his old studio in the Rue Notre-Dame-des-Champs, and a small farm in Normandy. He had been mobilized in September, '39, had taken part in the "phoney war", the campaign in France. ...

In June, 1940, he took refuge in a house belonging to an admirer of his painting. He came directly from the village where the remnants of his regiment were stationed to this smooth, white villa, all glass, slick and shining as the glossy photographs in a de luxe magazine. Alexis felt as though he had come to a different country, a sort of China where they spoke French. ... In the mornings, when he came into the dining-room, where a servant bustled round the table with the silver coffee-pot, where bees came in at the open door from the neat flower garden, as though they wanted to bring their honey to the table, and then caught sight of himself in the mirror, strangely attired in khaki shirt, breeches, puttees, and espadrilles, it seemed like one of those nightmares where one finds oneself naked at a large party. After a few conversational attempts he suppressed his inner turmoil and his war stories. It was not easy, because he was brimming with them. But nothing at all had happened in this Dordogne villa, and it seemed tactless to remind these people that he had returned from a war. He would have fled, as he had fled from the Germans, but, strengthening his sense of living in an evil dream, was the realization that he was unable to leave: he must wait here for Henriette, who was on her way from Paris to join him, bringing money, civilian clothes, and paints. He had been here for ten, then fifteen, days, and still she hadn't come. The war was over; and in this villa in the heart of the country life would have seemed perfectly normal, but here *he* was, dirty, without paints or canvases, without money, without a roof to call his own. Among these flannel trousers he felt alone and desolate; if the whole country was like this villa, he was an outcast. Even his passion had deserted him. Though he put on seven-league boots and rubbed Aladdin's lamp, the magic was gone. . . . Everything remained flat and ordinary, and in the raw, colourless daylight he was forced to look upon the ruins. This was defeat indeed.

On this particular day the house was even fuller of people than usual. How did they manage to get round in his paralysed country? Alexis, curled upon a sofa like a sick animal, stayed in his room by the open bay window. The gong sounded for lunch. From the back of the garden came the majestic mistress of the house, accompanied by two women and a man. Marc brought up the rear carrying a basket full of apples. Alexis rose and went to wash his hands. All this hot water, these switches within easy reach, oppressed him: he felt he had no right to them. He had been a prisoner in this villa for three weeks now: no one asked him to stay; far from it. . . . Well, it was time for lunch.

"Geneviève, how often must I tell you not to leave the windows open on the sunny side of the house? . . ."

The owner of the house, Alain Crispin (of the Crispin printing establishment), a large, dark, muscular fellow, lowered the Venetian blinds.

"Can't you give orders to the servants? I'm talking to you, Marie-Louise! . . ."

His wife turned her handsome, oriental head towards him, and shrugged her shoulders.

"Let's go in," she said. "Don't get excited, Alain . . ."

"Grandjean is always late," Alain remarked as he sat down. No one was in a good humour today. Conversation languished, through the chicken, beans, cream cheese, preserves . . .

"By the way," said Crispin, "starting tomorrow, we'll have to do without coffee after lunch . . ."

"Oh dear! But if you want it in the morning . . . There's hardly any left. It may take a little while for things to get straightened out." Marie-Louise peeled a banana. "Luckily we have enough fruit and drinks. . . . These bananas came this morning."

"They may be the last we'll get," Alexis remarked abstractedly.

"Why so?"

"The blockade."

"Ridiculous! . . . ." Marc was cracking nuts for Marie-Louise. "I'll get them, in any case!"

"More power to you. Being a simple mortal, I'll starve like the rest of the country . . ."

Alexis had said more than he meant, because the fellow annoyed him. In the old days Marc would never have dared to talk like that to him. Marc was one who couldn't help swimming with the tide; he'd always find himself naturally on the side of the winner. . . . Alexis was the defeated one. Let others change their rifle to the other shoulder, if they had ever carried a rifle:—not he! This war had been waged against him. He thought these people must already be thinking that his name was Slavsky, that his grandmother, whose portrait they admired, had been called Esther, and that they had perhaps made a bad bargain in buying his paintings. Who could tell whether or not they still had a market value? Meanwhile he walked among them in his dirty uniform, with a sad face, like a guilty conscience. No one likes his guilty conscience. Alexis was a sensitive man and imagined all sorts of things without foundation.

"Nonsense, nobody is going to die of hunger! There will always be ragout in Toulouse, because of the oysters. What could happen to the oysters?" The man from Toulouse, a cousin of Marie-Louise, in the pharmaceutical line, looked at Alexis without hostility—a big, handsome fellow, modest as a girl, he was incapable of any ill-feeling—but with an air as much as to say that since Alexis was not quite one of them, he could not be expected to know that there would always be oysters in Toulouse. . . . At east, so Alexis interpreted the look. Next to the cousin sat his young wife. She was pregnant, and it had already begun to show considerably.

Alexis rose and left while they were eating the fruit. . . . The next room was a large living-room, with straight, clean-cut furniture, as in the rest of the house, of white-stained wood upholstered in white leather. Although the red-and-white-striped linen curtains had been drawn in front of the bay windows, the heat was like that in a hot-house.

"This modern architecture—Le Corbusier," Alexis thought contemptuously. "In winter you die of the cold, in summer of the heat. Besides, it has all the intimacy of an operating-room."

The sun struck full upon the solid white wall, and the air was thick, sugary, viscous, like a cordial . . . Alexis left the room as soon as he heard the chairs move in the dining-room. "It's hot," he said to Alain Crispin, who came up the stairs behind him. Ruefully he caught the note of apology in his own voice. What was was there to apologize for?

"Alexis annoys me," said Alain to his wife in the bedroom, taking off his shoes and putting on sandals. Marie-Louise lay stretched out on the huge, low bed, the only piece of furniture in the white-walled room. Despite her large bust and the rolls of flesh on her stomach, she was beautiful, as she lay almost naked on the bed.

"He annoys me. He walks round here like a dying man. We all know that his situation is awkward, but it's not our fault that he has a foreign name and Jewish blood. There's a lot of talk about the Germans being anti-Semites, but perhaps there's nothing to it. They've fed us so much rot . . ."

"Yes," said Marie-Louise, yawning. "That may be true. Marc got a letter from Paris, and immediately told George that he should leave Toulouse and go to Paris. The anti-Semitic campaign has started, and they're suppressing the Jewish chemists. . . . There will be all sorts of openings. But George is so awfully fond of Toulouse. . . ." She yawned again. "Why can't Alexis have a name like everybody else? And all those stories he tells about the beautiful Esther! Nobody would have suspected."

"I would have liked to buy another painting. I like his work, and it's a good investment." Alain tied his sandals.

"If he weren't so pathetic I would have made it clear to him by now that it's time for him to leave. . . . After all, this isn't a hotel. It's incredible how people can hang on! I'm not mean, as you know, but think of the sugar he uses for breakfast! Hand me the *Masque*, will you?"

Marie-Louise read a detective story a day.

"You never know people unless you live with them." Alain shook his trousers to straighten them. "He's like a bird fallen out of the nest. We can't do anything until Henriette comes. You know very well that he's lost without her. . . . Here's your sleeping-draught." He put the little yellow book beside her and left hurriedly.

Henriette arrived the next day. She turned up laden with Alexis' clothes, his paint-box, under-linen. . . . Alexis could have cried with relief. Henriette, whom he hadn't seen for four months, hadn't changed; she was as she had become with the years, a strong, rather squarely built woman. Her body, her jaws, even her eyes were square. . . . She had on her ear-rings, her bracelets, her rings, her cape, and yet with all this paraphernalia she didn't look grotesque; it gave her style.

The day Henriette arrived lunch was gay. Alexis, dressed in trousers of navy-blue corduroy, a loose jacket, and a silk shirt, at once regained his air of a charming, eccentric, sorrowful, sulky prince. Henriette told them all the news of Paris, about the entry of the Germans into the empty town, about the people . . . the ones who had left, the ones who had come back, the prisoners, the dead, the ones who had been arrested. . . . M. Abetz, who had been deported as a spy before the war, had come back as ambassador. . . . Amazing! Are you sure it's the same man? Heavens? It's like a comic strip. . . . Do you think so? . . . The black-listing of books, the correctness of these Germans. . . .

"Haven't I always told you?" said Alain Crispin triumphantly. "Just wait and see; they'll put everything straight . . ."

"So you think, Henriette, that I could just go on back to Paris?" Marc asked.

"Why not, if you don't mind seeing them? . . ."

"What a stupid question!" Marie-Louise was annoyed. "You're not Jewish, so far as I know, and you've never meddled in politics. Everybody's going back to Paris when the holidays are over. Why not? If you're neither a German refugee nor a Pole, I don't see why you shouldn't go back."

"Et cetera, et cetera," said Alexis. "Nothing much to bother about. Just the plain German boot for good Frenchmen. You'll see them march down the Champs-Elysées. . . . A few swastika flags here and there."

"There are plenty of them," said Henriette.

"You're too touchy, Alexis. I wasn't referring to you. . . ."

"I never thought you were."

Marie-Louise rose. They had been having coffee. In honour of Henriette they had had coffee after lunch.

"Will you come up to my room with me, Henriette? We'll have a chat . . ."

Marie-Louise and Henriette were both from Toulouse. Not from the same *milieu*, of course, but compatriots nevertheless. They habitually nagged at one another, but in Paris they telephoned each other daily, and met often in Montparnasse.

"Alexis is intolerable," said Marie-Louise. "Stretch out, Henriette, you must be very tired . . ."

"You're telling me," Henriette sighed. "Has he been drinking a lot?"

"Not at all . . ."

"Are you sure? Perhaps he went into the village?"

"Never. He wouldn't even go to the village to oblige me. Once I asked him to take a registered letter down for me, and he said he was tired. In that drawling voice of his, you know. . . . You've spoiled him, Henriette. He's a terribly spoiled child. . . . Tired! He hasn't taken ten steps in the garden! . . ."

"He's been in the war . . ." Henriette thought Marie-Louise was exaggerating. She was willing to grumble a little, because it gave Marie-Louise pleasure, but she wasn't going to let Alexis be run down.

"This war hasn't been very tiring for our men. In spite of the running they did," said Marie-Louise.

"Well, that depends. . . ."

They were silent. The long white curtain, smooth as a cinema screen, was flecked with silvery shadows. In a corner of the empty room stood a lamp like a gibbet of steel wire. The mats on the floor were white, with an undertone of grey. Henriette thought this luxurious emptiness was of a sort to exasperate Alexis, and she felt herself melting with pity towards him. . . .

"We're in rather a bad day," she said. "Morot, Alexis' dealer, decamped to America. He's had it all planned since '38. He'll be denationalized. I don't know what's going to become of us. I don't dare tell Alexis. We haven't any savings—that's not our way. Nothing's left of the farm in Normandy, absolutely nothing. It was a direct hit . . ."

"Good lord!" Marie-Louise put her hand on Henriette's arm. "That adorable place! I forgot all about Morot. Somebody told me that he'd gone to New York. But you needn't feel embarrassed with us, Henriette. Alain would be only too happy to buy a picture from Alexis. . . ."

"You're a good sort!" They embraced.

Alexis was waiting in the pretty white bedroom with the big bay window.

"So she's been complaining about me?" he blurted out. "Well, I don't care. We're going to leave now. I'd go crazy here. I'm crazy already, or if I'm not, they are. . . . After all, is this 1940, or am I just dreaming? Tell me, has there been a disgraceful war, a terrible defeat, hell on the roads? When I got here, do you think they asked me what it had been like? Not a word. I might have come calling from the next château. . . . When I told them that in the villages Frenchmen were holding out their hands like beggars for cigarettes from German motor-cyclists, they couldn't see the point. Why shouldn't they hold out their hands? What did I mean:—like beggars?"

He talked on in this strain for a long time, in his thick, monotonous voice, happy to have someone at last to torment with his own torment, someone upon whom each word fell with the double weight of anguish and affection.

"But you're exaggerating. They did take you in, after all,"

said Henriette softly, because, although she agreed with him, she didn't want him to feel bitter. "Alain wants to buy a picture from you. He admires you greatly . . ."

"Damn Alain! Anyway, my canvases belong to Morot."

Thus she blurted out the news which she had meant to break gently, as though it had been the death of a dear friend.

"Morot has gone to America."

Alexis walked to the window, without saying a word. His eyes recorded the movements of the leaves, the layers of green foliage. . . . He felt as though a prison door had closed behind him. He had lost his freedom, because he depended on everybody. Nini and Alain were walking rapidly down the avenue to the right. . . . Little Jeannot was playing with the cook's son beside a heap of ochrous sand. Jeannot wore little white trousers with braces over his bare shoulders; the cook's son, who was rather older (four or five, perhaps), wore a black blouse, buttoned at the back. They were making mud pies and talking seriously.

"When you grow up," said the cook's son, "you'll be as ugly as a louse. . . ."

"Let's pack our things," said Alexis, sinking on to the divan. "Wherever we go it can't be worse than this. . . . At least I'll be able to get up and go to bed when I feel like it, be disagreeable, eat at midnight, feel at home. You've just arrived. You don't know what it means to live in a glass case, to be on exhibition every minute. We'll just clear out . . . I want to get drunk! I haven't had a drop since I came to this house. I don't want to drink with these people. ... ."

2

ALEXIS wanted to live in a big town. Well, he'd got what he wanted. From a distance the name Lyon-Perrache seemed to suggest the wild and multicoloured tangle of a jungle. But the big railway station was colourless, without any bright plumage. The only decorations in the broad, flat square in front were the tramcar lines, the pedestrians, the hotels. Yet if everything looked faded, it wasn't from having been exposed to the sun too long. The sky was a pall of grey drawn over its beauty. . . . Henriette and Alexis started down the stairway, the first of the Lyonese stairways. They boarded the Number 4 tramcar. Their life in Lyons had started.

The hotel had changed proprietors and been renovated, taking a step upward. The rooms facing the street had real carpets, and armchairs that looked like straight chairs with handles, upholstered in a peculiar kind of velvet printed with silver, effective if you didn't look at it closely, like theatrical material. Even the rooms opening on to a wooden gallery in the courtyard had nice white washstands, big brass beds, rather stiff sheets, and mirrored wardrobes of pitch pine. The fireplaces had been blocked up, but there were pretty radiators painted silver. You entered the hotel through a white hall with a chequered floor. In the evening this entrance hall was brightly lit by a large white central globe. The hotel desk was simply part of the counter of the *bistro*, raised to the rank of café, which belonged to the hotel. It was in this café that Alexis spent his best and brightest moments, drinking little glasses of cheap brandy. The proprietress at the cash register wore the expression of someone who has just had a quarrel. From time to time he saw the coloured glass door behind the cash-register open to let in the little bell-boy, dressed like a messenger, in a livery much too large for him. It was particularly noticeable in the collar of tarnished silver braid, into which he could have put both his hands. The new oilcloth of the springy window-seats smelled strong. The brass arm-rests shone. No one was ever there.

Henriette went out early to look for apartments: as long as Alexis wasn't installed in some kind of a home he wouldn't work. He went about with a sodden face, with a complexion like a turnip, and suffered from black, suffocating boredom. Such an extreme of boredom should have a medical name, *melancholia* or something. Some men came back from the war with a wounded leg or an injured spine; in Alexis the vital instinct had been wounded. To get up in the morning required an effort disproportionate to its importance. There was nothing to attract or stimulate him in the drab perspective of the day. In the end he got up, simply in order not to rot in bed. And because there was a radio playing in the next room . . . but there was a radio downstairs in the café, also. And when he went out into the street he could hear those sinister news bulletins from every open window. Whenever Alexis heard the introduction from *L'Arlésienne* he cringed as though he were about to be thrown fully dressed into icy water. The damned box went on emitting its serpents to roam the countryside, to bite right and left. Strolling aimlessly through the long streets of Lyons, Alexis seemed still to be fleeing from some danger.

How can anyone live in the neighbourhood of the Place du Pont! This rough, bristly heart of an immense starfish, with its misshapen, irregular limbs as streets . . . The square itself is shaped like the bridge of a ship, crowded with passengers waiting to arrive somewhere, although the ship is motionless. . . . Behind the bridge a swarming One Price shop figures as the poop. A tall building shaped like an axe, with its cutting edge towards the square, stands between two diverging streets. It is an hotel with several entrances, none of which dares to open on to the square: all of them are hidden in the little back streets, through which flows a squalid, sinister poverty. . . . Not that Alexis liked the Cours Gambetta any better; he chose it because it opened out wide and simple, surrounded by anonymous houses, ageless, faceless. He turned into the Rue Duguesclin, long and monotonous as life, leading to what? A fine testimonial for a hero! And what about the Rue de l'Abondance, which was brief as a good joke, flanked by doorless, windowless walls, with no gardens behind them. . . . But whether he turned right or left Alexis came out invariably at a corner of the Rue Garibaldi. Here was a small garden-court choked with scrub and refuse, behind a shaky fence, through which he could see rabbit hutches, strange, rusty objects, grass struggling up through the dust as best it could, and a sketchy arbour with rotting bench and table. This courtyard lay in an angle formed by two wings of a low brown house, covered with pink blotches. A sign on the blotched wall, at the level of the second storey, read *Au Bon Coin*, and underneath, *Café*. The letters were arranged in a semi-circle. Big, awkward letters with tan shading, the capitals embellished with scrolls, like the address of a letter from the country. . . . A wooden staircase, dangerously warped and rotting, led down from the shack into the scrub and sand of the garden. At the far side of the little house a long

picket fence made of tall, pointed grey stakes ran along a vast
rubbish heap. But the background to this desolate scene was
formed by the backs of big houses, high, narrow, like skyscrapers, oddly set together. . . . Alexis stood in front of the *Bon
Coin* a long time, staring at it. People came and went, small
business men, tradesmen, and clerks. These streets were cut to
their measure. They deserved nothing better.

Sometimes Alexis went in the opposite direction, towards the
Guillotière bridge. Sinister syllables; Nothing good could befall
him in the Guillotière district. "Guillotière," thought Alexis in-
sistently, "Guil-lo-tière . . ." He found nothing to admire, although he might have: a clear, transparent mist lay over the river
and the stone quays; the sky was just high enough to ride clear
of the houses which rose in terraces on the Croix-Rousse hill.
These houses were no more meant to be admired than the sky
or the Rhone. They were outlines of houses, with serried rows of
windows like the kernels on an ear of corn. The windows looked
at him unblinkingly, with menace in them, like the eyes of a crowd.
It was Alexis who lowered his eyes first. He crossed the Guillotière bridge. The original bridge had collapsed at the time of
Richard Cœur de Lion, and had been rebuilt with elegant towers,
a drawbridge, and arches extending to the Place du Pont. But the
people, wanting to improve on this, had built a new bridge, with
neither towers nor arches . . . "Guil-lo-tière," Alexis thought,
"Guil-lo-tière! . . ." and he refused to admire. He wasn't going to
be taken in by this dirty town.

The next day he started all over again, went to the Place du
Pont, Cours Gambetta. . . . One day Henriette saw him at a distance, planted in front of a house, a kind of shack, as though he
were expecting someone. He wasn't expecting anyone, he was
just looking. . . . On the crumbling wall was a sign, *Au Bon
Coin*. Henriette told herself that she must find an apartment. . . .

Quite apart from the fact that living in an hotel was expensive,
what little money they had was rapidly disappearing, particularly
since brandy was to be had at the hotel. Henriette was forced to
cook in their room, on an oil burner, and if she was able to prepare
appetizing dishes, it was only because she was a remarkable cook.
While she busied herself, her full, square shoulders thinly covered
by the silk of a housecoat which hadn't been fashioned for the

kind of life it now had to lead, her bare feet in cracked patent-leather slippers, Alexis lay on the brass bed repeating like a litany: "I am tired, tired, tired. . . . What possessed you to stick us away in this hotel? . . . I'm fed up with the Guillotière, the Place du Pont, with all these waiting people. . . . Good lord, what are they waiting for? Can you tell me? I'm sick of the proprietress. She keeps looking at me as though she wanted to say: 'I know you are cooking in your room, though it's prohibited. I know you won't be able to pay your next bill.' I'm sick of these shadows behind the curtains, drawn in broad daylight. I'm tired, tired, tired. I can't stand on my feet. . . .''

Shadows actually passed across the curtain of the window opening on to the gallery of the courtyard. . . . Alexis put his head in his hands. . . . The asparagus in the casserole, which left rings on the newspaper that served as a cover for the stand, smelled strong. Flowers were wilting in a vase full of stagnant water on the mantelpiece. A big powder-puff, yellowed with ochre powder, lay on the marble mantel beside a piece of bread and a face-cloth. . . . Henriette stirred the sauce, her tormented eyes fixed on Alexis.

"My poor darling! As soon as we move——"

"You say that every day."

"I have something in mind. Something you'll like, I'm sure. I'm making you a mousseline sauce."

"We won't find anything at all . . . I'm not hungry, but I'll eat because I'm bored, and it's a way of passing the time. . . . I'm getting fatter and fatter. How do these people live? What can they hope for? This herd of pigs, they're perfectly satisfied with their stupid affairs, as though nothing had happened!

. . . Nothing upsets the worthy Lyonese; they haven't been deprived of their furniture or had their habits upset. . . . Let Rome burn! I'm sure they would have been happy to keep the Germans. It would have meant good business. I'm absolutely sick of it. . . . Besides, I can't live outside Paris!"

"Why don't you go to the *Paufique*? The place is full of Parisians, journalists . . ."

"Do you want to make me cry? . . . When I think of money, our 'means of subsistence'! . . . We'd better learn to beg. I can just see us begging in Lyons. It's the last place on earth I'd want to be a beggar in."

"I've written to Morot again. If we don't get an answer by the end of this month I'm going to send a cable. Since you don't want to sell anything . . ."

"No, I don't want to sell! It's my last chance to prove to myself that I'm a free man. Everybody has claims on me: Pétain, the police, the hotel-keeper, the shadows on the curtains. . . . I'm not going to sell anything. Perhaps that's all there'll be of me, of my painting. Can you imagine me working here in this room with the curtains drawn? Suffocated between the mirror-wardrobe and the brass bed?"

Henriette got up every morning at seven o'clock now, to hunt for an apartment for Alexis.

3

THINGS always come out all right in the end. Morot sent them a small sum of money from New York, through an intermediary. He promised more to come. Henriette sold these dollars at a miraculously favourable exchange. Although they still had to be careful about expenditure (there was no telling when more would arrive) they could at least breathe freely again. Henriette bought two pairs of stockings (there was a rumour that silk stockings were about to disappear) and found a furnished apartment in the old quarter of Saint-Jean.

It was a funny old black-and-white house, like those smoke-blackened buildings close to the railway station. It faced the narrow Rue de la Juiverie and the Montée Saint-Barthélemy, which goes in the direction of Fourvière. By an underground passage from the Rue de la Juiverie you could reach an open courtyard on the Montée Saint-Barthélemy, as though a rectangular section had been removed from the cube of the house. By crossing the yard and opening a wrought-iron gate you found yourself in the Montée. The narrow façade on this side, partly encroached on by the yard, seemed to have been recently renovated, and its clear stone, its semi-circular balconies with chubby-looking, soot-stained balustrades, seemed to hide an older façade, as a new layer of wallpaper hides an old one. This impression was strengthened by the aspect of the same wing of the house from inside the court: a great stone staircase with worn steps went up into the heart of the house, supported only by stout half-columns one above the other, their Doric capitals level with the landings. From this side the antiquity of the house became clearly visible, the centuries it bore on its back, the patina of old, smoky stone. . . . A handsome iron wheel which served to pump water looked as though it were drawn on the wall with soot; the little door opening on to the Montée was black, fine, transparent as lace. The fourth side of the courtyard faced a roofless tunnel where the funicular to Fourvière started. From the court-yard the view was the same as from the Slavskys' apartment. The rails of the funicular disappeared beneath the pavement of the Montée Saint-Barthélemy, reappeared on the other side of the street, and dived into the black, yawning gulf of a tunnel. Above the tunnel rose high, narrow walls without windows. Although these were simply houses facing in another direction, being plastered over with a clear, light material they looked more like strange towers. A narrow, steep staircase rose between these walls, following the track of the funicular. All the rest was sky.

To reach home the Slavskys went by the Rue de la Juiverie. It was the nearest way from the centre of town. The entrance to the little passageway, or *traboule*, as they say in Lyons, leading to the court lay between the door of the funicular station and that of a small *bistro* called *Chez Thérèse*. The house had this peculiarity: that although the entrance was through this typically Lyonese *traboule*, the courtyard was light, and the flagstones were not only swept but washed. It was the only one of its kind in this ancient quarter, where the houses disappear beneath layers of century-old dirt. Once they had reached this handsome court the Slavskys climbed the majestic stone staircase, at the foot of which Henriette had insisted on placing a post-box, like all the other tenants of the house. Now she had her substantial letter-box of shining mahogany with a gleaming brass plate, attesting to the fact that all was well in the house of Alexis Slavsky, whose name she bore. However Alexis might grumble, complaining that she always had to install herself as if it were to be for life, and that the post-box was sure to bring them bad luck, Henriette wanted to feel at home; it's impossible to feel at home in Lyons without having your own letter-box like everybody else.

The apartment consisted of a single room which could be used as a studio, with a deep alcove curtained off from the studio. In the alcove was a door leading to a dark closet, which in turn had its recess, without a door. You entered the big room through a dark hallway; the kitchen was also dark, so that the big room seemed to monopolize the light. The magnificent oak parquet was patterned in stars; the paper on the old, wainscoted walls, a hot brown colour flecked with gold, reflected a smooth, unshadowed glow in the light from the large windows.

The unknown proprietor of the apartment had left behind him an iron bed in the alcove, and in the studio two beautiful, rather ramshackle sideboards, a round table with a marble top, white and cracked as a saucer, and a divan with a straight back-rest. . . . Everything was in bad shape. The nasty tag-end of a rug on the floor, the straw-bottomed chairs, the imitation Gobelins curtains all had a fatally dusty, worn look that discouraged any thought of cleaning them.

Such was the apartment when the Slavskys moved into it; after they had been there a short time it acquired the look and smell which all the places where the Slavskys lived had borne. Alexis categorically forbade any cleaning-up in the place where he worked. No matter when a cleaning woman came, she would disturb him, because he had no regular working hours. And the mere sight of a charwoman, with her intrusive odour, upset him so much that it took him hours to recover. Neither would he allow Henriette to come too often with dust rag and broom. However, Henriette didn't insist. . . . So the dust began quietly depositing a layer of grey velvet on the furniture, on the marble of the two handsome sideboards with their boxes and bowls, a gilded cup minus a handle, a chipped glass, all heaped full of pins, nails, thumb-tacks, Henriette's rings, bracelets, necklaces, ends of ribbons, pieces of lace, old garters, empty paint tubes, broken charcoal, a glittering paste stone, old letters, laundry bills. . . . There was dust on Alexis' canvases (which had arrived from Paris), on the round table, and on the parquet flooring. . . . The curtains and the divan seemed to absorb this dust; they felt clotted and greasy to the touch. However, in the middle of the room there was an oasis: the easel, and the palette on a footstool near by, the paint-box carefully arranged, the brushes washed and cleaned. . . . There was also the portrait of Alexis' grandmother, Esther, which had arrived from Paris at the same time as the canvases, and which never showed a speck of dust. Luckily, when they had installed themselves on the little farm in Normandy, Alexis had refused to have the painting sent there, or else it would have perished like the rest. More than anything, it was the portrait of Esther that made the Slavskys feel at home, so accustomed were they to having this great green-and-gold composition before their eyes. The light of Lyons intensified its effect; the green velvet dress looked greener, more velvety than ever; the hair and eyes more golden than the deep, tarnished gilt frame. The left side of the portrait, which in Paris had been in shadow, was here in light, showing the white hand of Esther resting on a book, which might have been the Bible or a prayer-book.

What a relief to have a home, after living for a month in a hotel, under everybody's eyes! . . . Alexis hardly went out at all. Henriette moved about the room, cooked, washed the dishes, cleaned the vegetables, darned the socks, made herself up at leisure before the mirror, mended a dress, washed herself in the kitchen, read novels, detective and otherwise, played with the little tabby cat she had picked up in the street (Henriette had a passion for alley cats), went out and came back, laden with packages. . . . Alexis, in slippers, his trousers sliding down his thin haunches, a cigarette stub in the corner of his mouth, stood in front of the easel or moved around the room. . . . He said without turning round, "Is that you, Henriette?" She unwrapped her packages and stepped behind him, curious to see what he had done while she was gone. "Don't you think . . ." she said, as though continuing a conversation. "Oh yes, just the same . . ." replied Alexis, who knew what she meant to say, as she knew how to follow the progress of his work. Perhaps Henriette was not an expert on painting in general, but she was an expert on Alexis' work, and she knew all its whys and wherefores, its developments, its successes, and failures. . . . "Would you like some coffee?" he asked after a moment. A coffee-pot appeared on the table, with toast, butter, jam, biscuits, cakes which Henriette had bought, or a pie she had baked before going out. They had a roof over their heads. The coffee was good. Everything Henriette prepared was always good, and the better for being eaten without a mob staring at them, thinking things about them, making mental reservations and judgments on their activities. . . . If the cups had no saucers, and the bread was put directly on the table, and there were ashes everywhere, that was their business. Henriette's dressing-gown, which looked now like a working-smock, could fall open over her breasts. She wore no brassière: Alexis knew them, she didn't have to pretend that they were the breasts of a young girl. Alexis could go without shaving, the red stubble showing golden reflections that matched his hair, giving him something of the look of an escaped convict.

It began to be very cold, rainy, and unpleasant. In spite of difficulties which would have been insurmountable for anybody but her, Henriette had procured wood and coal to last through the winter. Alexis feared cold more than anything on earth. Sometimes they walked out together into the Saint-Jean quarter, with its old, dirty, narrow streets and its houses which seemed to be the prototypes of the hermetic houses of Lyons. Short of crawling on hands and knees, nothing could have been darker or narrower than these pipelike passageways, which served as entrances and opened in turn into courtyards. If a house in Lyons ever thinks of decorating its windows, adorning itself with ribbed vaults, ogives, wrought-iron gates, galleries, spiral stair-cases, virgins in niches, it is only in such a secret court, hidden from the eyes of passers-by. Do the Lyonese wish to hide their modest luxury by allowing it to become encrusted with dirt? . . . Alexis and Henriette walked between the houses, often silent, indestructibly united by an intimacy like that between a mother and her newborn child, a nurse and her patient. . . . The ghastly bareness of Lyons agreed with them; it agreed with these bare times of which nothing remained but the skeleton of the calendar. Happy are those who live in a world which they carry in them-selves. . . .

Oil paint, canvas, and turpentine were becoming scarce, so Alexis took to doing little *gouaches* on any scrap of paper, often wrapping-paper, dirty and even crumpled. This kind of painting satisfied his inner anguish, the anguish of the times; he identified himself with it, delighted in it. . . . He made several *gouaches* each day, scattering them round him and looking at them while he paced the room, a glass of red wine in his hand, sometimes stepping on them with his heel and leaving a print like the print of a tyre.

They both liked to exaggerate their negligence, in order to shed it more gloriously on those rare occasions when they went into town, to a restaurant or the pictures. . . . Henriette heated big basins of water and they cleaned up thoroughly. Alexis put on his cashmere necktie and his brown shoes, while Henriette made up carefully and put on her bracelets, her ear-rings, necklaces, gloves. . . .

When they came back they had a cup of lime-blossom tea before going to bed, a biscuit, or a piece of cheese found in the kitchen cupboard, even when they had had a sumptuous dinner. . . . How comfortable was the large iron bed and its horse-hair mattress, with the groove in the middle! Two bodies turning at the same time, as in a well-ordered ballet, supporting and aiding each other to the very brink of sleep. . . . The breathing of the other, a guarantee against whatever things grimace at night, conversations like dreams swallowed by the night, trustfulness. . . . The trustfulness which soothes fatigue, relaxes the nerves, intervenes between man and the solitude of the grave.

The terrible winter of '40/'41 came with all its rigour. All day long Henriette fed the old black-toothed stove with coal. Its elbow-shaped pipe stretched the width of the room. The stove fascinated Alexis almost as much as the iron bed, which turned up again and again in his *gouaches*, like an obsession: its thin, black rods were curled to form capital S's and spirals, and through this open grillwork the mattress appeared, tan and dirty pink, and the cotton coverlet, the colour of wine lees. . . . The sham Gobelins curtains, drawn back to show the bed, complemented the picture with their greyish greens, their faded crimson, and dusty beige. When the curtains were closed these colours formed a hunting scene, just as the window curtains portrayed in their folds shepherds and shepherdesses, embracing beneath the foliage of great trees. Beyond the windows could be seen high, narrow walls like towers, and a great deal of sky. Alexis' interest in the iron bed seemed inexhaustible, and its black stem continued to curve across in one corner or another of his paintings. He painted with his back to the window, cut off from the world, stimulated daily by his new approach. Each canvas was a new experience for him, as each new experiment is for a chemist. Did he hope to find the Philosopher's Stone, the *perpetuum mobile*? He painted doggedly, feverishly.

The letters which the postman deposited in the pretty mahogany box were their only bond with the outside world. Thank God they didn't need anybody, they didn't have to ask for anything, from friends or from the authorities. Four walls and a roof protected them from the weather and hid them from people; they were like something that has rolled under a wardrobe. "If they would only forget us!" said Alexis. He still remembered the months at the Crispins', the war . . .

All the same, this life wasn't exactly blissful. There were days when things went wrong. A novelist friend of Alexis once said that between what he wrote and what he wanted to write, the disparity was as great as between a dream and the account one gives of it. The same thing was true for Alexis. . . . While he followed the progress of his hand on the paper, guided by skill, instinct, thought, and hazard (hazard which was the autonomous, insubordinated intelligence of the hand), the tension was so great that he remained oblivious to everything else, in a trance like that which enables an actor to perform his rôle in spite of a high fever, or a partisan to march on with a bullet in his body. . . . But when he emerged from this state he found exhaustion, doubt, disillusionment waiting for him. . . . Too often Alexis knew his limitations; he was worn down by the perpetual desire to go beyond himself. He thought he would have been a thousand times better off as a simple artisan. To carve a wardrobe door, a ring, to know the joy of plain manual work . . . His father, with his funeral monuments and his casts, had been happier than he was. The son had given himself up to creative work, to its terrifying demands. . . . Alexis was totally lacking in serenity. There were days when things went so badly that he was deserted by his passion; on those days he became aware of the world and its news bulletins, the war, the war, the war; of the spruce old gentleman who was charming the people with his white locks and his kind, grandfatherly air. "Frenchmen," he bleated, and immediately one sensed catastrophe; of the infamous Laval, who drove peculiar bargains, considering what a horse-trader he was. "Why do you take so little from us? Please take a little more. Help yourselves," he said, instead of bargaining. At this time a rain of bombs was falling on London. It seemed incredible. London bombed, London a war front. . . . Necessities were becoming scarce, and restrictions were no longer a threat but a reality. On days when things didn't go right Alexis went down more and more often to the *bistro* in the Rue de la Juiverie, while Henriette waited on the landing, near the half-open door, for his step in the courtyard, in order to help him up the staircase. He would collapse on the bed with a moan, and fall asleep. But these spells never lasted long. Work absorbed him again . . .

In this way they lived in the old Saint-Jean quarter near the Saône. In the intensity of their passion, each mouthful swallowed by Alexis, each word he spoke, was as important for Henriette as a brush-stroke for Alexis.

4

ON one of their walks into town, just as they were entering the *Grand Bazar* to buy some coffee spoons, they met Mizzi. Mizzi was the wife of a painter; they had drunk coffee with her and her husband on the terrace of the *Dôme*. They greeted her all the more cordially since the girl was German and must have suffered plenty of annoyances. They shook hands at length, jostled by the crowd.

"Where's Robert? How is he getting along?" Robert was in Brazil. He had left just before the war broke out. A friend of his, a Brazilian painter, had been begging him for years to come and spend some time there, but he had never been able to make up his mind. Then he had left finally, in August of '39. A lucky break. . . . Mizzi had spent some time at first in a concentration camp, like all Germans, but had managed to get out of it fairly soon. . . . And now? Well, things weren't going too badly. She couldn't complain. She hadn't been married to Robert, so she still had her good German passport. . . . "Oh, really?" . . . "And I'm not Jewish, you see." Mizzi was wearing a red fox coat, almost yellow, which made her look like a baby chick, globular, in its yellow down, with a little cloud of a veil on her head, pierced by the yellow of her hair. To anyone who had known the little Mizzi of Mont-parnasse, in her belted coat, hatless, a silk rag round her neck, the transformation was startling. . . ."I'd love to have a cup of coffee with you," she said. "But I have an appointment. Let's meet some other time." Why shouldn't she come to them? It would be easier to talk. They made a date.

It had been so long since the Slavskys had heard any news of Montparnasse that their meeting with Mizzi stirred them both. It brought back all their old life. The day before Mizzi was to come they decided abruptly to go in for a thorough house-cleaning. They spent all day at it, went to bed late, and rose early to finish. . . . They did a thorough job: not a nook or a cranny escaped the dust-rag and broom, to say nothing of the large surfaces of the floor, the table, the windows. They sluiced pailfuls of water over the floor, shook the fabrics, and polished the furniture. . . . Finally the apartment was gleaming, and they themselves were filthy as their dust-rags. They began their personal ablutions, going at them with the same zeal, and emerging like new pennies.

Henriette put on her black dress, which she hadn't worn since Paris; Alexis, closely shaven and powdered, in a light coat, and the trousers of navy-blue corduroy, was again the Slavsky of the *Dôme*. The two handsome sideboards, cleaned off and waxed, looked imposing. The few things left on their marble tops—two antique gilded cups, a little casket lined with satin, a leaden-hued mirror, an amber necklace in a bowl, a tortoise-shell fan—looked like precious bric-à-brac, now that they had been cleaned and the junk removed. The canvas-stretchers, placed on the floor with their painted surfaces to the wall, were dusted. The easel remained in the middle of the room, but the palette had been put away and the paint-box closed. Even the sham Gobelins curtains at the shining windows looked neat, and the alcove curtains, with their greenery and their huntsmen, seemed to blend their colours with the light of Lyons. There were napkins and a white table-cloth on the round table; plates shaped like green leaves, loaded with *petit-fours*, biscuits, and candy . . . enthroned in the centre was the tart Henriette had baked.

Twice already Henriette had heated the water for tea, but still

Mizzi hadn't come. . . . Perhaps she had lost her way, or been detained, and since they had no 'phone . . . She was a flighty creature. Perhaps she hadn't meant to come at all. She had simply forgotten. She was laughing up her sleeve at them. . . . To think that they had gone to all that trouble! Such a good tart! Henriette had put the last of the strawberry jam into it. . . . Alexis, pale with rage, was just about to take off his cashmere tie, when Mizzi arrived. They had to heat the water once more, but they were so happy not to have waited in vain with their hospitality that they were both in a charming humour.

Mizzi talked a lot about the camp, the women she had met there, the misery she had gone through after leaving it. . . . She told them astonishing news of their friends in Montparnasse. Pierre Lefranc had been arrested in May, '40, for carrying sixteen passports. Forged? Naturally; if a passport is genuine there's not more than one. They laughed. True enough, but it was hard to imagine Pierre Lefranc with sixteen false passports. What were they for? Gestapo. . . . But that was incredible—that simpleton! I can still see him with his pipe. . . . Pierre arrested! By whom? "Look here, Alexis, obviously it must have been the French. In May, '40, there were still German spies, and they were shot from time to time by the French. Not always, oh no, not always . . . Incredible! A fellow who painted like a school teacher! The others? Plenty of Montparnassians had left or were trying to leave for America. More power to them; Morot is frantically trying to get me to come to New York. Nothing doing. We live on a dung-heap, but it's our own family dung-heap. And don't tell me the dung-heap doesn't want me because my name is Slavsky; that I should call myself Durand or Dupont like everybody else. I like my name; I wouldn't trade it for any other. . . . Don't get excited now. . . . What else? Why, a lot of them have left the occupied zone. Have you any idea what became of little Kramen? Little Kramen is still there, walking along Montparnasse with a toothbrush in his pocket. 'If they arrest me I can at least brush my teeth.' How like him! I can just hear him. He hasn't changed, good old Kramen! But why should they arrest him? He isn't Jewish? It's a funny name, though. It might be Jewish. Well, it never would have occurred to me. . . ."

Mizzi seemed to enjoy the warmth of the room. She had taken

off her grey astrakhan coat, which was more becoming to her than the big, bushy coat she had worn the other day. Her navy-blue suit had square shoulders and a skirt so narrow that it showed her knees with every step she took. A white tailored shirt, a cravat, a little felt hat. . . . Everything was good and expensive, but, try as they may, German women never quite achieve elegance. Too much forethought goes into their toilette. They are best naked . . . they have good figures. But Mizzi wouldn't have appealed to Alexis even stripped: he didn't care for the servant-girl type.

She asked to see Alexis' new paintings, and they showed her the *gouaches*. She seemed disconcerted for a moment, but not for nothing was she the wife of a painter; presently she exclaimed that it was amazing, amazing, and that she knew of a collector, a real Maecenas, for Alexis . . . Alexis grew suddenly very grim, took his *gouaches* out of Mizzi's hands, and put them back in their folder. He didn't need a patron. He wasn't interested in selling. He had a contract with Morot. He didn't live on charity. . . . "A patron is a patron. That has nothing to do with charity; a collector makes his fortune by supporting artists . . ." This definition of a patron failed to put Alexis in a good humour. "Besides," Mizzi added, "you don't refuse money when it's offered to you. . . ." She left them after they had promised to come to her next Saturday. If they really couldn't come for lunch, they must come right after, and they would have coffee together. She was living in an hotel with her friend, a German.

"I wonder why she wants to shower her favours on us?" Alexis murmured, as soon as the door had closed behind her. He began rapidly devouring the rest of the pie.

"Why do you have to take it that way? She's not a bad girl."

"I know what I'm talking about. I can feel those things. I'm psychic, as you say. The moment she looked at my *gouaches* I knew something was up. . . . She's looking for an investment. It's some kind of scheme. I can just see him, her friend. Can you see a German living peacefully in a hotel in these days? I'll bet you anything he's a big noise in the black market. That's the Maecenas. . . . She makes me sick!"

Alexis finished the pie and attacked the *petit-fours*.

"Well," he said, stretching himself, when nothing edible

remained on the table, "I think I'll take a little walk; all this sweet stuff makes me thirsty."

5

MIZZI's friend was a big, sturdy fellow, with prominent teeth beneath a short upper lip, and teeth as extensively repaired as a pair of old socks. His handshake was hearty. He wore a suit of good material, with a thread of green in it. He received the Slavskys with loud demonstrations of joy, and rang for coffee. The room was as vast as the reception room of a diplomat. The bedroom, with two huge beds, could be seen through a half-open door. On the tables and the mantelpiece were boxes of sweets with trailing ribbons; baskets of glacéed fruits, glasses, and a bottle of chartreuse stood on a round table, other bottles on a tea cart . . . Mizzi looked very trim in black with a white collar and little red velvet bows on her hair-ribbon. . . . "So you knew my little girl in Paris?" asked Mizzi's friend, giving her a tender look. Appropriately, he had a fat neck and wore his hair short.

"Klaus is late. The coffee will be cold," said Mizzi.

"He'll take a drink instead. Ha ha!" laughed her friend, as if it were a good joke. "Madame Slavsky, I can't forgive you for having known my little girl before I did . . ." He pinched Mizzi's cheek. "You are living in Lyons? You're not thinking of going back to Paris? We're going back there in two or three weeks. An old Parisian like me can't live out of Paris——"

"You're in luck. We are old Parisians too," said Alexis.

"Here's Klaus at last. I want to introduce Monsieur Klaus Dietrich . . ."

M. Dietrich clicked his heels. He was a short man, and his eyes were of such a light blue that they seemed almost white, making his complexion livid, as a certain kind of lightning does. If Mizzi's friend had made the Slavskys uncomfortable, M. Klaus Dietrich removed their last doubts. The conversation wavered; then Alexis decided to adopt the haughty attitude of a Parisian of Paris, capital of the world. Slight and boneless, he lay languidly back in his armchair, his hands extended on its arms; what a pity there weren't lace cuffs to decorate the wrists! He talked about rain and fine weather in his drawling, monotonous voice, polite but nonchalant, crinkling his large eyes in his long, narrow, hollow-cheeked face. Henriette clenched her teeth. . . . The conversation turned to painting, and M. Dietrich asked about Alexis' work. He had seen it only in reproduction—a great loss—but he had heard it talked about so much, by Mizzi, and indeed by everyone in Paris . . .

"Your work is much esteemed, Monsieur Slavsky . . . I should be so glad if I might visit you and see your paintings——"

"I'm terribly sorry," Henriette intervened, very much the woman of the world, "but we are only camping here. We receive nobody . . ."

"Mizzi has told me, on the contrary, that you have a very interesting studio in the old part of Lyons, and very prettily furnished. But since you put it so strongly, I don't want to insist. Couldn't I see your work here at my friend's, Monsieur Slavsky? Or at my own place? I'm very anxious to acquire a few items for my private collection . . ."

"Mizzi might have told you that I'm not selling. Everything I do belongs to Morot."

"But Monsieur Morot is no longer in France. He made a get-away, like all the good patriots. Ha, ha, ha! That gives small collectors like me a chance. . . . I'll give you a good price, Monsieur Slavsky."

"Another cup of coffee, Henriette? Alexis? Klaus, you'll help yourself, won't you?" Mizzi said, thinking it might be wise to intervene.

"What a charming little hostess you are!" said her friend, squeezing her hand. "Charming—charming!"

"That was a trap," said Alexis, when they found themselves once more in the Rue de la République. "Poor Robert, if he knew what he had lived with for a year! What are those fellows doing in civilian clothes, anyhow? What kind of racket are we getting mixed up with? It's just damnable. What the hell does he want to get out of me?"

"That isn't the question . . ." Henriette was still black with rage; her level eyes seared the passers-by, the tramcars, the grey sky—everything she looked at. "She certainly hasn't lost any time, the little slut. . . ."

"We're in a mess," Alexis continued to wail. "What the hell do they want from me?"

Henriette didn't even pause to look at the handbags in the window of Lancel's. It was raining, and the snow was melting underfoot. Never had the people of Lyons looked more like dogs whom a good master wouldn't have put out in such weather. . . .

"I see the Boches everywhere," Henriette said morosely. "When I look at these Lyonese women dressed up in new clothes, looking so dowdy all the same . . ."

"Let's go to the *Cintra*," Alexis suggested. "We'll wash our mouths out . . ."

There was a big crowd at the *Cintra*. They stood waiting for seats, jostled by the wet people coming in and the overheated people trying to leave. Men and women crowded round the tables like sparrows all pecking at the same crust of bread. Furs open to show the lapels of tailored jackets, and jewelled ornaments. White hands fluttered, with their drops of coagulated blood at the tips. Smoke smothered the voices like cotton wool.

"This is lousy," said Alexis. "Let's go. We'll buy a bottle and get drunk at home."

They waited a long time for the Cordeliers tramcar, at the blue heart of the city, where the public markets, the Bourse, and the big stores, had been whitewashed in compliance with defence regulations. The lines seemed to buckle on the black, sodden paving; the little red tramcars followed each other so closely that they looked like trains; pedestrians waved their arms, ran, clung to the tramcars, made the doors of the big stores fly . . . The florists' carts were garish, like the variegated dresses of the women. . . . The sun was setting, suspended in a grey sky above the great Rhone bridge.

"Oh no, you're not going to stop to look at shop windows now! . . ." Alexis let go the arm of Henriette, who was attracted by the *Galeries Lafayette*. Henriette followed him. But the *Galeries* didn't interest her in the least! What was there to get mad about? Besides, here was the tramcar . . .

6

AFTER this bad day Alexis did almost no work. He would leave the house, drag himself along the Rue de la République, to the café, to Morel's, the *Café Neuf*, or the *Paufique*. . . And whenever he met anyone he would bring home a story. Either it was a Pole just out of concentration camp, who mentioned, among other horrors, that he had seen Kurt (known to everybody in Montparnasse), who had turned up there in German uniform as a member of a German commission. Or else it was a journalist talking about the director of the *Bonnet Phrygien*, whom everybody had thought an Alsatian Jew until he turned out to be an Aryan of Greater Germany, buying up hotels and cinemas on the coast on behalf of the Germans . . . Alexis again and again spoke of poor Robert, who had lived with Mizzi for a whole year without suspecting a thing, and of Pierre Lefranc, the holder of sixteen passports. . . . Henriette would wait for him on the landing, and help him up the stairs. "I don't know what to do with myself any more," he moaned while she undressed him; he fell asleep repeating over and over to himself, "what to do, what to do with myself."

And one day when Alexis was busy painting for a change, and Henriette was out, Mizzi renewed her attack. She arrived with flushed cheeks, in her grey astrakhan; she removed Henriette's girdle and a pair of socks from a chair, sat down and crossed her legs. Neither Alexis' reception—he didn't even ask her to sit down—nor the indescribable disorder of the studio disturbed her. She was unassailable, either from shamelessness or insensibility.

"If you don't want to sell us your paintings," she said, "why not sell this?"

She pointed to the life-sized portrait of Alexis' grandmother, regarding her in all its arrogance. There was a strange resemblance between Esther and her grandson, when he said:

"And my soul into the bargain? There's nothing for sale in this house. . . . Tell Monsieur Dietrich to buy Vlamincks or

Frieszes. . . . He'll like them best, and, good God, in times like these it's probably not a bad investment."

"How obstinate you are! Klaus has already bought some Vlamincks. It's yours he wants. He'll give you a good price."

"Just like that, without having seen anything?"

"You are disgusting. Do you want me to change your dollars at the best rate?"

"No, thanks. I get money from Morot through the bank at the regular rate." Alexis threw himself down on the divan. "God, how tired I am! I don't want to keep you, Mizzi, since Henriette isn't here . . ."

"You drink too much," said Mizzi. "You've got bags under your eyes."

She took out her compact and lipstick and began to make herself up, and then closed her huge, opulent, leather handbag, which snapped like an old folio.

"I'll get along better with Henriette. . . . I strongly advise you to see Klaus again. I realize that it was wrong of me to promise him your paintings. It never occurred to me that you would be sticky about it, but since I've promised him . . . he would be annoyed. Go and see him once, and fix it up. . . . Good-bye."

They had a long discussion as to whether they should go or not. Late at night, long after they went to bed, they went on talking in the dark depth of the alcove. About four o'clock in the morning Henriette got up to make tea, because something hot might make them sleep. . . . While the water was heating over the gas she shook up the coal stove and put on more fuel. Alexis smoked, leaning one elbow on the pillow. What a night! Finally they decided Henriette should go alone, be charming, and sell nothing. . . .

In the morning she went down to 'phone Mizzi, making an appointment for the afternoon. For moral support for the interview with Mizzi's accomplices she got herself up regally. She was nervously exhausted. She broke an ear-ring, and trampled on her dress because she couldn't get into the sleeves, which were inside out. . . . Such a tempest! Alexis kept handing her things with understanding sympathy. Finally she put on her cape with the fur collar, smoothed down her stiff, shining hair on her neck, put on a hat made of the rolled tail of a silver fox, which came

down to her gleaming black eyebrows, slipped a dozen bracelets on her wrists, kissed Alexis, and left. He waited for her in the
topsy-turvy room, with its unmade bed, with the remains of
lunch and breakfast scattered on the table, with scraps of mutton
on the starred parquet. By the time Henriette came back the ash-
trays were full of cigarette stubs, and Alexis was at work before
his easel. He didn't even turn round when he heard her step. He
was completely absorbed in a charcoal drawing. Henriette put a
big box of chocolates down on the table.

"There," she said. "That's off our chest . . . Alexis! Aren't
you going to ask me what happened?"

"Yes, of course," said Alexis, retouching the drawing with
his thumb. He hummed, "Night and day, you are the one . . ."

Henriette took off her cape, her hat, her shoes, which waltzed
across the room, her tight dress, her bracelets, slipped on her
warm housecoat, thrust her feet into felt slippers, and began her
story:

"Mizzi received me in a small boudoir-sitting-room; just
imagine, they have another little salon, beside the other, a whole
suite, my dear. . . . He came exactly on time, newly shaved,
stinking of lotions and Cologne . . . Mizzi left us alone, d'you see
the point? I thanked my stars I'm pretty hefty, but I wondered
what was up. . . . He started by paying me compliments. . . . How
I smelled good, of the French earth, how well he could imagine
me as Marianne, with a Phrygian bonnet, or as a Marseillaise of
the Arc de Triomphe. . . how he loves France . . . the Champs-
Elysées, the Tuileries . . . the art, the women . . . ah, the women!
. . . Finally I told him. I had to say something; after all, I hadn't
spoken for an hour, so I told him I'd known one or two Germans
in my life who were all right. He said that wasn't very many. . . .
So I said that perhaps it was because I hadn't known many, and
that my type was the slender, delicate type, *vieille France*. . . . He
started laughing like mad, and began talking about you and your
painting, and said that you were too conscientious about Morot,
that he's exploiting you like a gangster. I told him you were mad,
that all artists are mad, but that you mustn't be opposed because
it kept you from working. Then he started pestering me about
Esther, and that's when I had a tough time. He wanted her, he
wanted her! . . . I swore Mizzi knew nothing about it, and that

Esther had only a sentimental value. He said: 'Esther? That's a Jewish name. How does your husband's grandmother happen to have a Jewish name?' The dirty rat! I told him it wasn't a Jewish name in Russia, that it was as common in Russia as Marie is here. He teased some more, and then gave me the box of sweets, 'To efface the bad impression his insistence may have made on us' . . . and in homage to my beauty. . . ."

"He exaggerates!" said Alexis, drying his hands on a dust-rag, his eyes fixed on the drawing.

". . . And to your talent. Mizzi never came back. Did you ever hear of such a trollop? Anyway, I think he understood."

Henriette went to Alexis' side. He seemed satisfied with his drawing. . . . He had good reason to be . . . Henriette was already regretting all that he was going to simplify in this almost classical sketch. . . . "It's nicely balanced," she said. "Don't change it too much."

"It's not a question of anatomy," Alexis said, and went back to work.

But this spell of work wasn't to last. They knocked at the door about 5 a.m. There were five of them, the police superintendent in a slouch hat and the ribbon of the Legion of Honour at the head of the band. They quickly turned the apartment upside-down. They rummaged through the drawers, in the bed, lifted up the rug, inspected the inside of the stove, and knocked on the walls and partitions to see if they sounded hollow. Alexis, sunk in a chair, watched them apathetically, while Henriette, hands on her sturdy hips, her eyes rolling like wheels, her thick black hair tumbling about her forehead and ears, screamed at them at the top of her voice, followed them everywhere, got in their way whenever she could, asked to see a search warrant, stood in front of everything, shrieked that this wasn't France, it was just a jungle, where anybody could walk in on you, the French were worse than the Boches, and she wouldn't forget the superintendent in her prayers, he could be sure of that. . . . The superintendent loathed her, and when he could get in a word edgeways he commented on the perfidy of the Slavs, who stick knives in their brother's backs and poison their best friends. "You be hanged, you and your Slavs!" howled Henriette. The assistants looked more and more worried and began telling each other that if this termagant was allowed to go on at this rate she must be someone with friends in high places. . . . They grew more and more curt and offensive, and finally the superintendent, who would have liked to stay for another hour or two, yielded to their silent pressure and gave up. To finish it all off, Henriette refused to sign the report, and they left as though she had thrown them out.

The only thing Alexis and Henriette could imagine was that they must have found their address in the course of a search at Mizzi's friends, and that they were looking for dollars. The whole thing was incomprehensible. . . . Here they were, in the disorder of their home, a sinister disorder, a pogrom, and they couldn't understand what it meant. . . .

"Shall we go back to bed?" Henriette asked gently.

The bed-clothes hung down, the pillows lay on the floor. It was cold, because the stove had gone out meanwhile. They might just as well go back to bed. . . . The walls and furniture were no longer the same; they had acquired a strange, hostile, distant look. . . .

"My feet are frozen," said Alexis.

"Do you want a hot-water bottle?"

"After all that, I don't really care about going back to bed."

"I'll make some coffee . . ."

Alexis lay down on the divan, face to the wall, Henriette came and went, straightening the room, cursing those dirty cops under her breath. . . . They didn't even know their job. They hadn't found the niche in the alcove where she had put their last twenty-five dollars from Morot. A bad job. . . . But why should they be looking for their wretched twenty-five dollars? What did it all mean?

After coffee they washed very thoroughly, dressed, and went out into the street.

From that time they avoided the apartment as much as they could. They would have liked to leave Lyons, but they had to wait for more money to arrive in the spring. Besides, what would they do with Mistigri, Henriette's little tabby cat? Alexis was willing to sleep anywhere, on a bench in the square, in a doss-house, anything to avoid having to go up to the studio again. He had taken a violent dislike to the place, as though it were infested by vermin, or a dead rat under the parquet had poisoned the air. Henriette watched over him, and he always came back in the end, but as late as possible.

Wherever they went they met a great many people who told all sorts of stories. The execution of Mizzi's friend created quite a stir. He had been entrusted with the buying-up of dollars on the q.t. in behalf of those "gentlemen", but he had bought them primarily for his own use. Moreover, he had trafficked in anything that offered. They had found several hundred thousand dollars in cash in his hotel suite. He was taken to Paris and promptly shot by the Gestapo, who don't like being fooled. Mizzi, because of her youth, was only severely reprimanded and sent to Germany. The rumour was that Klaus Dietrich had informed on them, by way of settling accounts. . . .

"You don't know which way to turn any more," said Alexis.

He gazed at the houses in mortal anguish; these fortresses of privacy were no more inviolable than the shells of snails. They were as open to the winds as those half-demolished houses into which everyone can look and see the wallpaper and the lay-out of the rooms. . . . Private life shown in vertical section, storey by storey. The sense of security behind one's walls was a thing of the past. Nowadays, if it isn't a bomb that disembowels a house, it's a cop. Alexis washed his hands every ten minutes and acquired something like a nervous tic in his shoulders, and he jerked them like a person who can't get rid of a smell, or the memory of some filth he has stepped in. . . . He came home to the Rue de la Juiverie only to go out again.

7

THEY left Lyons long before the good weather came. But how could you tell in Lyons whether it was nice in the country or not? It was like living in a house with dirty window-panes. Henriette had heard of a family pension in the *Basses-Alpes*. Why should they go to the *Basses-Alpes*? Why shouldn't they? They left for the *Basses-Alpes*.

Alexis had wanted a spot as isolated as possible, and the family pension was, in fact, located in an isolated house on a wooded, mist-shrouded mountain. From the window of an irremediably cold bedroom they could watch the landscape shiver. There was no *bistro* within a radius of four miles, and the wine at the pension was prohibitively expensive. Alexis had hoped for solitude: what he found was a lepers' home at the end of the world. The other guests were dreadful comrades in misfortune.

They had their meals in an icy dining-room: depressing, dull, interminable meals. Then they had to live through the remainder of the day, and the evening. In the sitting-room, where everybody gathered because it was the only heated room, Alexis felt like a ship in a storm. There was someone fiddling with the radio all day long, the women knitted, the men read the papers, and everyone talked. . . . They were all waiting for the end of the war, and they said it was a good thing the Germans had come to straighten us out a little, to teach us discipline. . . . If they ever left Paris there would be a revolution, it would be the end of everything. . . . The easy ways of the past were over and done with. . . . Pétain, splendid old man . . . poor old man . . . they say he's negotiating secretly with De Gaulle. . . . Now that we've gone back to the soil . . . What a wonderful institution the *Chantiers de la Jeunesse* is! You really think so? They have nothing to eat down there. . . . What do you mean, nothing to eat? My son just came back from there in splendid shape. He used to have rather socialist ideas, too, but now he has a clear head and a proper view of things. . . . You are lucky. My nephew came by here a few days ago, and these ladies will bear me out that he's very thin. He says his friends steal everything they can lay their hands on from the villas around. . . . Several of them put their heads together, to whisper that the British were the finest nation in the world. . . .

They had a little unpleasantness with the proprietor over an electric plate. Since spirit could no longer be bought, Henriette had got a little electric plate. After all, you can't live without making something hot to drink when you want it, or a hot-water bottle. There was also the problem of the electric iron. And another scene over the newspaper belonging in the sitting-room, which Alexis twice took up to his room and forgot to return.

"Do you want to go back to Lyons," Henriette asked, "or anywhere you like?"

But where was anywhere? Travelling was expensive. They couldn't throw themselves into it blindly. . . . Alexis didn't want to go back to Lyons. Nothing on earth could have dragged him back. He hated the thought as much as he hated Mme Giraudon, who knitted socks for her war prisoner son, and threw out pitying remarks about how ill poor M. Slavsky looked. As much as he hated the fact that Mme Giraudon's daughter blushed every time she ran into him on the stairs. Nor did he like having old M. Roux, with his Education Ministry ribbon in his button-hole, who was so sure that the Germans were going to straighten us out, challenge him on the subject of modern painting and try to make him admit that it was all mystification, a method of self-advertisement. He hated it as much as he hated the fact that every time he went to the bathroom one or two old spinsters opened their bedroom doors a crack to see who was passing. If only the children would stop screaming and crying! If they could only be given their meals apart! Then there was the servant girl, who persisted in turning Alexis out of his room on the pre-text that she had to clean it, this cleaning consisting of a single stroke of the broom and a clump on the pillow. . . . He wanted to stop up his ears, not to have to hear all this talk about the war and war controls, or about Mme Carret, the wife of a war prisoner, whom they wouldn't leave quietly to her affair with the escaped war prisoner who had turned up the other day. These two never appeared in the sitting-room. Mme Carret didn't even eat at the pension. She left every morning, to go where? They wondered. Alexis suffered agonies.

By the time the good weather came he felt very low. There was a sudden burgeoning of beautiful days. As rapidly as in an animated cartoon, the landscape grew green, summerlike. . . . The sitting-room, dining-room, and corridor emptied. The guests disappeared into the garden, and the open country. Some of them missed lunch, others dinner. Mme Carret vanished for forty-eight hours. The escaped prisoner left the pension, perhaps out of decency. The children ran and shouted in the garden. Mme Giraudon's daughter was expecting the arrival of a cousin.

Alexis hated walking, especially climbing, and in this place it was impossible to take a step without either mounting or descending. Nevertheless he went out every morning, hiding his paint-box beneath his raincoat slung over his arm. He simply had to get out of that pension without having anyone say to him, with the smile reserved for lovers, children, and simpletons, "Well, M. Slavsky, I see you're going to do some painting?" As they might have said, "Yes, yes, go ahead with your love affairs; you're only young once!" or "Run along and play, there's nothing wrong in that. Have some fun. . . ."

"If I meet any of them, it's finished. I can't work again for hours," he'd say to Henriette before he left the room. The person he feared most was old M. Roux, of the Education Ministry. M. Roux never said a word, but simply pointed an accusing finger at the paint-box. He rose early in the morning, before anyone else, and since his rheumatism prevented him from walking, he installed himself on the terrace at the top of the garden, whence he dominated all the exits.

Once out of the danger zone of the pension, Alexis stopped, looked about him, and chose his direction. The landscape was romantic, with tall fir trees and lofty forest glades, and narrow shady paths disappearing into verdure, where one wouldn't expect to meet a soul. Presently Alexis decided to choose a path leading to a glade overlooking a valley, a real beauty-spot. He enjoyed resting under the trees, whose fragrant branches swayed like fans over his head. He sat down among the small rocks, with the view of the narrow valley in front of him, so luminous by contrast with the glade shadowed by great trees. Beyond the glade was a small stream, but it was necessary to climb for some distance along a pebbled path. The water cascaded down the slope over heavy stones, forming clear pools whenever it came to a hollow, dashing white and foaming over tiny falls, running calmly for a few yards where the ground was level, only to froth still more violently down an even steeper slope . . . Alexis ended up each day at this stream, wearing bathing trunks under his clothes. He had chosen a spot where a flat stone formed a small island, big enough to lie on. After hiding his paint-box in the shrubbery he would undress and lie down on the rock. His body was so slight that he might have been taken for a young boy. His skin, turnip-white in the beginning, like the skin of most red-heads, turned fiery red, and then took on a colour like glowing copper, which darkened as the days passed until he became brown from top to toe. He ate sandwiches for lunch and never went home until evening.

Henriette didn't accompany him, since she disliked walking; the garden of the pension was good enough for her. The people didn't bother her; she ignored them mentally, even though she chatted with them about all sorts of things. The women were very friendly. She and Alexis were artists, and these people were curious and flattered to approach this distant world, especially after old M. Roux's remark that he had heard of M. Alexis Slavsky, and that he was among the most highly esteemed of the young fantastics. Everyone boasted of his artistic connections, and the general opinion was that Henriette, in spite of her make-up and ear-rings, was a more decent person than Mme Carret, who, although a woman of their own world, behaved scandalously while her husband was dying of boredom in a Stalag. These ladies didn't consider themselves prudes, but a soldier, a prisoner, to them was something sacred! The two spinsters who embarrassed Alexis so greatly by opening their doors to see who was passing in the corridor would have enjoyed seeing Mme Carret stripped and pilloried . . . "Why," said M. Roux, sniggering, "it might not be a bad thing to see . . ." M. Roux often joined the ladies. He was suspected of having a weakness for Mme Carret; men were all alike, always ready for mischief. . . . Henriette said the pillory idea was so good, because the men would put all pretty women there on the pretext of misconduct. . . . Everybody laughed, but the old ladies wouldn't give up the idea: misconduct like Mme Carret's should be forbidden by the police; the government should protect those poor men who had been reft from their homes. . . . Henriette suggested that if the police had to worry about people sleeping together they'd never be done. There was too much of that sort of thing in these troubled times. . . . The ladies thought her a trifle indelicate, but after all she was right. The conversation turned quickly to the question of food. The rate at the pension had been raised from forty to fifty francs, they no longer served jam for breakfast, and everything was beginning to seem skimpy and to taste of grape-sugar. And the fare here had once been so sumptuous! Remember the ducks? There always used to be plenty of milk, big slices of bread-and-butter, and honey on the table. . . . The laundry question was becoming critical. The ill-fed servants were getting insolent, and the proprietress daily threatened to close the place. There was no lack of topics for conversation, especially after June, when the Russo-German war began. M. Roux said that the Russians were rascals who betrayed everybody, but Mlle Giraudon's cousin, who had just arrived, grew furious at this remark. Since it was the Germans who had attacked, evidently they, not the Russians, were the rascals. And what difference did it make, so long as the Germans were beaten and gave up? . . . Henriette had already been told confidentially by Mlle Giraudon that her cousin was about to leave to join de Gaulle. Anyway, everyone was glad that the Russians were in it too: when your luck is down, you want to see everybody else in the same fix. . . . It isn't fair for some to suffer and others not. . . . Particularly the Russians. . . . There was speculation as to the effect it would have on the food supply.

Ever since the twenty-second of June Alexis had been unable to work. Perhaps the end was near; perhaps the Germans were on the point of collapse. He listened to all radio broadcasts, as everybody did. . . . But the Russians were retreating. Couldn't anybody stand up to the Germans? It was enough to drive one to despair. There was a period of terrible dejection, when the fall of Leningrad seemed imminent, and the Germans were advancing towards Moscow. The Führer had promised the fall of Moscow for the fourteenth of July. . . . Alexis had a feeling that he would never see Paris again. But no, the Russian line held. They were making a stand. It was extraordinary. In any case the Blitzkrieg was a wash-out. The Russians had supplies, generals, and soldiers. . . . The clay-footed giant refused to budge.

Alexis first met Mme Carret far from the pension, in the little glade, in the shadow of the tall pine trees. There it was like being in a dark theatre, of which the little valley formed the brightly lit stage. Mme Carret was sitting on top of a big rock, dangling her legs. "Oh! Look out!" she cried, and Alexis stopped in his tracks, startled. "You're going to step on my mushroom! I've been looking at it, but I was too lazy to go and get it."

"Allow me." Alexis picked a big pink-and-white mushroom

at his feet and presented it to the lady. "What will you do with it, madame?"

"Throw it away."

"I see . . ."

"You look better in copper than in plaster," she said. "Where did you get that tan?"

"Down there, by the stream . . ."

"There's a stream? You can bathe?" She jumped to the ground.

"Don't you know these parts, madame?" asked Alexis, walking beside her. "It's a little cascade, not deep enough to bathe in. The water only comes to your ankles. But you might be able to get wet in it."

"I go about the country, but I never take a walk."

Alexis remembered that she returned to the pension only to sleep. If she didn't walk, where did she spend her days? But he didn't dare to ask any questions. She furnished the explanation herself:

"Some friends of mine have a place near here, but I didn't go to live with them, because I wanted to be free. I take the train down there every morning. . . . But they left yesterday, and now I'm alone."

"One is never alone . . ."

From the glade behind them they heard voices; a boy ran past, followed by others, a bevy of boys with knapsacks and heavy boots, led by a priest . . .

"I'll bet they're making for my stream!" Alexis was filled with rage and despair. When they reached the stream the boys were already there, but some distance above Alexis' flat rock.

"Here we are." Alexis did the honours. "If you don't mind, I'd rather go up beyond that thicket, where we'll be out of sight of those little ruffians. . . ."

They climbed over the rocks, among trees and shrubs, and settled down, the paint-box, covered by Alexis' jacket, beside his raincoat. The babble of children's voices spattered down on them through the sound of the cascade and vanished, like water-drops in the sun.

"They'll dirty the water," said Alexis resignedly. "I was going to offer you a glass of it. It's delicious . . ."

"We'll wait. They won't want to stay long. . . ."

Alexis pricked up his ears in sudden apprehension. Was she going to tack on to him? Mme Carret returned his look with one full of smiles. There were smiles in her crinkled eyes, gleaming slits edged with mischievous black lashes, smiles on her forehead, polished as the pebbles of the cascade, her fine, arched, plucked eyebrows, her high, round cheekbones, on her red butterfly mouth. . . . Alexis began to laugh, embarrassed because she had seen through him, and lowered his eyes:

"You hold your legs like a dancer," he said, "when her partner lifts her by the waist . . ." He looked at her legs, bent outward at the knees, and flat against the rock on which she sat; her feet, in espadrilles, were pointed like a toe-dancer's . . .

"I studied dancing before my marriage," she said. "My family let me take dancing lessons, because I threatened to kill myself if they didn't. Of course I had to promise never to go on the stage. . . . As long as I had to fight them I worked very hard, but now that I'm free to do as I like I don't even dance any more . . . I'm too lazy—terribly lazy . . ."

It was a magnificently hot August day, cooled by the foliage and the water near by. This woman was very good to look at. Alexis would have liked to question her, find out who she was and where she came from, but he didn't dare. He was surprised when she told him that she came from Lyons. . . . He'd never have thought it. She was so frank, so vivid. . . . But after all, there had been a precedent: Mme Récamier. Oh, I didn't know Mme Récamier came from Lyons. . . . Outsiders never knew anything about Lyons. . . . But she mustn't keep him from working.

"It isn't you, it's those little wretches up there. I've already done quite a bit of work this morning. I came out very early. I'll show it to you. . . ."

He opened his paint-box. On a little canvas inside the lid was a town scene—a dust-coloured wall covered with pink blotches, with the legend *Au Bon Coin*, and underneath, *Café*. In front of the wall a few shrubs, and in the background skyscrapers or towers. The whole thing was painted in minute detail.

"You did that this morning?"

"Yes," said Alexis, studying his little scene.

"Here, in the woods?"

"Yes, until now it was quite peaceful. . . . Henriette will have to scrape off this whole side of the canvas. I'll start again." ·

He unwrapped his lunch. Dry bread, two hard-boiled eggs, a piece of cheese, two biscuits . . .

"I can't help it, I'm going to eat one of your eggs. I'm starved . . . .Tomorrow I'll bring along my bathing-suit and something to eat."

Alexis looked away to avoid her laughing eyes. She was rather pert, but he would be glad to see her again tomorrow. The children's voices had stopped, without their noticing when.

"You see, we stayed longer than they," said Catherine, taking from his hands the glass he had filled from the cascade. "It's like the war: they'll go: all you have to do is wait. . . ."

How well her round head was set on her shoulders! She had the prettiest neck he had ever seen, long, smooth, and round as a column. . . . Her legs and arms, too, were long and round and smooth. . . . Beneath her shirt, which was unbuttoned down to her waist, her breasts were widely set. Thrust upwards by her wide belt, the globes of smooth flesh under the masculine shirt were fascinating. All the hinges of her body, wrists, knees, waist, small, delicate, round, and very smooth . . . she was made of well-polished ivory, a little yellowed and darkened. . . . Alexis told himself that it wouldn't be at all bad to "stay them out" beside her.

8

ALEXIS was no philanderer. An occasional brief infatuation, a chance encounter, or a woman who fell into his arms. . . . Besides, Henriette wasn't jealous. The idea that for her sake Alexis should forgo all the pretty women he might have, the pleasure that belonged to him, as to any man, made her feel a tyrant. At bottom she was very sure of him, very sure of herself: Alexis couldn't do without her. Still, she wanted to know what he had been up to, so as to be prepared for danger if need be. . . . During the summer of '39, just before the war, Alexis had been much occupied with a painter's daughter, a bright, delightful girl of sixteen. He had taken her out in his old car, gone on long excursions, and they had spent the evenings together at the cinema, or perhaps elsewhere, Henriette didn't know exactly. . . . She had seen so little of him that she ended up by taking the train to her little farm in Normandy.

She had a passion for this farm, of which Alexis might well have been jealous. When Morot had considerably increased Alexis' monthly allowance, they had bought a picturesque ruin in Normandy. Presently this delightful place, embowered in an apple orchard, had acquired an air of prosperity, with its turreted dovecote in the yard, the white walls of the house striped with russet timbers, the high, steep slopes of the slate roof, the white chickens pecking in the yard, the lowing of cows. They had installed running water, electricity, and even a telephone. The inside of the house was brown and white, like the outside: the walls white, the wardrobes, benches, and tables brown, the ceilings white with brown beams. The copper pots brought the sun into the kitchen, which was dim and cool in summer. Henriette spent her Sundays at the junk market, and whenever she went to the farm she took with her a new "find". The interior took on colour and substantiality. When, having risen at dawn, Henriette went down to the pump to wash, in spite of the hot water in the bathroom, when she busied herself with the cow, the chickens, her two dogs and three cats, or talked with the farmhand, or made jam and preserves, or arranged her gleaming jars in the cupboard, labelling each one "Strawberries", "Raspberries", "Apples", it would have been hard to recognize in this capable farm woman the Henriette of the *Dôme*, or the Rue Notre-Dame-des-Champs. . . . In August of '39 Henriette left her farm, and Alexis his lovely little friend. The war had begun.

So the appearance of Mme Carret, Catherine, didn't upset Henriette in the least. On the contrary, it proved to her that Alexis was all right, since he never had love affairs when things were going badly. Catherine, pretty as a little black cat, would have her time; she would last as long as summer lasted. . . .

Henriette actually made herself their accomplice, helping them to meet without the knowledge of the other guests. Alexis fled from the others like a conspirator in peril of his life. Whenever he thought about their remarks, their guesses, and their furtive smiles, he groaned. It made him sick. . . . The affair about the "escaped prisoner", who had only taken the same train with Mme Carret in the mornings, served as cover for them. No one must suspect.

Catherine hated walking at least as much as he did, but together they covered many miles. Neither of them cared much for rural love, for grass, sand, pebbles, or the sky for a canopy. And yet they spent their time in each other's arms under trees, among rocks, and finally in a hut, on straw. . . . The attraction must have been strong for Catherine to forgo comfort, and for Alexis to forget the thousand eyes of the countryside, lurking behind each tree, each shrub, each furrow, while the grass, the dust, and the millions of tiny cracklings, rustlings, and hummings, the concert of tiny noises, would muffle a step, a breath. . . . You can never be sure of being alone in the country. O for a hermetically closed bedroom, a locked door, closed shutters, a big bed! . . . They were drawn to each other, as by force of gravitation.

Catherine, at the age of eighteen, had married a young man of twenty-two, of good family, rich and handsome. When they had danced together a lot, travelled half across Europe in a beautiful car, bought clothes, jewellery, furnished an apartment in Paris, dealt with some property that had come to Catherine from her family, spent nights in Montmartre, gambled, flirted, played all sorts of games, and danced and danced and danced—the marriage had gone on the rocks. Cathie's husband had wanted a decorous home. Cathie didn't want to be bothered with anything. Her husband expected his meals on time. Cathie lay stretched on a divan with a book, and munched sweets all day. Her husband liked going out. Cathie didn't care a straw for social duties. Her husband was taken up more and more with his business, the stock exchange, conferences. Cathie, becoming lazier and lazier, dreamed on her divan, bored to tears, waiting for something exciting to rouse her from her stupor. At length something amazing did happen. Her husband began bringing young men home, and as time went on the men he brought home were of a lower and lower sort. At first Cathie didn't understand. Then she cried, then she despaired, and finally she revolted and surrounded herself with men to prove to herself that she was still a woman and desirable. At all costs she must have admirers, victims. She was always going out, receiving telephone calls, letters, flowers.

Then she took a lover, almost by chance, grew tired of him, and relapsed into her divan-and-sweets life, leaving her mortal ennui only to take another lover, and then drop him in turn. She had applied for a divorce, but the war had complicated everything, and she no longer knew where she was. For a girl of twenty-four, which was her age now, she had a strange store of experience, but as a precocious child remains a child still, so she had preserved, in spite of these experiences, the naïveté of a boarding-school miss. The strict principles which her family, rich Lyons manufacturers, had tried to instil in her had been forgotten so long ago and so thoroughly that she could be unprincipled in all innocence. Still, there remained a kind of general colour to her thoughts, so that she was troubled by the opprobrium which is cast on those women who take other women's husbands, fathers of families, women who break up homes. . . . And this judgment remained unchanged in Cathie, like her habit of brushing her hair for a long time before she went to bed, or drinking a glass of water on getting up, of making fun of her Uncle Georges, of cooking snipe in a certain way, as her mother and grandmother had done. . . . A married man was taboo. A decent woman doesn't sleep with married men. . . . Although it's very unlikely that such a principle had been formulated thus by Catherine's family, it was nevertheless true that Catherine didn't sleep with Alexis. She put into her refusal a remarkable strength of mind, which to Alexis seemed like foolish obstinacy. After all, she wasn't going to ruin his home or take him away from his children. . . . But such things weren't done, and Catherine didn't do it. And yet she was no fool, Alexis thought. She knew quite a bit about life and about people. . . . She had such a quick understanding, she was so amusing and so charming, there seemed to be a purifying flame in her. . . .

While they kissed each other beneath the trees on the mountains of the *Basses-Alpes*, the storm that shook the world hadn't stopped for a moment. But the Germans were no longer advancing in Russia, and there was reason to hope. Perhaps, perhaps, by next spring . . . Cathie's father was a violent collaborationist, but she and her brother, with whom she had stayed since the beginning of the war, were open de Gaullists. Alexis was not de Gaullist, he was nothing at all. He had only an ardent desire to see the Germans get to hell somewhere else. . . . Cathie agreed; her de Gaullism expressed itself above all in the exasperated impatience which seized her from time to time: if it would only end! This was like Cathie. She was either asleep or she was frantic. They understood each other perfectly.

9

CATHERINE returned to Lyons first. Alexis and Henriette followed shortly after. During their week's separation Alexis and Cathie found time to send each other eight wires and six letters. Lyons was no longer a dark cave with dripping walls and looming shadows, it was a city of delight.

When Alexis saw the Rue de la Juiverie again, the Montée Saint-Barthélemy, the façade with the little semi-circular balconies, the soot-darkened balustrades, the yard of well-washed flagstones, the mahogany letter-boxes, his own among them, with his name on the copper plate, which had grown tarnished during their absence, his heart contracted. . . . The big winding staircase, the door . . . Henriette took the key from his hands and opened the door. What met their eyes wasn't a pleasant sight.

"You might as well go out while I tidy up," she suggested.

"Oh no, I'm going to help you. You couldn't do it all by yourself. . . ."

How sweet and gentle he was, never complaining of being tired or bothered. . . . He looked splendid, like a gilded knifeblade, the hollows of his cheeks filled out a bit.

They didn't expect Catherine until the next day after lunch; she had to go to a family gathering. Her grandmother had come on a visit from her estate. But a day and a half was enough for putting the house in order. At last the parquet was waxed, the sideboards were polished, autumn foliage filled the big glass vases, and the house smelled pleasantly of coffee. . . . Mistigri, who had returned from *Chez Thérèse* in good shape, slept curled up on his cushion in a spot of sunlight. Alexis had gone down to get cigarettes, and returned in great excitement with a flask and little antique glasses. They had only ordinary glasses in the house, too common for the fine cognac which he brought up at the same

time. He would have liked to refurnish the whole place in the
half-hour before Cathie arrived. She came a quarter of an hour
early, but Alexis had already been watching at the window for her
for a quarter of an hour, and met her on the landing. They embraced in the dark hallway, happy to be reunited. But when
Alexis saw her in broad daylight in the studio, saw the manner in
which she offered her hand and cheek to Henriette, he grew suddenly bashful. In place of the Cathie in espadrilles, with a kerchief
tied under her chin, he beheld an elegant young woman in black,
with a short skirt, closely fitted at the slender waist, her shining
black hair plaited on her neck in an elaborate coiffure. The jewel
she wore in her orange scarf was so splendid that one might have
suspected that it was paste. . . . He let the two women talk. How
dewy were her lips, her eyelids, her tea-rose complexion. . . . He
felt more and more depressed: what could she see in him? . . .
"Cathie," he murmured, when Henriette had gone into the
kitchen. "Cathie, I want to tell you that I love you . . ." Cathie
took his hand and squeezed it with her smooth, hard, ivory hand,
until it almost hurt. Her nails were long, narrow, and lacquered
almost black. "At last! I love you, I love you, I love you . . ."

Henriette brought the coffee. She appeared to have heard
nothing. . . .

Catherine came every afternoon. In the mornings Alexis
worked. He went straight from his bed to the easel, his eye and
mind clear and alert. His morning work seemed inspired. He
achieved incredible successes. He felt a magical force in himself,
that passed his understanding, his ordinary potentialities.
Catherine's presence stood above his work. Henriette kept the
apartment clean and trim. They didn't dress until after lunch,
about two o'clock. Alexis shaved every day, and Henriette had
manicures and went to the hairdresser's. She had ordered a new
suit, and blouses.

Catherine came about three. As soon as Henriette went out to
do her errands, as she did often, Cathie stretched out on the divan,
and Alexis sat down beside her. When he knelt he looked like
one of the gilded angels in his father's studio, wings folded in
repose. . . .

"Cathie," he said in his toneless voice, very softly, bending over her as though he were afraid others might hear him. "We aren't made for this restless life, do you think? I can't get used to the radio, the newspapers, opening doors, staring eyes. Can you? We aren't made for these constant, unpredictable changes, either of us. . . . You know what I would like? I would like to have been living in some secluded spot in the days of stage-coaches. They would have brought us something unexpected every year. Perhaps a knight would have knocked at the door one stormy evening. . . . No, not a knight! He'd have fallen in love with you immediately, and I would have been ferociously jealous. I'm jealous enough as it is, without any knights. We would have had children, little ivory children like you. Does that sound good to you? From time to time, at moments chosen by us. Can you imagine our choosing the moment ourselves? We'd be seen by the people of the capital, in order to sell my paintings and display you to envious eyes. . . . You'd have beautiful dresses, and I'd have lots and lots of money, so that you could have absolutely everything you wanted, all that I want you to have. . . . You'd be the most beautiful, sweetest, the most virtuous of women. . . . Wouldn't you be virtuous? Or *would* you? People would bow very low to you and kiss the hem of your dress. I'd be a great painter, leading my twelve children by the hand. . . . And we would leave before things went wrong—because they always do go wrong if you stay with people too long. . . . They'd be sure to get inquisitive about your divorce, and about Esther. Then we would disappear as though through a trap-door, and nobody would ever find us again. Do you agree?"

"I want everything you want."

"Do you think we'll be able to escape them, Cathie?"

Cathie opened her bright, slitted eyes very wide.

"You'll end by frightening me, you dreadful spoiled child; you're afraid of the dark!"

Henriette came in, looking maternal and homely, loaded with surprises. . . .

10

CATHERINE had to go away for the holidays: another family gathering. Then she left with her brother for the winter sports:

there was no way of getting out of it. After all, she lived with him, and she couldn't refuse him every time. Then her grandmother summoned her urgently, believing herself to be dying. It was a false alarm, but again it was impossible to say no. Letters and telegrams flew back and forth. Two interminable months! A long and thrilling separation.

Catherine came back the day of a terrible storm. Her black raincoat and high rubber boots were varnished by the rain; raindrops rolled like pearls down her tea-rose face. The stove was roaring in the studio, and the vases had tulips in them. She stayed for dinner. When Alexis went down to *Chez Thérèse* to try to get some wine, Henriette said to Cathie:

"Cathie, you must stay overnight. It's raining dreadfully. . . ." She took Cathie's hands and looked at her with fervent, anxious eyes. "It's only a pretext, of course. You know that. When I look at you both, you so dark and he so fair . . . Why don't you, Catherine?"

Catherine blushed cruelly, she was near to tears. She was shocked, indignant, humiliated, a little disgusted; the whole thing was absurd and yet she wasn't sure that she oughtn't to find it sublime. . . . Catherine was beside herself, but being a native of Lyons, she showed her emotions very little.

"What about you?" was all she could say.

"You must understand that Alexis and I are like brother and sister."

Cathie, still aloof and hard, said:

"I don't understand!"

"There's nothing to understand. All that matters to me is his happiness. If you wanted to, you could even live with us. We'd rearrange everything. You could have the bedroom. We'd install you like a pretty little black cat in its basket." She kissed Cathie. "Your skin is soft. You smell good. You're like a plant one wants to take care of in order to see it grow, and become even lovelier. . . ."

Alexis came back with two bottles of red wine, very proud to have got them from Mme Thérèse. Cathie would stay overnight. Despite the torrential rain, Henriette went out. She told them she had an appointment with someone who would give her news of Morot, and that it wouldn't be wise to miss him. . . .

When she returned the studio was filled with silence and darkness. Mistigri, silent as the night, came to rub himself against her legs. Henriette lighted the little lamp on the sideboard. The curtains of the alcove were drawn, and her bed was made on the divan. She listened. Not a sound. She undressed, lay down on the bed, and turned out the light. Silence returned, as water becomes motionless after the fall of a stone. Nothing moved, nor did Henriette.

"They're shamming dead," she mused, "but I'm going to be so quiet that they'll think I'm asleep. . . . So she did stay! I wonder she didn't slip off at the last minute, with those 'principles' of hers. Principles, indeed! . . . A woman made to order for Alexis . . . physically. . . . She's ravishing. . . . Especially tonight: what skin, what a complexion! All other women seem oversize beside her. Beside Alexis, too. It's not that he's small. He's not small, he's middle-sized. . . . They're both slim and light, like bits of jewellery. . . . She makes you feel as if you had elephant's feet." Henriette was conscious of the heaviness of her square, solid frame on the broken springs of the divan. . . . "They don't stir. . . . That's the awful thing about this business, that they're so well fitted to each other. . . . Can I refuse to let Alexis have a woman who's made for him? Alexis' and Cathie's children. . . . And I who will never have any. . . . It's not fair . . ." Her throat suddenly contracted, and she felt the pain in her chest that comes before a burst of tears; she stiffened herself inwardly, appalled: what did this hysteria mean? "Love-children," she said, moving her lips without a sound, repressing the tears that had already welled up under her eyelids. "Why am I crying? Have I undertaken too much?"

Listening so hard made her ears sing; her feet were cold, and she didn't dare make the least movement lest the divan should creak under her. . . . Nevertheless, the evening spent in the café with strangers hadn't been funny at all. . . . Nor the lonely walk home in the rain. If times had been different she would have been less tolerant towards Cathie, but to take away from Alexis the little joy he might have, in these times when everything seemed to be conspiring against him . . . "But what would become of Alexis, with his luxury lady, if he didn't have me?" she mused, swallowing her tears. "He can't do without me. Still, he got along without me all right during the war. Yes, but the war was a simple matter. . . . He can't do without me. . . . This silence, this utter silence, is strange . . . Alexis will free himself more easily by sleeping with her than if she refuses the bait . . ." She imagined Cathie's naked body. "There's an exciting side to the story. . . . Much too exciting! Have I undertaken too much? Why don't they make a sound? They haven't gone off, have they? I'm sure she stayed. . . . No woman could resist him; he's handsome, intelligent, gifted. . . . Wait till Morot sees his last paintings! They'll all die of jealousy. . . . The only thing is for Cathie to live with us. I know Alexis: Cathie could never keep him, she's a ravishing little animal, but quite insignificant . . . . What's that? They're talking. . . ."

It was barely a murmur: "Do you think she's asleep?"

"Oh yes, she's asleep . . ."

"I'm afraid—and you, always afraid of eyes and ears . . ."

"Henriette doesn't count as eyes and ears. . . . Don't think about it any more . . . I love you, Cathie, I love you! I've never known anything like it, I didn't know such love existed! Swear you'll never leave me—never, never. . . . All your life long, do you hear, all your life long . . ."

"Alexis, what has happened to us?"

A great, dark silence enfolded Henriette like a crêpe veil: she had fainted on the divan. It was more than she could bear.

It was when Alexis went down to buy bread and a newspaper the next morning that Henriette talked to Catherine. It all happened very fast:

"Well, my poor child," she said. "What sort of night was it?"

Catherine's eyes, those shining, narrow eyes, filled with a kind of madness. She didn't answer.

"Listen," Henriette went on. "I told you yesterday that Alexis and I are like brother and sister . . . I hope you understood me? Lovers like us have the whole of life before them, and what comes after, too . . . Alexis can't do without me nor without my love . . . I wonder why I'm telling you all this——"

"So do I," hissed Catherine—one might almost have said she

had become Mme Carret again, despite the fact that she was wearing Alexis' pyjamas and padding about in his slippers.

"Shall I tell you? To keep from committing murder, from throwing you off the landing!"

Catherine emerged from Alexis' pyjamas in all the glory of her rounded breasts and long smooth limbs.

"Very well," she said, sending the jacket and trousers flying. "I don't know why you have done this to me, you and your Alexis!" She put on her stockings, slipped on her blouse . . . "I tried to be loyal, but you have lied to me, tricked me. . . . Keep your Alexis, I don't want him . . . I'm under a curse . . . I have no right to love . . . I don't know which way to turn either. . . . Why? What have I done to you? . . ."

"What have you done to me?" cried Henriette, but she silenced herself immediately: there mustn't be a scene. Cathie must be gone before Alexis came back.

"You arranged it all yourself, you put me in his bed . . ." Catherine slipped on her raincoat and drew up the hood. "If there's a divine judgment . . ."

She ran out, slamming the entrance door. Henriette clenched her teeth, praying that she wouldn't meet Alexis on the stairs or in the street . . .

11

FOR two months now Alexis had been silent. Dust invaded the apartment like grass sprouting in an abandoned garden. The paint-box and palette were messy with dried, mixed colours, and the brushes stood unwashed, stiff, unkempt . . . Alexis was always more or less drunk, but even when drunk he did not talk.

They got a letter from the owner of the apartment asking them to move. No explanation. The Slavskys were given two months to look for something else, but in the meantime the place had ceased to be a home, if it ever had been one. . . . One furnished place is like another.

They were still sleeping together in the same bed in the dark depths of the alcove. They went to bed in silence; Alexis turned towards the wall, Henriette towards the night table. He begged pardon when he happened to touch Henriette, as he might have done to a lady in a tramcar. Except when she had to undress him, dead drunk, or when he dropped asleep, sprawled across the bed.

The Germans had started their summer offensive, and hopes again were shattered. Laval was now in power. The noose was tightened.

She had no idea what he did in the daytime, or where he went....

He went to the big house on the bank of the Rhone, facing the Croix-Rousse, to the big house where Catherine lived. He stood motionless before it like a tree, but never saw her either enter or leave. One day he ventured to walk as far as the door. That day he had been to the barber, and he carried a new pair of gloves in his hand. He mounted the stairs and rang, and asked the servant who opened the door, "Madame Carret . . .?"

"Madame is out of town, monsieur! . . ."

"What a pity!" said Alexis. "I'm stopping at Lyons for only a few days. You don't know when Madame will be back?"

"I couldn't tell you, monsieur. It won't be for two or three weeks. Madame is in Paris."

"In Paris . . ." The wall between them rose higher and higher. . . . Next time she'll go to Germany. . . . Why shouldn't she? When he came home drunk that evening Henriette looked distrustfully at his haircut and the pair of new gloves in his overcoat pocket. Could Catherine have returned? She, too, knew that Catherine was away on a trip . . .

Alexis now went no farther than the Saône. He followed the bend of the river, the unbroken, semi-circular curve of the tall houses, like the grandiose wall of the Roman Colosseum, their high windows imitating its bays. With his coat collar turned up, Alexis roamed along the river bank. Desperate people are often attracted to water, even though they have no intention of throwing themselves into it.... But Alexis also went towards Fourvière, where about twelve years ago great houses had slid down the hill, collapsing at the foot and burying their inhabitants in the debris of their homes. Nowadays collapsing houses are a familiar sight; soon there will be more fallen houses than standing ones.

Catherine's house was standing. He had thought that she was a disaster victim like him. Not at all! Her house stood. She was in Paris, while he, Alexis Slavsky, with a grandmother named Esther, waited for his lodgings to collapse, one after another. How right were the people of Lyons to build their habitations in the guise of grottoes, mines, catacombs! . . . Alexis would have liked to live in a cave, a real grotto, and wall up its narrow entrance, which no one but he would know. The interior would be magnificent, just as he imagined the interior of Cathie's house, the houses of the big silk merchants of Lyons. . . . In his grotto there would be a big lake, stalactites, stalagmites, and pillars. . . . No bomb, no human voice or look, would ever be able to pierce the thickness of the rock; he would be sole master of it, and would choose the hour for walking out beneath the sky, the sun, and the moon.

The ruined houses of Fourvière had long since been cleared away, and the bare slope aped a sort of casual, rural air, with its vegetable gardens, its potatoes and cabbages, but it succeeded only in looking what it was, the site of a disaster. Ragged urchins played at its foot, in the Rue Tremassac, where the rubble had fallen. And lest anybody should forget what had given it its gloomy renown, there still stood facing the bare slope half-demolished houses of the kind that made Alexis shiver, displaying in vertical section their wallpapers and the other vestiges of private lives. There's nothing solid about one's four walls. But after all, what had happened one day to the buildings on the Fourvière hill only repeated what had happened earlier to the primitive chapel up there, which had collapsed in 1840. It helps little that at each disaster that visits Lyons (the plague, the invasion of 1870) the burgesses of the town make a pilgrimage up the hill and vow to redecorate the cathedral which replaced the chapel, or the basilica which now replaces the cathedral. . . . What have the burgesses of Lyons vowed this time? The basilica would soon be too heavy for the Fourvière hill. The immense gilded statue of St. Michael shone above the city, protecting the vegetables on the slope denuded of its houses, the Rue Tremassac with its ruins, the ragged urchins, the invaded town. . . . Pretty poor protection, Alexis thought sarcastically.

He went back to the Rue du Bœuf and plunged into the courtyards which had made him think of dark grottoes . . . Alexis

was like a poet who goes about repeating a verse that corres-
ponds to his state of mind, his eye roving in search of objects to
match his misery. He liked the square court, with a thin, bent,
gas street lamp, dark and useless, standing in the centre, surrounded at a distance by four crumbling walls and the dark lacework of the stair balustrades. . . . He liked all the courts, with their
black, greasy dirt, under which lurked mouldings and capitals.
But what fascinated him most about these courtyards at the
ends of dim, narrow passageways were the dark iron bedsteads
piled there. Why were there beds in almost all the courtyards
of the Saint-Jean quarter? What troubled him was that they
were all replicas of his own bed, with the thin, dark rods forming
capital S's and spirals, which haunted his paintings. . . . At first he
had found those beds beautiful, as depicted in his paintings,
but presently they began to worry him. Why had the beds all
been set out in the yards? Why were they all like his own? Why
did they keep sticking his own bed, his most personal property,
under his nose? Wherever he went he stumbled over his own
bed. But this wouldn't do: he must pull himself together. He
tried to find a rational explanation: perhaps they did it on account
of the bed-bugs. You had only to look at those walls to think of
bed-bugs. All the houses smelled of bed-bugs and rats. But the
days passed, and no one came to take in those beds; they
seemed to have been there always, rusting in the rain, the spring
rains now. . . .

One day Alexis visited a courtyard with walls salmon-
coloured, and where the far wall was replaced by terraces, with
the slope of Fourvière and the sky beyond them. . . . That day
Alexis decided to return to Catherine's house.

12

THE servant told him that Madame was out, but that M. Gilbert,
Madame's brother, was in. Should he announce him? . . . No, he
would come back.

He came back in the evening. He wouldn't have done it had he
been sober, but he had been drinking. He wasn't drunk, but he
had had several drinks. The main door of the building was not

yet locked. It must have been about nine o'clock. This time the cook came to the door. She was a stupid woman, so without asking any questions she led him into a little gilded and tapestried salon, full of bric-à-brac, mirrors, screens, and paintings, and left him there. "Is it you, Paul?" Catherine's voice came through a half-open door. Alexis went in the direction of the voice, pushed open the door, and entered.

Catherine lay on a straight-backed sofa upholstered in green satin sprinkled with gold dots. She was dressed in a high-waisted nightgown, her shoulders were almost bare, and her hair was piled on top of her head, with the hint of a parting in the centre. When she caught sight of Alexis she got up and slipped on a feathered robe that made her look like a bird of paradise. Alexis sat down, and Catherine also seated herself facing him, on the same sofa from which she had risen. Half reclining, one shoulder propped against the straight back, bending a little forward, she said, "Well, go ahead."

He said, "You shouldn't have left me; you shouldn't have left me. . . ." Alexis looked at her, dazzled. It was plain that she was not for him. . . . He thought it not unfair; she was too perfect for him. . . .

"Then you weren't worried about me," said Catherine, bending still farther forwards, and snapping the words right in his face. "Suppose your dear wife had thrown me from the top of the stairs?"

Alexis did not answer. She wore pink ballet slippers on her feet, the ribbons tied above her ankles. He could see her back and the nape of her neck in the tall mirror that hung between two small columns, where there also swam a vision of a large bed, which must have been behind Alexis.

"I don't like her smell," he said at last.

"You don't like her smell, and you've been sleeping with her for fifteen years," said Catherine acidly.

"She has promised to die with me . . ." Alexis lowered his head. He was like a man under interrogation, who cannot bear the torture and so betrays his comrades.

"So you want to commit suicide together!" Cathie laughed a false little laugh. "How romantic!"

"I didn't say commit suicide, I said *die*." He looked at her from under his lids, feeling terribly humiliated. He repeated: "*Die*. We'll take each other's hands and die." He looked at Cathie again and said very quickly and sharply: "We'll die together. . . . It's like whistling in the dark. . . . I'll hear her voice, and she'll hear mine. We're accomplices in the face of death. But I don't like her smell. . . ." He shrugged his shoulders in disgust.

"Well, then," Cathie said, bent almost double as though she were in pain, "there's no room for me between you two. I don't come into this conspiracy."

"You—I love you. I would like to die *for* you, not *with* you. Live with you, be always, always with you, do nothing but be with you, and wait for you when you are not there."

Alexis' eyes were closed, and his voice sounded even flatter and more monotonous than usual. Cathie began to cry; she cried violently, the tears streaming down her face

"I'll never get over it," she said through her tears. "Never, never. . . . What have you done to me? Now everything is over, for ever; I'll never be able to love anyone else; everything seems foul and wretched. . . ."

Alexis watched her cry. He wanted to get up, but all of a sudden he felt terribly drunk: he couldn't stand upright. Besides, Cathie wasn't crying any more. She stopped crying as abruptly as she had started, and her tears left no mark on her clear, smooth face.

"You can write to me at this address," she said in a calm, commanding tone. "I'll write to you at a letter-box which you must rent from a concierge in a *traboule*."

The concierge to whom Alexis applied was as dirty and discreet as her *traboule*. The letter-box was an old one that hung a little sideways, deeply hidden in a *traboule* which took a right-angle turn after the double row of letter-boxes, and was thus more than usually dark. He was glad to have the key to the sturdy little rusty padlock. And yet he felt a sudden pang: how had the idea of renting a letter-box occurred to Cathie? Still, it might be the usual thing in this odd town, where everybody seemed to be hiding. He wrote on a scrap of paper *Francis Alpe*, and fastened it to the box with a drawing-pin. Of course it wasn't as handsome as the copper plate on the opulent mahogany box in the Rue de la Juiverie, but he felt well pleased.

On the advice of Catherine, Alexis had chosen a *traboule* in the silk quarter. From Friday to Monday morning, and every evening, the place was deserted, and there was no danger of meeting anyone. How expert and prudent Catherine was! . . . The *traboules* in the silk quarter were like the dark, narrow passages in the Saint-Jean quarter. But while the passageways of Saint-Jean rarely become *traboules*, but simply lead to courtyards, those in the centre of the town pierce the blocks of the houses in every direction, so that pedestrians can dispense with the streets altogether and avail themselves of these dark short cuts from one point to another between the Saône and the Rhone. The fine network of *traboules* spreads beneath the houses, complicated as a sewer system and almost as dirty and malodorous. Once swallowed up by these dark corridors, you find yourself separated from the daylight world, with its tramcars, its shops, its noisy pedestrians, and in deep silence you enter the town's secret undercurrents. Through the stench rising from the gutter crossing a courtyard, from doors half open upon God knows what secrets, and what horrors, from all these stairways with their dark banisters, twisting about from cellar to roof, from these niches and nooks, through the impenetrable windows with their grillwork and iron bars, from all this arises a penetrating odour of secrecy, as intense as it is intoxicating. Whatever your secret thoughts, whatever you may have to hide, a suit-case with a false bottom, a desk with secret drawers, a safe with a coded lock, the whole thing reeks of conspiracy, of illegal printing plants, of adultery, or simply of unavowed vice and crime. . . . All the things that may lurk behind a door at the end of a *traboule*! Alexis felt dizzy: a refuge for Cathie and him! Think of opening one of these sticky doors and finding oneself amid the luxury of rugs and divans, the comfort of fresh linen, the profound relief of knowing that one is beyond discovery. In the meantime he had to content himself with the letter-box.

He went to his box ten times a day, ten times he took out his key and unlocked the little door. There was no one to see him do it, to think him ridiculous, strange, or suspect. Once a day, to his surprise and delight, he found a square white envelope in the box. The rest of the time it was tragically empty, and Alexis watched it with the patience of an angler above his line. But although

Catherine wrote every day, she still obstinately refused to see him. Her letters said: "Why have you spoiled and wrecked everything? Why have you done this to me?" Those of Alexis were simply a fervent prayer. "Come." This had been going on for weeks. It was spring, and Lyons was fragrant. This town is like an ugly girl with magnificent eyes, or incomparable hair. But the eyes don't make up for anything; those beautiful, useless eyes are just depressing. Very few towns have such trees as Lyons. The perfumes in the streets of Lyons in the spring, now delicate, now strong, take you by surprise, like the discovery of a warm, affectionate soul in a hardened business man. When the century-old trees in the gardens of Lyons, supported by stone walls as the Rhone is by its quays, put out shoots and leaves, when the towering acacias and limes become fragrant, when the fruit trees in the districts of *Monchat* and *Bron* begin to flower like big, lovely bouquets, amid vegetable gardens in the suburbs of workers' dwellings and cheap villas, giving the landscape a vaguely Japanese air, when masses of roses and gladioli cling like odorous fringes to the Lyonese walls, without relief or colour, then Lyons becomes appealing, like an ugly girl who has been lent the fairest jewels and bathed in all the perfumes of France. Its beauty moved Alexis to tears, and yet it was a poor, modest kind of beauty: to find Lyons beautiful and be content with it you must forget the perspective of the Champs-Elysées, the blue skies of the South, the stone tracery of the old cathedrals. . . .

Meanwhile Henriette prepared to move out of the Rue de la Juiverie. They were going to live in the same hotel as before, near the Place du Pont.

The shadows thickened in the tentacles of the *traboule*. Night fell vertically on to the courtyard, out of a remote sky, and the strange, vaulted arcades seemed to thrust more heavily on to the squat pillars, which already looked half sunken in the earth. The steps of the spiral staircase, seen from below, opened like a stone fan. Catherine wore not the veil of the adulteress but a silly pink hat perched on her head like a basket of flowers. She just missed stepping in her open-work boots, in which her painted toe-nails could be seen through her thin stockings, into a gutter afloat with milky water, but they fell into each other's arms over the ditch, leaning against the greasy wall. The evil-smelling *traboule* was their only shelter. Where else could they have met? Certainly not in her little golden-tapestried salon under the eyes of her grandparents on the wall, at the risk of having her mother or her brother appear and having to undergo questions. . . . Nor, of course, in the hotel. . . . All that remained to them were those dark grottoes, where the light came through the courts and passageways as though between the fissures of rocks. . . .

This quarter of an hour in the shadow of the stone was Alexis' last meeting with Cathie. Later he knew that she had come to say good-bye. A week passed without letters, and then the catastrophic news came:

I am leaving [she wrote]. *An American is taking me with him to his country. There is no use trying to be loyal and decent. I wanted to suffer with my country and with you. Thank Henriette for having put me back on the right road. You can also tell her that I hate her. . . .*

13

THERE was nothing to get drunk with. He returned to the hotel. As he passed alongside the wooden gallery, holding back his despair until the door of his room could close behind him, the Russian who lived next door, an old fellow who did his best not to look like a tramp, spoke abruptly through the open door of his room:

"Neighbour," he said, "won't you come in and take a cup of tea with me?"

It was the first time he had addressed Alexis. Alexis went inside.

"It tastes much better in company," said the old man, with a pronounced accent. He busied himself about a round table covered with a white cloth, fetching glasses, cleaning them with a long, narrow napkin embroidered at both ends with red cocks. "I have lemon," he said proudly, "and biscuits. And I don't wish to conceal from you that I also have some liquor. This is my day off."

Perhaps the old fellow wasn't so old after all—simply worn out. He was short, with a straggling, curly beard and hollow cheeks; his wrinkled forehead overhung his clear eyes like a roof. His gaze was unshadowed, perhaps because he had no eyebrows. . . . He wore a dark, shiny suit, and his shirt was clean, though unmended, with an ill-fitting collar that displayed his wrinkled neck in spite of the big studs. His tie looked like a piece of string, and scarcely served its purpose.

His room was exactly like that of the Slavskys, except for the wallpaper pattern of little flowers instead of stripes. Above the table, upon which Gordeenko had set glasses with saucers, lemon, and little biscuits, hung a magnificent map of Russia with little flags indicating the front line. Beside it hung a photograph of Marshal Timoshenko cut from *Sept Jours*, in a paper frame decorated with flowers awkwardly drawn in coloured pencils. "I see you are looking at my Marshal," said the old fellow. "I don't know what you think of him, but I regard him as a very great man . . ."

With his trembling, swollen-veined hand, Jean Gordeenko poured a colourless potion. "Your health . . . your health, dear neighbour . . ."

One hour passed, then two, then three, and they were still in the heat of a political conversation. When Henriette knocked on the door, attracted by the voices, one of which, to her amazement, she recognized as that of Alexis, the latter realized that the pain which had been dogging him like a toothache had vanished. "To the health of the beautiful lady," said Gordeenko, kissing Henriette's hand. "And your health, too, happy husband of the fair lady . . ." Henriette had to drink a glass of vodka and eat a biscuit.

When Alexis left his neighbour his forehead was moist and his ideas were clouded. "I've just met the Paulais," Henriette said. "They say they simply must see you. I've told them you're ill, but they insisted. You know how Paulais is. . . . They're going to wait for us until eight o'clock at the *Café Morel*. Well, it's their funeral, I can't help it. . . . "What time is it?" Alexis asked. "It's after seven thirty, we'd better hurry . . ."

Henriette put her hat on again, having just taken it off, and touched up her make-up. "I'm ready," she said.

They found them still at the café, on the point of paying their bill. "Ah, there you are!" everybody cried at once.

The Paulais had this habit of turning up in your life, monopolizing you passionately for a day, or a crowded evening, and then disappearing for months on end. Whenever they turned up they were full of projects, about to leave for the West Indies, or just come back from Hawaii, celebrating someone's anniversary, spending money they had won at the races, or dragging around in their car some immense chest picked up at a bargain in the junk market. . . . In the old days their big car was always waiting for them down the street. Paulais was vaguely connected with publishing, bought a masterpiece from time to time, financed a newspaper or a political party. . . . He seemed to have plenty of money, and owned some kind of mines somewhere. . . . Whenever one got together with them there were sure to be at least ten other people. Besides his wife, Paulais dragged round with him women he had picked up anywhere, according to the fancy of the moment. His wife didn't seem to mind; she was still good-looking, although there were lines about her eyes. . . . These chance encounters piled up like a snowball, until there was always a gang round the Paulais.

The war hadn't got them down. They had just come from Cannes, bringing among their luggage an exceptionally ugly young woman, incredibly thin, tanned to the colour of burnt toast, with splendid bare legs and vivacious, predatory hands. They also had with them a rather too handsome young man, quiet and well dressed, and another, fat and bald, with the journalist's loquacity and dirty fingernails. The Paulais were stopping over at Lyons on their way to Vichy. They had always managed to get along with the people in power, whoever they might be.

"Delighted to see you, Alexis," said Paulais, pushing a generous tip towards the waiter. "You look lousy. I hear you're drinking too much. It's public talk, I didn't get it from Henriette. . . ."

He was rather handsome: a thin face, lined, but not with age, and superciliously sly drooping lips. The few white threads in his raven-black hair made him look very distinguished.

"People should mind their own business," said Alexis, pouting. Gordeenko's liquor had been potent.

"All right, all right. Let's go and eat. I've been told of a little restaurant in a low-down quarter. A wretched little hole. This is Lyons, isn't it? . . . I have to give a special password to get in. . . ."

Everybody got up. Out in the street Paulais took Alexis' arm.

"Well, things aren't too good, eh? Let's cross the street, it's over there."

"Why should they be? I'm an exile, a vagrant, like everybody else . . ."

"You don't want to go back to Paris?"

"Want to go back to Paris? What a question! No, I don't. First of all, they won't let me. I'm not *persona grata*. Second, because I don't even want to ask for permission. I have no intention of going into long explanations about my name, and about Esther. I was always taught that it's impolite to ask people about their religion. Indeed, it's worse than that, it's in gross bad taste! . . . Just imagine my providing them with a certificate of baptism! It's like taking a Wassermann test and handing the mayor a certificate of good health before he's to marry you. If my papers were false, I might try, for the fun of cheating them, and because I enjoy absurdities, but mine are authentic, I have all the legal rights according to their own laws. I should merely feel disgusted. Besides I can't bear the sight of them!"

"You're too sensitive," said Paulais. "Pull yourself together, and live like everybody else . . . for the time being."

"That's what I'm doing."

It was only a few steps to the restaurant, which was a very dubious place. A dusky lane full of moving shadows, whispers; a back room, narrow and crowded as a tramcar; a young proprietor immaculately dressed; raw ham, olives, steaks and chips, wines; Paulais' thousand-franc note. . . . There was nothing frank or open about it, except the disgusted look of the waitress. Alexis sobered up completely. His thoughts turned to Catherine, who was lost, dead.

No, Alexis wasn't drunk now. He was perfectly aware of Henriette practising her charms on Paulais, and of the way the latter responded; jealousy of the cadaverous woman with the tanned skin, and the journalist's attentions to Henriette. Henriette laughed, throwing her head back, one hand on Paulais' hand, the other covering, in a magnificent gesture of despair, her great square eyes. . . . Henriette hadn't been like this for ten years, since the time when she was still a force of nature, and well aware of it. . . . The fat journalist, who had washed his hands in the meantime, applauded everything she said. Alexis ate and thought of Catherine, registering Henriette's conduct automatically all the while.

"Henriette says you've unsexed her," Paulais called loudly to him, interrupting his thoughts. "I've heard better testimonials than that, old boy!"

"Bedroom secrets," said Alexis abstractedly. "Hold your tongue, Henriette. . . ." He sank back into his reverie.

They were having coffee. A sugar bowl full of sugar stood on the table. Very doubtful sugar . . .

"Suppose we quit this black-market hole and get some fresh air?" suggested Alexis.

Paulais paid the bill, and everybody rose. . . . But there was no question of separating. The Paulais were staying with friends. Why not walk over there? . . . Henriette walked between Paulais and the fat journalist, Mme Paulais on the arm of the handsome, silent young man. The dark, thin woman fastened on Alexis, but he couldn't understand a word she said. At last he got fed up, and said to her:

"Can't you see I'm drunk . . ."

After which he could continue his silent conversation with Cathie.

They arrived at a big house, with, for Lyons, a sumptuous staircase. They amused themselves by creeping up it. . . . At each floor was a niche, and in each niche a life-sized statue of a nude woman, with one hand on her breast, the other across her middle. The niche on the third floor was empty. Henriette climbed into the niche, and lifting her dress, held it up and with one hand over her breast, and with the other across her middle, stood immobile. She wore nothing under her dress, and in the blue light of the

dim-out her flesh was pale as marble. The resemblance was
perfect. . . .

"Splendid!" cried the journalist ecstatically, and even the
handsome, silent young man said, "Bravo, bravo". Paulais
opened the door with his key. Inside were a lot of people and
many bottles. Alexis pushed a door open, and without having
the faintest idea where he was, without turning on the light,
lay down on the carpet. . . . They were making a terrific noise
in the next room. It was incredible that people could shout like
that. The radio was full on, and a gramophone. . . .

"Henriette, give me a cigarette," he shouted, without much
hope of being heard.

Henriette almost fell over him. "Are you ill?"

"No, I'm just sick of this. Let's go. . . ."

They walked back to the hotel across a moonlit town,
flooded with noises and colours. They had a long way to walk.
The big bridges. . . . The houses of the *Croix-Rousse* sleeping
with their eyes open, their artificial, fixed and glassy eyes. . . . The
cold river, austere in this moon-drenched masquerade where
nothing and nobody was any longer recognisable.

The moon penetrated even to the courtyard of the hotel,
lighting up amost insolently the little wooden gallery. They went
to bed quickly, the shutters closed, the curtains drawn. . . .

Lying on his back in the dark, with open eyes, Alexis continued
his argument with Cathie. Time moved slowly, like sand in an
hour-glass. Cathie, wearing a hat like a basket of pink flowers,
was saying, "Everything is dirty, spoilt and. . ." Like a hiccup
that can't be suppressed, a sob grazed the silence. Alexis heard
it but ignored it. "Why have you done this to me?" Cathie said.
"Everything is dirty, spoiled . . ." Then a waft of spasmodic
breathing, discreet as the scratching of a mouse, tickled his ear . . .
Alexis pulled the blanket up over his head: what was the matter
with her, anyway? But the little sobs penetrated the blanket.

"Why are you crying?" Alexis threw back the blanket and sat
up in the bed. He expected her to say, "I'm not crying". Then he
would lie down again and everything would be calm as before.
But Henriette began to talk:

"I'm crying because I have nothing left on this earth, because
I'm old, because I'm lonely . . . I was fond of my chickens and

rabbits. . . . There's not a feather of them left. . . . Nothing is left of you either, not a feather. Only grief and loneliness everywhere . . . I haven't even Mistigri. . . . I used to think that when I got old I would go to the farm. . . . Now everything is gone; I'm alone with my barren old age, and everything is wretched . . ."

Alexis said nothing, but he stretched out his arm and laid a hand on Henriette's naked arm. He had never realized how much the house in Normandy had meant to her. As though it were simply a question of a house, he thought. . . .

"It's the war," he said finally. "We're war casualties, like everybody else. . . . My dear."

Henriette was crying bitterly.

"But we are two, together," said Alexis. "Don't cry, my dear . . ."

He took her in his arms, and they embraced each other with a despair greater than the night. They found each other again, after a long absence, but it was upon the occasion of a death, over a grave. . . .

14

HENRIETTE had left for the country to look for a place where they could spend the summer. They were hoping she would find an isolated little farm that would keep them from starving, and at the same time preserve their solitude. She left no address, since she didn't know where she would go on to from Brive. It was said that there was still food in the centre of France. . . .

Alexis knocked on his Russian neighbour's door. His neighbour was just leaving for work (he was a dish-washer in a restaurant), but he asked Alexis to spend the evening with him. Alexis went to buy a paper and magazines. He had been feeling bilious for some time; every morning he woke up feeling sick. He tried to read, feeling very uncomfortable. . . . Perhaps he had really been drinking too much these last weeks. He had a bottle of Vichy water sent up to him, and for the first time in a long while he took out his sketch pad. . . . The preceding day he had been to an exhibition of paintings, one of those exhibitions which, in

Lyons, are held in the shops of interior decorators. As usual, it was full of sham Matisses, sham Bonnards, sham thises and thats. . . . From a distance you might take them for genuine! How shamelessness, impudent, and tedious they all were! Not a single live canvas; not a single one of these fellows, who were already well known, had anything to say! He at least had his own means of expression, whether good or bad; he had his own language, his point of view, his sensibility. . . . He wasn't going to jump along with his legs tied, like Matisse. That only made sense if you have gone through what Matisse has, and come out where he has. . . . That should be obvious. The clerk in charge, of whom he had asked the name of the painter of one canvas, since he had no catalogue, had come back with a list, saying, "Five thousand, monsieur". All the list showed were numbers and prices. Monstrous! He went out about five o'clock. How about going to a tearoom for some tea and cake? He hadn't had any lunch. He remembered a tea-room close to the Place des Cordeliers where as late as last year they had served good cakes.

Spring was thickening, and burgeoning into summer. Alexis' legs felt like lead. The walk over the bridge, in the sun, seemed endless. The noise in the streets, on the bridge, and especially in the Place des Cordeliers, seemed almost more than he could bear. . . .

He had to wait quite a while before he could sit down at one of the glass-topped tables, where a lady and a little girl were already sitting. All the tables were taken, and there were about twenty people waiting, watching you gulp down your drink, counting the number of mouthfuls left in your cup. These twenty, and all the rest, were women, without exception. The fashionable world of Lyons. . . . They all seemed to know each other. The waitresses smiled at their old customers, most of the tables were reserved, and the cashier held confabulations with customers who went out carrying parcels that were made up for them in the kitchen. Agelong clients, they and their mothers and their grandmothers, natives of Lyons, entitled by birth to chocolate and *petit-fours*. Besides the dowagers, there were quite a few pretty girls who were worth looking at. Strange how they all bore a family resemblance to Catherine. . . . It's dangerous, such a family resemblance. . . . It explains, underlines, exaggerates. Catherine was more beautiful than these girls. She was beautiful, not by the standards of Lyons alone, but by any standard of feminine beauty, still . . . There was her reserved and distant air, which had so greatly impressed Alexis. He hadn't thought about it before, rapt in admiration as he was . . . Desire makes you blind and dumb. Oh well . . . you had only to look at these tall girls with their haughty, superior manner, as though they had the world in their pockets . . . The flat-breasted ones behaved like duchesses! And yet, God knows, there was nothing aristocratic about them; they were no more aristocratic than they were Parisian. They didn't have the courage, even, to wear a cheap dress from the *Galeries Lafayette*. They were snobs, to the colour of their fingernails, their handbags, their jewellery. . . . They were all alike, even to their fashionable little eccentricities. Catherine bought her dresses in Paris, and yet . . . certain details . . . for instance her coiffure . . . That domestic touch. Amazing! She would never have worn a local costume with the serenity of a great lady or a factory girl. . . . What an abominable thing an environment is, it devours you body and soul! Oh well . . . Cathie was far away. *Bon voyage*, Mme Carret!

He listlessly ate his jam tart (last year's cakes had vanished without a trace), soaking it in a strange concoction made of cocoa husks. They didn't even serve tea any more in this place. The girl at his table was unhappy, because they weren't allowed to serve the cocoa-husk drink to children under eight, and she wanted some. Alexis eyed the red-brown liquid sceptically. So it was all right to poison adults! He felt rather sick, and hurried out. He was sure the waitress had taken too many of his ration tickets. Alexis didn't know anything about tickets. It had taken Henriette's absence to make him use them.

The air had done him good, and back at the hotel he took up his sketch-book again. Time passed with incredible swiftness. When Jean Gordeenko knocked on the partition it was already ten o'clock. Alexis washed his hands and went over to join him. His queasiness was gone.

They played a game of chess and then another. Since Alexis hadn't dined, Gordeenko prepared tea, and Alexis went to his room to fetch biscuits and tarts. There was some black-market sausage in the cabinet, too, but the very thought of sausage nauseated him. He let Gordeenko explain the relative positions of the German and Russian armies to him, and then he went to bed.

The next morning Alexis rose early. He still felt sick, but the feeling passed away as he worked. He went out for lunch, since he had to eat, but came back to the hotel soon, eager to take up his pencil again. At ten in the evening Gordeenko knocked on the partition. They sat down before the chess board, but Alexis played poorly, and complained a great deal about a pain in his stomach. Even Gordeenko's tea, with the last slice of lemon, was hard to swallow.

During the night his abdominal pain became intolerable. He had to get up and vomit. His belly was bloated, hard as a rock, and he had a high fever. He didn't dare to waken Gordeenko in the middle of the night, but as soon as dawn showed through the window he knocked on the partition, unable to endure it any longer. Gordeenko came in barefooted, his unbuttoned shirt hanging out of his hurriedly donned trousers. "What is it, neighbour?" He bent over him; a silver cross and a medallion hanging from a silver chain dangled against Alexis' chest. Alexis could only moan. . . . Something had to be done, he felt terribly bad. . . .

The doctor didn't come until afternoon. He threw aside in disgust the rags, shawls, woollen scarves, hot-water bottles, and napkins round Alexis' writhing body;—all the futile paraphernalia with which one tries to relieve suffering. Alexis couldn't even raise himself up. All he could see was a hand and a wrist-watch with a grey buckskin band. He heard: "Peritonitis, probably appendicitis. . . . Better have him taken to the Basile clinic. We must get an ambulance at once. Gordeenko, my friend, go and telephone quick, now. . . ."

"Will they operate on him?"

"I can't tell. We'll see. There's a chance. . . . If there's ice at the *bistro* downstairs, get some and put it on his abdomen at once, until the ambulance arrives. They're pretty slow. I warn you. A man could die before they come. . . . Run to the chemist and get an ice bag . . ."

"What if they don't have one?" Gordeenko exclaimed, and left on the run.

Gordeenko didn't go to work. The hotel proprietress lent poor M. Slavsky an ice bag. "It would have to happen while Madame was away! Don't worry, if you need anything at all . . ." The little bell-boy ran over to the restaurant where Gordeenko worked to tell them that M. Gordeenko wasn't coming, that his best friend was at death's door. All day long Gordeenko chopped ice for Alexis' stomach. Still the ambulance didn't come. The time passed quickly for Alexis, he was so immersed in pain. He saw Gordeenko moving about, and the proprietress, who came to the door from time to time with ice. . . . Was there nothing she could do? She went to 'phone once more for the ambulance. The student who lived in the room beyond the Slavskys', the last room on the wooden gallery, also stopped by to inquire how things were going: could he help in any way? If there was any errand to be done he would do it gladly. As usual, he had a girl with him, and Alexis heard him say "Shh! Shh!" whenever the woman's voice rose. All this now belonged to a different world, a world of people who came and went, who could stand up, and who didn't suffer . . .

Towards dusk the ambulance arrived. It was still light enough for a small crowd of people to gather, and look on eagerly while the man on the stretcher was put in the ambulance. Alexis ground his teeth: the pain, the onlookers staring at his pyjamas, at his wretchedness . . .

The clinic was in a courtyard. The only attendants were a male orderly, who helped take the stretcher off, and a nurse, who walked beside Gordeenko while the stretcher was borne through the corridor.

They carried him into a large room: a public ward! While they lifted him up and put him to bed, with the busy, attentive gestures of nurses handling someone mortally ill, Alexis thought, with limitless despair, that he was going to have to suffer in public, vomit in public, relieve himself in public, and perhaps die in public. . . . Once in bed he verified the location of the pain—which, while he was being transported, had lost all human shape, overflowed, and deprived him of consciousness—and reconciled himself to suffering in an orderly fashion. He longed ardently for death.

"They'll operate tomorrow," Gordeenko whispered to him.

"It's too late to do it today. I'll go now, but I'll be back tomorrow, neighbour, may God keep you. . . . What a pity your wife is away. . . ."

The nurse gave him a morphine injection. "If it gets worse," she said hurriedly, gathering up her utensils, "call Ivan . . ." Ivan, the male nurse, stood at the foot of the bed smiling and nodding his head. "Ivan," he repeated, pointing a finger at himself. He was a big fellow, whose face was disfigured by a scar on one cheek. Alexis didn't answer, lying on his back, oblivious of the ward. He was nothing but a belly racked by suffering, upon which floated the cold discomfort of the ice bag, the stiff sheets, the bulky pillow, the board-like mattress. . . . There was a stone in his belly too big for it; it stretched the skin to bursting, and kept turning, wounding him first in one place, then another, with knife-like or serrated edges. All the time he kept thinking about the war, about the wounded; at last he understood the horror of unaided suffering, of dying in that hell. . . . The war, the war, the war. . . .

When the immense, grinding pain began to ebb like the sea, he hardly dared believe it. He hadn't even noticed when the easement had begun. . . . The bed grew more comfortable, the blades in his stomach were blunted: the morphine had begun to take effect. By the light of the night lamp he divined a shape in the next bed, a shape that moved, with a bandaged head. He saw eyes like a puppy's, and knew that those eyes wouldn't embarrass him, whether in suffering or in dying. All of a sudden his heart overflowed with tenderness, a kind of happiness. His body lightened, his pain rumbled in the distance. He would have liked to glide into death just like that. There had been a time when the very thought of death had filled him with panic, with a mad, paralysing terror. But today, being so close to it, he awaited it with something like impatience, now that his hour had come and he was exhausted. He was moved with joy at the thought that he would be delivered from all evil. Neither his past life, nor the void before him, had any existence. There was only the moment itself. And yet the thought of his painting brought tears to his eyes. He had not said all he had to say. He was just midway along the road. . . . So much lost and squandered time. . . .

Ivan, the attendant, was gliding between the beds, bending over a patient. . . . Alexis heard breathing, a discreet cough that tried not to waken anybody. He would have liked a drink. . . . He stretched out his arm but couldn't reach it, and the young patient next to him rose up, leaned over, and pushed the glass towards him. "Thanks . . ." breathed Alexis. He drank eagerly. A large white shape appeared above him. "You're not asleep? Are you in pain?" Ivan was saying. He touched the ice bag. "That's not ice, it's a hot-water bottle!"

He returned very quickly and replaced the hard, heavy ice bag on Alexis' belly. "Your feet aren't cold, are they?" He ran his hand under the sheet. "Oh your poor, cold feet!" He took Alexis' feet in his warm hands. "Poor, poor feet . . ." he said, and the glow of his hands passed into the feet and mounted to Alexis' heart. He began to feel drowsy, while Ivan stood motionless by his bed. He didn't hear him leave. . . . His feet were warm, the bed was good, and he himself felt good and well-disposed. Henriette wouldn't be here to take him by the hand, but there was the helpful hand of his neighbour; always, everywhere in the world, there was a neighbour to come to your aid, a human being always turned up when you couldn't manage any longer by yourself. Alexis wept.

In the morning his suffering reached its peak. The stone that swelled his belly had started to turn and was threatening to break through his hips and loins. The nurse arrived at eight o'clock, and immediately gave him another injection. As the morphine began to set floats beneath the burden of his body, he noticed indifferently and yet with astonishment the grey colour of his skin. He lifted the bed-clothes: his stomach and thighs were grey . . . Ivan prepared the patients for breakfast. Alexis watched their pale, thin hands, and their efforts to sit up. . . . The nurse came to fetch his young neighbour with the bandaged head for his dressings; he could walk slowly, leaning on her arm. Ivan started to sweep the room. When did he sleep? Alexis listened to all the movement, and was glad he wasn't alone. He began to feel drowsy.

It was Ivan who woke him, lifted him in his arms and put him on the hospital trolley. "How light you are!" he said. . . . Here was the corridor through which Alexis had come in. . . . Two men in white coats and the nurse were talking loudly and laughing. . . . Ivan stopped the cart in front of a door, opened the door: the operating-room appeared in glaring, pitiless light. The time had come. Something terrible was going to happen. He was in for it!

15

WELL, he did not die. Slowly he began to live again. . . . He had several postcards from Henriette, who was moving from place to place looking for a house. She gave no address, and had no inkling of what had happened. When she returned, eight days later, Alexis could already smile and eat. Gordeenko had been to see him daily, bringing news and little gifts.

"I've brought you some flowers, neighbour," he said. "We are men, but why shouldn't men enjoy flowers?" He tugged at his straggling beard.

The patient in the next bed, a builder's man who had fallen from a scaffolding, had completely recovered. His mother, who had hastened from the country, and who had been unable, ever since first hearing the dreadful news, to get over her fright, brought her son some chicken, rabbit, and butter, sighing and weeping all the time. . . . They gave Alexis a chicken wing. The injured man absolutely insisted on it. It was a great day!

Henriette was a little like this mother. While she had been looking around, taking trains and buses, walking miles so that Alexis could at last work and live in peace, he had nearly died! She couldn't get used to the horror of the idea. She even had to take to her bed. But fortunately she recovered quickly. It was just a bad migraine, without after-effects.

But the dream-place which she had found after so much trouble was no longer suited to the convalescent Alexis. It was an isolated house, without any conveniences whatever, in the depths of the country: four miles distant from a baker! But the landscape was splendid, and supplies could be had from the surrounding farms. . . . Well, it was out of the question now, they might as well forget about it. All they could do was go back to the hotel. After all, the hotel wasn't so bad. The room was cool, and Mme Zoppi, the proprietress, had offered to cook for Alexis. Besides, there would always be a doctor at hand.

Lyons was stifling and sticky with heat. Alexis remained stretched out on his bed, his door open on to the wooden gallery. He recovered very slowly. Mme Zoppi made the bell-boy (who had grown considerably since the Slavskys first knew him, and promised soon to fill out the braided collar of his uniform) bring a deck chair on to the wooden gallery, and Alexis was quite content to gaze at the blue lid of the stone shaft which formed the yard. The student in the back room had to step over him every time he came home with his women, but nobody minded. Alexis spent the days idly, unable to concentrate on anything, to read or play chess; the most he could do was to play cards with Henriette, while awaiting Gordeenko's return. He lived only for the news, and the news was very bad. The German tentacles were lengthening, and reaching out towards the Caucasus. Oh, God, if the war would only end! Since his illness, Alexis had been unable to think of anything else. He had been patient, had tried to come to terms with this life, but it had grown intolerable, impossible. . . . He who had formerly detested the radio would have liked to buy one now. But it wasn't feasible, even if they could have found one. They had to be careful. Now that they were living in the hotel there was always the possibility of some excited Legionnaire running and denouncing them to the police for listening to foreign broadcasts. Fortunately there was Gordeenko, with his unshakable and heartening faith in the Russians. Listening to him Alexis grew animated, and a nervous tic made his eyelids jerk. . . . If it would only end!

He went out for the first time between Henriette and Gordeenko. They didn't walk far, but it was very hard for him even to reach the Place du Pont. The sight of the square moved him as if it were his native land. They led him back and put him to bed, pitifully weak, and pale as death. How would he regain his strength? He slept poorly, and though Henriette and Mme Zoppi used all their ingenuity to tempt him, he hardly ate at all. The only thing he liked was the tea Gordeenko prepared for him, which the latter had procured through a series of complicated and costly deals among the clients of the restaurant where he worked.

Henriette, in an ecstasy of gratitude, was not far from thinking Gordeenko a saint. "You have only to look at his eyes," she told Alexis. "There's something almost superhuman in them!" Despite Gordeenko's modest protestations, she got hold of his three shirts, two pairs of socks, and even his underpants, and gradually covered them with a positive embroidery of darns. It was quite possible that she gave the choicest bits of food to Gordeenko. After all, Alexis didn't eat, and Gordeenko was entitled to them. Henriette herself had grown terribly thin. She still had enough to eat, but at what a cost of shopping, journeys, queuing, and shifts of every kind. Lyons seemed to be living on what was left over on a tablecloth. . . . And then the money question. Money vanished in a terrifying way. Where did it go? Alexis' illness had been a financial disaster, despite Gordeenko's connections, and the Russian surgeon with whom he had served in Wrangel's army, and who had performed the operation gratis. There was the clinic, operating-room, dressings, medicine. . . . And now there were the little amenities from the black market. Henriette worried so much that in three months she lost fifteen pounds in weight. However they looked at it, they must leave Lyons.

16

THROUGH Mme Zoppi, the proprietress of the hotel, they at last succeeded in renting two rooms in a village one hour from Lyons. The house belonged to a blood-cousin of Mme Zoppi, a very proper person, the widow of a highway inspector, with a small income. But living had become so expensive, she didn't need all that room, now that she was alone, and the lady and gentleman would be comfortable . . . "I'm not saying there'll be meat at every meal or all the butter you'd like. But there's goat-cheese, eggs, and vegetables. It's the country, you know. . . ."

The cousin had laid in wood for the winter. It was the wood that determined Henriette. She couldn't face the thought of winter in Lyons with a shivering Alexis, in an hotel which would not be heated this year, and with the food problem grown quite impossible. For once she really insisted that they should leave, despite Alexis, who didn't want to budge. Gordeenko came to Henriette's aid: couldn't Alexis see how his wife had changed? They must go away, recruit their strength, and really eat. . . . There was no doubt of final victory, but it wouldn't be before '43, one mustn't count on '42.

It was a tiny village, but an important railway junction. A single street, and the Rhone with a great, shimmering metal bridge. Mme Loiseau's house was close to the station; it had only one floor, a tiled roof, and a little garden where a few vegetables grew. When M. and Mme Loiseau had retired here to their native district they had bought this little house. But poor M. Loiseau hadn't enjoyed it for long . . . Mme Loiseau went on to say that she was quite lonely in the house. She hadn't any children. ("You have none either, have you, madame?") Life is so lonely without children. So when Mme Zoppi had written her about her invalid guest, she had agreed right away . . . Henriette scanned their future home: the kitchen to the left of the central corridor, and behind the kitchen the room belonging to Mme Loiseau. They were to have the two rooms across the corridor. But of course they would have the use of the kitchen, as had been agreed by letter. In fact they could stay there all day if they wanted to. It was the custom of the country to live in the kitchen, especially in the evenings, now that the days were getting short and one had to be careful about electricity. There was the risk of fines. Everything was so strict these days, it was easy to get fined. And neither M. nor Mme Loiseau had ever been fined in their lives, either over electricity or anything else. This was no time to begin. . . . So they would spend the evenings together. It would be very pleasant.

The room to the right, opposite the kitchen, was the dining-room. It was for them. As you see, it gave on to the street, like the kitchen . . . "And here's your bedroom. It looks out on the garden and the railway lines," like Mme Loiseau's own bedroom. "At first the trains will keep you awake, but you quickly get used to them, and then they actually send you to sleep." The linoleum was waxed: very few people could still afford that luxury. Wax was unobtainable, but Mme Loiseau had a little, very little. "You'll need to be a bit careful, though. Perhaps you could make yourselves little felt overshoes, but we'll see about that later. Everything's clean, as you can see, the windows, the curtains, the wardrobe mirror, the sheets, the dining-room tablecloth . . ." Madame Loiseau told them how as a young girl she had dreamed of having a dining-room in light oak, and that when they moved here she had finally had her wish, but her poor husband hadn't enjoyed it for long. She showed them the inside of the buffet, the dishes, glasses, cups, and the little pot of preserves which she had made for her lodgers; they must try it and tell her how they liked it. The flowers came from the garden. Mme Slavsky should be careful always to keep a saucer under the vase, so as not to make rings on the light oak table. She hoped they would find the bed comfortable. It was large, and the mattress had just been remade; they would find everything they needed in the two nightstands. She had added a lampshade especially for them. Without a shade the light might be too glaring, and pink would go well with a dark complexion. She must have guessed that Mme Slavsky would be dark! A door opened directly from the bedroom on to the garden, but Mme Loiseau had preferred to have it nailed up, because whenever it was open at the same time as the hall door there was such a draught that twice now she had had to replace broken panes, and just think of trying to replace panes these days! First of all there are none, and then they cost a forttune! The Slavksys should be careful always to keep the two bedroom windows closed (they were difficult to nail up on account of the shutters) and only to open those in the dining-room. To reach the garden they could go by way of the dining-room and the corridor. . . .

When Mme Loiseau left them she was still muttering like a tea kettle that continues on the boil after being taken off the flame. . . . Henriette sank down in tears into the crimson armchair in the bedroom, but Mme Loiseau came back to talk to her about the kitchen and the casseroles, and Henriette had to jump to her feet, surprised while still sobbing, and pretend that she had hay fever, rather out of season. But Mme Loiseau was quite uninterested, being completely absorbed in her casseroles. . . .

Henriette must have been very tired to cry so incessantly. Alexis, on the other hand, had been very calm all day, and tried to console her, while she arranged part of their things in a wardrobe, on one side of which hung Mme Loiseau's dresses, exhaling an odour of camphor and curds, and the rest in the drawer reserved for them, the other two being occupied by the effects of the late M. Loiseau. Henriette upset one of the two tiny vases, each with a heavy dahlia in it, which stood on the dresser, and the water flowed over the waxed wood and the embroidered runner. When she tried to remedy the disaster she upset the second vase. . . . Alexis mopped up the water carefully with his big cambric handkerchief, while Henriette sat in the chair crying. "It's nothing," he said. "It doesn't show any more. She won't notice it, I tell you, she's as blind as a mole. Look, I've wiped it all up."

Mme Loiseau wouldn't let them go out to eat: it wasn't worth going out and spending money on a poor meal, when there were eggs, potatoes, and cheese at home. But Alexis insisted. They hadn't seen the country yet; family life would begin tomorrow, but today she must let them play at travellers still. They wanted some air . . . which was quite true.

In the main street were grocery shops, two drug-stores, two cinemas, and a great many vegetable stalls with beautiful displays of fruit and vegetables. Henriette couldn't get over it. This was something very different from Lyons. The apples smelled good. The road led to a little bridge over a small, nameless stream; beyond it were some insignificant hills, copses, and fields. They had seen enough in this direction, and decided to go back by way of the high Rhone bank, parallel with the main street. The quay was not impressive, in spite of its shady trees: it was simply a deserted, dusty road, with a few closed garages, littered with old iron and tyres. The Rhone, beneath them, was fringed with sand and filth; it seemed hardly possible that this was the splendid, turbulent, imposing Rhone of Lyons and Avignon. They reached the big, metallic bridge for pedestrians and cars. Across the Rhone, which seemed too small for such a large bridge, they could see rolling country with orchards. But they didn't cross over. Right after the bridge came the station, and the end of the open country. They followed the main street again, passed their little house near the station, and entered the station restaurant. "Nothing to eat," they were told. At the *Café de la Poste et du Sauvage* a voluble, gesticulating woman gave them the same answer. In the third, and perhaps last, restaurant the proprietress suggested that they should cross the bridge. Over there they would have a better chance. . . . There seemed to be something odd in the suggestion, and in the proprietress's rather meaning look at Henriette. Alexis grew insistent. They weren't particular, and they were very tired. The landlord came out of the kitchen and sized them up, and apparently judging them differently from his wife, led them into the back room, where they had an omelette and string beans for a hundred and eighteen francs. It is true that two glasses of wine were included.

Mme Loiseau was waiting for them. She had to explain how the locks worked, and how to go out to the garden at night, and where to find matches and the paraffin lamp that held a little, a very little, paraffin. . . . They must use it carefully.

They finally went to bed. The bed was good. They had a moment of excitement when Henriette's head struck the head-board of the bed, which reverberated like a gong! It wasn't wood, as they had supposed, but metal painted to look like wood. Alexis caressed the nape of her neck, and pointed out to her how handy it was to have the light switch within reach of one's hand when one lay in bed. He turned off the light: the chain-pull fell back against the bed head with a faint vibration. Presently the trains began to file past, long, interminable. . . . The rasp of brakes. . . . Now they were starting up again. . . . Shrieks, shrill, lugubrious whistles. . . . Sighs. . . . Asthmatic gasps. . . . A sound of a de-railing train, the authentic sound of disaster, was repeated so often it seemed to be something normal. . . . Henriette lay crying in Alexis' arms.

17

HAD Mme Loiseau been mean, everything would have been simple. But because she was so kind, they were at her mercy. How could they avoid eating with her, when she had changed her lifelong habits in order not to inconvenience her lodgers, and when the idea of separate meals didn't even occur to her? For the first few days, in the hope that she would get tired of waiting, the Slavskys came to lunch at three o'clock, but it was no use. Mme Loiseau even tried to hide from them the stomach-ache it had given her. There was no question of taking their meals in the light oak dining-room; Henriette would never have dared lay places at the immaculate table where no one had ever sat down to eat. Nor did she dare to use the dishes in the sideboard; her hands trembled when she touched one of the gilt-rimmed plates or one of the ruby glasses, and felt Mme Loiseau's anxious eyes upon her. She used only the odd pieces of kitchen crockery. What could you do with a person who went to so much trouble to be agreeable? Henriette had only to light the stove in the kitchen for her to run in and move her pots, to give Henriette all the space. She wouldn't let Henriette wash the dishes: "Leave them, I'm used to it. . . ." She often took advantage of Henriette's being away on an errand to clean the vegetables for her, and often prepared a lather for her with her own soap, soap that was so hard to get, so precious. Just think if it should disappear, like lard and sugar!

So kind she was that she knocked on the dining-room door every ten minutes, always for a perfectly good reason. A cousin had come with some cheese. Would Mme Slavsky like some? She had taken the rabbit off the stove. She thought it was done, but if Mme Slavsky would care to come and look? Would Mme Slavsky give her her husband's silk shirt? She just happened to have some hot water . . . her combinations, too, while she was about it. . . . She trotted round the house in her black dress patterned with little white flowers, thin, white-haired, with a dental plate that gave her two rows of impeccable, ferocious teeth.

Alexis, entrenched in his room, perforce resigned himself to the appearances of Mme Loiseau. He was up against the wall; the bedroom was a cul-de-sac. He had tried the garden. But apart from the fact that in the garden Mme Loiseau hadn't even to knock, there were too many flies. He also often went to the *Café de la Poste et du Sauvage* and drank quantities of wine, but he didn't seem to be gaining any weight. Mme Loiseau whispered to Henriette that her husband was very thin, that he needed a tonic. . . . Alexis was indeed emaciated; there was nothing left of him but two profiles glued together. At mealtimes Mme Loiseau stuffed him with everything she could find, and made him clean up his plate. Alexis preferred to stuff himself rather than argue

with her. When Mme Loiseau set the casserole in front of him for
him to soak up the sauce, he had the look of a cornered animal.

It was the only apartment that had ever resisted the atmosphere
of the Slavskys, taking on neither their colour nor their smell.
Alexis' canvases, together with Esther, had remained in Lyons.
Mme Loiseau did the cleaning herself, and everything remained
stiff and immobile as on the day of their arrival. The rooms looked
uninhabited. When Alexis dropped ashes from his cigarette he
jumped up to remove them; if there were ever any on the night
table, he cleaned them up with the sleeve of his pyjamas. But he
did no work. How could he violate this interior with paints,
the smell of turpentine, the dust of charcoal, and art-gum? . . . The
furniture would have had to be moved. Alexis resigned himself.
It would have meant shifting a universe, and he was incapable
of such a feat.

He was completely idle without being bored, being so weak.
Henriette had the kitchen and all the rest to occupy her. They
began to find this perpetual constraint natural; they got used to
talking in undertones, since every word was audible throughout
the house, and to getting up early, since they washed themselves
in the kitchen, where there was always "water in the sink", and
since Mme Loiseau waited for them to finish before beginning
the hundred little tasks she had to do there. It was impossible to
know when she made her own toilet. Did she get up at dawn, or
did she wait until after they had gone to bed in the evening, or
didn't she ever wash herself? They never found out.

They got used to hearing her talk with emotion of the
Marshal, and to her indignation whenever attacks against the
Germans provoked sanctions. It was a double crime: the crime of
assassination, and of inflicting suffering on innocent people. It
was also dishonest, making a liar out of the Marshal, who had
accepted the conditions of the armistice. Yet despite Mme
Loiseau, the attacks and sabotage continued in ever growing
intensity. . . . "Have you noticed, Mme Loiseau, that the Germans
aren't taking hostages any more?" Alexis insinuated. "I won't
say there aren't any executions—I don't want to exaggerate—
but not of hostages as such. . . . What do you think it means?"
Mme Loiseau said excitedly that she didn't know about that, but
that the people who made the attacks were hot-headed revolu-

tionaries, and just as well out of the way! . . . She also grew very excited on the subject of forced labour; the government was acting in our interest, and since the promise was made, they should keep it and go; it was only fair that some of our poor prisoners should come back! "You really think they're being fair about the exchange? I have a feeling the Boches are cheating . . ." said Alexis, revenging himself on Mme Loiseau for the potatoes that she piled on to his plate. Henriette gave him a severe look. Once they started arguing it would never end. . . . "This isn't the time to try to do them down," continued Mme Loiseau. "We've been defeated. All we can do is to keep quiet. . . ." "And start all over again when we've recovered?" Alexis couldn't refrain from saying. The potatoes were choking him, especially since there was no wine. Mme Loiseau shifted her false teeth (was her conscience stirring?), but finally she said, all the same, that we'd have to learn to get along with the Boches while there was still time, so the war would be over sooner; otherwise there'd be no end to it. . . . She said "Boches" like everybody else.

There was only one thing that roused Henriette: Mme Loiseau's rage on the day when she brought home a disreputable alley cat which she had picked up somewhere. . . . Mme Loiseau didn't want any animals in her house. The lady and gentleman were going too far. She never objected to anything they did; they were more at home in her house than she herself was; but this was too much: she couldn't tolerate cats in her clean house, where there were no fleas, germs, or bad smells. . . . Neither cats, nor dogs, nor birds. Henriette, haughty and dignified, left with the cat under her arm, carrying a big piece of blood sausage, which Mme Loiseau had been counting on for the evening. There was no further mention of the cat, but its skinny shadow continued to hover between the two women.

The cold days precipitated a conflict between Mme Loiseau and Henriette. Henriette wanted some heat, but Mme Loiseau thought it was too early. They were soft. Weren't they ashamed of themselves at their age? Didn't they have any blood in them? M. Slavsky should force himself to eat a little more. He'd feel the cold less. Alexis sat with chattering teeth, in the crimson armchair in the bedroom. Why did he always stay in the bedroom, when the oven was lighted in the kitchen? He could sit there.

Nobody would bother him. And if he wanted to rest after lunch, they'd put an armchair close to the stove. Mme Loiseau did, in fact, encumber the kitchen with an armchair dragged from her bedroom, the door of which was always closed. "Look," she said, opening the oven. "It feels good. It will warm your knees . . ."

One day Alexis was so cold that he didn't get up. He didn't get up the next day either. Mme Loiseau tightened her lips, clicked her dental plate, and didn't yield. It wasn't until the third day that she brought in logs. The little stove smoked, smelled strongly of varnish, and settled down. Henriette brought Mme Loiseau a handful of green coffee that she had been hoarding jealously for two years. Mme Loiseau adored coffee as cats love valerian. She was crazy about it. "Oh no, I don't want to deprive you of your coffee. Oh no." She began getting the pan ready to roast it. These Parisians were eccentrics.

Since they had no radio, the echo of events came to them only by way of the newspapers. Roosevelt's speech, and the landing in North Africa, hadn't the same effect as if they had been in Lyons, especially with Gordeenko at their side. . . . O for Gordeenko! Henriette was obsessed with the thought that Morot might not be able to send them money any more, that the arrangement with the person who was sending them francs, while Morot deposited dollars to his account, might cease to function. The thought terrified her, but she said nothing to Alexis, who was still ailing, and seemed unable to recover.

When, on the eleventh of November, they heard that the Germans and Italians had overrun the frontiers and the de- marcation line, they only half believed it. Nothing had changed in their little corner. They believed it on the day when Mme Loiseau returned to the house in a state of indescribable excite- ment: on the bridge she had encountered a German soldier with helmet and rifle, a sentry! Henriette and Alexis ran out. It was true: a German sentinel was pacing the big metal bridge. They hadn't time to comment on this incredible fact, for when they got home they had Mme Loiseau to take care of.

She called in a weak voice to Henriette, who went into her room and found her in bed. Henriette could barely recognize in the pale invalid with the ghastly blue lips, who lay on the narrow bed, the once active Mme Loiseau. The air in the room was stifling from the closed windows and the kitchen nearby. The room was filled with furniture like a lumber room, and redolent of catastrophe; the wash-bowls with their spilled water, the wet towels lying everywhere, and Mme Loiseau's clothing cast helter-skelter over the chairs. Mme Loiseau told her, in a voice that was barely audible, that she had had an attack in the kitchen. Henriette straightened the dress and picked up the petticoats, wiped up the spilled water from the floor, and changed the compresses on Mme Loiseau's forehead and heart. Poor Mme Loiseau! In bed she looked like an old, skinny chicken, plucked after its neck has been wrung. She was so thin without her clothes, her head hanging pathetically, her skin yellow and crinkled. . . . It's a mercy that people cover their nakedness, so that it needn't be thought of all the time. She sighed gently, while Henriette passed a caressing hand over her tangled white hair. Alexis ran out to find a doctor.

The doctor gave her an injection and recommended rest. It had really been a slight heart attack, but they didn't tell her. Soon she was trotting round the house again, taking the work out of Henriette's hands. She never mentioned it, but she was deeply grateful to Henriette for having taken care of her; indeed she had spent the night in an armchair by her bed, emptied her chamber pot, made vegetable broth, and given her her medicine. . . . And poor M. Slavsky, who had had to run for a doctor! He had been quite out of breath when he came back. Mme Loiseau had never been spoiled. She wasn't used to such attention. . . . When Henriette mentioned to her that they might be in financial difficulties she almost flew into a passion, and told her not to give it a thought, it could be arranged somehow; she would lend them money which they could pay back at their own convenience. Nevertheless, when Alexis, with a sudden access of energy, suggested that they leave, because he couldn't endure to be idle any longer, Henriette had to tell him that it was out of the question, and he accepted the blow. Events were moving so swiftly now; perhaps everything would be over by the spring. They must hold out until then, and not lose patience, now that the end was in sight.

It was with interested motives that they made the acquaintance of their neighbours, who had a radio and listened to London. You could tell from the garden that it was London.

It became a ritual for them to go next door every evening after supper. All day long Alexis waited for the moment when he could batten on the British news, as someone might wait for a drug to dull a pain. At about nine-fifteen they walked into the neighbour's kitchen to hear the radio sputter out, "This is London." The neighbours, man and wife, worked in the silk factory, the boy went to school. Mme Loiseau didn't join them. She stayed home to wash the dishes and read the paper, which she hadn't time for during the day. She no longer talked about her political opinions, and whenever the Slavskys returned more excited than usual, and told her about the Russian advances, or about Stalingrad, she retired quickly into her bedroom, to "lie down," she said . . .

They passed the peak of the winter in Mme Loiseau's kitchen, with the oven heating their knees. Mme Loiseau was right, it was pleasant. Alexis barely left the house, even for air. They might have passed a Saturday or Sunday evening at a cinema, but the cinemas weren't heated, and it would have interfered with the broadcast at nine-fifteen. Alexis did little jobs for Mme Loiseau. He held up his hands for her to wind the wool ripped from an old sweater, wrote letters for her to her cousin, and stirred the soap she was making with the oil in which formerly she had kept sausage; it had now turned rancid, and was no longer good for anything but soap. Watching the soap on the stove, and stirring it unceasingly, was something of a task. Towards evening Alexis would begin to get jumpy and tell Henriette to hurry with the supper, lest he might miss the beginning of the broadcast.

The good weather came. The windows on to the street were open, there were flowers and strawberries. . . . Yet the Russian advance had halted and Alexis was gloomy. Their village still hadn't been occupied. The sentry on the bridge had become part of the landscape, and occasionally a few Germans passed through on bicycles, from across the bridge. . . . The other bank of the Rhone belonged to a different district, and there were Germans there.

Alexis and Henriette took little walks. Alexis was feeling better, after all, than he had done in the autumn when they arrived; at that time he wouldn't have dared cross the bridge: it would have been too much for him. They both despised walking, so they didn't go far. If there had only been pleasant walks, but where could one go in this country? ... During the winter they had never ventured beyond the main street, but now they pushed as far as *California*, as they called the other bank, where the scenery was entirely different, with magnificent fruit trees. *California* began for them just beyond the iron bridge and the sentry. The bridge connected with the national highway, wide, straight, and smooth, flanked by great trees, with such thick foliage that they formed a green canopy over the road. Just beyond the bridge, on either side of the road, were two café-hotels, whose terraces and gardens faced the high Rhone bank littered with refuse. Before the building on the left were often one or two cars. People could be seen on the terrace, with its rusty iron tables. But at the one on the right was a strange apparition: a shabby prostitute standing and knitting an orange sock! Beyond the hotel the orchards began, apricot trees, peach trees, already covered with ravishing little wool balls, light coloured and gay as confetti. Trucks passed, loaded with fruit crates, blue-clad workers pedalled or walked by, and handsome, buxom girls, their bare legs and arms tanned by the sun ... Alexis was feeling more contented. He took a sketch-pad with him, even though he didn't work yet, and he looked at the scene composed by the sentry, the peeling hotel, the harlot with her orange sock, and the little, light-coloured woolly balls. ...

The fine national highway, flanked by big trees, ran straight and flat for three-quarters of a mile to a little place proclaimed by a large signboard as "*Le Beau Fruit*". But first they had to cross a railway line. It annoyed them to have to wait for one of those interminable goods trains to pass, open flat trucks with huge wine barrels, and closed, secret ones, bearing away the wealth of France. At last the fringed barriers lifted and they entered the little village with its few houses, a lemonade factory, a goods station. They sat down in the café on the little circular *place*, fried in the sun like a pancake, drank a saccharine lemonade in the fly-blown room, and returned by the same road, beneath the century-old trees.

Since the beginning of the warm weather they had gone every Saturday to the pictures. They went in spite of the bad air, and the echoes in the barnlike theatre, and in spite of the old films which they had almost always seen before. On Sundays they listened to the radio twice, at twelve-thirty and in the evening, always with the same impatience and the same hope, like people with a lottery ticket who are about to hear the results of the draw. They had already drawn one prize—the Bizerta and Tunis film— and there would be others if they were duly patient. On Sunday afternoon the neighbours would ride eight miles by bicycle to go swimming; Alexis and Henriette had no bicycles, so they had a good excuse. Mme Loiseau also left on Sundays, first to go to Mass, and then to visit some farmer relatives, whence she returned loaded with foodstuffs. This was in fact the best day of the week, since for a few hours Alexis and Henriette had the whole house to themselves. Right after the twelve-thirty broadcast they came back to the house. Henriette took off her dress, washed leisurely in the kitchen, and then went round in her slip, played patience on the dining-room tablecloth, prepared a drink at an unwonted hour. . . . Henriette hadn't gained any weight since they had come to the country, despite the good food and little exercise. Her body showed its square frame; her face had lost it feminine roundness and displayed hard planes and angles. . . . Her square jaws and the exaggerated eyes in her thin face made her look remarkable. What had become of her breasts? Her fingers were bony, roughened by housework, and she had not made her face up since a short time after their arrival, when Mme Loiseau had returned in excitement from the grocer. She had been asked why her lodgers had come to settle here. And why not? she had replied. They were much too superior people to bury themselves in a little place like this, where no one ever came for a holiday, especially for the winter. But M. and Mme Laborde came here too. That wasn't the same thing; their factory was only six miles off, and they owned a beautiful house in the neighbourhood. . . . The lady wasn't a Jewess, by any chance? The woman whose little girl Mme Slavsky thought so pretty had thought she looked a little like one, but M. Giraud, the retired policeman, who had come to get his wine, said he didn't think so, that to him she looked like a Provençal woman, from Toulouse or some such place. Nevertheless the grocer's wife hadn't been reassured. Besides, these people had a foreign name. Mme

Loiseau was unable to account for these conjectures; she thought they might be caused by Mme Slavsky's make-up. When Henriette retorted that all the girls in this region made up, Mme Loiseau said that it wasn't so noticeable in the young ones, it wasn't the same thing. Whereas if she, Mme Loiseau, were to put on rouge . . .! This last argument was decisive. It struck home with Henriette: she left off making up, and put away her cloak, ear-rings, and bracelets. Those things were only for the "young ones". . . . Alexis shrugged his shoulders. Ridiculous! Besides losing fifteen pounds in weight, she had gained twenty years. What was all this nonsense, anyway? She shouldn't pay attention to Mme Loiseau. Oh yes, said Henriette: Mme Loiseau knew. She was a simple soul, the clear-sighted kind. Henriette's eyes took on a pained expression, her eyes were noticeably large, and made people on the street turn round to look at her.

18

IT was an amazing coincidence for them to find someone they knew in this hole! And yet it happened one day in the main street. A woman on a bicycle turned twice to look at them. It was impossible to think who she might have been. They were still talking about it in their creaking bed.

Next day, when they were just about to enter the *Café de la Poste et du Sauvage*, she addressed them.

"Alexis Slavsky, isn't it?" she said. "We may as well not try to dodge each other; we'll run into one another twenty times a day on the street . . ."

It was Louise Delfort, the journalist, But, oh, God, how she had changed! Here, for once, was somebody whom the war and its restrictions had improved. She had been a rather heavy woman, with a mottled complexion, tousled peroxide-yellow hair, indifferently dressed, and almost slovenly. And now, though she wasn't slim, she was at least not fat, held herself very straight, had a trim waist; her muscular legs looked longer in their wooden sandals, her blue-black hair was done up in great, shiny curls that revealed charming ears. . . . The heavy eyes went well with her complexion, in which the pink underlay a dark, rich tan. Her

teeth were brilliantly white, the two front teeth slightly separated.
. . . Her white cotton flowered print dress looked cool and smart.
. . . She was absolutely unrecognizable. . . .

"I must tell you that I rather intended to make myself unrecognizable," she said, glancing around her. "And I thought the
best thing to do was to disguise myself as a well-dressed woman.
If anyone had ever told me I'd spend hours in a beauty parlour!
That's the way it goes. . . . I've had a great deal of trouble. . . . I
don't know whether you know that my father is in England. He
often talks over the radio. . . . So they arrested me."

She turned round two or three times. No, there was no one
to overhear them.

"I'd rather die than go back where I've been! . . . Do you mind
if we move on a few steps? I don't like that fellow behind me. . . ."

Alexis and Henriette followed her obediently. She walked
ahead, wheeling her bicycle. "Let's sit here, if you can spare a
moment," she said, sitting down on the little stone wall that
skirted the dirty Rhone bank. Yes, they had time. . . . To conclude
the story—she had been here a week and had already run into
them several times. They might have recognized her, despite the
beauty treatments. . . . Yes, but she had done it so thoroughly!
They still couldn't get over it. . . . Well, she'd decided she'd either
have to leave the district or trust them. . . . Something told her
that she could confide in them, that their views would be almost
identical; and even if that weren't so, there are some things that
certain people don't do. She didn't think she would involve them
in any danger. The Gestapo seemed to have lost track of her. She
had been living in Cannes under an assumed name for a year.
But after the eleventh of November she had had to leave the
coast, and finally she'd been washed up here . . .

It was a blessing to have met this woman! It's always like that.
When you think you've reached the end of your tether, something
comes along to save you . . . Louise Delfort was living by herself
outside the village, in a villa belonging to a local manufacturer,
who was then on holiday. The manufacturer had made a lot of
money in the last three years. . . . To put it bluntly, he was a black
marketeer. Louise said quite simply that she was safe there with
him, because he was one of those people who always manage

to be on the side of the winner, who realize that the wheel always turns, and who take their precautions; and to have accepted someone like her as a refugee might stand him in good stead. The villa was quite new, and there was a radio, books, and a garden with big trees. On hot days they stayed inside the house where it was cool. . . . Between news bulletins, the radio murmured tuneful, silly songs, and Louise smoked like a chimney and told stories. . . . Before the war she had worked for a large newspaper, so she knew a lot of things the Slavskys didn't know, and a great many people. . . . In the old days they had sometimes criticized intellectuals and Parisians, but now, what a relief it was to run into a woman like Louise Delfort, after Mme Loiseau, and the neighbours with the radio! They were fed up with peasants and provincials, who were so alien to them! Fed up with provincials, even when they were intellectuals, and with petty bourgeois, even when they were Parisians. . . . In a word, they were sick and tired of having no one to talk to but people who belonged to a different world from theirs. It's all right for a short while, may even be instructive and interesting, but what a blessing to regain freedom of speech and judgment, not to have to be on one's guard, to take into account the knowledge and possibilities of one's interlocutor, not to feel that what one says stops at the threshold of a brain, and gets no farther! To be able to speak without "footnotes", as Louise Delfort called it, to make real allusions. . . . It may not be essential in a man's life to have heard of Picasso, Matisse, and Maillol, but unquestionably those who know of them, and have undergone their influence, bear the mark of it. Alexis was convinced of this and preferred such people. . . . How glad he was to be able to speak of Arno Brecker in the proper terms, to somebody who knew what Brecker was and could appreciate what was said, who could share his indignation at the empty grandiloquence of his sculpture, which was like one of those huge melons that always look so uncommonly like a pumpkin! What a pleasure to be able to laugh about the same things, to share the same habits of eating, of washing! What a relief, what relaxation! . . . To the Slavskys, so long deprived and starved, it seemed that Louise had, in addition to her own qualities, all those of the Parisian: the intelligence, the culture, the polish, the beauty, and the knowledge of how to use her beauty, now that, for unpleasant reasons, she had consented to be attractive. . . . What a lively, cynical mind; what elegance of word and gesture; what calm frankness; what daring! Despite Mme Loiseau's afflicted countenance, the Slavskys spent all their time in Louise's villa. They ate most of their meals there; Louise was a great gourmet, and vied with Henriette in cookery. . . . One day Alexis carried his paint-box up to the villa, installed himself in the pavilion at the end of the garden, and began to work feverishly. He was almost happy. He gained weight while you looked at him. . . . Henriette, too, was happy, because Alexis was so, and because he had started to work. If only there hadn't been the perpetual worry over the money which didn't arrive, the fellow who didn't write . . . Louise was always the same, smiling, affable, and friendly. Nevertheless, there was a slight upset between her and Alexis one day, when he said, speaking of the day of victory, that he was going to get even with the people who had done the dirty on him, and that everybody had his own little black-list. . . . Louise's face took on a new expression, and her warm voice shed its velvet.

"So you expect to leave your retreat on the day of victory, and count the scalps? You want to satisfy your thirst for vengeance, but without getting in any danger yourself, after others have paid with their lives to give you the chance? You'd better keep still about it. You haven't any right to vengeance. To hear you, one would think this war was being fought simply to annoy you, that every measure was being taken against you, personally . . . It's ridiculous, outrageous! What do you know about the sufferings of the war!"

The speech left Alexis breathless.

"But . . . but . . ." he said finally, "so I won't have any rights, even after victory?"

Louise gave him a long look. There he was, stretched out in the armchair, like a rag, without muscles, his cheeks hollow and lined, a vicious schoolboy, pretending to look old. . . .

"Yes, you'll have the right to paint fine pictures," she said, turning away her eyes.

All night long Alexis tossed on his bed, unable to sleep. What did Henriette think about it? Henriette thought that not everybody could carry a rifle, and she couldn't quite see what Alexis could do to further victory. . . . Besides, what were they doing exactly, the people of the "Resistance", as it was called? Where were they? How could they be known? They had met Louise, but that was the first time they had met anybody whom they suspected of being active. What did she do? What could she do? Did she do anything? If so, she certainly didn't talk about it, any more than she talked about the prison or camp where she had spent eighteen months. She pretended that it frightened her. "People are brave," she said, "as long as they haven't had their fingers burned. But I assure you that when one has been where I have . . ." All the same, she was twice away for forty-eight hours at a time without explanation. She took her bicycle and went. . . . If she had ever asked them to do anything, perhaps they would have done it. . . ."I think so," said Alexis, "if I could do it. I'm not very strong yet. . . ." But nobody had ever asked anything of them. How did this Resistance business work? They didn't dare question Louise, it would have been indiscreet. . . . In great agitation Alexis came back again and again to the notion that he must do something, that he couldn't let himself lose all claim on his country . . . "It's not a question of your rights, but of the liberation of the country," said Henriette, with a certain vehemence, which died away presently: Louise didn't make sufficient allowance for the illness he had just recovered from, or for the fact that he was a great painter, and must safeguard his work. . . . Painting was not Louise's domain . . . His work? Alexis was hesitant. He wasn't so sure of the value of his work. Henriette objected vehemently. . . . They didn't sleep until dawn. . . .

But the next day Alexis forgot his scruples: he had done a little canvas that satisfied him completely. The same day news came that the Allies had occupied Pantellaria! There was hope! . . . Louise half-closed her eyes, which looked more tired than ever, as though strained by glare. Yet there was hardly any light in that shuttered room. . . . They had got all the information they could out of the radio, and now they were resting, just the two of them, she and Alexis, lying back in long chairs. The radio hummed like a tea-kettle in the wide, rural stillness. Alexis took Louise's hand, and so they remained without moving or speaking. . . . Perhaps fearful of frightening away an illusion of past times, when one had still had a right to illusions . . .

Henriette came back out of breath, red in the face, and perspiring. She had returned to their house on Louise's bicycle, to see if there was any mail. Presently Louise got up to take her to the shower and give her a towel and some powder. . . . It was over.

What was over? Nobody mentioned it.

One day, as they were making their way to Louise's villa, they saw her in the distance signalling to them: the landing in Sicily! Yes, it's true, with parachutists and three thousand ships, miles of ships! Louise was so excited that she was going round in circles; she shifted the furniture about and drank huge glasses of water. . . . Alexis forgot canvas and brushes, and they spent the day with their ears glued to the radio. A real landing, at last!

Every day now brought its good news. But Alexis had begun working again, and trusted Louise to give him the news accurately, in detail. She never forgot anything; she had a prodigious memory and power of concentration.

Henriette went on worrying about money. It was melting away. Taking advantage of these days of good news, she finally brought up the question of selling one of the canvases. . . . And, to her great surprise, Alexis said: "I don't care. Sell as many as you like. I'll do others!" This happened on the road across the bridge. The three of them had gone for a walk, and now they were sitting on a low wall at the side of the road, with the basket of yellow apricots which they had bought at the roadside standing beside them, resting from the heat, enjoying the freshness and peace in the shadow of the big trees. It was then that they saw in the distance a German silhouette. . . . Yes, it was a German all right, and a non-commissioned officer to boot. He came nearer. . . . He wasn't alone. . . . Behind him walked a civilian and a second German, a helmeted soldier.

The three men approached and passed them: the N.C.O., well fed, tall, and sturdy, carrying a leather brief-case under his arm; the civilian a young man of twenty at the most, as pale as any living man could be, carrying with difficulty two wretched little suitcases of which the handle of one had come loose; the soldier with his rifle slanted across his chest. From the front the youngster appeared correctly dressed in a dark suit, but when they saw him from the back they saw two large, light-coloured patches on the seat of his pants. He walked with difficulty, dragging shoes much too big for him, and his naked heels were bleeding. The N.C.O. stepped briskly, talking in a loud voice: ... "When you speak to them," he said in German (Louise understood German), "they always pretend to be half-witted. They don't understand a word of German. But they always understand you in the end. ... How old is this one? What do his papers say?"

"Twenty," replied the soldier.

The people who met them lowered their eyes. ... "He's a good fellow ..." said an old workman, whose blue overalls were so patched that it was impossible to tell where the original cloth left off and the patches began. The young man walking beside him said nothing, and wiped away the sweat that ran down his forehead.

"My God, that broken handle! ... How dreadful!" said Henriette in her deep voice. "They take a man away under everybody's eyes, in broad daylight. ..."

"A few bold fellows ... and a bicycle thrown at their feet ... I wonder how many there are round here?" Louise had the dry voice and hard look that appeared in her from time to time, like a rock beneath the smooth surface of water. This time it comforted Alexis: he felt protected; but ordinarily it made him a little afraid of her. ... She was so womanly, with her shoulders and slim waist, the charm of her two slightly separated front teeth, her lips that looked so soft, and her heavy eyes, the eyes of love, and then all of a sudden this harsh expression, this dry tone. ... But when the harshness was directed towards the Boche kidnappers Alexis thought it quite in place.

They returned to Louise's villa in silence. There was nothing special on the radio. Louise left them, and they heard her walking up and down in the next room. The National Radio was giving a chamber-music concert. The National Radio was a disgrace! You might have imagined yourself on the terrace of a provincial café, the orchestra and audience in celluloid collars and cuffs ... considering the real talent we have in the country! ... "Oh, dear," said Henriette, "my heart's like lead." She put her two hands over her heart and closed her eyes. "My heart has leaden wings. ..." The shadows round her eyes were corroding her pale cheeks. Alexis felt a vague uneasiness: she wasn't going to be ill? He had never seen her ill! Then Louise opened the door, with papers in her hand. "Read that," she said, scattering them over their knees.

It was the first time they had seen any of the underground tracts. They fingered them with pious fear. There was something electric about these leaflets—something that went to one's head. The half-effaced letters on cheap, greyish paper, the poor words they carried across the country, whose object was achieved by their mere existence. These leaflets which command respect, which attest to the tragic courage of a disarmed people. . . . Alexis turned them over with emotion. He had no desire to read them. He had a feeling that they were not meant to be read. . . . But Louise insisted. "Read," she repeated. . . .

Auschwitz . . . the camp of "slow death" . . . ten thousand deportees from all the occupied countries, men and women, a great many of them French . . . three hundred to a room, seven sleeping in the same straw bed, which is never changed, wearing convict dress, with the serial numbers stamped also on their bare chests. . . . They are not allowed to have their own spoons or cups, or given any light in the evenings to eat their bread by. . . . A fourteen-hour working day for everybody, including the ill, the infirm, the women. The inmates work on the demolition of the towns of Bleiwitz and Auschwitz. . . . The women separately, guarded by soldiers with police dogs. . . . Three lavatories for ten thousand internees, few washrooms, one shower per month. . . . Their clothing never changed. . . . The overseers are former German convicts; corporal punishment left to their brutality; the horsewhip is a favourite instrument. . . .

In a preceding pamphlet we told how one hundred French women were deported from the Romainville camp, among them intellectuals. . . . Twenty-six of these hundred are widows of hostages. . . . They are in Auschwitz. . . .

FRENCHWOMAN BEHEADED WITH AN AXE

THE Nazi axe has made its appearance in France.

In the yard of the Fresnes prison, for the first time it has made a French head roll; the head was that of a woman, an intellectual, a Protestant, and a mother. . . . Mme Albrecht was well known in university circles in Paris. . . . Who, one asks in horror, could have denounced to Hitler's henchmen this distinguished and intelligent woman to be the first victim of the hatchet of Hitler's executioner, as though, in her person, the instrument of barbarism had intended to proclaim the beheading of our civilization. . . .

This was written to be read, to be read and remembered. . . . They left earlier than usual.

It happened the next morning. They were still in bed when Mme Loiseau thrust the letter into the close-shuttered room. "It's from the village," she said.

Louise wrote that the manufacturer who owned the villa had returned and brought her news which made it necessary for her to leave. She sent them her love and affection, and a thousand kisses. . . . They would hear from her through her host. . . .

"So they haven't tormented her enough!" Alexis cried in a sudden rage. "The besotted creature's going to get herself killed!"

Henriette closed the shutters again, and lay down out beside him. She was crying. . . . She had never been like this. Nowadays she cried at everything. A thousand kisses. . . . She had never been so demonstrative. . . . Mme Loiseau came several times to knock on the door. She had already warmed up the breakfast twice, and was beside herself. Well, it couldn't be helped.

The manufacturer was a man of about fifty, with glasses and a heavy moustache. He offered Alexis a glass of iced grape-juice, and explained that he was about to leave again, and that if Alexis wanted, he could go on working in the pavilion, it wouldn't bother him. But he said it all in such a peevish tone that Alexis gathered up his things and left the pavilion and the villa, not intending to return.

Mme Loiseau sulked; she was jealous of Louise, and although she said nothing openly against her, she insinuated that an un-attached woman was a danger to the community, especially in times like these. . . . She didn't explain why, but she seemed quite sure of herself. . . . "Eat as much as you can," she said, serving Alexis almost by force: his plate was heaped up. "Perhaps it isn't as nicely served as at your friend's—that is, at M. Blin's." (M. Blin was the manufacturer.) "One doesn't know what to say, everything seems so mixed up . . . I can't understand an un-attached young woman daring to stay at M. Blin's, with the re-putation he has. . . . The king of the black market. . . . But then, it has a good side too. . . . It isn't often that a young woman knows how to cook, especially if she's single. . . . If she has never been married. . . . It's like the divorcees. When a woman is divorced you can be sure there's something wrong. . . ."

When Henriette asked, "Is Louise divorced?" Mme Loiseau was annoyed: how was she to know? She knew nothing. Nobody knew anything about Mme Louise. . . . One fine day she turned up and installed herself in M. Blin's house, and that was that. It was people like that who made it so you couldn't buy anything in the country, not an egg, not a quarter of a pound of butter! They come and buy everything, no matter what the price. "But look here, Mme Loiseau, Louise bought nothing, ever!" "But of course not; what I said wasn't aimed at her. I wouldn't allow myself", etc., etc.

The neighbours, whom they had deserted since they had been listening to the news at Louise's, were now less hospitable. They hardly dared to go there. And yet how could they miss the news from Sicily? Things were going well, very well, though still not quickly enough to please them. And since Alexis had agreed to sell some paintings they might as well get busy right away and leave this place; they were so fed up with it, especially since Louise was no longer there.

19

It was well over two weeks since Louise had left. Alexis was alone in the house. Henriette had gone to Lyons to handle the sale of his paintings, and Mme Loiseau herself had left for a week to visit her cousins. Henriette had had to wait for her departure before she herself could leave, since Mme Loiseau was capable of staying at home simply to look after poor M. Slavsky, and Alexis felt that a *tête-à-tête* with Mme Loiseau would have been more than he could have borne. Louise's departure, and the fact that he would now be unable to work for God knows how long, depressed him. On the day Henriette left, taking the train at dawn, he didn't get up until afternoon. What was the use of getting up? Lying naked on the unmade bed, his arms and legs, slender as a boy's, thrust as far from his body as possible, he examined his ribs, which striped his torso and seemed about to pierce through the pale skin. . . . They reminded him of the neighbour's black cat, and of the white dog with russet spots which roamed the streets: they too had ribs just under their skin, ribs that swelled out above a hollow belly. He moved his finger along the cicatrice which ran down his abdomen. It felt tense: which meant, no doubt, that rain was on the way. This heat couldn't last; there'd be a storm. the half-closed shutters, fastened with hooks, rattled in the wind. . . . The trains were rasping and bumping along, emitting cries of terror and fear. . . . Alexis lit his last cigarette. Louise had always had cigarettes, she had gone without food to have them. He ought to go over and see the owner. Mme Loiseau had said he had come back. To think that he had been unable to work for God knows how long! . . . He began to think in detail about the canvas he had begun. He was still thinking about it when he dozed off. . . . He fell fast asleep.

He dreamed of Louise, and woke up abruptly. He hoped he wasn't going to have erotic dreams now. . . . He stretched out. How hot it was! She was a charming, adorable girl. . . . He wondered how old she was. Probably not as young as she looked. She had a long life behind her. That trip she had made all alone, to the depths of the Ivory Coast . . . What journalistic talent! What courage! He hadn't noticed her in Paris, because she had been ill-dressed, ill-kempt, and had her yellow hair . . . Alexis detested yellow hair. . . . Besides, she had been too fat. No wonder, with her appetite! Alexis smiled, thinking of her look of interest and satisfaction whenever she and Henriette had prepared a gala meal, on a day of meat or butter. She had such a pretty waist . . . "I'm a simple soul," thought Alexis. "Intellectual stimulus is not enough for me . . . I like girls who are very young and very pretty. Louise isn't as young as all that. Not quite young enough. But what brilliance she has! . . . It's like Henriette. . . . Henriette is something else again. . . . In any event, she satisfies me, I like her, Henriette. . . ." He felt anguish at the thought that she wasn't there: what if he should fall sick with her away? The very thought made his scar smart. He was sure he wouldn't sleep a wink to-night; he couldn't sleep without Henriette. This heat, this stifling heat . . . He fell asleep.

He slept all day long, waking only when somebody knocked

on the door: a boy with a letter. It was a note from the manufacturer, asking him to come. He got dressed quickly.

Although it was already eight o'clock, the heat hadn't lessened,
and the sun, caught among the houses, burned as steadily and
intensely as live embers: but after Alexis had left the village the
wind licked his face like a flame. . . . The sky, everywhere blue
and clean, had only a few spots of clouds. Yet this submissive
countryside, which lay prostrate all round him, was parched for
water. . . . Alexis felt a faint emotion as he opened the little garden
gate: two weeks, yet it seemed already so long ago—Louise, and
the good days they had spent together . . .

This time the peevish manufacturer didn't offer him any grape-
juice, but received him in a businesslike manner, sitting behind
his desk. Louise had been picked up in Lyons, worse luck. . . . She
had been taken in a routine raid and identified, and apparently
sent away immediately. This time she would't be able to extricate
herself: when they catch you for the second time. . . . He gave
Alexis a notebook, a few books, and a suitcase which Louise had
left behind. These things would be safer with Alexis than with
him. There was nothing secret among her belongings, clothes. . . .
He might read what was in the notebook; it was probably the
beginning of a story which she had amused herself by writing;
those things are sometimes interesting, especially as souvenirs.
He rose and offered his hand to Alexis, by way of dismissal. It
would be better if Alexis didn't visit him again; and anyway, he
was going away . . .

The sky was zebra-striped with white; the wind drove Alexis
homewards, blowing into his back, overturning a fruit-stand, a
bicycle, banging the shutter of the *Café de la Poste et du Sauvage*.
. . . A few heavy drops fell from the sky like tears that must needs
fall. Alexis arrived panting. The suitcase was heavy.

He collapsed again on the bed. Really collapsed. . . . Louise!
Louise! What a fool! God, what a fool! . . . Why did she have to
put her head in the lion's mouth? Alexis hadn't dared ask the
manufacturer what he meant by saying she wouldn't be able to
extricate herself. Surely they wouldn't shoot her? You don't
shoot women. . . . No, but you behead them with an axe, like
Mme Albrecht, or send them to the salt mines, or make them dig
ditches in the camp of "slow death". . . . You don't shoot them,

no, no, you don't shoot them. . . . Louise! On rotten straw, in convict dress, a number branded upon her lovely breasts. . . . Alexis groaned. He took the notebook in his hands as though it were a relic. This jumbled yet legible handwriting, whose link was still fresh . . . Louise's voice came to him from these scribbled pages, Louise's voice speaking to him in confidence, an intimate voice which he had never known. . . . It spoke to him as though they had been lying beside each other in the half light, with her characteristic cynicism, the frankness behind which she concealed herself:

This time [she wrote] *I'm writing as a woman attracted by a man, using the written word as a means of seduction. I must put it down quickly while it still means something to me; that is, while the man still means something to me, because, frankly, I don't care a rap about him. I don't mean as a friend—of course he's a very dear friend. . . . But I've always been told that the best cure for seasickness is to embrace the first sailor you meet. I've tried it crossing the Mediterranean, and I know from experience that it works. . . . Of course it wasn't a sailor exactly, but at least there's something in the sailor story, because, as I said before, it works.*

"*Well, just now I'm in a state something like seasickness, and the first man who came along would do. What I want to recover from, speaking of seasickness, is this perpetual anguish . . . I want the air I breathe no longer to be poisoned by threats, a house again to be a shelter, and the word shelter to have its old meaning. I want to be able to walk in the street without turning round, not to have to run to the window to see who is ringing the bell, not to be shattered by sleepless nights, full of mysterious noises, a honking motor-car—is it going to stop? No, it's going on. Footsteps . . . countless footsteps . . . . Not a patrol? Are you sure? Voices, cries . . . and in what language?*

The first man would do. . . . Not quite, because I have to get just a little bit sentimental first. . . . It began the other day when we were left alone in the half-light, with the radio playing sweet music. As soon as my hand was in his, all the anguish, all the trouble, went. The "sailor's charm" worked! Am I a lucky person? Not as lucky as all that, because I can't make the forgetfulness last. It's high time I put a person into this story. . . . But it isn't easy, because if he shouldn't feel for me what I feel for him— which is nothing . . . And if the sailor's charm simply worked because of one of those little things I know so well: a glass of wine too much, the storm, sweet music, a particular mood. . . . And I know experience of this kind doesn't come off, the deception is too cruel, the humiliation too deep.

For the first time in my life I mean to amuse myself, to go about it coolly, deliberately, like an experienced coquette. Rather an odd occupation at this moment in my life, when I can think of nothing but him, and all the misery I so enjoy, all that I cannot put down on paper. But I must rid myself of this seasickness. It's a question of moral hygiene. If I can only keep my ideas straight and remember that he pleases me, and that I intend to act like an experienced coquette. So now I'll try to write so as to attract him. . . . Once I wrote an article about harems and almost needed to get myself raped afterwards, but this was quite incidental, nor do I know why I should have felt that way. The difficulty about this affair is that I want to hurry things up, and at the same time keep up this air of not interfering, of noticing nothing. . . . How restful it is to think of something else! He held my hand, and we stayed that way for a long time, without speaking. . . . It made the sailor's charm work, but I didn't say anything, and what isn't confirmed by words doesn't exist. There's even a question whether it ever existed—those two clasped hands. . . . We looked at each other candidly, without embarrassment. If it weren't for this mania for speaking, nothing would ever become real. It's the perfect system, if one doesn't want to have any worries. . . . What was he thinking? That I believed in affectionate friendship? He shouldn't think anything else; if he did it would be very disturbing, and bad for me, since he's not alone. . . . Really, I don't quite know what to think; is it really affectionate friendship, touched with a little emotion, or is it just his manner with women? There are men who can't be alone with a woman without making love to her. But we had been alone together many times; what made him act that way this time? Curiosity, desire, or bad habits.' That's it exactly. Curiosity, desire, and bad habits. I ought to ask him how I am to take this friendly gesture. . . . But, then, the lies would begin.

My whole life is at stake, and I'd rather not think about it. I'm brave so long as I lack imagination. But I can't close my eyes to the fact that the other day they almost caught me again. I'm about as well suited for secret work as the Eiffel Tower! Conspicuous, talkative, open to every wind that blows. And here I am in this business up to my neck. When I see the way most people detach themselves from events, I don't understand how they do it. How do they keep from becoming involved?

... And when you are, how can you help being in a constant state of panic and pain for those you love, for the whole world? As for me, I'm on the alert all the time. Only under the influence of music can I understand young people who cry out and go swimming in rivers or into the woods to make love. ... Yes, music makes me long for some immediate happiness, which would make me forget my troubles for a while. But I'll hold out, all the same, hoping for our hands to join, then my seasickness will be gone.

He doesn't look at me differently than before, except that there's a hint of animation when he mentions our tête-à-tête the other day, the news we listened to together. The promiscuous women of old had their lives before them; mine may end any moment. And that's really the crux of the matter. That's what I try to camouflage by the sailor's charm. But if he should offend me by keeping his distance, and if I should hold a grudge against him for it, it would ruin everything. Things rankle in my mind. Oh no! Not when I'm in love. ... But there ... I know why I want him: because I want to keep my head above water, and because I know myself, and that I need him for that. ... And I have work to do in life. I haven't time to let myself be drowned. But why should he want it? There's no reason why he should. He has a wife, a profession; why should he risk destroying our good relationship? Is the temptation for him greater than I believe, or smaller than I fear? It's nothing, nothing at all, neither one nor the other. ... Because I also am honest. For me, too, in certain cases, a man may be sexless, so much so that I have nothing to boast of if I have no "guilty thoughts". But suppose we had really been meant for each other? If Great Britain weren't an island, it would be kinder. ...

"He doesn't even try to be alone with me. ... Dream, poor girl, dream; cram your head with boarding-school dreams; cling to your dreams; go on telling yourself that he's a sweet, tender, perverse boy; let go of the reins; perhaps the horses will end by running away. ... No, no, and no ...

That was all; Alexis finished reading. These pages were so remote from what had happened. They were pages from the middle of a life; one doesn't die after writing something like that. ... What was it all about? Not about him, certainly. This was unimportant now. Louise, who was life itself, what had she got herself into, unhappy creature! Alexis turned abruptly over, put his head in the pillow, and began to cry like a baby. The trains ground their teeth and moaned, while he went on crying.

The trains ground their teeth and moaned while he slept, and after he woke up. But now it was black night and raining, to judge from this continuous sound like rustling tissue paper. A clap of thunder rumbled through the noise of the trains. Alexis breathed the freshness which came in through the open windows of the dining-room. A shutter in the bedroom, poorly fastened no doubt, tapped against the window. A small noise, a persistent, timid knocking. . . . Alexis listened: knock, knock. . . . The thunder rolled like a great billow over everything, drowning the rain, the sighs and moanings of the trains. But before the last roll had died away, the knock knock came again. . . . Alexis got up; undoubtedly somebody was knocking on the shutter. What time was it? Three o'clock. . . . He slipped on his pyjamas and went through the corridor to the garden door. What could it mean? He listened again, upright, near the door. Knock, knock. He tried to see through the glass pane, but the black night beyond made a mirror of it, and he could see only his own reflection, blurred and broken, streaming with water. . . . Knock, knock, knock. . . . He decided to open. . . .

It was like a film. . . . A gust of rain came in, and behind it emerged a human form which halted on the threshold. By the dim light of the corridor lamp Alexis could see a young man. "What is it?" he said. "Monsieur," whispered the youngster, "please let me in. I can't go any farther. I jumped off the forced labour train . . ." "Oh—come in." The youngster entered. He was drenched, as though he had just been dragged from the river, and he left great wet tracks in the corridor. Before turning on the light in the kitchen Alexis hung up against the window the cover which Mme Loiseau had kept from the days when the blackout had still been serious. The young man waited, motionless, leaning one shoulder against the wall, dripping like an umbrella that has been closed after a downpour. The little suitcase at his feet was a sodden pulp, as though it were made of cardboard. . . . Alexis stepped down from the chair and switched on the light. The young man's appearance was alarming. His face was wet with blood as well as rain. "What are you going to do?" asked Alexis. "Luckily I'm alone in the house. Take off your things. Dry yourself. . . . I'll give you a towel." The young man took off his jacket and shirt, sniffling and wiping his bleeding nose with the back of his hand. The handkerchief he drew from his pocket was a red ball, soaked with fresh blood. He washed under the tap: most of the blood came from a cut across his eyebrow; the bleeding from his nose had almost stopped. "Wash it well," said Alexis. "I'll make you a little dressing . . ." He went to the bedroom and came back with hydrogen peroxide and compresses. He told the young man to sit down, and made him an expert dressing. He had seen so many of them made while he was at the clinic. . . . "Are you a doctor, monsieur?" asked the young man, and Alexis felt extremely flattered. Now that his face was clean, his straight blond hair combed, you could see that he was a nice boy; he wasn't the one they had seen on the road the other day, but it was all the same thing. . . . "Well, what are we going to do now?" asked Alexis. "I suppose we should light the stove to dry your things, but I don't know how to do it. I always burn up all the kindling before the logs start. . . . Do you know how?"

The young man crouched down in front of the stove. "Put the small pieces in first," urged Alexis. "It will start quicker. . . . Tomorrow we'll chop some more. Lucky I'm alone, the landlady isn't here to make a fuss. . . ." "May I take off my shoes?" asked the youngster. "By all means. Your trousers, too. I'll bring you some pyjamas. I hope there's a clean pair left . . ." He went to get the pyjamas but found only the trousers. Fortunately the boy had an extra shirt in his suitcase. What a shame there wasn't a drop of liquor, not even wine! Surely there must be some somewhere in the house. But they hid it from him as though he were a chronic alcoholic, as he often . . . How the boy shivered! He would make him a cup of tea. Tea was also a rarity and would do him good! He put a kettle on the stove. The fire was well started. Come to think of it, wasn't he hungry? "I don't want to make any trouble," said the boy gently. Alexis was at a loss: what could he give him to eat? "Have you had any dinner?" he asked. "I haven't eaten since yesterday," the boy confessed. "I don't know this part of the country . . . I'm from Saint-Étienne. I jumped off the train yesterday. I could only think of getting away. The others said I was crazy, but I wasn't going to let myself be carried off like cattle! So I jumped . . . I said to myself: 'I have two hundred francs, I'll be all right.' But afterwards I didn't dare walk into any place. When you don't know your way around . . . I kept to the back roads on account of the police . . . I don't even know whether there are any Boches around. . . . I fell asleep on a little wall, and when I woke up suddenly, what should I see but a policeman on a bike two steps away. I rolled down the other side of the wall, and that's where I got my cut. Nothing happened when I jumped from the train, and now I jump off a wall a yard high and cut myself all up! . . ." He shook his head sadly. "Are there still any Boches left round here?" "No," said Alexis, opening the cupboard, "but that doesn't make any difference . . ." What on earth could he give the poor fellow to eat? Then he found on the top shelf of the cupboard a tray with cutlery, and beneath a napkin cold meat, hard-boiled eggs, tomato salad, cheese, and a nearly full bottle of wine! Henriette had prepared all this before leaving, and he had forgotten to eat . . .

They sat down to eat, both of them famished. "So they're pretty bad round here?" the young man asked, after the first pangs of hunger had been appeased. "I wouldn't say that. I really don't know much about it. The other day I saw a boy of twenty between two Boches on the road, so evidently they hunt them down here. That's all I know . . ."—"It's not good to be twenty years old," said Jean. "If I could only join the *maquis* . . .!" The food, the wine, the fatigue had gone to his head, and his cheeks were flushed. Alexis didn't know what the *maquis* was. The youngster put down his fork and looked at him sceptically: not know what the *maquis* was! . . . Where did he come from? Was he serious? . . . "What is the *maquis*?" repeated Alexis, ingenuously. If he really didn't know, Jean wasn't going to be the one to tell him. He felt disturbed. This red-head had acted like a brother, taking him in, but all the same there was something not quite right about him. . . . He didn't know how to light a stove, which was odd, and he didn't know what the *maquis* was. "The *maquis* is the *maquis* . . ." he said, and would say no more. Alexis didn't insist. He was thinking that Mme Loiseau would be absent for another week, and that during that time there was nothing to fear. "If anybody should come," he said, "I'll tell them you're a cousin of mine on an unexpected visit." Jean laughed: unexpected was right! They both burst into a peal of laughter. But there was nothing left on the tray, and now Alexis thought of the tin of peas which Henriette

kept in her suitcase as a reserve, on no account to be touched.
. . . Henriette would be angry if she found it gone. Oh, well,—
or would she? . . . Alexis began rummaging in suitcases, setting
everything topsy-turvy, and came back with the tin. They
ate the peas without heating them, and found them delicious.
"I was going to say," said Jean, "a *maquis* is a place where the
forced labour men hide. It's a centre of resistance, of what are
called Partisans, who prepare for guerrilla warfare. They get
orders from officers. Like military training. They show you how
to use weapons, teach you discipline, and all that sort of thing . . ."
He explained it all very clearly to this rather singular little
red-head, who was a good fellow all the same. . . . Jean evidently
had not received his military training, but when it came to
weapons, he knew all about them; every member of his family
worked in an arms plant at Saint-Étienne, and he knew how
to dismantle and care for and use every sort of weapon. . . .
Alexis greatly admired him, but he was very sleepy. It had long
been daylight. He took Jean into the bedroom; the two of them
stretched out on the bed and slept the sleep of the just.

They didn't wake up until noon. Alexis would have liked to
sleep a little longer, but Jean had already got up. He could hear
him running the water in the kitchen. Besides, they would have to
make their plans. . . .

They made their plans. It was Jean who made coffee, although
it was the hour for lunch rather than breakfast. The rain had
stopped, and it was glorious outside, fresh and blue. What should
they do next? Alexis said to Jean that the best thing would be to
ask the advice of the manufacturer. . . . He had a woman friend
who had stayed there, but she had gone to Lyons and got herself
caught. A tragedy. Why did she have to go and put her head in
the lion's mouth? Alexis thought the manufacturer must be a
resourceful man, and besides he knew the district, and Louise
had trusted him for reasons of her own. . . . Well, if Alexis
thought the manufacturer could get him out of this mess, they'd
better see him. . . . But after lunch they lay down again and had
another nap. The real trouble was that Alexis didn't fancy facing
the man again. . . . But something must be done, and he didn't
know whom else to turn to. If only Louise had been here. . . . But
she wasn't.

The manufacturer was at home. No, he hadn't had any news from Louise. His manner was curt, as much as to say,—you're not going to come back here every blessed day to ask for news of Louise, are you? Well, really, that wasn't what he had come for exactly. There was someone, a youngster . . . You know it's not a good thing to be twenty these days. . . . In fact, he's in considerable trouble. . . . So he'd thought, since Louise had spoken of him, and since he was a local man . . . In short, would M. Blin know, by any chance, of any place he could be hidden?

The manufacturer let him flounder, but then suddenly he seemed to have had enough of it. "I don't know what Louise could have told you. I don't meddle with these matters. I keep my hands clean. I've already had enough trouble on account of Louise. You'll see, they'll worm things out of her one day, and come here. I can give you a hint, however. . . . Is he a sound fellow, or an intellectual like you? Oh, he's a worker? That makes it easier. . . . Is he reliable?" "Yes," said Alexis. "Absolutely. I haven't known him long, but I'd vouch for him. He's a person who——" "Well," the manufacturer cut in (he had a nasty way of cutting you short), "do you know the Valliers' house? Take your friend over there. . . . But not before midnight. By that time everyone will be asleep. There's no point in rousing the countryside. I happen to have heard—it's amazing how people gossip—that they have hidden youngsters like that before. . . . They might be able to find a way of arranging things for your friend. They might have some cousins—everybody is related in these parts—the manufacturer and the carter; I'm everybody's cousin myself, since I'm a local product. I'll tell my cousin the policeman to fetch the boy right after midnight at the Valliers'; he'll tell them about it. . . . Don't look at me like that! Don't you know yet that the policemen in this region are capital fellows? Where do you keep your eyes and ears, my dear sir? The policeman will come on his bike. They'll surely lend another to your friend . . ."

Alexis thanked him. And since the man was a brute anyway, he decided to speak out. The boy had a cut on his forehead, which perhaps a doctor or pharmacist should see. . . . "I've told you that I don't handle that sort of thing," snapped the other, "I'm simply giving you hints, which anybody in this region might do. I'm not going to see this 'boy', as you call him. But you can rest assured that they're very well organized there, and they have a doctor at their disposal . . ." "And how about shoes?" Alexis went on, much relieved. "His soles are gone. He couldn't walk two miles on them . . ." "They have a shoemaker. Come now, don't be upset. Everything will be taken care of. When he gets to the policeman's cousin's house, he can tell her what he needs." Alexis thanked him again and took the manufacturer's hand. The man seemed anxious to appear a bit more human. "Why don't you come here to work any more, monsieur? I'm leaving again tomorrow morning. You'll be alone. I think you would greatly appreciate the solitude. . . . You'll find the key to the pavilion behind the shutter." He accompanied him to the garden gate. "If you should have anyone else to hide, don't hesitate. It's as I have told you. The *maquis* round here is very well organized. They had some trouble in the beginning, but now everything is running smoothly. But you probably know all this better than I do. I have no doubt you have already sent fellows there. . . . Now with Louise gone I guess you find things a little more difficult. . . ." He winked at Alexis. Louise had been right when she had said that as far as politics went, her host was simply a black marketeer, but that he was an excellent barometer, and impeccably discreet. "Incidentally," continued the manufacturer, "if there's anything you want to communicate to Louise—you understand what I mean by Louise—there's a Letter Box in Lyons. I needn't tell you that the address is secret. . . . But perhaps I'd better let you have it, because if your communications went through Louise they would now be cut off . . ." Alexis thanked him, without committing himself; he had no need of the address, things went well enough. . . . He was a little moved. . . . The Letter Box revived memories. So that was what the letter-boxes in the *traboules* were used for now!

On his way home Alexis chuckled to himself. So M. Blin suspected that he had become an active "worker". Did he suspect him of being an important person? Well, he would profit by it to "work" in the pavilion. . . . But what a strange story about the Letter Box! . . . He almost regretted his discretion. He would have liked to know if it wasn't, by any chance, the same one. Alexis delighted in strange coincidences.

The boy was sleeping on the bed with his mouth open. It seemed a pity to wake him. Alexis explained the situation to him, and had him light the fire, while he himself went out to buy food. How was he going to manage on a Sunday? Everything would be closed. . . .

"Doing your shopping, Monsieur Slavsky?" The grocer's wife was all smiles; it was the first time M. Slavsky had been seen with a shopping bag. "What can I give you?" she went on, letting him in through the back door of the shop. Alexis asked at random for six pounds of tomatoes, and was stupefied at the price. He pointed with his finger to what looked like a large pumpkin; it must be something edible, and there wasn't anything else in the shop. "Would you like some runner beans, monsieur? I've kept some for a customer, but I'll gladly give you a pound if you wish. You mustn't starve while your wife is away! . . ." Alexis took the pound of runner beans which the woman drew from beneath the counter. He felt a little embarrassed, but he was enjoying himself. At the *Primeurs* (he had already learned to knock on the back door) he bought a pound of big peaches, which turned out to be a small amount, and two pounds of pears. . . . This time he had guessed right. He went home, well laden and content. Fortunately, Henriette had left him a whole loaf of bread and Jean had another in his suitcase. Bread would have been more difficult, since it was a question of ration points, and Alexis had such a holy fear of ration points that he had hardly ever tried to use them . . .

Jean had already lighted the fire and swept the kitchen. He greatly admired Alexis' purchases. At Saint-Étienne there was literally no food to be had. There was no question of simply going and buying provisions in a grocery. When he thought of the trouble his mother had getting everybody fed! He had two younger brothers, and his fiancée was staying with them. How they must worry about him! His father had been completely prostrate the day he had left. Undoubtedly it had made him ill. As for Maryse . . . Nevertheless, he had promised them that he wouldn't let himself be taken out of the country . . . Jean knew very well what a pumpkin was, and he showed Alexis how to string the beans.

After dinner they played a game of *belote*. Alexis tried to hear the neighbours' radio, but there must have been a lot of atmospherics this evening, for he couldn't hear anything. So he returned to the card game. Towards midnight they ate the remains, and all the tomatoes vanished. Six pounds wasn't so much after all.

The night was as black as they could have wished. They met no one on the street or on the path beyond the little bridge. The vine-covered house of the Valliers was silent, but a light could be seen between the cracks of the shutters. The old grandfather opened the door. "So you're getting away," he said, patting Jean on the back. "That's right. . . . Ernest is here. He's been expecting you for an hour. . . ." The policeman was drinking with the younger Vallier. The granddaughter was ravishing, a genuine product of this land of luscious fruit. . . . Not more than eighteen. The policeman's uniform made Jean wince, but what can you expect— he wasn't used to it. . . . "So," said the policeman, "we must be off. We still have quite a way to go . . ." "Ernest, don't forget to tell Marie that I've brought a yard and a half of that sateen for the little one, and that she must send me one of her old pinafores— I like that better than measurements . . ." Mme Vallier, the mother of the beautiful girl, tied up a package. "Are you going to put it at the back, or on the handlebars?" "Don't worry, I'll manage . . ." The policeman put on his cap. Jean pressed Alexis' hand. "I would have liked to stay with you," he said, pressing the hand hard. "Come on. Good-bye, everybody . . ." The policeman was in a hurry.

Alexis walked home slowly. He might have thought himself alone in the world in this black night. As soon as he turned his back on the Valliers' house everything disappeared. There were no more houses or tilled fields; he barely remembered that beneath his feet was a path that men had made. How still the air was, empty now of people and of things; how peaceful! The house seemed stifling. Oh yes, there was a Mme Loiseau, who would not allow the windows to be opened. . . . Well, he wouldn't open any. Alexis undressed and lay down, although he wasn't a bit sleepy. He felt as wide awake as possible. . . . But he was glad to be in bed, in this empty house. He felt as though he had just returned from a long, delightful journey. . . . No place is as delightful as home. . . . And yet he had had human contacts with people who suited him.

In the old days he had had many cronies, in the days when life had still been worth living, when one could devote oneself to painting, stroll through Paris, and eat without a thought, before life had become a continual heartache, a continual waste of time. . . . Cronies existed to nibble away your time and decry your pictures, but you could manage very well without them. Human contacts ought to be reduced to chess games. Except for real comradeship! Yes, those were the true human contacts, a medal without a reverse side. But you had to think of the things that engender comradeship. There had been comrades in the clinic. And Jean was one. . . . But you couldn't be at death's door every day. And Gordeenko? Gordeenko was something else, something more complicated. Gordeenko was a friend. And Louise? Poor dear girl. . . . Tomorrow, thought Alëxis, he would go and work in the manufacturer's pavilion. The man wouldn't be there. No one would be there. . . . Perhaps he would succeed in feeling sheltered the whole day long. Then he could work; perhaps he could produce a masterpiece, with the isolation he needed so as to be immune from people: from their thoughts, their reservations, their words, their looks, their distrust, their malevolence, their interpretations, their opinions, their habits, their way of seeing things, their vices, their ideas, and their desire to impose those ideas upon you, and to impose themselves, to dominate you by guile, by brutality, by the right of the strongest, by force, force, force. . . .

On the morning after that night of peace he was awakened by rapid knocking on the door. It was not yet seven o'clock! He was paralysed: had something happened to Jean? He ran to open the door, dishevelled, in his crumpled pyjamas. . . . It was the neighbours; they had heard on the six-thirty news that Mussolini had resigned! This was the beginning of the end! They vaulted on to their bicycles and pedalled off as fast as they could. They were already late for work.

Alexis went back into his room, weak with emotion. What magnificent news! How splendid of these people to have awakened him to tell him about it without delay! It seemed as though he could already see the end of this four-year-long tunnel. His ears still rang with the thunder of the wheels, the cries of the locomotive, he was half asphyxiated by the smoke which filled his throat, his nose, his eyes, and the blackness was so complete that for a moment he was seized by panic. What if he had grown blind, and he alone was unable to see! But now the whiteness of dawn shone on the windows of the train, as it hurtled on its way, shrieking. . . .

Alexis took his easel and paint-box and walked towards the manufacturer's villa. The grocer's wife, on her threshold, bade him good morning, and asked if his wife was still away, glancing at his easel and box. "Yes, yes . . ." said Alexis affably. Just as he was leaving the village he met Grandfather Vallier, who hailed him, and the granddaughter, even sweeter and more charming in the morning air than the night before, who said to him: "Well, monsieur, your cousin is in good hands. . . . He won't have long to wait now, things are moving fast! Today is a great day for people like us."

"For people like us . . ." Alexis chanted. He pushed open the gate to the garden, with its big trees, found the key of the pavilion behind the shutter, and set to work.

It didn't take Henriette long to find him. The grocer's wife had seen him pass with his easel, and at the *Café de la Poste et du Sauvage* he had also been seen, talking with the little Vallier girl. . . . Surrounded by cigarette stubs, Alexis leaned over his canvas and straightened up, humming, "For people like us . . ."

"Aren't you going to ask me how I got on?" asked Henriette, looking at his canvas with passionate curiosity.

"Oh yes," he said, getting up and wiping his hands on a rag, his eyes on the canvas. "I'll even say 'hello' in a minute . . ." He sat down again. He was pretty well satisfied with this picture.

Henriette stepped to the right, and then to the left, to judge it better. A fine canvas. . . . It was still barely a sketch, but you could already see what it would be like. Provided he didn't spoil it! He really oughtn't to touch it again. . . . Henriette thought it a remarkable canvas, one of the best Alexis had ever done. Morot would be ecstatic over it this came close to his "golden period", which Morot had so much admired. . . .

The canvas represented a hotel. Before the hotel a German soldier was knitting an orange stocking, while a blowsy-looking girl watched the bridge, against a background of peach trees scattered with little bright balls, gay as confetti.

Standing beside Henriette, Alexis examined the canvas.

"I think I've got it this time . . ." he said. "You know, it was my picture at the Art Gallery, the one with orange discs, that gave me the idea. . . . Look at the trees in the background . . . eh? This whole corner will have to be scraped out, though. You'll do it right away, won't you?"

They went on looking at the canvas for a long time, in silence; Henriette admired it more and more. And Alexis wasn't at all dissatisfied. He thought he had done well.

Saint-Donat,
September, 1943.

NOTEBOOKS BURIED
UNDER A PEACH TREE

IT has been going on for four years now. Four years of separation from some person or thing, four years of a world devoured by nostalgia. A meeting, a return home, only means more suffering when you have to tear yourself away again. Life is spent in partings, in waiting for absent ones. . . . However you pass your time—in killing, trimming your nails, carrying dynamite—what is simply an expectation of castrophe doesn't deserve to be called life. Between those who are waiting for each other stretch miles of horror, burning forests, blood-soaked earth, wrecked trains, ruins, mangled bodies, prison walls, whole miles of them. . . . Today does not exist: there is only the sweetness of past days, and an uncertain tomorrow. And what if, on the day the waiting ends, one should have nobody left to love, to find? What if one of the parted ones no longer exists, and the other remains, single, useless, heartbreaking as one glove when the other has been lost? And they were still quite new! . . . If we could only be sure that while we ourselves are rotting, there are young ones growing up to take our places.

I can't sleep. Ideas as black as the sleepless night whirl in my head. I've always felt uneasy going to sleep, losing the consciousness of myself, even when I was a child. I can even say that I sleep better now than I did then. I go to bed more exhausted. Think of all the years left behind, the things done, the movements made, the effort to keep alive. . . . With each day that passes we are more worn out. And one day the fatigue will be so great that we shall not wake up any more. Ever since I have been living alone and waiting, life has seemed like a continual process of getting up at dawn, just in the middle of the soundest sleep. But the alarm rings, and I've no right to miss the train; the water is icy, there's no time for a cup of barley coffee, the suitcase won't shut; and at the station I realize that I've left the most important thing behind in my room! All this effort beyond one's strength, things all done through fatigue, gaps in the memory . . . But you have to go on and take the train, if you have a scrap of human dignity left. I dream about luxury. It wouldn't really be luxury, but a medical treatment. Not to have to get up unless I felt able, to forget the straw mattress, the vermin, the brutality, the ghastly hunger, the cold. . . . But I've promised myself not to talk about this. The luxury of a bed with smooth sheets, of housework done by invisible hands. I would eat only things I liked, things that don't upset me, it would be warm, the window would open on to spaciousness, a beautiful landscape, the door would be open, everything would be lovely, and everybody friendly . . .

I can't sleep. The walls of this little house bear the weight of night. I'm alone here, in a little house in a village in the heart of France. What I said about luxury was just flummery. Actually, I'm quite content here. I've been told to cover up my tracks, to stay in a corner without moving, and I've been here for a month now. In peace and warmth. Nobody can surprise me here. I can write as I like, without risk, and just to please myself! I've never been able to do this before. Writing has always been a task, undertaken for practical ends. I've written in order to communicate, explain, get something, help or show someone up. . . . Now I write without purpose, the way you dream through a sleepless night or lying in a hammock, looking at the sky, watching the clouds move past. Before I leave this place I'll burn what I've written, but meanwhile this exercise book will keep me company. It's my only privacy, my only solace in this life, which has been nothing but duty—and I want this to be a sublime duty. But there are days when I feel like letting things slide, when I long for a friendly hand, a caress, for a life of ease and pleasure. . . . People think me strong, brave, and hard.

I've come to await insomnia with impatience. I go to bed as I used to go to a ball. Every night I play at being Cinderella. But while the squalid, peeling kitchen is a reality, my nightly excursions lead me only into the palaces of memory. It's been a long time since a little glass slipper brought me a charming prince. Dawn finds me alone in the kitchen once again, in my woollen slippers, my old dress.

How extraordinary is the capacity of our minds to compress our memories! What was that novel dealing with the life of a man as he remembered it during the few seconds of falling from a window? Hundreds of pages to set down the thoughts of a few seconds! Memory is like a coiled paper streamer, which, when you throw it, shoots over the heads of the dancers. Memory, speedier than light and sound, astonishingly complete, in colour and relief, composed of innumerable minute details! What can you convey of it in writing, more than tiny fragments? When I write, "I wore a maroon-coloured uniform and a black pinafore to school . . ." I feel the woollen dress on my skin, Nounou's hands buttoning my high collar, the crossed shoulder bands of the pinafore, like the uniform of a lady's maid; I see the window turning blue with sunrise, the little paraffin lamps, the soft, unmade bed . . . I see and feel a thousand things. It's a professional failing to wish to set down a memory in writing, to fix poor fragments of it, instead of being content to dream luxurious dreams. What a strange urge, to say, "I wore a maroon-coloured uniform and a black pinafore to school . . ."!

I'm a little girl. A white table, set with linen and dishes and sparkling glass, rises out of the black void which preceded it. I think this is my earliest memory. I pass from the arms of Paulette, with her Breton coif, into Grandmother's arms. Grandmother wears a black knitted cape and a wide black skirt. Big diamonds flash in her ears, one at the lobe, the other pendant. They cast blue lights that blend with the gleaming objects on the table. Later I was to discover that Grandmother's big skirt had pockets, from which she drew lace handkerchiefs, and bonbons wrapped in fringed paper.

We went to the beach in the donkey cart; my sister Odette cried "Get up!" The bath-house smelled of sweat, of wet wool, of salt water. When we were in the water Papa took me on his back and swam far out. He wasn't a cabinet member yet. Mama didn't swim. She sat in her deck chair and made wild gestures to us to come back. Poor Mama! She was always afraid. She spent her life worrying about Papa, Odette, and me.

When Mr. Krioukov appeared and wanted to take us all back to Russia with him I felt very sorry for myself, because I was so afraid of never seeing the ocean again. "But of course you will!" said M. Krioukov. Nevertheless I distrusted him, in spite of the big doll he had given me, a doll so big that I couldn't lift it by

myself, so Mama took it away from me and gave it to Odette.
M. Krioukov was fat and had a round beard. His son was beard-
less.

Unless my memory paints him handsomer than life, Vladimir
was the handsomest man I have ever met. I was thirteen years old
—the age of reason—when I saw him for the last time. . . . Like
his father, Vladimir believed that he owed his life to my father,
and it's true that my father was a great lawyer. He could make a
crime of passion out of any sordid murder. Not that I then suspected Vladimir, nor do now, of having committed a sordid
murder; but a crime of passion was just his mark. When he fell
in love with Odette, Mama grew ill with anxiety, especially since
Odette was only fifteen. Poor Vladimir!

We lived in Moscow until 1917. During the war years we
didn't go to France at all. I became almost a Russian girl. Papa
was rejected for the army, and M. Krioukov was only too happy
to have him stay. Papa was not only a great lawyer, but also a
remarkable man of business. M. Krioukov, who in the beginning
had simply invited Papa to visit him after the trial and acquittal of
Vladimir, found that he had discovered a gold mine: Father
doubled, tripled M. Krioukov's immense fortune.

Father is a self-made man. When he first knew Mama he was
a notary's clerk, without a penny. Mama, who was the daughter of
the manor, the best match in the district, left her home to follow
the little notary's clerk. When I say "little" it's not a mere figure
of speech. Father is very small, and it must annoy him a bit, as
he wears heels like a juvenile lead on the stage. Of course, Napoleon
was a small man too. . . . Although he's past sixty, Father still
has all his teeth and all his hair; he's still spruce and slim, with a
rather forbiddingly lined face. He's very well dressed, wears a
morning coat and striped trousers, a pearl pin in his tie, the
ribbon of the Legion of Honour in his buttonhole. . . . My sister
Odette was born while my parents were living at Rouen, during
the first, romantic years of their marriage. She's a child of love;
but I was born after Grandmother had already agreed to receive
my father, and after we already had our own house in the Rue de
l'Université, which my mother inherited from an aunt. However,
during my childhood the lovely rooms of the mansion were still
almost empty, and the damask upholstery of its antique furniture

was falling to pieces. Not until much later did the mansion become the sumptuous residence of *M. le Ministre*. Odette was always clinging to Mama's skirts, while I had a nurse in a Breton coif, and Mama never had much time for me. Mama was always a little absent-minded and vague with everybody, always a little dishevelled, with her lorgnette in one hand and a book in the other, a long scarf of fur or silk sliding from her sloping shoulders. She was charming, irresponsible, crammed with liberal ideas—"a revolutionary", my grandmother called her. I don't know what Mama had been like before we were born, or whether her liberalism was natural to her; but in our time she held her ideas stubbornly, even rigidly, as though she wished at all costs to keep "ahead of the times", gorged herself with philosophy, read everything that came out on education and pedagogy. . . . But I'm not sure that she wouldn't honestly have liked to send her daughters to a convent.

Father had become M. Krioukov's partner. His property in Russia had gone up in smoke in 1917, but he had invested a considerable part of his capital in France and England, to such advantage that, even now, although he's in London and has lost his citizenship, my father is a very rich man.

In Moscow M. Krioukov—Nicolai Nicolaievitch—had put an entire house at our disposal. To reach it you had to cross the Moscova River; the bridge ran into a shopping street, full of tramcars, pedestrians, and vehicles. . . . A narrow pavement, very high above the street in the summer, became during the winter, when the snow raised the street level, just the right height; ancient cornerstones marked the edges and corners of the streets. Its flesh-coloured surface was paved with stones as round as fists, terrible stones that jolted the carriages. The hackney coaches and vans filed past at a walking pace like an interminable caravan, with a deafening, metallic clatter. Only a few of the private carriages and de luxe cabs had rubber tyres. But during the winter the sumptuous, silent snow covered everything with a white blanket, and the town was suddenly plunged into a deep silence, barely broken by the muffled sound of horses' hooves and the gliding of sleighs. You turned off the shopping street at St. Clement's Church, a flaming red building with white baroque ornaments and green cupolas; you turned the corner, and at once Moscow

—low, squat, vast, silent city—took you to its heart, into its white, downy arms. Churches, convents, low-roofed houses, trees . . . and in the winter the snow was immaculate, so rarely did anyone pass through these wide streets and curving alleys.

Like many of the houses, ours had only one storey, a rather lofty ground floor. It was more like a pavilion than a house; yellow, with white pillars and a triangular gable. The entrance led into a courtyard, behind a wall, where were a little garden, a stable, and the servants' quarters. . . . The children's room had a big window, à l'italienne. Odette's and my playthings were piled in the embrasure, on a wide board which formed a window seat about the height of a low table. This board filled the width of the embrasure, and was about a yard wide. Through the window, across the street, you could see a little church, with gilded onion-shaped cupolas, and crosses that caught the sun.

It was through this window that I saw death for the first time. Snow was falling. Standing on the board with my nose pressed against the glass and Annouchka, my Russian nurse, behind me, I saw a casket borne by four men, and in the open casket the motionless form of a woman, white as snow, shining as though made of ice. She wore a white dress, and snowflakes fell on her cheeks, on her crossed hands, and on her white dress. I watched her, entranced; I'd never seen anything so beautiful! They carried the dead woman into the church across the street, the church where Annouchka took me without Mama's knowledge. If Mama, who had never even had us baptized, to say nothing of confirmed—the matter was never broached except with contempt —had found out that Annouchka took me to an orthodox church! As recent atheists, my parents had no truck with religion, Mama was much too much afraid of being caught by it, of falling into its trap and losing the whole conception of the world which she had built up with so much care. As for Father, I don't believe he cared about it one way or the other, but atheism was a delightful memory of youth, when he and Mama together had planned to transform the world; this was his reason for adhering to it. The orthodox church was as beautiful as the woman I had seen through the window. The velvet, holy darkness, lit by precious stones, gold, silver, candle flames, and the lights in front of the ikons. I can still smell the incense and feel my hand rise to make the sign of the cross, as Annouchka had taught me: the joined thumb, index, and middle fingers touch the forehead, the breast, the right shoulder, the left shoulder. . . . In the name of the Father, the Son, and the Holy Ghost.

My parents and Odette often went out in the evening. After she had undressed me and put me to bed Annouchka would go into the kitchen, and I would be left alone, surrounded by dark rooms. Then my hours of fear began. Through the open transom of the window came the icy smell of winter; in the left corner of the window, over a roof thick with snow, and glistening with cold blue and white sparks, hung a huge star. The door of the room was behind me, and through it the "black monk" came from the depths of the house . . . I knew he was behind the door already. And while I leisurely waited, my eyes on the star, there would come from across the silent town, muffled in white snow, a long, unbroken cry, a blue cry, an icy, indifferent, transparent cry. . . . The cry came from a locomotive in one of the town's huge railway yards, but to me it was the voice of space. This cry anteceded the siren, which speaks, however, to everyone; its terrible wailings are the laments of a beast already wounded, crying that evil is upon us, upon all of us. . . . But the isolated cry of my childhood reached me alone. Space cried out for me alone, to tell me that the world was vast and that I was alone. Distraught with fear, barefooted, in my nightgown, I ran to the kitchen, braving the black monk, who pursued me across the living-room, through the narrow corridor, and down the stairs that led to the kitchen. . . . The door was closed. And Annouchka had sworn by all the saints that she would leave it open, so that I could call her! The air in the big, warm kitchen was close, the shadows cast by the flame before the ikon moved. I bumped against the white stove, which was still warm, and big as a bed. I glided behind the cotton curtain surrounding Annouchka's bed (the other servants slept in the little building in the yard). "Nounou, wake up, I'm frightened!" I whimpered, and kissed her soft, lined cheeks. I was trembling. I didn't know whether she had really been asleep, but she got up at once and wrapped a big woollen shawl round her. "Blessed Virgin!" she said, making the sign of the cross before her yawning mouth. "Go back to bed, you child of midnight!" But she would respect

my fear and accompany me back to the bedroom, sit down on a
chair by my bed, and stay there until steps could be heard on the
staircase. For Mama didn't approve of my being frightened, and
if she had found Annouchka sitting with me she would have
explained at great length how disgraceful it was, now that I was
ten years old; and she'd have scolded Annouchka in her incredible Russian. Even when I was quite little I despised fuss.
So Annouchka had to get away while there was still time. While
she dozed in the chair by my bed I listened for my parents' step.
I didn't sleep much. Already I had the rings under my eyes which
have been there ever since.

2

I HAVE no one but Annouchka to keep me company at night in
the little house. There's no one, no one, anywhere around. Yet
I'm not afraid. It's years since I've spent such comfortable, peaceful nights. Yet here, too, cries waken me at nights when I'm just
about to fall asleep: at the end of the blind alley where my house
stands, on the corner, there's a little shack inhabited by a madwoman, who shrieks every night.

If you've ever taken part in a domestic scene you may know
the paroxysm of fury which makes you scream and break things;
perhaps you may even have felt crime brush you with the tips of
its wings. . . . That's the way my mad neighbour acts, all day long,
all night long. She's never been able to reconcile herself to the
fact that her husband deceived her; no more, now that she is old
and he dead, than when she was the prettiest girl in the village and
he got her children. The legend had it that she went mad after he
plunged her head into a pail of icy water while she was pregnant.
Through the quiet country night I hear her scream, "Oh, you
cuckolds! Oh, you whores!" in a paroxysm of fury, an intensity
of rage that should exhaust her. It would kill an ox, but she seems
to live a charmed life, and the thing goes on day and night. I see
her walk by our house, her feet thrust into man's boots, dressed in
a black jacket with seams basted together with white thread, as
for a fitting. Sometimes she wears a bit of bright embroidery,
sometimes she goes bare-necked, one arm and one breast bare.

Her ashy hair is done differently every day. She shouts to the row of Legionnaires parading past the alley, "You bloody old crocks!" and to the grocer who gives her her rations, "You dirty thief!" And when she meets a woman on the way to the well she stops and screams, "You trollop!" Once in a while she gives herself a shower; does she perhaps realize that she's going too far? Yesterday I saw her drenched, the water already starting to freeze on her, and she didn't even catch a cold! This woman will never die; she's pickled, hermetically sealed in her rage; and when I die, somewhere in the world she'll be here still in the alley, filling the night with her cries . . .

We never really got settled in Moscow. During all those years there was the thought of eventually returning to France for good, but we were never in France for more than two months at a time; M. Krioukov would wire or write, imploring us to come back, and we would come back to the yellow pavilion with the white pillars. And anyway, my parents adored Russia. It's impossible not to love Russia and the Russians. Then when the war started in 1914 there was no longer any question of getting our own furniture and settling down. We went on using the furniture of M. Krioukov, or rather of his nephew (who had gone to Siberia, where he owned some mines in which my father held shares). It was odd furniture, a mixture of beautiful things, like the salon in Karelian birchwood, honey-coloured wood, whose intricate carving I loved to trace with my fingers, following the little veins on the rounded backs of the armchairs and of the Russian Empire sofa with its gold edging and royal-blue satin. But there was a nightmare of a buffet in the dining-room, with a crackled surface like crêpe, the crevices filled up with pistachio green, like wrinkles filled with rice powder, the glass panes of the doors representing some kind of mauve lilies. The square table was covered with a green plush cloth, tinged by hot tea-cups. The chairs, of the same crackled wood, were oddly shaped, and were covered in leather of a sickening green colour. My father's study had a magnificent Persian rug that offset the shabbiness of the armchairs and sofa, with blue plush backs and seats embroidered with squares in the manner of a Persian rug. On the book-case doors and the heavy oak writing-desk were sculptured lions' heads. In the little salon, papered in white moiré, a crystal chandelier hung down from a rococo ceiling, and chairs with gilded backs stood all round the shining parquet. There was a gold-and-white grand piano, too. But the bedrooms were furnished only with iron beds, with cotton piqué covers over satin down quilts. Mama had taken out the night table that stood between the twin beds, and moved the beds together, in the French fashion. The bathtub in the bathroom was made of zinc, and the big water heater burned wood. The whole house was heated by great white-tile stoves, built into the walls. In the winter Piotr, the coach-man, brought in logs every morning, and stuffed the stoves full. When the logs were consumed, and nothing but embers remained, the stove doors were closed hermetically, and their smooth white walls stayed hot for twenty-four hours. All the windows were double, and kept closed all the winter, their joints stopped up with putty, so that only the transoms could be opened for air. A Russian house feels good in the winter; like a closely curtained bed, warm and cosy.

Then the Russian spring! The wonderful fragrance of melting snow, the return of colour to the town, after the eternal white-ness, the scraping of picks and shovels, cutting the hardened snow away, so the carriages and sleds can carry it off and the town won't be plunged into too deep a footbath! The joy of spring, the air blowing through the windows, opened for the first time, the dried, powdery putty on the windowsills, and the sound of the awakened town, released from the smothering snow, no longer mute; it's like the sound of an immense fair, shouts, blows, the clink of iron. . . . The joy of the Russian spring can only be com-pared to the delight of the first snow. Is it only the child's attach-ment to the house enclosing her, to its reassuring familiarity, that makes me think even today of this Russian house as *the* house? No, there was really something human about the yellow pavilion, something all-inclusive and sunny, which I've never found any-where else.

We had two horses, a dappled grey and a black, and every morning Piotr, the coachman, took Odette and me to the "gym-nasium", as the schools are called there. The sleigh had a heavy fur rug that fastened you down like a baby in a pram. Annouchka, with a woollen scarf over her head, ran out of the house to tuck in our coats, and fasten the rug, because once installed on his seat Piotr wouldn't budge. Oh, how I loved this morning ride! ... "Faster, Piotr, faster!" The trotter flew, and the huge back of Piotr in his wadded garments (the more thickly padded a coach-man was, the more elegant he considered himself) protected us from the flying snow kicked up by the horses' hooves. Piotr, with a cap adorned with peacock feathers on his bearded head, a narrow, coloured belt circling his immense waist above the dark garment which he wore over two or three lamb-skin great-coats, sat leaning forward, the reins continuing the line of his outstretched arms. ... We glided over the perfect snow of our street. The cold. The smell of invisible smoke. The spark-ling air. The opaline sky, upon which a diamond might have cut a design of branches and telegraph wires, like a restaurant mirror. Each branch, each wire, was covered with white needles, and so transformed into a thick nap of white velvet; the snow un-derfoot lost its softness, becoming compact and hard as macadam. The horses' long winter coats hung beneath their bellies in small, icy stalactites, and clouds of steam came from their nostrils, encircled by white needles. They were veritable steam horses, locomotives. They galloped hard, because they were so cold. Piotr's beard and moustache were frozen like the horses' hair. "Hey!" he shouted. "Hey!" But the coachmen in their sleighs didn't hear him, their heads were wrapped in thick shawls. You could see them throw down their reins and clap their hands, enveloped in huge warm mittens. As for the people sitting in the sleighs, they looked just like big bales of fur and wool. I can still feel my cheeks freezing, and the cold filling my nose with tiny, icy hairs, that kept me from breathing. I feel a strange ache in my forehead, and my whole face is cold; even my eyes seem about to turn to ice.

Past the glowing red façade of St. Clement's Church the metallic runners of the sleigh began to scrape on stone and rasp over the tramcar lines. This was a street of heavy traffic. The snow was a dirty brown colour, like sand, and the horses' hooves dug through it down to the bare stone. The people, stiff in their fur coats, all looked blooming, their cheeks reddened by the cold, hair white with rime, as though they wore the wigs of marquises and march-ionesses. Strange marchioness, with her felt boots and the red, checkered woollen scarf over her head and shoulders; strange marquis, too, dressed in sheepskin, with a fur cap! Urchins enjoying the snow, rolling under the feet of passers-by, screaming, blue with cold, their gloves drenched and frozen, the strings of their caps untied, their little overcoats unbuttoned in the heat of the game. . . .

Then came the bridge over the Moscova. As it is impossible, in Paris, to cross the Seine without emotion, because it can never become a matter of every day; just as, each time, one's heart is struck by the magnificent shades of grey, the delicacy of water, stone and sky, so crossing the Moscova is always like a fairy tale. Above the river the white walls of the Kremlin rise, and behind these walls are the serried cupolas, cheek to cheek, the flames of their crosses flashing in the white sky, dazzling and streaming like molten gold. Above the cupolas the high clock tower of Ivan the Great lifts its giraffe neck, and the broad palace façade vies with the snow in whiteness. . . . A fairy tale, a beautiful coloured illustration in a book for bright, good children, rather given to dreams.

Then there's the great plaza, Red Square, long, vast, and empty as a ballroom with no dancers, bordered on one side by the long wall of the Kremlin, embellished by the church of Saint Basil, set down at the corner of the square like a barbaric gem, like a dragon with cupolas for its multiple heads, each one decorated and resplendent in its own fashion, and all crazy, like spinning tops upside down. This church is so beautiful that one understands why Ivan the Terrible gouged out the eyes of his architect lest he should build one equally beautiful for somebody else.

Odette and I sat with our arms about each other, because the sleigh wasn't very big, and it tipped so much on the turns that we were in danger of being thrown out, in spite of the fur rug fastened on both sides of us. Now we were in the commercial district, with its low and high buildings making a broken skyline. All kinds of signs covered the façades from top to bottom, like paintings at an exhibition, so that you could barely tell what the walls themselves were like. There were large black signs that hung out from the wall like pictures or mirrors, lettered in gold: *Tailor . . . Books . . . Watchmaker . . .*; little ones, black or white, square or oblong: *Accordion pleating . . . Shoemaker in the Yard . . . Midwife. . . .* The handsomest ones were made of huge gold letters in relief and hung flat against the façades: *Creamery . . . Bakery*, or simply *Tchitchkine . . . Blandov . . .*, names requiring no explanation, like *Heinz*, or *Kellogg*. From what you could see of the houses you could guess that they were made of red brick, unpainted, or lime-washed white, yellow, or pink. . . . The snow broadened all outlines: roofs, projections from the walls, window-sills, shop signs. . . . On Saturdays you could see the men standing in queues in front of shops that bore rainbow-coloured signs: *Liquor Shop*. Only vodka was sold there, a state monopoly; you could see them drinking it right in the street, out of the bottle, without stopping for breath, heads tilting farther and farther back. The mass of signs and all the snow seemed too heavy for the houses, just as the tramcars (like jars of preserves, their doors and windows heremetically closed, the panes white and impenetrable) were too cumbersome for the street, where so many sleighs passed that they almost climbed on top of one another. I was dreadfully afraid of the muzzles of the horses that breathed in my ear, and also that the runners of the sleigh would get caught in the lines and we would be thrown out under the horses' hooves, or in front of the tramcar. . . . Yet the sleigh kept upright, as though by a miracle; the horses didn't bite. Piotr, without slowing up, turned into the school yard, stopping right in front of the big door, from which appeared the porter in gold buttons to unhitch the fur rug and extricate us from the sleigh.

The school was housed in the ancient palace of Prince G——. The big schoolroom had choir lofts, like a church, and a ceiling painted with clouds and cupids. A ceremonial stairway of white marble led up to the room. This stairway was reserved for the teachers, and of course the headmistress, a monumental lady in a blue satin dress with a long train. The students had their own stairway, leading up from a large, round vestibule, with a stove heated to white heat humming in the centre. The overcoats and furs hung on the wall, and each student had a bag for his felt overshoes, which all looked exactly alike.

The classrooms were large and handsome, painted over to hide the sumptuously decorated walls, just as the floors of the wide, vaulted hallways had been covered with linoleum. Nevertheless the big house retained an air of pomp. It was haunted by shadows, and our great game was to climb the hidden staircases, hide in the alcoves, mount to the large, low room with square pillars, under the roof, dash through the maze of little rooms where we were absolutely forbidden to go, and where the teachers' assistants hunted for us in vain.

I draw from memory each step I took in the immense park; I run breathlessly to hide behind trees and snowdrifts, and come back with wet gloves, my bonnet of otter's fur (with ear muffs and a black ribbon under the chin) askew on my head, my furs full of snow, from having rolled about on the ground or climbed up wherever it was possible to climb. At the end of the school ground, behind high palings, were more trees. They belonged to the garden of a lunatic asylum. In winter time, when the snow raised the level of the ground, the big girls could see over the fence. As for me, I could only peep through a crack between two boards of the fence, to see dreadful madwomen shouting and gesticulating, and others sitting quietly in the snow with their backs against the wall. One day my eye, close against the crack, met another eye glued to it on the other side—one of the most horrible things that has ever happened to me. Further off, also behind the fence, but separated from the women, were men—chronic alcoholics, as they themselves explained to us. . . . These were not insane at all, and some of them wore student uniforms and were very polite; the bigger girls used to engage in long conversations with the alcoholics, while the little girls stood on guard.

During the winter you could also jump over a wall into the yard of a ruined, uninhabited house. You entered it through the cellar, beneath a staircase, by hoisting yourself through a gap left by two missing steps. God is good to children, who are natural adventurers, and fills up the gaps in their knowledge with imagination. The staircase was shaky, the doors hung loose on their hinges, and the floorboards swayed underfoot. The wallpaper, which was half torn from the walls, was patterned with miserable little flowers, and the corner bedroom was inhabited by a black dressmaker's dummy, with a bulging bosom, a tiny waist, and a stomach as prominent as its posterior. Out of respect for the headless and armless black lady, we walked on tiptoe, stumbling over empty spools which sounded, when they began to roll, like carriages without tyres. There were all sorts of inscriptions on the walls: *Resolution of the Revolutionary Committee. . . . Down with the bloodthirsty Czar. . . . Victims of the fateful battle. . . . Comrades. . . .* Tiptoeing from one inscription to the next, we began to dream, and felt a little awestruck. The house was strewn with cigarette ends, ashes, and overturned boxes that had served as seats.

Our Russian teacher was a poet. We, the students, had found a poem by him in an anthology of "Decadent Poets". I could more easily forget my mother's name, or the day of the week, than these lines:

> Universe of chaotic mirages
> In the night of the coiling dream . . .

How we laughed over them! At that time I was still in primary school, with the little ones, but Odette was already fourteen. . . . She was remarkably precocious. The professor-poet was thin, pale, and vain.

I don't know when I first became aware of Odette's beauty. My mother liked to tell us how, on the day Odette was born, my old aunt Céline had bent over the cradle and cried, "Isn't it a pity she's so ugly!" Mama had burst into tears. One summer, by the seaside in France, at a children's party, a beauty queen and her maids of honour were selected from among the little girls. Mama thought this was a mistake, scholastically. However, the other ladies were convinced that my mother's concern arose from pique, because neither of her girls had been selected, so at the next party I was chosen to be a maid of honour. Mother must have been wrong, because I'm sure I felt nothing but delight during the promenade in a cart decked with flowers, drawn by a donkey, and that I didn't attribute this good fortune in the least to my personal merits. I was about five or six at the time. . . . During the drive we met Odette, with an odd, strained smile on her face. My sister had red hair, and the female organizers of the party could hardly put a little red-head in their flowered carts, even to make my mother happy. I don't know exactly when Odette became beautiful. Her red hair darkened, she had round, hazel eyes, a large mouth with perfect teeth, and a dazzling complexion that seemed to be lighted up from inside. She had a slight bust, round hips, long legs, and very small hands and feet. She had nothing to conceal. She could have walked round quite naked. Every part of her body was admirable. In fact, she liked to walk round naked. She had no modesty. Later on, when she went to dances, Mama and I loved to watch her dress herself, put on her fine underclothes, her silk stockings, her lamé slippers, her lavender ball gown. . . . I was speechless with admiration.

My life would have been torment if I had not, from an instinct of self-preservation, refused to be in the least jealous of Odette. It was she who taught me to admire gratefully, she who gave me the joy of going through childhood with living beauty before my eyes. I doubt if I would ever have become Elizabeth's friend (she was the personification of love) had I not undergone Odette's apprenticeship.

Once when I went to take my music lesson in a district at the other end of Moscow, I ran into Odette in the company of the decadent poet. Piotr had gone to fetch my father, and had let me out at the corner of the square. I couldn't believe my eyes when I caught sight of Odette in her little black velvet coat, her beige boots, with her cheeks all pink from the cold, and her red hair showing beneath her fur toque. She crossed the square and whispered, "You won't say anything to Mama." "Of course I won't say anything to Mama. I don't meddle with your dirty affairs!" Her burst of mad laughter left me speechless; the poet was watching us from across the square. I was a stickler for virtue, and I thought Odette's conduct very objectionable. . . . To meet her with a man, so far from the house! She must have meant to conceal herself! "What's the matter with you, Louise?" the piano teacher demanded. "That C is lower down—lower! What are you thinking about?" She dug her bony finger into my shoulder to indicate where the C was, while I wondered whether Odette wasn't a bad girl. . . . Again I recalled the phrase I had heard the summer before when the three of us, Vladimir, Odette, and I, had been out walking together: "I would like just once to have my fill of kissing you, and then die. . . ." For several nights afterwards I had been unable to sleep. What insolence! And Odette had permitted it. She had listened to it. Then there was this encounter today. . . . I restrained my tears; the piano teacher became indignant: "The left hand, Louise, the left hand! Come now, what's the matter? . . ."

It's six years now since I saw Odette last. What is she doing in Brazil, a place I can't even imagine? Odette with a husband, children, a house that's not our house. . . . Does she still listen to lovers who whisper in her ear on beautiful summer nights, "I would like just once to have my fill of kissing you, and then die . . ."? I won't tell Mama, when she lies under her tombstone at Père-Lachaise. The words of love are never "dirty affairs". . . . If I hadn't realized it myself, Elizabeth would have made me do so. . . .

3

I STOP writing, and drift away into dreams. I smile stupidly, lost in my happy childhood. I go out into the village street with my eyes full of too distant images, and can barely believe that I'm in a small French village, with a war on, the country occupied, misery all around me, and the daily worries that are as exasperating as the itch. All the lies that must be told. . . . I mustn't forget my name, that I'm a widow, that I don't get along with my mother-in-law. . . . The bombing at Boulogne. . . . I don't know why my family insist on staying there, but I've had enough of it. I prefer a small place like this. You get enough food here, compared with Boulogne, but I would like to have a little milk. . . . "You're very kind, Madame, but you mustn't deprive yourself." I utter meaningless words, while I think of something else. Yet even those few words, that slight constraint, are too much. . . . I, who was such an epicure, have come to eating nothing, because it bores me to bother about food. Good food goes with other creature comforts; if I have to worry about it I let it go, and easily at that. I've lost quite a bit of weight, and it has improved my figure. I would like to stay this way, and I would like to meet Jean again soon, so that he could see me while I'm still beautiful. . . . If only it weren't for conversations, the words that must be spoken to neighbours and shopkeepers, I would be quite happy here. It's just the right kind of a place for waiting—a place where it's hard to imagine anybody doing anything else. This little village in the heart of

France harbours me compassionately, and I'm grateful to it, as I'm grateful to the grocer's wife who gives me butter without ration points, to my neighbour who comes to saw my wood, and the plumber who repaired my roof when it leaked on to my bed. Discreet and obliging, they seem to wish nothing more than to do me services, and the words of gratitude and politeness come so hard that I must indeed be tired. I let the rain come into my bedroom for two days, only moving the bed into the middle of the room, just to avoid having to call someone, and having to talk.

A trip of three hours to the nearest town entails for all of these people a preliminary week of excitement, minute and anxious calculation, and the preparation of food and clothing. There are quite a few who have never been as far as the nearest town. All their lives they've been doing the same things, day in and day out, getting up at the same hour, going to a little country factory, men and women alike, returning at the same hour to cook dinner, go into the garden (always some distance from the house, near the fields), gather vegetables or grass for the rabbits, feed the chickens. All the houses are small like mine, with kitchens level with the street—kitchens containing only black stoves, sinks, gleaming casseroles, which are never used, faded linoleum on the floor covered with almost varnished floral designs, a table with peeling oilcloth, cane chairs, a cabinet that serves as buffet, and on the mantelpiece a row of flowered porcelain jars inscribed, *Pepper*, *Salt*, *Tea*, *Flour*. The jars are empty—not only now that there's nothing to put in them: they always were being meant to serve simply as ornaments. The bedrooms are all upstairs, like my own; strangers never get to see them, so I can't tell whether they're all furnished like mine, with a comfortable bed and a big counterpane, a blurred mirror on top of a table, a wardrobe, and the same kind of cane chairs as those in the kitchen. Except for the walls, covered with a mauve-grey wallpaper and decorated with photographs and mountain landscapes, my bedroom is pleasantly empty.

The country around is empty like the houses, the colour of scrubbed lineoleum, neither yellow nor grey nor green. . . . A slightly undulating country, reduced to essentials: fields, vegetable gardens, orchards, roads, lanes, and houses. I'm beginning to find a certain beauty in this lack of display, in this self-sufficient, unmeretricious land, so sensible and simple. I like the little river with its shrub-covered banks, the cultivated earth, which owes everything to man: irrigation, ploughing, grain, cabbages, potatoes, orchards. . . . A soil as appealing as poor children's clothes, the little bit of lace on the knickers, the patches on the little boys' trousers, the knitted gloves, the wide hems of the dresses, the pinafores, so eloquent of care and a watchful eye. . . . All the fruits of this earth are got with labour. When I think of the tropics, the riot of flowers and fruits, the luxury, the profusion, the outrageous abundance flung so lavishly by the earth at the feet of the firstcomer, who has done nothing to earn it . . .! When I think of the sunsets over the blue and green ocean, the intensity of the sky . . .! And then I look at the landscape before my eyes, sucked bare as a fishbone by the winter, the light mist in the thin poplars, like umbrellas shut after a shower, the light mist in the trees, bunched into faintly russet shapes like porcupines, in the ghosts of orchards, of which only a frail skeleton is left, the mist above this workaday surface now worn as lineoleum or oil-cloth—I look at this landscape and almost feel ashamed of the splendours that stuff my head, as though I had come into this village decked out in velvet and satin, ostrich plumes, and shoes with gilded heels. . . .

Now I've grown fond of these broad, colourless, open stretches reached by paths and roads and treeless lanes, where you are roasted in the summer; I like the rolling country, the neutral tones, the faint green of the meagre woods, the earth-coloured, dust-coloured, sand-coloured fields, the scattered farmhouses, hidden behind a few ancient trees. I like the illusion of emptiness in the landscape—certainly an illusion, because men have made of it what it is. . . . But how rarely do you see any men! Now and then one walks slowly behind his oxen, or another trims his vines, or another passes on his bicycle. It's easy to dream against this grey background, almost as easy as in the vast Russian forests. But over there, in the tropics, the imagination is so far outdistanced by the delirious reality of flowers and smells in infinite variety, that dreams grow pale and mortified and numb. . . .

But the landscape one has loved in childhood speaks the true language of the heart, and whatever it may be, it always remains

the most beautiful. The landscape of my childhood contained a
huge park with avenues, groves, pavilions, little humped bridges
beneath which no water ran, and a sheet of water with a tiny
island where a toy wooden hut stood, with figures of peasants
dancing around. The huge park tapered off into forest, and nobody could tell exactly how far the forest extended. . . . It was
already there when you got out of the train, surrounding the little
town with its unpaved streets as wide as boulevards, lined with
little log houses. The carriage rolled through the forest along a
rutted lane, where it was in danger of overturning any minute.
We understood that there were bears in the vicinity, and the danger
of getting lost in this forest was more than just a tale to frighten
little children. . . . Vladimir seemed to know each tree-trunk there,
and yet he got lost very easily with Odette, when they went to
hunt for mushrooms or strawberries (how I loved gathering mushrooms!) From time to time we had picnics. M. Krioukov's big
country house was always full of guests, all of whom seemed to
be members of the family and to have lived there always. The
table was set out under the trees in front of the house and was
always loaded with food. As soon as the samovar cooled off,
another boiling one was brought out. Between meals there were
little home-made rolls, white cheese, cream, and bowls of milk on
the table. Mme Krioukov looked almost like the peasant girls
who waited at table, barefooted, with bright kerchiefs on their
heads, wearing pink, sky-blue, and white blouses that hung out
over their cotton skirts. Mme Krioukov wore the same kind of
blouse as the peasant girls, but like my grandmother in Normandy
she had big diamond ear-rings. By and large she resembled my
nurse Annouchka, only she was even more fleshy, and I loved her
almost as much as I did Annouchka. For days on end the whole
house was busy making preserves. This was done in front of the
house, close to the table that held the samovar. Sitting in a circle,
the women removed the cherry pips and the green stems of the
strawberries, while the preserves bubbled in a great copper
cauldron set on a kind of stove. I was allowed to taste the foam off
the preserves, which I liked much better than the preserves themselves. The women sang, and their piercing voices rose high into
the sky.

It was warm and mild, golden weather. Vladimir wore wide

khaki breeches, high boots, and the fullness of his high-collared Russian blouse was gathered in at the back and tucked under his belt . . . . He had extraordinary Asiatic eyes, the sockets flat and level with the cheeks, sky-blue eyes, Asiatic and Nordic at the same time. . . . Odette's two hands in his . . . the little round yellow leaves, like gold coins falling from a horn of plenty, sticking, as they drifted down, to the thin, chalky birch trees. . . . Whenever I think of Vladimir, my first love, it's in that autumn forest, by Odette's side. I had such a strong sense of reality, of the place I occupied in the world, that I never felt any jealousy. It's at the age of thirteen or fourteen that one best understands love. You need the courage of un-selfconsciousness to bear that paroxysm, that steadily mounting curve. . . . It's a disgusting comparison, but I can't help thinking of the mad woman in my alley. Yet even she has moments of lull, whereas love as I understand it, as I experienced it at the age of thirteen, as Elizabeth has realized it in her life, knows no break. I loved Vladimir with all the freshness of childhood, which allows complete and spontaneous concentration on a single being, asking nothing in return, knowing nothing of one's own unhappiness, steeped in the immense joy of presence, content with a fugitive encounter, the sound of a voice; without jealousy, reproaches, without insistences, clashes of wills or ideas, without rivals and rivalries, and with one sole anguish—absence, one sole hope—to see and hear him; For two years I had no thought that was not linked with Vladimir. I never went into the street without thinking that I might meet him; I lived only in relation to him. It was he who taught me everything about love, even physical love.

I lovingly re-enact the minute incidents of my thirteenth birthday: the presents, the chocolate with whipped cream, the cake with thirteen candles. . . . We were in Moscow at the time, and that evening I was allowed to go with Odette and Vladimir to the theatre to see the ballet. I wore a pink dress and my first silk stockings. I had worn curlers all night, and my black curls were smooth and shining. I didn't look at all like the little Russian girls with their long blonde pigtails: Paris was in my blood. . . . Enveloped in furs, with fine, white wool shawls about our heads, we got into the sleigh that was waiting before the door, with Piotr upright on his seat. Once in the narrow sleigh, Vladimir sat me on his knee, put his right arm round Odette's waist, his left round mine. "Hold her tight, *barine*," said Annouchka, who looked on. "Don't lose her on the way . . ." The sleigh left the courtyard slowly, and then Piotr let the horse gallop. At the first curve the sleigh tipped, and Vladimir pressed me very hard against him. Then something strange happened, something upsetting. I thought I was ill; I was very much afraid. Yet at the same time I realized that this feeling came from Vladimir, and I looked forward to the next curve. . . . Vladimir pressed me against him. . . . He was talking in a low voice to Odette, his lips against her ear.

In the huge red-and-gold theatre, in the darkness of the box, with Odette beside me and Vladimir behind her, I watched the ballerinas flutter through the strange silence of the ballet. The absence of voices, this silent group moving like little transparent clouds in the sky, the delightful absurdity of the pantomime, quite enchanted me. There were times when my heart almost stopped beating. The ballerina, shimmering white, like a diamond, stiffened her sturdy legs and stood poised on her toes, arched her slender torso, her swan-back, her thin arms, a miracle of suppleness and dancing grace, flying, whirling, swept along on the current of the music. . . . Her partner, sheathed in white, slanted across the stage, flashing his legs as a barber flashes his scissors before a haircut, seized the dancer, lifted her above his head, where she seemed to hang miraculously, her crumpled ballet skirt revealing her marble thighs. Behind the couple the dancers moved in transparent lightness of ballet skirts, their pink, firm legs bending and stretching, quickened by the music, by the violins, which made me tremble. Interval. . . . The smell of the theatre, the feverish, festal atmosphere, the heat rising from all that red and gold, from all those lights . . . the box of chocolates, Odette's hazel eyes, the string of pearls round her neck, the red velvet bench in the seclusion of the box, the big mirror, where, by the light of a small lamp, I could see Vladimir's image smiling at me. . . . He looked very handsome in his uniform. Down below, in the orchestra, many officers were standing among the red rows of seats. . . . In the great semi-circle of the boxes I could see bare necks gleaming with diamonds, elegant head-dresses, furs. Vladimir was mad about Odette, but I could see in the mirror at the back of the box, where it smelled of chocolate, perfume, and the velvet of the draperies, that he was smiling at me. It gave me a pain in my chest. Yes, I was beginning to have breasts, which I kept tightly laced because they embarrassed me, and I wondered if they weren't going to bother me when I tried to sleep. Had Vladimir noticed my breasts, and my love? . . .

4

"Oh, you cuckolds! Oh, you cuckolds!" My life in this village consists only of nights. They are more real than the days. These demented cries seem more suited to the time and to myself than my days, empty of events, friends, work. . . . I have no radio, and the world aflame is reflected for me only in the stupid little newspapers. I tell the neighbours that I buy them to light the fire with; otherwise they would never understand such a strange expenditure . . .

I began to gain weight when I was fourteen. Until then I had been a slender child, with heavy eyes and curly black hair, dressed in very short Parisian dresses. The awkward age became me. Then, just when we returned to Paris, I began to gain weight. I was fat until my marriage and after. Odette, what with the dresses, and all the things Paris can do for a woman, grew even prettier. We got along very well together: Odette a woman of the world, I a bookworm; Odette always frivolous, intent upon her love affairs, quickly taken up by Montparnasse; I, dressed anyhow and looking at men askance, since Vladimir was no more, and from the age of fifteen behaving like a student.

When I hear people complain about their environment, pretending to be its victims, or talk of their struggles to escape from it, I'm always amazed, and somewhat sceptical. I don't understand how anybody can endure anything he doesn't like, since it is harder to bear it than to reject it. Odette and I created our own environment at thirteen or fourteen, or even earlier, when we chose our school friends for ourselves. We both found the wealthy *bourgeoisie*, among whom our parents and relatives moved, tedious, ridiculous, and ugly. So we simply avoided them. Our parents' attempts to impose this environment upon us were foredoomed to failure, just like their efforts when we were small to give us cod-liver oil, except by force. Short of detaining us forcibly, bound hand and foot, there was no way of making us attend their receptions or accept invitations to their little parties. Of course Father tried to thunder, but we both put up a passive resistance that was polite but unshakeable. We were both very fond of our parents, but we found it hard to forgive such absurd demands as that we should accept their friends, as though friends were something that could be handed down or inherited. Still, our parents were democratic, and our victory hardly deserved to be called one, so much was it a foregone conclusion. We simply allowed our father's fits of rage and our mother's laments to pass over, like a shower. Certainly we would have preferred fine weather, but there's nothing to be done about the climate. . . . Besides, very soon Odette married a magnificent Brazilian, who was very rich and treated her like a goddess. About the same time I took my Bachelor of Science degree, but next year I changed my mind and entered the School of Arts. Mama didn't need to watch over me; I was always sensible, always thinking of Vladimir, killed in the war, I didn't know where . . .

I was the daughter of a cabinet minister, with a considerable dowry, which still wasn't as great as you might think, for although Father made a great deal of money he also spent lavishly, and Mama was not a very careful housekeeper. The way she wasted money was ridiculous. Besides, she had her charities. . . . I don't know why Gaston was so bent on marrying me. At that time he was a kind of lion in the fashionable salons of Paris. He was a gifted young lawyer, a remarkable orator, cultivated, wore British clothes, and spoke of love like a lover. You might almost have taken this papier-mâché man, this walking sham, for a human being. But in fact he was emotionally shallow, and neither truly learned nor really handsome. A face at the mercy of the merest trifle, easily put out of countenance, when his skin would glisten, his eyes redden and bulge, all about nothing; the crease of his trousers took the place of good looks in his intellectual person. . . . He worked for my father, and if Odette hadn't been married already I'm sure he would have fallen for her. But Odette was already in Brazil.

He began to turn my head with invitations, theatres, wild car-rides, dinners, and incessant talk about love. . . . It was a great change from my examinations and tennis matches, from my excessive prudence, liberty, and simplicity. Flirtation was banished from my own circle as something ridiculous and un-worthy. Lovers were feeble creatures: with us the great thing was friendship. We even exaggerated a little. It was the fashion then, and I admit that it was I who set the key, in spite of my friend Elizabeth. But Elizabeth was the exception that confirms the rule, and it was generally agreed that everybody was in love with Elizabeth. It was a devoted, faithful group, and I was just a plump, dark-haired girl with a passion for work and sports, dressed in an old tailored suit, my only beauty culture consisting in a cold shower every morning, living on the outer rim of a luxurious household, of my father's politics, and my mother's activities. I was sceptical, condescending, and tolerant towards my parents, with the indulgence usually shown by ripe age for the pranks of youth.

But all the same I was only nineteen, and under the expert hand of Gaston I lost my self-possession. All the more, since I got nothing but encouragement. Father was delighted at the prospect of my marrying a young man with a future, and Mama was already worried that I might remain on her hands, and what in Heaven's name was going to become of me when she was no longer there to look after me, especially since I refused to wear woollen underwear, and had already been caught in an avalanche once, when I was skiing in the Alps? Poor Mama! She really thought she was taking care of me, just because she worried me about woollen underwear now and then!

There's nothing in the world like the strange fantasies of innocent girls, and no vice can compare with that inspired by the fear of physical love in a virgin. The obstacles to love were not invented to protect virtue, but to make the pleasures of love more poignant. I'm sure that Gaston owes his greatest physical pleasure to me, but after two or three months he let his nerves get the better of him. He pushed me back suddenly one day, on the large divan where we had spent endless hours, got up, and hissed, "You won't give yourself, because you think you'll get me to marry you. . . ." When the German officer slapped my face during an interrogation I had the same feeling of defilement. Years have passed since Gaston said to me, ". . . because you think you'll get me to marry you . . ." and still that memory disturbs me. What an idiot the man was! I undressed, lay down naked on the cold leather of the divan, and clenched my teeth. . . . A fine afternoon of debauchery! Then I told him: "Now get out of here. I don't want to see you again, ever!"

When the Boche officer slapped me, I spat in his face. The thought of it makes me tremble, though I didn't tremble at the time. . . . He wiped it off, and said to me, "How sorry I am that I can't have you executed right away!" But he seemed calmer, and didn't strike me again. Perhaps he liked to be spat at; perhaps it gratified his sexual instincts. They took me back to his room one night, after they had performed a mock-execution on me. I had done like the others, I had shouted "*Vive la France!*" But they fired blanks. I collapsed, nevertheless, sliding down the wall. . . . When they led me into his room after that, and when I saw his bulging blue eyes, his almost bald skull, and his manicured hands, I spat in his face again. . . . And God be praised, I disclosed nothing! Compared with the moral torments of those who have betrayed what they knew, death, I feel, would be preferable by far, at once, without even time to look at the sky, to say farewell to my past, my future, my youth, my loves, to hope, to Jean. . . ."This beautiful child is a veritable devil," he said finally, and pushed a chair towards me. "Sit down, *gnädige Frau*. I heard your father talk tonight over the London radio. He talked a lot of nonsense. . . . Odd that he should have had a child like you. . . . To prove to you that we aren't barbarians, we'll send you to a camp instead of shooting you." They didn't send me to a camp, but they put me in solitary confinement. It was a lie, as usual. Enough! Enough, O Lord! I don't want to think of it any more, I can't. . . . If they would only let me leave this hole! No, I won't stay here any longer, twiddling my thumbs, while *they* go on torturing and killing. . . . I won't stand this cursed quiet any longer, those stupid cries: "Oh, you cuckolds! Oh, you cuckolds!"

A whole year passed before I consented to see Gaston again. This complicated cynic was, in fact, as simple as a village lad. Since I no longer wanted him, he had to have me. And they all conspired against me. Mama was touched by Gaston's "constancy" (oh, these perspicacious mothers!). And Father, and all their friends . . . Tired of the struggle, I accepted my fate.

Once we were married there was nothing cheerful about our home life, and when we went out it was among Gaston's circle, where I stayed awkwardly in a corner while he scintillated. Even if I had been a genius it wouldn't have made any difference. Nobody would have noticed or spoken to me. I weighed twenty pounds too much for Gaston's wife, and those twenty pounds were too heavy a handicap. . . . Gaston was really a provincial who had never lost his awe of Paris. He had chosen as his *milieu* the fraction of Paris that sets the fashion in all things. His friends were people of taste, but they thought they had a monopoly of it, and they maintained their monopoly by dictatorial means. Certainly Gaston was terrorized by them. A passing remark by one of his friends would have outweighed his esteem, his love. . . . I remember the evening I arrived at a party in satin shoes and a sports coat. He would have liked to repudiate me. Then there was the story of the purple dress. I'm very fond of purple, mauve and lilac, but all self-respecting women wear black; therefore. . . . To succeed in this environment I would have had to start out with a new body. I've always felt hostile towards celebrities, but it was during this period of my life that I learned to hate everything acquired, established, already discovered—yet famous people themselves are often not to blame: they are famous simply because they are better than others. But what I really detest are the people who bow down to them, without understanding why. There must be something sexual about this which I can't quite fathom. I'm like those men in love with virginity; I need to make my discovery and choose before the others. Anything or anybody who has already had success automatically ceases to interest me; I like to swim against the tide. . . . Gaston was the opposite of everything I liked. But if he was ashamed of me in the salons, he knew very well how to take advantage of me when nobody saw us or heard us: he had used me up to the point where I could no longer leave him, just as you can't escape from someone who has taken away your dress and shoes. . . . If I hadn't lost my little Jean in that dreadful accident I would still be with Gaston.

We were living with my parents in the Rue de l'Université, on the first floor, which my father had furnished for us. That ghastly accident! I would rather face the rifles of the Boche soldiers a thousand times than the moment when I saw the blood-stained body of little Jean. . . . Mama, half-crazy with grief, roaming all night from room to room, cradling the little corpse in her arms. I'm crying. . . . So many years have passed, and I'm still crying, but more, perhaps, over myself than over the little body. He was one year old, such a sturdy child, and then this irrevocable, inconceivable thing happened. . . . I left Gaston, the apartment, the servants, the fashionable fools who cast me out. . . . Just when I had slimmed down by twenty pounds!

I owe everything to my friend Elizabeth. She walked into my hotel room, leaned over my bed, and said: "I detest unhappy people if I can't do anything for them. . . . But you'll come out of it, and it's worth the effort, my dear. . . ."

She made me give up my hotel room, the room which had known my empty days, my sleepless nights, all that odious, monotonous, wasted time, in the middle of a Paris where everybody knew where he was going, where everybody seemed in a hurry to get to a business appointment, a lovers' meeting. . . . Mama had left for the country. After the death of my little boy, she, who had loved us so much, seemed to have forgotten all about us; she took refuge in mysticism. There had been a change in the Cabinet, and Father, though he was deeply upset, was occupied with other things than looking after me. I had left all my own friends since my marriage; they hadn't had the luck to please Gaston, and they'd held it against me that I was unable to leave his circle. Elizabeth came into my bedroom, with a waft of her own subtle perfume, and said: "I detest unhappy people . . ." in her thin, gentle voice. I felt terribly humiliated as she bent over me, sweet as my child had been. She came quite close to me, and in this sudden intimacy there was so much warmth that I melted into tears, like snow in the sun.

5

Now for the second time I'm a well-dressed, slim woman. I don't mean to say that I'm like one of those lissom reeds, like those skeletons so easy to dress—would that I were! Even when I'm nothing but skin and bones I still possess majestic shoulders, the torso of an empress, or an opera singer, no collar-bones showing and breasts as round as though they had been drawn with a compass. . . . I never had a really small waist, I was never really flat, and my legs are plump. A beautiful body, if you like, but I don't care for it. Today I'm perhaps even thinner than on the day Elizabeth came to get me out of the hotel. It's almost a year now since I left the camp; well, I'm in better condition than I was, but I don't think I'll ever be plump again, I left the camp in such terrible shape. . . .

The peasants who took me in after my escape, after my thirty miles on foot, had quite a time with me. My beige silk dress which I had been wearing when they arrested me, and which I had never been able to change, my underwear, my overcoat, were reduced to rags and swarming with vermin. My hair was awful—long locks full of lice, the ends of it still yellow, as it was bleached when I went in, and the rest of it jet black. . . . No stockings, the sandals they had given me at the camp—the most precious present I have ever received. Everything had to be burned: dress, coat, underwear; and I had to cut off my hair, which hung below my waist. It would have been impossible ever to clean the teeming mass. The old peasant woman, Marie, spent all her time heating water in a black cauldron hung over the fire. I sat down in the little tub, while Marie's daughter (a woman who looked as little like a peasant as can be imagined, with her straight hair and spectacles) washed me, soaping me over and over. . . . Then I went to lie down on a straw mattress upstairs. It was a luxurious mattress: the straw had been put in a large and very clean white canvas cover with buttoned slits through which you could put your hand to rearrange the straw. And sheets! It had been eighteen months since I had seen any sheets. The women were worried for fear I should be cold. . . . Cold! There was a fire in the kitchen, and it was already March, with spring almost here. I've never tasted anything better than the *café au lait* in the mornings, the big slice of bread with butter and honey. . . . I must have been a sorry sight! While she heated the water for me, Marie kept muttering prayers, tears streaming from her faded eyes. They were a closely united family: Marie, her daughter Andrée, her son-in-law, whom I seldom saw because he was always out of doors, and her two grandsons, fifteen and eighteen. They all shared the same ideas and they all stuck to them; solid, serious people. . . .

This was in '42, when there were still passes between the zones. I didn't know how to go about finding Jean again without either compromising him or giving myself away. I got Andrée to write to his friends without mentioning me, and then the waiting began. I had already waited so long at camp, thought of him so much, tried so hard to be worthy of him. . . . Finally, after three weeks, an answer came. Nothing was known of Jean. But that might or might not be true. There was no way of finding him without mentioning my name or involving some of our friends.

Eventually I had to think of leaving. The farm was completely isolated, and I was of use there, but the country folk were already gossiping about the presence of a stranger in the house. So I thought of some old friends of my parents, the D.'s. . . The D.'s were from Lorraine, and I counted on that. People from Lorraine are like the Jews, there's little chance of their being pro-German. They had a piece of property in the South, and provided they wanted me, the place would suit me very well. The main problem was how to manage so that I could arrive without attracting too much notice. I had lost all my clothing, and if I were to present myself at the grand establishment in Marie's or Andrée's clothes I could never pass for a guest. We finally decided to send the oldest boy to the D.'s to sound them out. I started out with him; he helped me over the demarcation line and installed me with some other peasants, where I was to await the answer of the D.'s. It was heart-rending to have to leave Marie, Andrée, and the others, and the house which had been like paradise to me.

Mme D. arrived very shortly, with all the necessary clothing, with kisses, caresses, and tears. . . . That's how I came to be settled on their estate, and how, after a while, I went into Cannes to disguise myself as an elegant woman. . . . I had my hair done

becomingly in black ringlets, my finger- and toenails enamelled
pink, got bathing costumes so I could lie in the sun and get
tanned, tailored suits from Hermés, furs, and even jewellery. . . .
but the jewels belong to Mme D. . . . Dear Mme D.! It was with
her that Mama found refuge when she ran away from home to
marry Father. Now, under very different circumstances, she was
taking me in. Soon my skin grew smooth, my hair shone; and
I glistened all over like a well-fed, well-groomed horse. . . . But
I had still heard nothing from Jean.

Until the day I met Pierre, or rather someone who now calls
himself Pierre, as he gave me to understand. A contact at last!
. . . And news of Jean. Fantastic though it seemed to me, he had
seen Jean in Paris, with his own eyes. Pierre, heaven-sent, would
take him news of me.

I began to work again. We had blown up six Boche cars
equipped for repairing radio transmitters, etc. . . . I thought we
were doing good work. Jean let me know that he would come to
see me very soon. Then one of our men was caught and tortured.
. . . That was the beginning of November. I'm sure the comrade
didn't talk, but what with his arrest and the Italians spreading out
on the coast, our friends became very nervous. I was asked, as
Jean's wife, for whom they felt responsible, to go into hiding. So
I came to this house, which belongs to a comrade who had left
it to go and work somewhere else. I haven't seen Jean again.

But to return to the days when Elizabeth roused me out of my
despair—those blessed days of Elizabeth. . . . I rented a furnished
apartment in the Boulevard Saint-Germain opposite the post
office. Elizabeth had come to live with me, and the merry-go-
round began.

The house looked like all the others on the boulevard, but
behind the staircase leading to the apartments on the street side
there was another staircase, made of wood, in the unexpectedly
deep vestibule. This second staircase was covered with a red carpet, and had a handsome hand-rail and large wooden balustrades.
It ended at the first floor with a landing, a door, and beside the
door a small, curving corridor that led to two small staircases to
the right and left, creviced between the walls, and carpeted. At
the top of these staircases was still another door of the same light

chestnut wood as the first staircase. I rented the rear apartment at the top of the second staircase. But if you knew the place well you could descend by the back way directly into the vestibule of the Saint-Germain house. The apartment had a big living-room with a nailed-down carpet and draperies; above the divan were bookshelves, as though to show that this was not simply a temporary refuge. . . . There were also small, square armchairs around the table, a bureau, a folding table, ash-trays, and vases. Everything in the bedroom was low: the bed, the night table, the huge, varnished wooden dresser. . . . Behind the well-equipped bathroom (with tiled walls, pier-glass mirrors, lights everywhere, and a large toilet table) there was a second small bedroom just big enough for a bed. A tiny kitchen, fully provided with dishes and pots, opened off the living-room. The rug was stained, the plush of the armchairs seemed to have been brushed the wrong way, yet I've never lived in a more congenial, more convenient place, or one that lent itself more easily to topsy-turvy days, getting up by electric light, going to bed by daylight; cold meals, armfuls of flowers, drinks, evening dresses taken off at noon, jewellery thrown pell-mell among banana skins and cigarette ends. . . .

Elizabeth installed herself in the little bedroom behind the bathroom. She had an apartment in the Boulevard Montparnasse, gas-lit, with a rubber bathtub in her little kitchen, a bare, white apartment that recalled a convent cell or an actress's dressing-room. The walls were whitewashed; her fur coat lay on the divan, there were plenty of flowers. . . . But I was so anxious to have Elizabeth close to me that I begged her to come and stay with me, and actually the thought of living in Paris like a visitor didn't displease her. She was about thirty at the time, with little lines at the corners of her eyes, which emphasized her fresh complexion. Yet, when she came into my bed, dressed in a long nightgown, her fair hair in curls drawn back over her round head and fastened with a black ribbon at the neck, she was so childlike, so appealing, that I could have devoured her with kisses. But I didn't. She intimidated me, the strange child, and I refrained. I think today that I shared the life of the god of Love. Elizabeth wasn't beautiful as Odette was, yet I recovered with her the great joy of my childhood, the joy of living near a person who was continually attractive. Elizabeth was like a landscape which pleases you in any kind of light, in all seasons. She had lovely legs and arms, ravishing grey-blue eyes, the most beautiful eyes I have ever seen. . . . When we were all students it was the great game of all her friends to watch a newcomer approach her, and watch him gradually fall a victim to the malady of love. Nobody could ever resist the mere presence of Elizabeth. And all those who ever loved her, happily or unhappily, remained grateful to her throughout their lives, their marriages, their children, and their diverse destinies. Elizabeth was always the high point of their lives.

She had many flaws: she was capricious, excessive in her likes and dislikes, extravagant, careless about getting into debt, accustomed to doing as she pleased at every moment, and, on top of all this, impatient and short-tempered. She was reckless with money, time, her health, her splendid gifts. . . . But she managed somehow to scatter happiness with open hands. In her presence people became intelligent, almost brilliant; they lived their lives to the full. . . . I'm not the only one she has lifted out of the depths of despair. To leave Elizabeth was a little like leaving Paris, and nothing can replace Paris; away from Paris everything is flat, vacuous, and petty. All the other cities of the world are simply branches of Paris. You can find virtues, excellences, talents, beauties there, but to appreciate and exult in such glories, and then forget them, you need to be in Paris. Once under the spell of Elizabeth . . .

I'll never get over the loss of her. I'm sure she married Stanislaus Bielenki in a moment of despair; I'm sure love had played her a nasty trick. Perhaps it started the way it always did, with Elizabeth throwing herself into it as you might jump into an abyss. . . . Perhaps the man had not yet understood, had not yet realized, and Elizabeth already despaired, and said to herself, "He doesn't love me!" She had already given it up as too late. I can still hear her small voice: "I don't want love at a reduced price. . . ." I think the name of the man who had got the better of Elizabeth was Vigaud—Michel Vigaud.

When I came back from my first big assignment for the paper, I had told no one the hour of my arrival, and before going home I stopped at Elizabeth's apartment in the Boulevard Montparnasse. But Elizabeth wasn't at home. I had to leave again the next day, and my evening was taken up by Father and my chief; I dined with them in the Rue de l'Université. During dinner my chief insisted on my looking in for a moment at Bielenki's, where there was a big party that evening, and I consented. I had drunk a little at dinner; my father had had the best wine brought up from his cellar: he was proud of his daughter. . . . The fever, the excitement of being in Paris. . . . I was still pitching a little—the air journey had been very rough—and I still had minarets and desert sand before my eyes. . . . My chief told me that my articles had been a big success. In my mail was a letter from a publisher suggesting that I should bring them out in a book. Life was full to the brim. To go to Bielenki's I put on my most eccentric dress, one I had never dared wear before, because I could only keep it up by hitching it somehow over my breasts. But before I went I had to see Elizabeth at all costs.

She hadn't come home. My message was still there, tucked into the keyhole. I found her in the bar of the *Coupole*. . . . She was gloomy, abstracted, and more appealing than ever. She looked at my platinum hair, gently opened my evening cloak, and said, "Very pretty . . ." I would have preferred to stay with her, unless she had wanted to join us at the Bielenki party . . .

But I couldn't very well run out on my chief, who stood there hypnotized, gazing at Elizabeth, chewing his cigar, saying, "I'll be delighted and honoured to take you both."

"No," said Elizabeth, without bothering to be polite. "I won't go, but I want Louise to go . . . I want you to tell me your opinion of Michel Vigaud, Bielenki's friend. But you're too beautiful to be trusted with such a mission . . ." I had so strong an impression of distress that I'll never forget it, any more than I'll forget the white, dead woman I saw through the Italian window in my childhood. . . . "Come back here, it doesn't matter how late, I'll wait for you." We exchanged barely three words in the chief's Rolls, which took us from Montparnasse to Saint-Cloud, where Bielenki lived.

All Paris was at Bielenki's house. His parties were always successful—no wonder, with the buffet and orchestra he offered his guests. There was a mob in front of the buffet, but in the large white hall with white columns and a floor of black-and-white marble that reflected the light, people were dancing with such ordered elegance that you might have been looking on a cinema screen, at the projection of an elaborate, artificial party scene. All the female extras were delightfully dressed, and the males were in keeping. In the other rooms people chatted, standing, sitting, lying. There was champagne everywhere. And if by any chance a little nook remained unoccupied, the music came to fill in the empty space like a ground colour. I didn't want to show myself right away. There would be too many hands to shake, too many questions to answer about my trip. So I hid in a recess of the little salon next to the dance floor, where I listened, ensconced in a huge armchair, abstracted and delighted, to my companion's comments. . . . But then the voice of a singer came from the hall, and gradually everybody in all the rooms grew silent, and the dancing in the hall stopped. From my corner I could see clearly the platform for the orchestra and a singer now standing in front of the musicians. He was in evening dress, and young. . . . This night-club music affects me so strongly that it's disgraceful. I can't judge it sensibly, but I still think that for this type of singing the fellow was unrivalled. Everybody went crazy, shouted, applauded. In the room where I was hiding a couple embraced passionately, and for the first and last time I allowed my chief to kiss me. The young singer was Michel Vigaud.

When he stepped down from the dais I tried to approach him, but there was such a mob around him that I gave it up. I hoped to have a chance to see him later, but I had no luck: he disappeared. Not even Stanislaus, who had given me a wonderful welcome, could find Vigaud, although they lived together. "Listen," I said to him, "I absolutely must see him. It's very important. Or at least, you tell me—is he all right?"

"This fellow will be the death of me," Stanislaus answered in all seriousness. "Haven't you got eyes? He's just sent from heaven to worry me." And then he turned his attention to a Spanish nobleman, who looked very Parisian.

I returned to the *Coupole*. But I wouldn't let my chief kiss me in the Rolls, and he couldn't understand why one time it was yes, and then *no*. . . . Everything had dropped back into place, and I felt terribly ashamed. I still am. Elizabeth was at the bar; she seemed desperately tired. "Well?" she said. I had to be honest:

"I've nothing to say. I'd like to ask you questions myself. He sang, but I suppose he does something else, doesn't he?"

"Did he dance?"

"I didn't see him dance."

"Was he a success?"

"Yes, terrific!"

"All right," saïd Elizabeth. "Thanks a lot. . . ." We said goodbye. I left the next day and didn't return to Paris until months later. Elizabeth was no longer there.

Elizabeth had a strange impulse towards destruction: how otherwise could she have married Stanislaus? Though at the time I knew nothing about Michel Vigaud, I knew Stanislaus Bielenki very well. He had often been to our house, and Father had often kept him for dinner. He had brought Odette and me fancy toys, and he had sat me on his knees. I don't think he was always bald. Later on my family sometimes entrusted me to this old family friend, who took me to concerts, to eat cakes at *Poiré Blanche*, to the Louvre. . . . The man was a veritable charmer, in spite of his baldness. He was an excellent talker, with encyclopaedic knowledge and a disturbing agility of mind. He not only knew innumerable stories, but also knew how to listen attentively and gallantly. When I was barely fourteen he began treating me like a lady, paying me compliments and kissing my hand. I loved going out with him! When I think of it, he seems the perfect person to keep a woman, better than a husband, because she takes no responsibility for the way he gets his money and needn't bother about whether or not it's inconvenient for him to spend some of it on her. . . . The perfect man to keep a woman, created to anticipate her desires, to shower her with pleasures and gifts; disburden all her worries and unpleasantness. . . . I've never been a kept woman myself, and I'm afraid it's too late, as far as Stanislaus goes, because I've heard he's at the Gurs camp. I don't know that he's done anything to "deserve" it, unless it was his pre-war connections with the Soviet Embassy, or unless he has Jewish blood. Poor Stanislaus, I owe him a great deal; he gave me a helping hand at a moment when I was about to lose my footing. He had a passion for taking care of other people's affairs, and with his wide understanding of human nature he often succeeded. But, Gurs or no, he was finished before the war; Elizabeth had gone out of his life. He couldn't resign himself to losing her, and since he's an enterprising man, he fought. But he lost her all the same. . . . Elizabeth, child of nowhere and everywhere, returned to her native Sweden just before the war broke out. Does she still think of us? Or has France, where she lived all her woman's life, already become for her what China is to us, an unhappy country where people are always fighting?

But at the time Elizabeth stayed with me in the Boulevard Saint-Germain there was no question yet of either Michel or Stanislaus.

Two single young women living together attract men and women to them like a magnet. Life then was one continual surprise party, surprise encounters, surprise chicken-in-aspic, with no account taken of time, lived in a haze of alcohol, fatigue, and music—which has always stirred me more deeply than drink or men. Night clubs, dances, the *Deux Magots* and *Lipp's*, where you got coffee, crescent rolls, and sausages, because you had got up too late for lunch and too early for dinner. . . . Always the same faces in the same dense smoke, and the hope of finding someone, and something to happen. . . . I was so fed up with myself that I tried to lose myself in this disorderly, chaotic life, and never find myself again. I spent fantastic sums; Father refused me nothing. I ordered dresses right and left, simply so as not to have the same face in front of me, which I had come to loathe. Sometimes I dressed like a elegant woman, sometimes like a choirboy, with extravagant make-up. Then I changed to stark black clothes and went without make-up . . . I was twenty-three, heavy-eyed as though I made love day and night, with the skin of a baby; my bleached hair looked very striking, and I was delighted. But it hadn't occurred to me that once it was bleached I'd have to go on bleaching it, or dye it black while it grew out again. That's how I happened to remain a blonde all those years, with either bleached or platinum-dyed hair. Later on I didn't pay much attention to my looks; half the time I went around with the roots of my hair black, and the rest of it all colours. Not until I was in prison could my tortured hair quietly grow black again.

I ended up, of course, by taking a lover. I did it because of that wretched Gaston, whom I ran into at the *Deux Magots*, and

who tried to make up to me: I had my startling white hair, and I
was dressed to attract notice. Gaston depressed me so, that that
very evening I left with another man. I can't define him more
exactly than by calling him a man. Anyway, after this unexpected
adventure he dropped out of my life. Two days with him in
Brussels were enough to restore my poise.

When I came back I went to see Stanislaus, and I really should
burn a candle to him. Almost at once he got me the job at the
paper, where I worked for ten years until the war broke out. As
soon as I started to work I went back to the Rue de l'Université.
Gaston had left. Anyway, I returned to the bedroom I'd had as a
girl. I ran the household, which had been going to pieces without
a mistress (Mama still hadn't come back), and took care of Father.
A few months later I left for a big assignment, the first of my
trips across the world. It happened that every time I returned to
Paris Elizabeth was away. Or else Stanislaus was hiding her. And
I met him only rarely, at my chief's house. He stayed away from
me, he was afraid of me on Elizabeth's account, of the influence
I might have on her. I didn't insist, because my life was so full,
so hectic, so thrilling. Then I met Jean, the one whose real name is
Jean.

6

ALTHOUGH it's December 24, Christmas Eve, my crazy neighbour still shouts "Oh, you whores!" People think I'm plucky,
hard, strong; if they could see me crying over my turkey stuffed
with chestnuts! A poor, poor woman, no longer very young,
parted from everything she loves, from Paris, her comrades, from
Jean . . . I've been here for two months now doing nothing but
wallow in my memories. It's Christmas Eve, and here I am, with
my hands in my lap, my eyes turned inward. But today I did some
real cooking. If there is anything Gaston misses me for, it's my
crayfish *à l'Américaine*, my duck with orange sauce, and my
desserts. I'm an epicure—that's why I'm twenty pounds over-
weight . . . I shared a turkey with my neighbours for my solitary
Christmas Eve. It was I who paid for it and they who fattened
and kept it. They invited me to spend Christmas Eve with them,

but I preferred my own company to a family party (their child is the noisiest youngster in the street) and their conversation, as monotonous as my days. They think me strange, but not terribly so, because the village is full of crazy people: an old man who always walks round with an open umbrella; a small and gentle woman who sits on the steps of her house, with tanned skin and greying hair, looking at herself in a cheap mirror and talking unceasingly in a quick, low voice; another woman who always imagines her house to be full of people (Claude, who has come to put a joint in the oven; the policemen, who have gone to bed in Maurice's bedroom; little Dédé, who goes about on all fours), while her house is actually empty and no one has set foot in it for days; the old chemist in his dark shop, where the jars throw poisonous reflections on the sinister walls, sitting in front of the stove all day long washing his feet—I wonder how he finds time to write his anonymous letters: "Monsieur, you are a fool. Vote for the socialists . . ."? To say nothing of Marthe, the madwoman in my alley. Yes, the women of this staid village are irrepressible, and if I were a writer of fiction I'd find plenty of material here. Nowhere have I seen women wait for their war-prisoner husbands with such passionate intensity as these.

Midnight. The mice are scurrying about in the attic over my head. I went up there once to examine the window, by which, if the need should arise, I could escape over the roofs and into the fields. There were some old bottles and cartons, and a big funeral wreath. The clock strikes twelve, the mice scamper overhead, the lamp is out. The only light comes from the tiny wax candles burning on the Christmas tree; the demented woman shrieks. It's rather terrifying, but I'm not afraid. I'm no longer afraid of the emptiness, the silence, the funeral wreath. I'm only afraid of the Boches—naturally, because they're Evil itself. To escape them I would even run into the arms of the black monk of my nightmare. . . . What can make me forget those blue eyes, that bald skull, that mincing, pederastic gait? The Russians have said all along that it was the Germans who invented the monkey. They're not as shrewd as they think; they're always well satisfied with themselves and ready to teach the rest of the world a lesson, sometimes even when they're being duped or laughed at. That's why they win victories but lose wars, why the devil gets their souls. . . . No, I won't stay here twiddling my thumbs! I've already written to Pierre, and even if he doesn't answer me, or simply tells me to stay where I am, I'm going to do my level best to get out of this cursed quiet. I'll simply go to Lyons or Paris. . . . They'll see.

I've been to Valence and seen Pierre. I came back here to get my stuff and then left for Paris. I travelled first class, in great style, with a fur coat and one of those high hats, something between a turban and sugar loaf, by way of disguise. When the Boches entered the compartment and asked for my identity card, I had an unpleasant sensation, but it all went smoothly; my card seems to have done the trick.

The train was four hours late and I missed my appointment. My friends hadn't thought of giving me a second appointment, just in case. I must have cut a fine figure wandering through the streets of Paris wondering how long it would take me to re-establish contact, or if I would ever be able to. But by a lucky accident I managed to do it the very next day. What an amount of time one loses over all this segregation and secrecy! I slept in an icy little ground-floor room whose keys had been given me in Lyons. Then they sent me to ring door-bells to collect money. I walked through the streets of Paris with taut nerves in the insensate hope that I might run into Jean. I'd been told that he was on the point of leaving for Algiers and that it would be impossible to get in touch with him before three or four days.

During one of my visits (a fruitful one) I met one of Father's friends, M.L. . . . It seems Father is moving heaven and earth to find me and make me come to London. M.L. is an important de Gaullist leader. He invited me to a restaurant near the Porte Saint-Denis; they still serve excellent food there, just as they did in the old days, when my boss entertained actors there after benefit performances given under the auspices of the paper. We looked like a couple who would want a private room, and it's so much easier to talk in one. The private room was so small that, once inside, we filled it with our limbs, our gestures, our voices, as though we had been the mechanism inside a grandfather clock. M.L. made me think of Stanislaus at the height of his glory, although he's less bald and pale, and I should imagine his eye kindles easily. . . . I kept my distance, and everything went well. The bill was terribly high. I enjoyed the luncheon very much, but at the same time I felt deeply ashamed, thinking of my comrades in their unheated rooms, their numb fingers barely able to hold a pen, without ration cards, dependent on gifts of food. . . . To say nothing of the young fellows rounded up for forced labour. It seems that some of them are hiding out in the Savoy Alps. . . . I wonder how anyone manages to hide himself in this country, exposed as an open palm, with its good roads, and railways . . . France is not Russia. Still, I'd much prefer to join the precarious *maquis* in the mountains than to hide this way, behind a curtain of lies. Am I going to turn into one of those women who wish they were men? I think of Elizabeth, of her air of revulsion when she said, "Imagine not having breasts, and doing military service! . . ." Elizabeth was full of odd notions.

M.L. has a son in the navy, with de Gaulle. I could guess how deeply he was worried about him from the warmth with which he urged me to rejoin my father. He told me that Father has aged, lost most of his teeth, that he's bent and lonely, and that my arrest was a terrible blow to him. Poor Papa! I certainly shan't leave France, I can't tear myself away from its woes, I'm tied here, unless Jean . . . "So you're working with the communists?" M.L. asked. "Of course I am." "Yes, it's more risky, but they're more careful." M.L. gave me news of Odette. She couldn't be better; the children are delightful. Papa carries their photographs about with him and shows them to everybody. It seems that Father is really turning to his family. While I . . . M.L. said it would be easy to get me to Brazil from London. It's simply another of those ideas. Brazil, indeed! . . . M.L. was upset because he wasn't able to convince me, and, indeed, told me I was pig-headed; he ended by giving me some money, which he pretended was from my father. After all, it makes no difference to me where the money comes from; it will help us a great deal; I've rung a good many door-bells without result.

During those two hours in the private room I completely shed my imaginary personality, which had come to seem real to me. Once again I was my father's daughter, born in the sixth *arrondissement*, with grandparents in Normandy; I was someone who had gone to work every day in the newspaper office in the heart of Paris, Louise Delfort, the journalist, with her network of occupations, ideas, and friends. . . . I was so carried away by this new personality that I went straight from the restaurant to my old friends, the S.'s. . . . They nearly fainted when they saw me. From their reaction I could gauge the distance between me and Louise Delfort.

Paris seemed outrageous to me, engulfed in the occupation and the black market, complacent, bloated, shameless. . . . Jean left for Algiers without even knowing I was in Paris.

I'm back in my hole again, sitting before the table with the peeling oil-cloth. It's hot, and I can smell the leeks in my soup. Physically I'm relaxed, yet my heart is heavy. . . . I'm well off here, but I must move in order to be closer to the railway. I lose much too much time getting out of here.

I've just come back from Lyons. It's full of police, barriers, helmets, carbines, German 'planes overhead. And since Lyons is about as attractive as a prison door, anyway, it's not a pleasant place to be in now. I preferred not to go to the hotel, but slept here and there on divans. . . . It's very tiring not to have anywhere to rest for a moment during the day, comb your hair, wash your hands. . . . It's really more dangerous to sleep at the comrades' houses, who are always more or less in danger of a raid—especially when you carry a false identification card. But that's the way everybody does it, so I did the same. It's all chance, anyway. It was terribly cold in that dirty city. The houses are unheated, and the streets are filled with slush that's neither snow nor water. . . . And the violets are so fragrant that they make my heart ache; they remind me of all the things that are not included in discussions about *maquis* politics. But violets are supposed to turn work-girls' heads, and what am I but a girl waiting for her man? I can tell myself honestly now that I don't succeed in losing myself in my work: I do what is necessary, the way you kill a rat, even though doing it disgusts you; as you empty the bed-pan of an invalid; as you do housework because you can't live surrounded by filth. . . . I've never been primarily interested in a good time (the short interlude in the days of Elizabeth hardly counts: it was a kind of illness), yet here I am longing for parties, champagne, gipsy bands. The more denuded life becomes, the more I long to waste my time; I can think of nothing but enjoyment, luxury, of closing my eyes, stopping up my ears. The festival that goes on in the midst of the plague, while the stricken die, our brothers and sisters, splendid victims of that plague. But how can I think of a festival? It's totally unreal, a mere fantasy . . . God knows I was never tempted by the kind of life led by a certain fringe of the "Resistance": the wild spending in black-market restaurants, the strange excitements, feverish noise, restlessness, want of caution; the mishaps brought about by the romanticism, the dilettantism, the stupid chatter of people quite unfit for their work. And among them, too, there are so many frauds who dream of landing a good job and getting on, as if that was all that mattered! A fine prospect for the future. . . .

And, lord, how tiresome these people I work with can be! How cautious they are when they have to deal with a communist! Ridiculous and odious, like people who are afraid someone's going to rob them, who stay sitting on their precious treasure. Especially when the treasures are such trifles that nobody would think of trying to steal them. Their heads are stuffed with trash as if they had a bad cold, and yet they think their minds are cool and clear. They take their filthy trash for treasure, while the true treasure, the true liberty, is to have a clear head. They're like a suspicious housewife, who locks everything up because the working classes are all thieves. . . . This is what makes my work so hateful: I go to it wholeheartedly, thinking of nothing but how to get rid of the Boches, and all I meet is trickery, foul blows, and prejudice, all because of my connection with Jean! "She's working for him, for the communists. Be careful . . . " It's true, I work for the communists, and against the Boches. I've almost come to believe that among intellectuals there are organic anti-communists, just as there are pathological anti-Semites. They always think you have designs on them, that you're trying to get the better of them, and the more they're wrong the more complacent they are. Jean used to say: "First of all it isn't true: Péri was an intellectual, Barbusse was an intellectual, etc., etc. . . . Besides, we must work with people as they are." But Jean is a perfect person. He could work with the Devil incarnate. He's patience and reason personified. Even his faults are perfect, given him lest he overwhelm us with his perfection, to make him perfect in a human

way, and not like a god. I love Jean. I am waiting for him. . . .
The Boche will go away and Jean will come back. If I'd had one
or more lovers while Jean was away (for intoxication is sometimes
as like love as two drops of water, and you long to unite your
misery with someone else's) I would tell Jean about it, and he'd
take me in his arms, console me, and I'd forget everything that
was not him, everything outside him, looking into his wise eyes,
the eyes of an omnipotent lover, like God. . . .

Jean would say, "We must work with people as they are. . . ."
and I try to act as though he were here. I take my courage in my
hands, I return a sour look with a sweet one. But everything
about them rubs me the wrong way. Wherever I tell anything
that sounds the least picturesque, they look uneasy. In the first
place, if it were anything remarkable I wouldn't tell it. And in the
second place there's not material for a story in my present situation. A story might be made out of the dung-heap of our cheer-
less days, of ration tickets, news items, identity cards, tears,
despair, grief, impatience, revolt, fury, indignation; but not from
the dead-level of time wasted. And what am I doing if not wasting
my time? The agony of impatience is less painful than the
atrophy of heart and mind that goes on throughout the days that
leak away, as through a hole in your pocket. Is this only a story?
I seem to know in advance the stories people are going to write,
are writing right now. And I recoil in advance from the horror
they will make us re-enact. . . . And the greater the writer's
genius, the more repellent will that story be. Jean would tell me
that I'm wrong, and I know that I am wrong, undoubtedly.
Besides, the heroism and squalor of our days are destined to
become subjects of an art that will long survive us. Certainly. . . .
But, God, how I long for a glass of champagne, a gipsy band!

In the large café opposite the Place des Cordeliers, sitting
before my sixth cup of *Viandox*, I watched the people arriving,
leaving, or seated, and I said to myself, "This one is waiting for a
woman; and that one is waiting, like me, for someone who doesn't
come; he's upset, because nowadays when a person's late for an
appointment it makes your heart throb . . ." I envied the amorous
couple terribly. . . . "People who talk with heads close together
look like conspirators, and perhaps are. All France is conspiring.

Some prostitutes over there. Really, that young partisan shouldn't look so agitated, or else he should find another job." I waited . . . I didn't know the person I was waiting for, nor did he know me. Was he late, or had we missed each other? I displayed my copy of *L'Effort*, and fingered my bunch of violets.

The man, when he came to interrupt my thoughts, was dark, and looked as though he had lost quite a bit of weight; the rings round his eyes came half-way down his cheeks, and his hands were pale, thin, very weak. He spoke the prearranged words, "Violets are my favourite flower. . . ." Among other things, he wanted me to visit the *maquis* and write an article about them. Perhaps later on, when I have more time. I left him in a hurry, not without regret, but I had an appointment on the outskirts of Lyons. One of those appointments that entail hours and miles of walking. If it rains it's impossible to find refuge anywhere. There's not a café or a doorway, only smooth, interminable walls, and you must submit to being drenched. But there's never anybody about, which has the advantage that you can see people coming from a distance. Nobody can approach you in this desert without being conspicuous; there's nobody to overhear you or surprise you. . . . Each of these appointments results in a pair of worn heels and torn stockings.

Today's appointment was rewarding in every respect; it promoted our work, and gave me news of Jean! He has arrived safely in Algiers.

I haven't much time to fill my exercise books, I have so many more important things to write. The material must be ready for the printer in three days. I'm going to Valence to give it to Pierre, and when I get back I'll take it easy for a few days, and indulge myself up in what has become a kind of vice, my journey into memories of the past.

There was a period of my life when my travels were not at all confined to memory. Africa, North America, Asia. . . . I love water as much now as I did when I was a child, perched on my father's back, when he swam out to sea. There's no place where one can breathe as freely as on the deck of a ship. The marvellous monotony of the water, the briny sunshine, the deck chairs, the polite stewards, the *consommé* served on deck, the novel that drops from your hand, the passenger who retrieves it for you. . . . The careful comfort of the cabin, the vast expanse of water which you see through the round porthole as through a magnifying glass, the jagged lacework of the foam. . . . Or a sailing ship, sometimes, the straining ropes and sails. . . . The journey without fatigue, with taxi, porter, and sleeper; journeys by motor-car, 'plane, on camel- or horseback, on foot—I've known them all, enjoyed them all . . . I love the cadence of an unknown language, the strange food, all the surprises of a strange town, and my own impatience and curiosity . . . I love travelling as others love the gaming table; I look forward to a new place as others look for the next number to come up. I love the desert sand, the perils of the jungle, and the scum of big cities, the English loam, and the tropical flowers. . . .

I loved to return to Paris, to come home, too. What bliss to discover the little casket of home, where everything is so well-adapted to your body, made to your measure: the language, the temperature, the countryside, the street, the bedroom, the bed, every sound! . . . I loved my job, the big office building, the smoke-grimed desks, the bustle of sallow, cynical, overwrought journalists. I knew these gentlemen inside out, both in the printing-room and when they came to interview my father first as a Cabinet Minister and then as Premier. And the boss, like the executive in the movies, who never stopped asking me to marry him. It was his own idea. . . .

I met Jean aboard ship between London and Leningrad. It was a small ship where everybody stuffed themselves with caviare, and sang and danced all night long, including the entire ship's crew, the captain, and the stewards. Five sunny days, five moonlit nights—I almost said honeymoon nights. . . .

Leningrad is the most beautiful city in the world. Flat as the ocean, without hills or skyscrapers, endless perspectives, streets so long and broad that you cannot take them in at a glance, paved with wooden blocks, a pavement as soft and luxurious as a rug. The tremendous Neva, the granite quays, the vast, sumptuous palaces painted pistachio green or russet, with white columns and gables. The pallor of those white nights, when you can read by the deceptive light that seems to come from nowhere. A somnambulists's city, where the pallor of day and night are confused, and confuse you. We spent every night on those fantastic quays, and day came without bringing us to our senses; we lost our foothold in the crazy city, which immersed us in a cold delirium that had a taste of rusty iron, of fog, of marshes. . . .

There was a large hotel in Leningrad, the *Astoria*, a palace hotel, but the people who stayed there were not at all like what one is used to seeing in such places. For instance, there was Jean's friend, who wore a white smock and boots, and came to my room to tell us about the mountains and the marvels we should see in his country. His words seemed innocent enough, but they were as heady as new wine. It was he who started us on our trip to Moscow, bought our tickets, and accompanied us to the station. Without him we might have foundered in the white nights of Leningrad. On the way he showed us the broken pavement and the peeling walls. He said: "We don't bother to repair anything here. It's not worth it; there will be another war." That was in '36.

How odd and charming Jean was in the sleeper between Leningrad and Moscow! He had never travelled by sleeper before, and he had to touch everything with a sort of admiring curiosity: the pretty blue fabric of the seat, its velvet brocades, the nickel-plated hooks that hold up the berth when it's closed, the straps that fasten it, the adjustable lights, especially the little lamps in the wall, close to the pillows, shaded so that one can read in bed without inconveniencing one's companion. The dressing-room between two compartments, with a nickel-plated wash-bowl and running hot water; the odd, long, narrow stool! I had never realized before how ingenious, solid, and well-constructed it all was. The conductor brought us two glasses of tea with lemon, biscuits, and caviare sandwiches. . . . The conductor was genial, neat, and hospitable as though he had been entertaining us in his own home. If you got sleepy you had only to call him to make the bed. The door closed like a lid, and crammed together in that blue brocaded box we rolled across an unknown, beloved country, towards the city of my childhood. I anticipated with emotion and excitement both the new and the old that awaited me, both what I would rediscover and what I would discover for the first time. Jean was my guide, for, while I was the one who spoke Russian, he was the one who knew Russia. And we already hoped that we two would always be together. . . . I've never been so supremely happy as I was for those few hours on the train between Leningrad and Moscow.

In Moscow there were no longer streets paved with stones as round as fists, and horse-cabs were almost as rare as in Paris. Asphalt and motor-cars everywhere, and the streets so crowded that the city seemed to lose its equilibrium, like an overloaded car. There were big, new houses, the names of the streets were changed, and I couldn't find my way any longer. Jean teased me, asking if I hadn't lived in Moscow in another incarnation. Perhaps that had been so, after all. . . . People lived intensely there. Every day they wore a different dress, and their work seemed to stimulate them like a football match. In Moscow, in the Urals, everywhere there was a new generation who wanted, at all costs, to learn, to know, jealous of the greater advancement of the other countries, hardening their muscles in order to catch up with the others and outstrip them, taking pride in the future of their country, in all that science, effort, courage, genius held in store for them, in the well-being they would achieve, the leisure, the comfort—even luxury, the clothes they would wear, the houses they would have. . . . What though, in this festival of hope, you stumbled now and again upon filth, disorder, graft, and treachery! We see today how the ocean of the Soviet people has washed away everything that was not its faith and its hope.

I should have continued my trip, but I returned to Paris with Jean. I could no longer live without feeling his hand in mine. The world, which had been full and inexhaustible before Jean came, had taken on even deeper meaning through him, a new harmony. This chaos, which I had vaguely searched for an idea, a landscape, an injustice, a crime, an exploit, grew harmonious through this interdependence, this new meaning. . . . But really now, I must get down to work. I have important things to write.

7

I THOUGHT SO. The mad woman has insulted me at last, like everybody else. She's been very excited ever since morning, when

I heard her whetting her knife against the stone wall of her house, shouting, "Blood must flow! Blood must flow!" When I went out to buy bread I saw a group of people gathered in the alley; there was Marthe insulting all women in general, menacing those who passed with a pitchfork. I hoped to pass unnoticed, but she threw herself at me. "Look at her! With her harlot's eyes!"

"That's enough," said a man, trying to drown her voice, embarrassed that such a thing should befall a stranger. "That's enough. Shut up, or we'll get the police."

"Go to hell, the whole pack of you!" howled Marthe, turning on a respectable-looking woman. "You bitch, I'll teach you!"

I went on to get my bread without stopping to listen further.

Have I really got harlot's eyes? Jean said almost the same thing once. I like my eyes, I'm grateful to them for having impressed Jean, but I like Jean's eyes better. I wonder where he got his yellow eyes—a Frenchman born in Toulon of a fisherman and a working woman? They are a little like Vladimir's eyes. . . . Jean was a war orphan, and ward of the nation. He got scholarship after scholarship, and became a great scientist, a great physicist, and a militant communist. He has a handsome Asiatic face, smooth, calm, swarthy, with ears set close to his head, and cropped black hair. He's tall, rather stocky, with shoulders strong enough to carry the world's weight. He's mad about fishing and shooting. One of those men who show their measure even in normal life, and who, under exceptional circumstances, surpass themselves.

When I first met Jean he was already parted from his wife. Their little boy had gone with the mother. I don't know why or how they parted, and I never asked him; the only thing I cared about was to make sure he no longer loved her. His wife and the little boy were living with her parents. Jean had kept their Paris apartment, a small ordinary apartment with a Provençal dining-room. . . . I lived part of the time in the Rue de l'Université and part of the time with him. I took along my pots and dishes, because ever since he had been alone Jean hadn't eaten at home, and the kitchen was empty, except for an old stained coffee-pot. Jean drank a lot of coffee, and never washed the pot. He worked and slept in his study, where there was a divan, with a back-rest and very hard cushions, and a hard bolster at either end. A big

American desk stood by the window, and there were books strewn everywhere, on the shelves that lined the walls, piled on the floor, on the chairs. . . . In the corner stood a baby's high chair, left behind, probably, because the child had outgrown it. And when I went into the bathroom I couldn't help imagining a baby's napkins drying on the square clothes-dryer above the bathtub. Jean's mother came from time to time to clean the place and mend his clothes. When I arrived with my dishes and clothes I had to spread out beyond the study, into the bedroom and dining-room. The first time we had dinner together in the Provençal dining-room Jean was gloomy, and hardly said a word. But he grew used to it very quickly. I didn't touch the high chair in his study, but I put away the little chamber pot in the bathroom, and the armless teddy bear perched on the clothes hamper.

I was reluctant to leave Paris now, to resume my travels, and my chief, sensing that there was a man behind it all, tried his best to suggest tempting assignments. Jean was almost snowed under with work, what with the Sorbonne and his Party duties. Yet things did work out somehow, and we were outrageously happy. When one is sure that every possible free moment is for the other . . . One day Jean came to see me in London by 'plane, pretending that he had work to do there, just because he wanted to see me. The two of us were close accomplices in life. . . .

During the war I grew closely attached to Jean's mother. I went to see her every day. We were both terribly worried about Jean; at first he suffered petty persecution, but after the tenth of May we were afraid there would be designs on his life. Everybody said his number was up. If the "phoney war" hadn't ended as it did, they might have been right, what with the police on his track, and all kinds of dodges. Indeed they were not above planting evidence among his belongings. Then the rout started; Jean wasn't taken prisoner, and he came back to Paris. He came back to his old apartment and returned to his course at the Sorbonne. As for me, I had never left Paris.

Soon after, the trouble began in the Rue de l'Université. Papa had disappeared during the exodus, and was suspected of having been among the passengers of the *Massiglia*. So the police started pestering me, and ended by searching the house in the Rue de l'Université. I didn't wait for any more, and on the day

Father first spoke over the London radio I had already moved to Jean's mother's. When they came to arrest me they found the house empty.

I started working for the Party in '41. (I wasn't a Party member: it's possible to have faith and yet not feel in oneself the apostle's vocation; it's possible to love a woman, and yet fear the humdrum of married life. Jean didn't insist.) We rarely saw each other now; it was too dangerous. Yet one day we decided to have lunch together at his place. And on that day, of all days, I had from morning the disagreeable sensation of being followed. I never really saw anybody; it was uneasiness rather than certainty. At Jean's, the table was laid; there was mimosa, and the Provençal dining-room was so bright with sun that the log fire in the fireplace was scarcely visible. Jean had on a navy-blue pullover and a very white collar. But we had to keep watch from the window, and remember the sword hanging over our heads.

There was a queer fellow down below, walking to and fro. I'd barely had time to fill in my identification card, which I had received only that morning, and the ink wasn't even dry on my finger, when the door-bell rang.

The police inspector was alone, and polite. While he asked Jean a few questions, he stole glances at me. "And this lady?" he asked finally. "Will you please tell me her name?" Jean pretended to be amused. "But she's my wife, Monsieur."

"Oh, I see," said the policeman. "Do you happen to know Madame Louise Delfort, Madame?" I lowered my eyes indignantly. "What a question, Monsieur! . . ." He was obviously embarrassed, because if I were Jean's wife it was quite natural that I should be jealous of this Louise Delfort. "Will you please show me your identification card, Madame? Excuse me, but I'm simply performing my duty." He left. The mimosa on the table hadn't wilted, the logs were still crackling, as though they were amused. What a wonderful, reckless day! It was to be the last.

A week later they came to arrest Jean, but he escaped by way of the balcony and the neighbouring apartment, which was empty. About the same time I stupidly let myself be caught at his mother's, where they weren't even after me, having come simply to search his mother's house. My record was bad: to be my

father's daughter and Jean's mistress was too much for one
woman. They had plenty to ask me.

Much later, when I was in camp, I learned the details of
Jean's escape. During the interrogations they told me so many lies
that at times I believed Jean was dead. You must not believe what
they say, never.

And here I am, writing, instead of doing a useful job.

8

I've been in Lyons for two weeks. It's spring, with storms, colds,
packed tramcars, and every kind of wretchedness. When I got
back I spent forty-eight hours in bed, immersed in silence,
solitude, and sloth. . . . Marthe has killed herself. Today was
Sunday, and I went to have coffee with my neighbours : I couldn't
refuse. . . . They are dreadfully boring, like children who prefer
the stories they already know, and they repeat the same things
every time I see them, laugh and grow angry in the same way. The
war has just managed to introduce a little variety into their conversation. There's gossip about my frequent trips to Lyons, and
that bothers these decent, good people. They don't like seeing me
travel in these "troubled times". My presumed recklessness upsets
them as greatly as their caution stupefies me. But I realize that
people have begun to gossip about me here. Discreet as they are
(so much better bred than people in the great world), they've
thought fit to hint that I'm being discussed. . . . In any event, I've
decided to leave as soon as I can find another lodging. I've heard
of a villa belonging to a M. Blin, a manufacturer, which sounds
just the thing. I can't understand why my friends take so long
renting it for me; surely I would be much safer in the house of
a business man engaged in the black market, than in a comrade's
house. The business man, on his side, knows what he is doing
when he offers his house to someone like me : he wants to get on
good terms with us. This honest scoundrel may be very useful.
And I'd be very comfortable in his villa, which seems to be
brand new, with all modern conveniences, and without the
owner, who lives in Lyons and seldom stays in V——. But my
friends, who have found the place for me, are still hesitant; they

wonder if it's safe enough—and then the black-market aspect puts them out a little. When I return from Paris I'll stop there. It isn't far from here.

The villa is perfect! The manufacturer happened to be at home, he offered me a first-rate lunch, and he strongly urged me to move in. I suppose he would prefer to stay there himself and share it with me; he made it only too plain that he liked my looks. But he quickly understood that I wasn't his cup of tea and took another tack, emphasizing that I would have the villa all to myself, and that nowhere would I be safer than there, where he knows everybody, and where everything passes through his hands. Even while he's in Lyons he keeps in touch with everything that happens at V——. If I should decide to go to this villa it would be a great advance in the matter of luxury. It's not palatial, but nearly so. . . . The owner seems to love his house and care for it. Everything is run by electricity—kitchen, bathroom, heating; the rooms are spacious and comfortable, like the furniture, and neither ugly nor beautiful. No paintings or knickknacks—the owner hasn't had time to acquire any yet. The garden has a lawn, flower beds, and a few old trees. But the acme of comfort is provided by the housekeeper, who is deaf and dumb. If I hadn't been set on the place before, this housekeeper would have determined me.

These are my last nights in the little house, and I feel depressed. I've never suffered from either cold or hunger here. The little house has done its best for me. It has helped me to populate my solitude. I can still hear the shouts of the boys bowling in the alley; and Marthe's strident voice. . . . This is summer, '43, and the war continues. Lord! When will it end? When shall we be delivered? Each season brings new hope; we think it must end, simply because it can't go on any longer, and yet it goes on.

I'm taking my copy-books with me. I must. After all, they compromise no one but me. I possess nothing on earth; I sleep on divans here and there; the faces surrounding me are strange faces; that is why I need these copy-books, this refuge which is mine alone. I'm aware that the deaf and dumb housekeeper is not also blind, but I'll find a safe place for them. . . .

9

I LIKE it here. I tried all the armchairs before I chose the one to push up next to the radio. I listen to all the broadcasts; it's fascinating. In my little house I was deprived of this narcotic. The owner's radio is very good, and so is the bed. There's a bathroom with a separate shower: what luxury! The garden is filled with fragrant roses. I've put them in all the vases.

The landscape is just the same as that round the little village —just as sensible and commonplace. But this is the peach and apricot season, when the country displays its abundance. Trees and market stalls are nearly breaking under the weight of magnificent fruit. The villa is just outside the little town, which is barely larger than my village and yet has the air of a town. There is a main street, with shops, four pharmacies, two cinemas, and several hotels. The Boches rush round in cars and on bicycles, crossing the Rhone by a great steel bridge to poison the atmosphere for us. Still, the bridge is only for vehicles and pedestrians: the railway bridge is a few miles further down. But it's a huge bridge; it's guarded by a Boche sentry armed to the teeth; although V—— has only one business street, this bridge makes it a town. Moreover, it's an important railway junction where many people come and go, and a lot of money is spent here. . . . All this takes place outside the real life of the town, which goes on living its half-rural, half-industrial existence, without bothering about the affairs of railway and bridge. Perhaps there have been times when motor-cars brought an air of the open road and cities, but today the garages along the desolate Rhone bank alongside the main street are closed, and old tyres and junk are strewn over the filthy bank. The houses of sin, banished from the town to the other side of the bridge, look as rusty as the garages, but they are not closed. Boche motor-cars park in front of the "hotels", and a solitary woman, duly made up so there'll be no mistake about it, and absorbed in her knitting, attracts customers. The contrast between this country of orchards, with beautiful fruit hanging like ornaments on the branches of the trees, and these "hotels", from which gramophone music can be heard at all hours, not to mention the poor girl on duty, who surely must be half-witted, judging from the derision of the German sentinel, is beyond description.

There's a bicycle in my host's garage, and I take advantage of it for roaming about. It's very handy for my appointments. It saves me waiting for buses, uncomfortable journeys standing up, and stifling in the crowds.

The owner has come on a business visit and asked me to lunch with him at the *Restaurant de la Poste et du Sauvage*. Between chicken and steak (when they want to treat you well here they double or triple your courses) he asked me to marry him. A catastrophe! I already saw myself turned out of doors, without a lodging, pursued by the ill will of a man of questionable integrity. But I was wrong. He told me right away that he had never really thought I would accept, that he wasn't worthy of me, but had wanted to try nevertheless—rank folly, he realized. In any event he was at my service, all his possessions were likewise mine, as he was, body and soul. This corpulent personage was not without a certain dignity. When he took off his glasses there was something childlike about his near-sighted grey eyes that went to my heart, and made me want to cry. . . . He said he wouldn't come back unless I asked him to, and only if he could be of service to me. I had already used him as an intermediary in Lyons: this tender-hearted bandit was in the other war and hates the Boches. Besides, he's as crafty and cautious as a Sioux; he has made large profits on the black market, and in turn has helped the *maquis*. Money doesn't smell.

He let me return to the villa alone, in order to avoid gossip, even though his car was waiting outside the restaurant—a petrol car, of course.

When I reached home I felt languid from the luncheon and my foolishness. I sank into the big armchair by the radio and turned the dial. I shouldn't listen to those sentimental songs, which quickly get the better of me. A desire for love! I stayed in the armchair until the music changed to an advertisement for a blood tonic. Then I went into the bedroom to stretch out. It's true, I have harlot's eyes; Marthe must have judged me correctly. I slept heavily, without dreaming, until evening.

Everything happens by threes. Good God, what's going to happen next? Yesterday a proposal, today an unlucky encounter. At least I think so. I ran into Alexis Slavsky, the painter, with his wife. She was carrying a shopping bag, and he had a loaf of bread under his arm. They evidently live in this town. They didn't see me this time, but we're sure to run into each other eventually. What shall I do? Leave? Where can I go? After all the trouble my friends took to find me this quiet spot, which seemed so perfect. What business have they to come here? Only eccentrics could bury themselves in a hole like this, if they had any alternative. Slavsky sounds Russian or Polish, but I'm sure Alexis Slavsky represents everything that's most French. And certainly neither he nor his wife is Jewish. Let's see, now, what was her name? Henriette, yes, Henriette Toulac. If your name is Henriette Toulac you have nothing to fear from the National Revolution, unless you go out of your way to ask for trouble. But I'm sure they are people who mind their own business. This pale greyhound of a man had talent, plenty of it. Henriette had a hellish temperament. She has changed so that I didn't recognize her at first. She used to be a rather sturdy woman, with lots of make-up, eccentric, very Montparnasse. Now she's pale, skinny, and wears black in midsummer. They are bound to recognize me, despite my black hair, my slimness and my grand clothes. I met Alexis during Elizabeth's time. Later on I saw him several times at the *Deux Magots*. And just before I left for the U.S.S.R. I spent a whole evening with him at the D.'s . . . I remember now that he wasn't anti-Soviet; besides, it's quite out of the question that this couple are collaborators. If they were they wouldn't be here, but in Vichy or Paris. Moreover, he has his painting. True, that didn't prevent Derain or Vlaminck . . . But Slavsky is a man of such refinement and delicacy, and Henriette is so intensely French. I'm going to tell them: "I call myself Louise now, that's all. I've been in prison because my father was a Cabinet Minister, so keep your mouths shut!"

The manœuvre worked. I met the Slavskys and talked to them. I think I succeeded.

Yes, I succeeded. We have become friends, and not only holiday friends (on this absurd kind of holiday) but friends by choice, whom a benevolent chance has set on the same road. They are completely outside everything, in spite of their passionate hatred of the Germans and their strong desire to see them get out. Alexis speaks of them with astonishing violence, dropping his plaintive air, while his narrow, greyhound nose blanches with fury! To say nothing of Henriette, who acts like a madwoman, ranting and gesticulating. She's a genuine orator. An admirable, marvellous tragic actress! Especially now that she's thin, flat-breasted, with a few lines on her forehead, and those eyes that seem brimming with the South, its passion, cunning, and talent. . . . Dear Henriette, completely absorbed in Alexis, who is her sole passion, joy, and interest, both a husband and a child. . . . If she had had any children I'm sure she would have farmed them out lest she be distracted from Alexis. . . . What would have become of her without Alexis? For Alexis is not just an accident; she needed this sorrowful prince, consumed by his own passion, which is painting. She needed the intensity of Alexis' passion, his ignorance of life, his beautiful hands, his white complexion that goes with slightly carroty hair, his nonchalance, his whims, and his re-finement. She needed someone who couldn't cross a street with-out her, or pay at a restaurant, or telephone, who hasn't yet learned how to use ration tickets. Someone who is as he is only because his vocation is absolute. Alexis loves nothing except his painting.

We spend whole days together. They never bother me. They come and go, engrossed in their own affairs, he in his painting, she in Alexis. When we are together it's a diversion for us, full of echoes of our true lives and passions. It's a three-dimensional life, not a sham; our mysteries are not false mysteries. . . . I'm glad to have given Alexis a chance to work. They live in a little house close to the station, bullied by their landlady, a good old country woman. Alexis, that modest, sensitive person, is unable to work under the woman's vigilant eye, on her polished floor. Since I gave him the key to the little pavilion at the end of my garden, and since he has begun working there, he's a different man. He's willing to take walks, to eat, he's getting sunburnt, and looks less like a corpse. . . . He listens to the radio now with-out the nervousness that irritated me: he used to throw himself into an armchair, get up, twiddle the dial, trying to get rid of the atmosperics, swear, and complain. . . . Now he doesn't care if he misses most of the news, and is satisfied with the summaries I give him. I have to explain everything to them, as if they were children. They don't even know the names of the politicians, let alone their records or their present positions. They know nothing of what is going on in our country, sabotage, derailments, bombs . . . They approve of it all, because they are against the Boches, but they seem to think that these things are done by abstractions somewhere in the void. Sometimes I feel like scolding this Alexis, so distraught by the war, so shattered by the derangement of his passion, the loss of the protective laws and walls that are necessary to his work, by living exposed to millions of eyes, to every hazard. Alexis, dying of shame, like a virgin thrown naked into the street. It has come to such a pitch that I, who have a ready hand, deserve credit for not having slapped him some-times when he started complaining of all his troubles, brought upon him by his foreign name and his having a grandmother named Esther. But what have they really done to him? Nothing whatever. They haven't killed his loved ones or deported them, he hasn't been left alone in the world, he's not parted from someone, exposed to the horror of absence; he's never been thrown in prison, humiliated, tortured, nor does he die with each soldier who dies for us on the eastern front. He isn't grieved by all that is being destroyed, the schools, the harvests, the Dnieper dam, the hopes trampled underfoot by German boots. He doesn't know what it means to love a people, the people, to worry over every boy in the *maquis*, over every runner who carries tracts, over all our "Jeans" lost in the fog. . . . Yet when I see him before his easel I'm able to gauge his passion, and I tell myself that people like him are probably necessary to our country's survival.

They have landed in Sicily. Hope once more!

For a week now I've been doing nothing. My host has sent somebody to advise me to keep quiet, there has been trouble in Lyons. . . . If the Allies don't hurry, the Boches will do for us yet. Yet, since those are my orders, I must resign myself to idleness, with only this new hope to keep me alive. It's beautiful warm weather, but I'm ill at ease. Now that victory is so close, panic seizes me, and I'm almost dying of fear lest I should never see the

end, never see Jean again. I'm afraid, yes, afraid. . . . Even
these notebooks disgust me. My impatience and nervous exhaustion are too great. Unless . . . unless I should write for someone
besides myself.

10

THIS time I'm writing as a woman attracted by a man, using the
written word as a means of seduction. I must put it down quickly
while it still means something to me; that is, while the man still
means something to me, because, frankly, I don't care a rap about
him. I don't mean as a friend—of course he's a very dear friend.
. . . But I've always been told that the best cure for seasickness
is to embrace the first sailor you meet. I've tried it crossing the
Mediterranean, and I know from experience that it works. . . .
Of course it wasn't a sailor exactly, but at least there's something
in the sailor story, because, as I said before, it works. . . .

Well, just now I'm in a state of something like seasickness, and
the first man who came along would do. What I want to recover
from, speaking of seasickness, is this perpetual anguish. . . . I
want the air I breathe no longer to be poisoned by threats, a
house again to be a shelter, and the word "shelter" to have its old
meaning. I want to be able to walk in the street without turning
round, not to have to run to the window to see who is ringing the
bell, not to be crushed by sleepless nights, full of mysterious
noises, a honking motor-car—is it going to stop? No, it's going
on. Steps . . . many of them. . . . Not a patrol? Are you sure?
Voices, cries . . . and in what language?

The first man would do. . . . Not quite, because I have to get
a little bit sentimental first, just a little bit drunk over it, just a
tiny little bit. . . . It began the other day when we were left alone
in the half-light, with the radio playing sweet music. As soon as
my hand was in his, all the anguish, all the trouble, went. The
"sailor's charm" worked! Am I a lucky person? Not as lucky as
all that, because I can't make the forgetfulness last. It's high time I
put some content into this story. . . . But it isn't easy, because if he
shouldn't feel for me what I feel for him—which is nothing . . .
And if the sailor's charm simply worked because of one of those

little things I know so well: a glass of wine too much, the storm, the sweet music, a particular mood. . . . And I know that experience of this kind doesn't come off, the deception is too cruel, the humiliation too deep.

For the first time in my life I mean to amuse myself, to go about it coolly, deliberately, like an experienced coquette. Rather an odd occupation at this moment in my life, when I can think of nothing but him, and all the misery I so enjoy, all that I cannot put down on paper. But I must get rid of this seasickness. It's a question of moral hygiene. If I can only keep my ideas straight and remember that he pleases me, and that I intend to act like an experienced coquette. So now I'll try to write so as to attract him. . . . Once I wrote an article about harems; I almost needed to get raped afterwards, but I hadn't done it on purpose, nor do I know why I should have felt like that. The difficulty about this affair is that I want to hurry things up, and at the same time keep up this air of not interfering, of noticing nothing. . . . How restful it is to think of something else! He held my hand, and we stayed like that for a long time, without speaking. . . . It made the sailor's charm work, but I didn't say anything, and what isn't confirmed by words doesn't exist. There's even a question whether it ever existed—those two clasped hands. . . . We looked at each other candidly, without embarrassment. If it weren't for this mania for speaking, nothing would ever become real. It's the perfect system, if one doesn't want to have any worries . . . What was he thinking? That I believed in affectionate friendship? He shouldn't think anything else; if he did it would be very disturbing, and bad for me, since he's not alone. . . . Really, I don't quite know what to think; is it really affectionate friendship, touched with a little emotion, or is it just his manner with women? There are men who can't be alone with a woman without making love to her. But we had been alone together many times; what made him act like that this time? Curiosity, desire, or bad habits? That's it exactly. Curiosity, desire, and bad habits. I ought to ask him how I am to take this friendly gesture. . . . But then the lies would begin.

My whole life is at stake, and I'd rather not think about it. I'm courageous so long as I lack imagination. But I can't close my eyes to the fact that the other day they almost caught me again.

I'm about as well suited for secret work as the Eiffel Tower! Conspicuous, talkative, open to every wind that blows. And here I am in this business up to my neck. When I see the way most people detach themselves from events, I don't understand how they do it. How do they keep from becoming involved? . . . And when you are, how can you help being in a constant state of panic and pain for those you love, for the whole world? As for me, I'm on the alert all the time. Only under the influence of music can I understand young people who cry out and go swimming in rivers or into the woods to make love. . . . Yes, music makes me long for some immediate happiness, which would get rid of my troubles for a while. But I'll hold out, all the same, hoping for our hands to join, then my seasickness will be gone.

He doesn't look at me differently from before, except that there's a hint of animation when he mentions our *tête-à-tête* the other day, the news we listened to together. The promiscuous women of old had their lives before them; mine may end any moment. And that's really the crux of the matter. That's what I try to camouflage by the sailor's charm. But if he should offend me by keeping his distance, and if I should hold a grudge against him for it, it would ruin everything. Things rankle in my mind. Oh no! Not when I'm in love. . . . But there . . . I know why I want him: because I want to keep my head above water, and because I know myself, and that I need him for that. . . . And I have work to do in life. I haven't time to let myself be drowned. But why should he want it? There's no reason why he should. He has a wife, a profession; why should he risk destroying our good relationship? Is the temptation for him greater than I believe, or even smaller than I fear? It's nothing, nothing at all, neither one nor the other. . . . Because I also am honest. For me too, in certain cases, a man may be sexless, so much so that I have nothing to boast of if I have no "guilty thoughts". But suppose we had really been meant for each other?

He doesn't even try to be alone with me. . . . Dream, poor girl, dream; cram your head with boarding-school dreams; cling to your dreams; go on telling yourself that he's a sweet, tender, perverse boy; let go of the reins; perhaps the horses will end by running away. . . . No, no, and no. . . .

.   .   .   .

No more games, no more "sweet music"! My host came this morning with bad news: our printer has been arrested, and our plant seized. The pressman too. Everything's a mess. I'll leave today. I think I can find something else through the man who "likes violets". My host has told me how I can get in touch with him. This M. Blin is priceless! Once this matter is settled (what a way to put it! My heart bleeds . . .) I'll visit the *maquis* and write that article about them. The prospect of victory upset me strangely, but now I've pulled myself together again. I've put my note-books in a metal box to be buried under the peach tree in the garden. The last notebook won't go into the box; it isn't large enough, worse luck. I'm going to tear out this last page, and leave the notebook in my bedroom. There's nothing compromising in it.

Tomorrow I'll leave for Lyons, and then for the *maquis*. I promised the man who "likes violets" a long time ago that I would do it.

11

THE revolver, that cold, heavy, black, murderous object, affects me like a scorpion. The driver put his in the glove-box beside the ignition, and the two men in the back slipped theirs into their pockets. I sat next to the driver. At the feet of the two men in the back was an odd black case containing a dismantled sub-machine gun.

For some time we had been rolling along the narrow departmental roads, which are as smooth and well kept as the national highways. What a civilized country France is! Alternating sun and shade. . . . The car climbed. . . . Horned cattle, like stags, stood immobile as monuments, staring at this dark, gliding apparition, but the sheep galloped away like mad, moulding themselves into a single undulating mass. We passed through hamlets with steepled churches, which seemed, at our approach, to gather beneath their wings the little squat houses with their solid walls. Men and women stopped work and turned their eyes away from this dark, evil-smelling beast that roared past them. This country of stone and brown tile was already familiar with the

Gestapo cars, and my companions had hardly bothered to change the look of theirs, merely daubing some black paint over the number and the WH. We were riding cross-country in a car stolen from the Gestapo, without licence or papers, with a parachuted sub-machine gun at our feet. The car climbed higher and higher, and a kindly mist began to envelop us until we could barely see the road.

The mist made me sleepy, and the blind ride made me feel sick. My thoughts were drawn irresistibly to another ride, seven years back, along a strange road into a strange night. . . . From time to time a bright light barred the road as stark as footlights, revealing a barricade and an armed militiaman, with a blanket thrown round him, levelling a flashlight at us. That was 1936, in Spain. Fatigue, the foreign language, villages filled with strange, jagged silhouettes of guns, and moving, quivering, exulting shadows. A man jumping on the running-board . . . armed with a gun, a revolver in his belt . . . his brown, deeply wrinkled peasant face appearing at the window. "*Salud!*" he ejaculates. "French? *Salud!* Well, and Blum? Well, when?" "*Salud!*" we reply. We can't tell him anything about Blum. . . . First encounters with armed civilians, men and women with revolvers in their belts and in their hands. . . . The first dimmed lamps, the first blacked-out nights. Phantom cars, windows, and doorways all in league together. Bullets crossing the night, corpses. . . . Dead bodies, bodies of heroes.

Now they have come into our French villages to trouble the peace of our streets and squares, named after the Republic or Jean-Jaurès, where the constable as town-crier used to announce in his stentorian voice the cinema programme and football matches. . . . Where people ran to their doors to catch a glimpse of the bride all in white and the stiff bridegroom, followed by their hatted and gloved family . . . the slow funeral processions moving towards the sunny cemetery . . . the recruits, who went by singing, beating the big drum, kissing the girls . . . the oddly garbed Parisians. There were market days, holidays, the vintage, the corn-husking, the seasons of heavy toil, the constant exertion, the cares . . . the evening gatherings with pipes, clicking knitting needles, hot coffee well sugared, small glasses of brandy so heartening in cold weather. . . . Summer, with the sun burning

down on the backs of fields and men, shady paths, cool streams.
. . . The sky, the air, the day, the night, were familiar, every noise
had a known meaning: here's the five-o'clock bus; that's the
doctor's car; that's Robert sitting up late to mend his little boy's
shoes; that's Marthe going to the well; this is X's son coming
home from the café. . . . No need to watch out for every unfamiliar
sound: good God, what does that creaking mean? Whose steps
are those? They sound like marching boots! . . . Then they've
come! God preserve us! . . . If they come again to take away some
of our people, young men, or hostages. . . . Yesterday they went
to the S.'s farm, but the two fellows who were hiding there had
time to get away. In the afternoon they went through the village
in a small truck, stopped at the police station, and threatened the
policemen with sub-machine guns, because they don't do their
duty and round up the young men hidden on the farms. Mirliton,
the policeman, arrived out of breath at the tobacconist's where
there's a 'phone, to try to send word that the Boches had started
in the direction of L——, where there is a *maquis* unit—but they
had already cut the wire. At R—— they took ten more hostages
because a train had been blown up in the neighbourhood. They
entered the homes, kicking the doors in, and took ten people at
random . . . God preserve us!

We were rolling along the beautiful roads of France in a
stolen Gestapo car. The armed men with me were: the military
leader of the *maquis*, in civilian life a mathematics teacher; a
chemistry student; a former garage owner. Gilbert, the student, is
a communist; the ex-garage man is a socialist; the military leader
belongs to no party, but has a leaning towards the communists.
All three come from the same village, a rather large village,
almost a small town, with here and there a Gothic window, a
carved door, an arched bridge. . . . The church is beautiful, and in
the distance the ruins of a château can be seen. I arrived there late
last evening. Gilbert was waiting for me at the station and took
me to a house, where the woman led me on tiptoe to a bedroom.
It was after ten o'clock, and her husband was already asleep. This
morning I heard them listening to the English radio at seven-
thirty, before they left for work. By daylight, and well rested after
my interminable journey, I could see that it was a pretty bedroom, with crossed pink muslin curtains and a mahogany dresser.

This girlish room belongs to a friend of Gilbert who is away. His father works in a bank, his mother is a schoolteacher. It's one of the cosiest places I've been in, radiating neatness and peace. Gilbert came for me rather late, so I had time to get a good rest in my bed with its fine linen sheets.

We walked along the half rural, half urban streets. The weather was heavenly. The transparent water formed a clear little pool beneath the arched bridge. Gilbert greeted everyone we met, and stroked a dog that followed him. . . . "You're coming tonight, aren't you?" a cyclist called out to him. A man with his hands in his pockets stopped him. "Just a moment, Gilbert. . . ." They had a whispered conversation. We went on our way. Some boys dressed as mountaineers, with knapsacks and heavy boots, hailed Gilbert cordially but discreetly. "You know everybody here, don't you?" I remarked. . . . True, I envied Gilbert for being as much a part of the village as the stones of the houses, the water in the river. . . . "Yes, everybody," he replied. "I went to school with our worst collaborationist. His mother owns a grocery store, and she used to give me a sweet every time I went there on an errand for my mother. . . . Our present mayor, a thorough-paced scoundrel, taught me to fish . . . I love fishing. . . . To say nothing of the fellows I went bowling and played football with. . . . We have only three militiamen, and one of them, of course, is the son of the woman who gave me the sweets. . . . And the head of the Legion was one of my parents' marriage witnesses."

We had lunch at Gilbert's house. His mother is a small, bent woman, with eyes still young; his father a solidly built, ruddy-faced man with completely white hair. He's an old, militant Party member. They've already been raided twice, and that's why they prefer putting me up elsewhere. The military leader, who goes under the name of Renaud, and M. Noiret, the ex-garage man, also had lunch with us, and I took the occasion to ask them several questions about the *maquis*. I didn't want to be completely ignorant when I got there. . . . They maintained that in this region one-third of the youths evading the forced labour call-up—the defaulters, so called—are in the *maquis*, where they receive military training. It's very heartening, for if our boys don't want to go to Germany, and prefer to go into hiding (which is already a first step towards resistance), there's something negative about this attitude that makes you think of stealth and desertion. Those defaulters who are scattered among the farms, doing nothing but wait until the storm passes, must be transformed into combatants, lead martial lives, learn military discipline, become part of an army that is preparing to fight and free the country. That is why it's heartening to hear that thirty-three per cent of the defaulters in this district are in the *maquis* . . . I wanted to know how the boys go about finding their way into the real *maquis*, and what is done about rounding up the isolated defaulters and getting them to join the Resistance. But this problem, which is a very difficult one in the towns, seems to be non-existent in the little villages, where everybody knows all about everybody else, where cousin X's son is hiding, on which of the deserted farms the nearest *maquis* unit is located, and who is the go-between in the village. . . . But things shouldn't be handled this way! It's terribly dangerous! True . . . but people don't know how to keep their mouths shut. After they've burnt their fingers once or twice they may learn to keep quiet. . . . Meanwhile everybody in the village is in the secret, and few people ever come here from the outside. I still think more could be done about the isolated ones, but I don't like to insist. They tell me that everybody here knows that these three people handle the affairs of the *maquis*, and that Renaud is their leader. Even though he wears a Tyrolean hat with the brim turned down, dark glasses, and a brand new moustache, everybody knows that he is really Monsieur B., the teacher. His disguise is effective only outside a radius of fifteen miles. Incidentally, this teacher is good at his job, as military commander, with his calm gestures, his measured, penetrating voice. He seems to have no nerves, and you can see by his round, brown eyes fringed with black lashes that he's used to being obeyed, and expects it. You don't have to scratch very deep to encounter solid rock, both physical and moral, beneath that amiable and polite exterior . . . I can well imagine that our commander stood no nonsense in his maths classes.

Gilbert is blond as wheat and looks like ten Aryans, and has a laugh that rattles the window-panes. He plays this perilous and exciting game of risking his life for a just cause with passion. I feel an anxious tenderness for him . . . I can see his mother folding her hands to keep from wringing them, since she's neither able nor willing to prevent her son from risking his life. She admires him, and helps him as best she can, and agonizes with fear.

M. Noiret, the ex-garage man, might also be an ex-bar-loafer. He's about thirty, something of a dandy, with great black eyes and wavy hair, a handsome Southerner, with a passion for fair play.

After lunch people began dropping in. I felt a little lost among all those people drinking coffee and small glasses of spirits. There was a boy four or five years old who climbed on everybody's lap and shouted "Police" at the top of his lungs, every time steps sounded on the stairs. There was a pregnant young woman with a handsome, healthy face, a man in a military coat with civilian buttons, another, very dignified, with white hair and a black, wide-brimmed hat. The arrival of a chubby-faced fellow who looked like a wrestler caused much excitement. "What's happened to you, Maurice? How you stink!" In fact, he gave off an over-powering fragrance. "I was carrying a bottle of scent for some-one, and it broke and spilled into my tobacco." That tobacco! Whenever anybody took some of it to roll a cigarette the reek of scent brought up the story of the scent bottle flask. Before the war, Maurice was a lorry driver. You could see that he was very strong, and I was told he was a dare-devil. When he arrived at the *maquis* dressed in a policeman's uniform, driving a light lorry borrowed from his own police chief, bringing all kinds of food, everybody was delighted. But his enterprises hadn't always been so tame.

We left after lunch, the military leader, Gilbert, M. Noiret, and I. I'll see the others when I get back, or perhaps *en route*.

The black Gestapo car came out of the fog, the landscape gradually flung back its white sheets, and the sun appeared once more on the grass and stone plateau. No sign either of man or beast. We were going through a country where it seemed that nobody had ever been before us. I was wide awake. The car had left the main road, and we were pitching and rolling on a little grass-covered path, among trees and shrubs that crackled and lashed the car as we passed. We penetrated ever deeper into the verdure, which seemed to close irrevocably behind us, obliterating our traces. A turn, and then an armed man dressed in khaki. He gave a military salute: it was the first *maquis* sentry.

The tricoloured flag with the cross of Lorraine floated in the sky behind a high stone wall. We stopped before the gate and were saluted by a sentry. Renaud, the commander, got out of the car, and I followed him, while behind us Gilbert and M. Noiret carried with all due honour the sub-machine gun in its black case. . . .

A grassy courtyard, a big white house on the edge of a chasm edged by a chain of mountains. The men stood in ranks in the courtyard. The commander stepped forward:

"Company, attention!"

They wore leather jackets and khaki breeches. They stood with chests out, heads high, their arms glued to their rigid bodies. . . . The sky was blue, the calm unbroken.

"Stand easy. . . ."

I heard Renaud introducing me to the company, but my thoughts wandered. I was thinking about those boys lined up before us. . . . I was thinking that each of them had had an address, a job, a bed with sheets. . . . They had worked, gone to cafés, caught the bus, played with their children, and been spoiled by their mothers. . . . Now they live in hiding with the comrades. That's a thing that makes your heart beat.

Renaud finished his little speech, and we went into the house. A large, dim room, earth floor, a table, benches, a fire on the hearth, a smoking cauldron. They slept in the next room, the light room that looked out over the chasm. The straw was clean, and the country beautiful. There were twelve lads, handsome, well built, neat, shaved, and clean. No illness, no boredom, no vermin, and they complained neither of the discipline nor the solitude. . . . They had no time to become bored, occupied as they were with drill, problems of supply, and changing their location whenever the *maquis* was spotted. They would barely get installed before they'd have to move on again. They were well fed; the peasants denied them nothing, although they asked exorbitant prices. In a few cases they had been forced to pay black-market prices. Black-market prices? Wouldn't it make the stones of the hamlets blush? Yes, but now that's how things are, and besides, there has been some progress. They willingly sell us everything we need now; they no longer treat us like thieves. Yes, unquestionably there has been progress. It's a strange thing. . . .

Their sons, brothers, husbands, whom they tremble for, are here, willing to fight for them and us, yet they treat them in the same way as they do those gentlemen who glut themselves with steaks and "extras" in the restaurants. . . . Oh, these peasants! The "people of the plains", to use the expression which distinguishes the large population of France from the *maquis*, are often rather below the mark, even though I don't always share the arrogance and conceit of some of the young combatants, the heroes of today and tomorrow. . . . But can you imagine a front without support behind it? Who would furnish the combatants with all they need? It's a truism, after all. The people of France needn't emigrate in a body to the *maquis*. . . . There's a certain air of nobility about fighting with firearms, but there are different kinds of conflict, and there are heroes in the plains quite equal to those in the *maquis*. Granted that the people of the plains, who are so ready to knit sweaters for young soldiers and send packages to the war prisoners, don't go out of their way to help the defaulters. It's more difficult, too, because there's no postal service to the *maquis*. Yet a large proportion of the population is behind them, because (as all agree) they've left with the approval of their families. In fact, even today, there are probably more people in the plains who daily risk their lives in opposing the occupation forces than there are in the *maquis*. To each his part.

And so it goes on—training, supplies, fatigues: but what they really live for is a raid. In this *maquis* all the equipment comes from a Youth Depot. They actually eat food that has been "provided" by a branch of the National Relief Fund. (They gave me some excellent spice cake to try.) These raids enable the *maquis* to live, yet they limit them as much as they can, since it's really the ones directed against the Germans that are their true *raison d'être*. They get excited and start talking. . . . Raids are the spice of their lives, raids which teach them how to act like partisans, to harass and attack the occupation troops and make their lives impossible. Some are scarcely more than boys, and these are the ones who delight in playing Indian, whose desire for danger and adventure finds satisfaction in these hazardous attacks, while for the others it is the exalting idea of liberating the country that comes first. In this *maquis* the great problem, and the only cause of demoralization and depression, is the lack of arms: twelve men have, between them, only three revolvers and four old hunting rifles. The arrival of the sub-machine gun is a great event. They have only one demand: arms, arms!

12

WE rolled along at full speed on the narrow departmental road. It was getting late, and the sky had lost its brilliance. . . .

"Yes," said Renaud, who was in the driver's seat, beside me. "We should have received some parachuted arms. . . . I don't know how it happened, but they disappeared under our noses. Somebody else got them . . ."

He spoke calmly, without passion, his eyes on the road.

"I'm responsible for their lives, and I can't let them go into danger with bare hands. . . . Not to mention that the *maquis* may be surrounded and they'll be killed without being able to defend themselves. . . ."

I have too vivid an imagination: I can see the twelve of them going out in a body, tall, clean-cut, handsome; I can see them advance. . . .

We reached the village late in the evening. It was a tiny village— just a few houses nestling against the mountainside. I had the feeling that I was cut off from the world for good. . . . Two deeply tanned youngsters from the neighbouring *maquis* took me to a kind of barn, where there was a room in the back filled by two big wooden beds. "There's an inn in the village, but it's full tonight, and besides you're better off here. Whenever one of us goes sick he comes here to sleep." They stumped off in their heavy nailed boots. The madly flickering candlelight made me dizzy; I blew out the candle, and then felt free to open the shutters. It was unbearably beautiful outside, with a full moon. I lay down on the bed fully dressed; I could see the sky over the roof, and between the cracks of the floor a fresh wind came in. In the house which I could see through the window lived the only collaborationist in the hamlet. It was because of him that the boys told me to keep the shutters closed. I couldn't go to sleep, but it wasn't on account of the collaborationist. . . .

I got up very early and was ready at seven o'clock. Renaud

had said he would come for me in time for hoisting the flag; this *maquis* unit was just three-quarters of a mile away. But at nine o'clock nobody had come. . . . I made a tour of the village, not daring to go too far afield, or to show myself too much, on account of that cursed collaborationist. I was afraid of causing a sensation, of having people ask who I might be. It's not often that anyone turns up here who is so conspicuously *not* from this part of the country. I roamed behind the houses until I came upon a big, friendly peasant woman, who said, "They're keeping you waiting. . . ." So she was in the secret—but then she owned the barn, and was quite distressed because they hadn't told her the night before, and because I had had to sleep in a dusty room that hadn't even been swept. It was a good thing the boys had at least remembered to bring me some water. . . . She told me all the details of how she had nursed a boy with tonsillitis in that house, and another with influenza. In short, it's the infirmary of the *maquis*. For one boy, she told me, they had had to call the doctor from C——, and the doctor had asked a lot of questions: But where is this young man from? Surely not from the village? A cousin? Whose son? All the same, the doctor had been very kind and had come back twice. Surely he must have known what was up. . . . The only worry is the village black sheep, the neighbour—oh, that neighbour!—and his wife, who is even worse than he. . . . The other day somebody happened to mention in front of her that the Gestapo had come. . . . And she exclaimed: "Gestapo? What's that?" He travels for a firm of grocers, and he's still travelling. I wonder what he has to sell, in these times. . . . It seems he has bought a plot of land at X——, forty miles from the village. But that isn't far enough off. He'll have trouble all the same, though he thinks he can hide himself! But in the meantime . . . The boys aren't careful. If you tell them to be careful, they say, "If he doesn't keep his mouth shut we'll teach him a lesson! Damn the fellow. They didn't see you, I hope." The conversation with the peasant woman began to repeat itself. I didn't know what to do next. . . . Also I was uneasy, and no longer able to admire the picturesque village, this splendid country of rock and grass. It began to get hot. "Haven't they come yet, madame?" the wheelwright shouted as I passed by his shop. "Well, he's in it, too," I thought. I entered the shop, which was stacked with wheels, a mechanical saw, boards, and old iron. . . . At the back, astride a chair, his chin on the back-rest, sat an enormous man having his hair cut by the wheelwright. The wheelwright was also the barber, and on the wall there was a small mirror, a very white smock hanging on a nail, and towels on a table covered with white oilcloth. . . . "Do you want the paper, Madame?" asked the large man. "Not that there's anything in it, but you may as well look at it while you wait. . . . They'll be here soon now, it's quite close." Evidently it was known why I was here and whom I was waiting for. "He owns the house where the *maquis* are quartered," the wheelwright explained by way of introduction. But I had read the whole paper, and the haircut was almost finished, and still they hadn't come. So I decided to go to the inn, especially since I was ravenously hungry.

Our black car stood before the inn, abandoned among the chickens, geese, and dogs. . . . "They'll be here soon," the innkeeper said encouragingly. So she too . . . Well, since they all knew. . . . She served me magnificent coffee with milk, snow-white bread, and butter. It's like the forgotten pre-war days in this lost village. . . . In the room, which was dusky and humming with flies, there was a wooden table, covered with crumbs and dishes. A very old woman, still vigorous, seemed to be the innkeeper's mother. In the corner sat a boy from the *maquis*, with an injured leg. Beside him was his wife, who had come to see him. A man in airman's boots, who had come out of one of the bedrooms, the doors of which opened on the common room, called out to me in a jolly voice, "So you have come to visit the *maquis*, Madame!" Taken unawares, I muttered something unintelligible. "Perhaps you take me for the Gestapo?" he said, teasing me. So I began to be confidential; evidently I had been tactless and hurt his feelings. As I was to learn later, he was the book-keeper at the inn. The innkeeper herself was the supply agent for the *maquis*. I got on to my pet theme again: "Why do you think there are so many on their own? Why are there still so many who are not in contact with the *maquis*?" The young book-keeper got very excited. "It can't be helped. There's too much politics in the *maquis*. The royalists say confidently, 'Today we march with the communists, but tomorrow we'll give them the boot,' and the communists, on their part, say the same. . . . How can you expect anything better? Fortunately it's different in our district. Besides, if they played politics here my boss wouldn't supply them. It's as simple as that!" To judge from his conversation, the book-keeper might have been a socialist. However, I didn't believe that it was an excess of politics that kept the youngsters from joining the *maquis*. He didn't convince me of that.

Ah! here was Renaud at last. "What happened? Did you forget all about me?" It turned out that the night before a fellow had come to the *maquis*, where the three of them, M. Renaud, Gilbert, and M. Noiret, had slept, with information about where the parachuted arms had come down. . . . They were going to go and look for them. It was absolutely necessary to do it this very day. However, they would still show me the *maquis*, and afterwards they would take me somewhere where there was some means of communication, and leave me there. Since they had promised that I should see the flag hoisted, they would take me there: the fellows were waiting for us.

But while yesterday they had had only me to think of, today they had other things on their minds, and it was still quite a while before we got started. Renaud, Gilbert, and M. Noiret came and went, reappeared and disappeared. . . . To increase the general agitation there was the fact that two fellows who had left on a mission the day before, and should have returned that same evening, had not yet turned up. There was talk of 'phoning, but nobody 'phoned; instead, someone was sent to the father of X——, who had been to C—— and might know something about it. But I can't remember why it was that the messenger never returned from his errand. Strangers kept arriving at the inn, all evidently implicated, among them the two boys who had showed me to my room the night before. There was also a huge fellow with a bare hairy chest, trousers that were too short, and dirty feet in espadrilles, and another with a big nose, a beret, and velveteen trousers. He was dressed like a peasant, but was evidently a worker, a mechanic. He was the one who had brought news of the parachuted arms. The black car panted outside the inn. Renaud tinkered with the motor, dogs barked, hens cackled.

We went on foot across the lovely, scented fields. . . . They told me that it would be a ten-minute walk. Already we could see the smoke rising from behind the trees where the house was hidden.

There it was, a large building, looking like a church without a cross, in the middle of a clearing, at the bottom of a hollow surrounded by mountains. We approached the house without meeting a single sentry. We had to walk in and announce ourselves before they took any notice of us. . . . It was evident that they no longer expected us.

"Company, attention!"

Here they were, chests out, heads high, arms glued to their stiff bodies. . . . Thirty-five of them. Big and small ones, straight and crooked ones. All dressed in ragged clothes. They wore espadrilles and sandals, and some were barefooted, while a few had nailed boots. Now it's summer and they are tanned—the sun takes care of them—but they could not spend the winter like that. . . . Peasant faces, poorly shaved, hair hanging down their necks. . . .

"Raise the colours!"

The tricoloured flag with the Lorraine cross, a poor, faded rag, jerked up the pole, which was only a thin, twisted tree from which the branches had been lopped. . . . I felt very much like crying.

"Stand at ease. . . ."

Renaud made his little speech. . . . Then we went into the house. It was almost eleven o'clock, but the huge room had not been swept, unwashed mess kits lay about, and filthy playing-cards were strewn over the table, among crumbs and peelings. When I asked about the sentry they said with great assurance: "We don't need a sentry here. The village watches out for us, and if there were anything up we would know . . ." Perhaps. But a *maquis* half a mile from a village seemed rather too close. "But it's the village that watches out for us!" How about the traitor, the commercial traveller? "Oh, him, we'll take care of him. Just wait and see . . ." Well, it's not my affair. Here, as in the other *maquis*, different though that was, they don't complain, they get good food, and they're not bored, especially since they are close to the village, which, as they say, is the best village in France. They lack only one thing: arms. They were absolutely frantic on that point. What would they do, for instance, if the same thing were to happen as had occurred at their previous encampment, forcing them to leave? There was a fellow who prowled round the camp every night. They could see his lighted cigarette, and they found German cigarette butts all round the camp. . . . He was a daring fellow, coming so close all by himself. The sentry fired at him, but missed, and he got away. . . . If they hadn't left in time, if they had been encircled, they would have had nothing to defend themselves with. And, in fact, those old sporting guns I saw on the wall would have been of little use. "Especially since they're never cleaned," remarked M. Noiret. . . . All right, all right. . . . It wasn't my job to take them to task. I who sleep in a bedroom all to myself, with linen sheets. I got up to leave, and all I dared to say to them was that a *maquis* bearing the name "*Maquis Guy Mocquet*" could not fail to prove worthy of its name . . . I shook their hands. They were so charming, so appealing in their rags. God only knows what's in store for these lads. . . . They went with us as far as the great trees that bordered the clearing, and a little fellow with a blond beard, one of those young beards soldiers like wearing in this war, asked me suddenly, "Who is Guy Mocquet?" Poor devils! They grope in the shadows, seeking a cause to live and die for, without even the comfort of knowing who Guy Mocquet was—seventeen-year-old martyr who gave his life for France.

We returned to the village. It was noon and very hot, and I had a headache and felt depressed. It's all very well to say *Keep off politics*; but would it involve politics to explain to them who Guy Mocquet was? The flies stuck to us afterwards in the little parlour of the inn, behind the bar-room. Everybody was there. We were about to have lunch. Nobody paid any attention to me, nor did I bother about anybody. I was busy enough with the thoughts running through my head. . . . The two youngsters who had left the day before still hadn't returned. Somebody should surely telephone. . . . The meal was excellent, although it was eaten in a constant bustle and uproar. Renaud was called away between two mouthfuls, and Gilbert and M. Noiret were doing some complicated reasoning. When the two missing men arrived at last they were received apathetically: nothing had happened to them after all. They had been delayed, and were asked to stay overnight, and then they weren't allowed to leave today without their noon meal. The *maquis* will get a lorryload of potatoes: that's a promise. It was after two o'clock. We were drinking coffee. It was really much too hot. "Will you excuse us,

Madame? We must make a little trip. Half an hour at the most . . ."
said Renaud. But if I had happened to object it would have made
no difference.

Half an hour at the most! It was six o'clock, and still they
hadn't returned. I had reread the paper and gone back to the
peasant woman, who told me all over again about the doctor, and
the commercial traveller who was a collaborator. . . . But the wheelwright was no longer in his shop. I found him in a little shed,
busy shoeing some oxen. I no longer felt embarrassed to be
strolling through the village. The countryside looked smiling,
but I didn't dare go too far afield. The "half-hour" might end any
moment. The village, plunged in a silence punctuated by the
clink of the wheelwright's hammer, dozed quietly and peacefully.

The black car arrived almost at the same moment as the
gasogene car, the latter bringing Maurice, and Gilbert's father,
with grave news. The militiaman (he whose mother, the grocer's
wife, had given Gilbert sweets) had furnished the Gestapo with a
list of ten persons, including Gilbert. They had discovered this
at the prefecture. There was no doubt about it. We were in the
little back room once more . . . Maurice was crimson with rage.
"I've told you a hundred times that he should be got out of the
way! But you kept on insisting that he was the only son of his
mother. . . ." The little room buzzed with talk. The man in the
wide-brimmed hat was also there, evidently an intellectual, and
the fellow who had come the night before with news about the
arms, and the big fellow with the bare, hairy chest, and the
cashier at the inn . . . "I'm an only son myself," Gilbert said at
last, very gloomily, "and I suppose my mother is fond of me . . ."

His father took no part in the discussion. "Give me some tobacco, Maurice," he said. "Good God, how it does stink!" In all
this excitement he and Maurice almost forgot to mention that the
roads were blocked by the police. Not only two or three local
policemen—that would be nothing—but reinforcements brought
from a distance, and overturned carts blocking the roads. . . . As
for them, they had been allowed through with their gas-car,
because their papers were in order. . . . "There's no doubt that the
B—— *maquis* made the raid they planned," said Renaud with
satisfaction. "That's excellent. It's eight o'clock now. Let's get

going . . . Maurice, you come with us. You drive. You can take us to C—— by side roads. You know the country. Once we get there we'll drop you, and you'll manage. . . ." "I don't want to go to C——. Why to C——? I have no business there." "That'll do," Renaud cut in. "Have a look at the car. There's something jammed. See what it is . . ." Maurice left the room. Renaud suddenly seemed to remember my existence. "I'm sorry, Madame, but you'll have to go back in the gas-car. I daren't take you with us. We have no licence or papers. . . . If we should be stopped we couldn't wait to explain, but would have to either shoot or bolt, without bothering about you. I'd rather you returned quietly in the gas-car. Gilbert's father and M. Moiret will take you back. You'll be safe with them. . . ." So out I went to the gas-car.

Gilbert's father was struggling with the broken-winded old contraption, which stood panting outside the inn, while Maurice tinkered with the engine of the black car. . . . "So we are to take you back, Madame?" M. Noiret asked. "I'm afraid you'll have to wait another hour. We must return those two youngsters to their *maquis* first . . ." Alas! I went down the street. Maurice was wiping his hands. He had finished. The car was ready to go. . . . "Oh yes, I know the road!" he said with tears in his voice, "but why the hell should I go? You've got business there, but what about me?" "That's enough; get in," said Renaud. "Don't talk so much and give me some of that nice tobacco. . . ." I opened the door of the car and said, "I'm going with you." "As you wish, Madame. But I'll ask you to sit in the back for safety." I had been afraid that he would protest, but no, he had told me what the risk was, and it was my own business. I was no longer a child.

I sat between Gilbert and the man with the big nose and the velveteen trousers, who had the news about the parachuted arms. They would take me to C——, where I could sleep and get a bus the next morning.

Night was falling. I felt stifled between Gilbert and the other man, both of whom were dozing. The lovely sunset was hidden by the backs of Renaud and Maurice. The animals were coming in from the fields. The peasants waved their arms to keep them out of our way; the oxen stood still in the middle of the road. Sheep stood in an undulating mass, herded by barking dogs. . . . "Well," said my neighbour with the big nose, "I've just had a little nap. . . . It's five nights now since I've slept. . . . They almost got me, the swine. They ambushed me at every crossroads, and I only abandoned my bike in the nick of time. I didn't dare go to sleep in the barn for fear I might snore, and I can hardly keep myself from coughing! It seems they were prowling round the barn all night long. It's a good thing I didn't cough!" I didn't know the beginning of the story, but it made no difference. It was clear enough without a beginning, and well suited to the night through which we were now driving, hoping to avoid the police. When we came to a large village, Maurice leaned out of the door and talked in dialect with a peasant: "Any police by the bridge?" "No, it's all quiet round here. . . ."

A very large village. We stopped in front of one of the houses. Gilbert and Renaud got out. I've no idea what they did in the house. The man with the big nose slept, while Maurice walked up and down in front of the car. . . . I too got out, it was so stifling inside. Again I couldn't help thinking of Spain. "If the Spanish war hadn't been lost . . ." I said to the air. . . . But Maurice heard me. "Yes, you're right." In a sudden fury he added, "That bastard Hitler again!" The air and Maurice's fury did me good. Renaud and Gilbert came back. We got going again. . . .

It was night now. We passed through little hamlets with lighted windows, nestling against the mountains. The roads were full of ruts. . . . "Before we hit C—— we'll have to go along the national highway for three hundred yards. It will be impossible to avoid it." There were many hairpin bends. Our front wheels seemed suspended in the void above a chasm. Maurice was a remarkable driver. . . . We drove slowly down a kind of goat path where normally we would have had a smash. "Listen," said Maurice. "I'll tell you something funny. You see that cabin?" Indeed there was a dark shape that might well have been a cabin. "That's where I had my first girl!" We all laughed madly. . . .

The car was still descending the hill slowly. Below us we could see the national highway, like a broad river behind the trees. We were only fifty feet from it when a light, white and pitiless, leaped out. . . . It was the headlights of a big car standing some distance from us on the road, and by their light we could see another car, with its lights switched off, standing at the foot of the road we were descending. . . . Maurice put on the brakes. "What's up?"

said Gilbert, opening the door. "What's up?" A revolver appeared in the hand of the man with the velveteen trousers. I had already dived towards the open door behind Gilbert. . . . But the two cars started and drove away rapidly. I hadn't had time to be afraid.

We drove at full speed along the national highway. Here was the beginning of C——. This was where I got out. The car stopped and all four of them shook my hand. "Thanks, I'll manage. It's just as well for me not to be seen with you in this ghastly car. . . . Thanks again, and I'll be seeing you in a better life!"

I was able to find a room; cool, with the window wide open on a magnificent, starlit mountain landscape. What if I were to give up my job and work only for the *maquis?* . . . Renaud is no longer a teacher, Gilbert is no longer a student, M. Noiret no longer cares about sports and motor-cars, Maurice no longer drives a lorry, and all the young men in the *maquis* are no longer what they used to be: they are all fighters. . . . At first I saw only their faults, but now I've lost my heart to the *maquis,* with their daring, their high spirit, and their hopes. . . . I was with them in theory before I went to see for myself, but now I want to be really with them. I want to know whether the wart they cut open with nail scissors became infected, whether the lorryload of potatoes ever reached them; I want them to have a radio; I want . . . What can I do to help them? They must be helped at all costs.

Here I am in Lyons again, sleeping in the back room of a grocer's shop, and feeling very well and safe.

The new printing office functions smoothly. The new press-man is managing all right.

No news from Jean. I keep on repeating to myself, the Boches will leave, Jean will come back. But do I really believe it? This waiting is getting to be too much for me!

I must go to the *Galeries Lafayette* to try to get some handker-chiefs, and if possible some espadrilles, anything light to put on my feet, they hurt so. . . . Also some elastic for garters. . . . A very domestic day. . . .

13

*Monsieur Blin was still in bed when his deaf and dumb housekeeper
knocked at the door of his room: she uttered sounds and pointed
towards the garden. He looked through the window: he saw a stranger
in the middle of the lawn, holding under his arm a wicker basket
like those used for sending flowers. He pushed the housekeeper towards
the door and shouted through the window, "Come in!" As he was,
in his pyjamas, he ran towards the man who was already walking
up the steps into the parlour. "You come from Louise?" he said
hastily.*

*"Yes," said the man, opening the little wicker basket with his thin,
pale hands. "She was picked up in a raid in the street close to the* Galeries
Lafayette. *By some horrible mischance, she was recognized. . . . It's all
up with her." He opened the lid. The little basket was full of violets, and
under the violets lay an exercise book. "I've brought you this," the man
said, drawing out the notebook. "I've kept her clothes, in case they could
be got to her."*

"Is there nothing I can do?" Monsieur Blin stammered. . . .

*"If anything can be done it will be done. . . . We'll do everything
that's humanly possible for Louise. Good-bye, Monsieur; you know our
Letter Box."*

*He went down the steps of the porch. Monsieur Blin's pudgy fingers
groped among the violets. Louise! . . . Louise! . . .*

*Louise Delfort was deported to Germany. News of her execution
did not arrive until the autumn of '43, which was not the date of
victory.*

". . . I've put my notebooks in a metal box, to be buried
under the peach tree in the garden . . ."

*Louise! Louise! The personification of Life. It was unthinkable.
Leaning against the wall, the owner of the house watched the man digging
the earth beside the peach tree, a big, strong man, digging the earth in a
kind of desperate affection, as though it covered Louise's body. . . . It was
a big black box with gilt lines on the lid. Jean, the one whose
real name was Jean, lifted the box out of the hole. Yes, the little
pile of notebooks was there: School . . . Headmistress . . . Note-*

book . . . Belonging to. . . . They were a little damp, but otherwise undamaged.

"I'll take them along," said Jean. He didn't even stop to shake hands with Monsieur Blin, who was still leaning against the wall; he walked off, his booty under his arm. It was the manufacturer who filled up the hole and sealed Louise's grave.

Saint-Donat,
   April, 1944.

A FINE OF
TWO HUNDRED FRANCS

EPILOGUE

EVERYTHING'S in a terrible mess: railways, the minds of men, and food supplies. . . . Will it be over tomorrow; will it last another winter, another month, or a century? The hope of peace hangs over us like a sword. Housewives have ceased sweeping and making soup. Everyone eats cold food, drinks any sort of liquid. Writers no longer write—is there going to be a censorship, or not? The factories are short of raw materials, the owners are afraid of raids, half the workers are idle, the peasants look upwards as they reap the harvest, watching for the 'planes that swoop down and machine-gun anyone in sight. . . . There's an all-pervading smell of rotting peaches. Peaches sell one franc a pound, or seventy-five francs. The black markets serve their customers beefsteak, butter, and trout in the front room, oblivious of decency and prudence; ration points are like deflated currency, people queue up in front of bakeries at dawn. There's a hail of orders against driving cars, leaving the house or coming back, harbouring strangers, hiding, hurrying. And yet people are doing all these things with impunity. . . . Broken-down lorries rumble about, with or without authorization, until they are caught and taken over by the *maquis*, or the Boches. Motor-cars do a hundred miles an hour, terrifying the villagers. There are arrests, tortures, executions by the thousand. The danger lies not in doing this or that, but in happening to be on the spot where a raid occurs. There's a continual mutter in the air, punctuated by explosions. The stormy sky, the azure blue sky, is streaked by a thousand lightnings—what fire is setting it aflame? Thousands wait with ears pricked and watchful eyes. Those who fight, and those who help the fighters, and those who tremble—all of us are waiting.

"A poor sort of invasion," somebody said. That was in June. The great hope had turned sour, like milk at the approach of a storm. After twenty-four hours everybody's joy had drooped and wilted. You had to start waiting again, in an ever-deepening bath of blood, surrounded by an heroic community now going rather to seed. Life was bitter, down to the smallest details. It was bitter to see the cowardice and pettiness that survive on this storm-tossed raft, the black market, the monstrous egotism, the stupidity, the darkness, the heroism that should be as pure as the Vercors snows, graft, and poverty, ambition, slander, trustfulness and treachery, ghastly execution, the bitter, sleepless nights, noisy with mosquitoes and idiotic shells. . . . "A poor sort of invasion. . . ."

And yet it had been a great feeling to see the modest words "A fine of two hundred francs for the first rip," turn up among the welter of personal messages. No, it was neither oracular nor funny, it was clear and sensible, like a French phrase in a foreign text. What it meant was "Go into action!"

"Go into action," said the message. The chief was in the *bistro*, standing on a chair, his ear glued to the radio, which had been put up very high. His face was red. His adjutant and the quartermaster came running from the other end of the village; they, too, knew that there was "a fine of two hundred francs for the first rip". They were on tenterhooks, and they talked very loud. The night, which had merely misted over at first, became turbulent and restless. . . . There were some who did not know, who had no idea, that there was "a fine of two hundred francs for the first rip", but the night knew, became turbulent, and restless. . . . At the inn, where the wounded man from the last skirmish was being cared for, the proprietress looked on, silent and uneasy, while people mounted and descended the stairs, carrying their joy like brimming cups. The upper corridor, partitioned with thin, wooden walls, rumbled like a loudspeaker. Steps and loud voices stopped at the door, and there was a terrific knocking: they came in, already in uniform, helmeted, wearing tricolour arm bands, revolvers in their belts. Caution was a thing of the past. They had waited two years! That was long enough! A fine of two hundred francs for the first rip!

At dawn they brought back the helmeted cherub, pink and white, dainty as a chocolate soldier, visibly fated to be broken.

Did he achieve his mission? History saw only his departure and his return, and the bed in the first-aid station set up in the baker's house.

They brought him back at dawn after the troubled night which passed into a mad day. The first rip: the invasion.

There were armed men on the roads, in the villages, armed men getting in and out of lorries, armed men in the streets and *bistros*, women on the thresholds, children screaming. A long convoy of lorries blocked the main street and the town square: the whole French personnel of an airport, leaving for the *maquis*, and their commandant standing by helpless and bewildered. Our officer, who the night before had stood on his chair to listen to the radio, and his adjutant, were in glittering uniforms. And beneath the general sense of relief there were sudden shocks of surprise that the country was still crowded with Boches. It was almost beyond belief.

The next day things started to go wrong. The men were on the road for twenty-four hours, and nobody thought of relieving or feeding them. People didn't know how to use their weapons. No one would listen to anyone else. The officers could scarcely be induced to stop swaggering and lead their men up into the hills. You see, it isn't the victory yet, it's just the beginning of the conflict. Men departed, amidst tears and curses of wives and parents; others came down from the hills. They had had enough of the heroic life already. The sun still shone brightly, but the enthusiasm was turning sour.

All sorts of things went wrong. A youngster whom no one had remembered to relieve on the first day got pneumonia. A policeman who had left for the *maquis* came back in terror from up there, saying that they looked at him unpleasantly, and wouldn't take orders from him. . . . The butcher complained about the defaulters. Nothing happened. The men grew bored in the *maquis*, and the civilians did nothing but incessantly criticize. The first-aid station in the baker's house was never empty. The young fellows didn't know how to handle arms, and shot themselves. "Life is hard," said the little chocolate soldier, sitting on the table while they probed his wound again in search of the pieces of his helmet. . . .

The weather was fine, blue and green beneath a golden sun.

There was no sign of Boches or Vichyites. Everyone was waiting, and wondering how things were going to turn out. What were they doing in the *maquis*? What were we all doing? Euphoria had died a beautiful death. "It's a poor sort of invasion!"

Two officers fell out of the sky, one English and one French. The radio operator who jumped with them was killed: his parachute failed to open. "He didn't know how to work it," said the heart-broken Englishman. But the parachute bearing the radio equipment and clothing also failed to open. The two officers came just as they were, their hands in their pockets, in uniform. The Frenchman wore a blouse, braid, and *France* stitched on his sleeve; the Englishman, without blouse or braid, wore khaki shirt and trousers, nothing on his sleeve. He was in command. He was blond and handsome, like the pictured Englishman. The Frenchman was grim, dark, and spectacled. What was he—people asked: priest, Jew, Freemason, professional officer, aristocrat? . . . But about the Englishman they all agreed: Intelligence Service.

They spent the night with the *maquis*, and arrived in the village next day. The car stopped in front of the doctor's house. The doctor received and transmitted the messages of liaison agents; he had organized the first aid post in the baker's house, and found hideouts for the youngsters, the Jews, men on the run; had set up the sending station and a man to operate it; he was the one who possessed all the rubber stamps for forged papers. People watched the two officers and the leader of the *maquis* get out of the car in broad daylight, in the centre of the village, before the doctor's house. They watched tactfully, in silence. "This is a strange sort of occupied country," said the French officer, mounting the steps.

There was a crowd in the doctor's dining-room: the doctor and his wife, another doctor, the doctor's son-in-law, the leader of the *maquis* where the two officers had spent the night, a couple who were friends of the doctor, and the doctor's children, who kept running back and forth through the room to the garden. The table was strewn with English staff maps. The Englishman, affable and cordial, had everything explained to him. The Frenchman kept silent. Whenever he found it useful, the Englishman no longer understood French. The Frenchman understood, and said nothing.

The two officers went back to the car; they left directly for the *maquis* in the hills, to meet other leaders and men, to hear tales of prowess and exploits. The handsome Englishman congratulated everybody, and then went for a walk. The Frenchman gathered the leaders round him. "You've told us about the things that are going well; now tell me your difficulties." He was deluged with grievances.

They dined at the aid station in the baker's house. It was very late. The baker himself prepared the dinner, and the nurse, who was the daughter of the owner of the sawmill, waited at table. They had cold veal and cream buns. "Whose big bed is that on the left as you go upstairs?" asked the Englishman. He ate neither the cold veal nor the buns, and he tried desperately to keep from falling asleep at table, while he dreamed of the big bed he had seen. He hadn't slept for two nights, not a wink. . . . He had his troubles: he had been sent to France on the day he was supposed to have been married. The Frenchman pretended not to be tired, and talked about Algiers with sinister animation. The leader, the one who had swaggered so on the day of the landing, and had since subsided, rose before the end of the meal. "You see, sir," he said, "I can't even eat in peace. I must attend a political meeting." No one could tell what the officers thought of it, but the English officer had to stay awake, because they too were to attend a political meeting a little later. Then they would be taken back to the *maquis* for safety. In a sudden access of good sense, the villagers would not permit the English officer to sleep in the big bed.

The officers had left. There was nothing to do but wait through those grand, hot days. "Well, it was a poor sort of invasion . . ." The doctor continued to distribute forged papers (here are the stamps, help yourself . . .); the Red Cross ambulance parked in front of his door was used to transport arms; there was a rumour that a woman assistant who slept in his office had arrested the prefect of the department; two men who arrived drenched, after swimming the river, were the ones who had killed a militiaman and escaped from the police; the *maquis*, arriving on foot and in cars, invaded the doctor's house, and sometimes at dawn one heard loud voices. That was when they came back from the parachutings and had their breakfast. The doctor's whole family, aided by his patients, were busy ripping up the parachutes to make shirts and clothing for the boys. The silken cords were taken apart and knitted into socks. A strange sort of occupied country! Nevertheless, the doctor was able to conceal the existence of the radio transmitter in the village. The village, in turn, kept quiet about the parachutings. There was a vast silent conspiracy between the hillside and the valley, between the day that organized, and the night that did the work, between the men and women here and up there. . . .

Gabriel Chevalme and his friend came home along the crest of the hill, their jackets over their arms, their feet trailing in the dusty road. The friend was singing. They were walking pretty straight for people who had had a good deal to drink.

The Chevalme farm was the one with the big poplar tree, the house set back a little in a hollow, so that from the Bord farm across the path you saw only its roof. But the poplar tree could be seen from everywhere, from all the steep hillside wheatfields, from any little patch of ground where the goats grazed, from behind the little copse on the ridge, from all the slopes covered with wheat, vines, fruit trees, from the depths of the ravines, from the distant farms, from the mountain paths, and from the highway down in the valley—from everywhere you could see the tall slender poplar tree of the Chevalme farm, or at least its top, outreaching ridges and woods.

Chevalme and his friend walked towards the poplar where Chevalme's wife stood, holding little Marie-France by the hand. Chevalme's wife stamped her feet impatiently. Ordinarily she didn't much care what hour her husband came home, or whether he was drunk or sober, but today was different. She saw them quite a distance away, with the beautiful red sun, nearly spent and already half sunk behind the hill, at their backs.

The wavering voice of Chevalme's friend reached her, now stammering and now shouting, borne on the wonderfully clear air. It may have been this voice which brought a little girl in a white dress running from the Bord farm across the field, followed by a dog. She came to the edge of the path, looked towards the men, and vanished at a run, behind the sloping field, like the sun dipping behind the hill.

"Hurry!" called Chevalme's wife, as soon as they were within earshot. "Be quick!"

She stamped her feet and gesticulated, and little Marie-France, who was just big enough to walk, tried to copy her. Chevalme's wife reached the height of impatience. Even ordinarily she was a very nervous woman. There was nothing to do but listen to her talk interminably, like a tap that someone has forgotten to turn off; you felt you would soon lose your foothold in all that water. Her husband hardly talked at all, as though each word might be the last drop that would overflow the bucket.

M. Chevalme and his friend were now quite close to the poplar, and the latter had stopped singing.

"So you're bringing a friend home," Mme Chevalme began, running to meet her husband. "Let him go ahead, I have to talk to you; please go on ahead, monsieur. Why did you have to bring him along, Gabriel? Why did you have to bring a stranger? Some of the boys have been here (Marie-France, don't pull my skirt—what a plague the child is!); there'll be a crowd tonight. The little blond fellow was here with the big bearded man. I told them they have nothing to be afraid of here, or across the way, but to keep their mouths shut. They're decent people, but Jeannette is getting big, and she's so terribly curious. Just now she came all the way up to the path to see who was making the row. If she were to say anything . . . And today of all days you have to bring a stranger. Who is the fellow, anyway? I've seen him before. He came to the Blanc farm for food. Perhaps he's a militiaman? They caught a militiaman like that the other day, coming for food. . . ."

"Maybe," said Chevalme.

"What shall we do? Send him away. Just imagine if he stays the night; drunk as he is he'd be sure to stay overnight, and then what if he should talk? There was a fellow at Saint-B—— who talked, and the militia came and arrested everybody and burned the house."

"Maybe," said Chevalme.

When they entered the house the friend was already stretched out on a chair in the middle of the room, before the big table. It was quite dark; the shutters were closed and the lingering daylight entered through the door. A small red fire, coloured like a sunset, burned on the hearth. Fly papers hung from the ceiling like sausages, heavy with flies. You could just make out the big brass pendulum of the grandfather clock tick-tocking against the wall like a sentry. Chevalme went up to his friend and gave him a terrific blow. The friend collapsed without a word. Chevalme picked him up, set him against the wall beside the grandfather clock, and hit him again. The fellow, drunk and surprised as he was, had no idea of defending himself. Chevalme hit, his wife talked, and Marie-France hovered near by, enjoying it all.

"Why hit him, Gabriel?" asked Mme Chevalme. "You might have turned him out politely. Perhaps he's not a militiaman after all. You've hit him enough—stop! The little fellow said it would be round eleven o'clock, or midnight. I told him there was nothing to worry about—any time. I guess there'll be a big crowd. You'll give them a hand, won't you? I'll put Marie-France to bed right away, I'd rather have her asleep—not that there's any danger of her talking, poor darling! You'll kill him, Gabriel, stop now! Put him out, right away! . . ."

Chevalme lifted his friend under the armpits and dragged him outside. It was no small matter to get him even as far as the poplar. He couldn't have dragged him any farther. Chevalme seemed satisfied, anyway, to have got him thus far. And the man must have been satisfied, since, before Chevalme had walked the three hundred yards back to the house, he was snoring magisterially. He was a sorry sight, with a split lip, his nose clotted with drying blood, his black eye ripening beneath the moon.

There was a full moon. She appeared like a huge, antique, gold coin, full-orbed, its edges worn thin, the image effaced by the centuries. This beautiful collector's piece flooded the fields and meadows with its white splendour, and its light grew so bright that it gradually awakened the fellow at the foot of the poplar.

He opened his eyes and received the moonlight full in his face. The silence was immense. There was the moon, there was the sky;

there were the vast expanses of moon-white fields, shining like
still water, and in their midst, a building like a castle, disquietingly
white. . . . The fellow shivered. He knew neither what had happened nor where he was. His mind was confused, he was in
pain, and he would have liked to hide himself somewhere in the
shadows away from all that strange brilliance. He boldly crossed
the path, glided over the white grass of the meadow which
sloped towards the white house, almost fell down on the little
steep path into the yard, and opened the rickety gate. The yard
of the Bord farm was surrounded by low buildings, into which
the moonlight fell as into a pit-shaft. A moonstruck dog rubbed
himself against the man, but didn't bark. The man prowled
round the house. On this side it looked out over an ocean
of fields and meadows to a mountain-chain on the horizon. But
just under the windows of the house was a clump of trees, and the
man reached the shadow of the big branches, where he stretched
out, moaning gently. He felt sore all over. Soothed by the darkness,
he fell asleep.

You could have heard a pin drop. While the fellow slept under
the trees, Mme Bord and M. Bord, Jeannette's grandparents, the
young Mme and M. Bord, and Jeannette, all slept in their beds. . . .
A noise, like a sound of big drums, cymbals, and little bells,
broke the silence. It came from the Bord yard and echoed
across the fields. The whole house awoke with a start.

Young Mme Bord jumped out of bed and ran to the
window.

"It's the Curé," she whispered, her head between the shutters.
"He's picking up his bicycle . . . he ran into the pail. . . ."

"You're still dreaming," said her husband, putting on his
trousers. "The Curé in our yard in the middle of the night!"

"It's the Curé, I tell you. He must have come down the path
and run into the pail. He's rubbing his knee."

M. Bord went to the window. "It's the Curé all right," he said.
. . . "Why, there's a whole crowd out in the field. They're coming
by the back way."

Jeannette sat up in her bed and began to cry. "Mama, who are
they? Mama, I'm afraid!"

"Hush. I've told you it's the Curé." But she too was
trembling.

"I'm going down," said M. Bord. "They keep on coming. There's something very odd going on."

"Paul, don't go out! Paul!"

Mme Bord ran after her husband, who was on his way downstairs, and Jeannette ran behind her mother. "What's the matter?" cried the grandmother's toothless voice, and the grandfather appeared on the landing.

Now the whole family huddled in the black kitchen, with just one half of a shutter ajar.

The silence was gone for good. Gasogene lorries puffed in the middle of the meadow, behind the clump of trees where Chevalme's friend had hoped to find peace. A small, fast car came and went across the field. Motor-cycles passed, pounding like machine-guns. The sub-machine guns gave strange, misshapen contours to the figures of the men who were arriving from all sides. The air was filled with the sound of subdued voices, speaking in calm, even tones, as in the theatre before the curtain rises. The moon was so bright that you could see a great distance.

"It's parachutes, that's what it is," said Jeannette's father, opening the window wide. "It's parachutes, right out in the open . . ."

"What's that?" The hairpins were dropping out of the grandmother's tiny grey chignon.

"You'll see in a moment. We're right in the middle of it. The English are going to drop parcels and men."

"Here?"

"Yes, right here. Right in front of our eyes."

Jeannette had stopped crying and trembling. Grandpapa, a little old bent fellow with a drooping white moustache, stayed a moment, and then went back to bed. If they had to parachute they could do it without him.

"When the Boches find out they'll come and kill us all. They'll burn the house." Jeannette's mother was still trembling all over.

"If they come they'll have to deal with me." Young M. Bord was filled with new pride, as though he himself carried a sub-machine gun.

"Mama, look, Mama, a man's coming from under the trees. He's coming here. I'm frightened!"

The drunk came towards the house in full moonlight, a sorry sight, with dried blood all over his face, a split lip, and black eye.

"Madame," he said, in a thick, appealing voice, "where am I?" The family looked at him.

"It's an Englishman," whispered the grandmother with her toothless mouth. "A parachutist. Good lord, he's been badly knocked about. He should be brought in and taken care of."

"I know him," said her daughter-in-law. "He's the fellow who came to the Blancs' for food. Just wait till he starts talking!"

"He's drunk," her husband said. "He won't say anything. He'll think it was a dream. Can't you see, he's drunk as an owl."

"You're at the Blanc farm," said young Mme Bord. "At the Blanc farm." She repeated it to impress it on him.

"At the Blanc farm," said the man, looking about him. "At the Blanc farm," he repeated in an anxious voice, his eyes searching for something to remind him of the Blanc farm. "Oh, Madame, the Blanc farm . . ."

He walked off without asking anything more, shaking his head woefully. "He's probably saying, 'I must be even drunker than I thought'," said M. Bord.

The fellow lay down again under the trees, in the same spot, and they could still hear his hoarse litany, "Oh, Madame, Madame, Madame . . ."

"Still, he might be an Englishman," began the grandmother. "Shh . . ." said M. Bord.

There was a distant droning in the air, growing louder. . . . Lights flashed up from the meadow, glowing pencils of light turned against the sky. Thunder filled the countryside, thrilled the onlookers, passed over their heads, and died away. Presently the voices in the meadow became audible again, the drunk man's litany, "Oh, Madame, Madame", and the grandmother's muttered prayer. Then the same droning began again, growing ever louder, drowning every other sound with its ghastly din.

Three times the 'planes circled the meadow. Not until the third time, when the noise was loudest, did a black fringe appear against the sky and slowly descend, while the noise of the engines died away into the distance. The containers, released above the field, as a hand lets a letter fall into the post, came down slowly over their heads.

"Take cover under the cars!" cried a piercing voice in the meadow.

There was a great deal of running and starting of engines. . . . Tossed by the breeze, the containers descended, swept past the meadow, and disappeared in the night. The lorries got under way.

The commotion lasted until dawn. The family didn't wait for the end, but nevertheless they didn't get much sleep, except for the grandfather. From their beds they heard excited voices shout orders, heard the cars leave, the voices die away beyond the house.

When young M. Bord left the house at six o'clock, nothing remained of the Walpurgis Night except the deep wheel tracks, the trampled grass, the overturned pail, and a bicycle leaning against the stone bench in the yard, under a vine-covered trellis. The oxen were stirring in the stables. "Hey!" shouted M. Bord, opening the stable door. "Hey!"

While he followed the slow, majestic oxen through the field, shouting as if he were given them a stirring oration, the grandfather chopped wood in the yard, the grandmother tended the animals, young Mme Bord worked in the kitchen, and Jeannette slept. The sunny day, growing ever hotter, advanced and receded like other days, and everybody was ruled implacably by the needs of the earth and the animals.

The Curé arrived towards six o'clock, while they were eating. He had a large head, spectacles, and muscles that illbefitted his cassock. Jeannette was delighted; the Curé had brought her some holy pictures, very pretty ones. After the meal they went out to pick cherries, and from the top of the ladder the Curé said, "Just imagine, I've lost my bicycle . . ."

"We've kept it for you, Father," said young Mme Bord, without turning her head.

The Curé, who was breaking off a branch fringed with magnificent, shining red cherries, said nothing for a moment. It was very hot. He wiped his forehead and started to descend the ladder.

"How do you know it's mine?" he asked, stepping to the ground.

"How could we help seeing you, after all the racket you made last night, Father?"

"Well, I won't lie to you," said the Curé, choosing the ripest cherries from the branch to give to Jeannette.

When they went into the ravine to rest, they found a parachute caught in a tree, and, showing no surprise, they began to disengage it from the branches and gather up the weapons which lay scattered about.

The doctor had learned that Doriot's men, from the neighbouring town, were preparing to blow up his house. One shouldn't feel that the danger was over simply because there were no Boches in the offing, or because the policemen of a whole department had taken to the *maquis*, or because of the landing. The doctor had found an empty château in the vicinity of the village and had sent his wife and children there. He had even tried to do so without letting anyone know about it, although in that neighbourhood it was considered low and cowardly to hide oneself and take precautions.

It might have been called a château, but really it was just a big, deserted house, full of mildew. The little boy lost his way in the great rooms, on the vast staircases, in the corridors, cellars, and hidden corners. They heard him cry, but they couldn't discover where the crying came from.

The park was a lawn bordered by tall trees, with a dried-up fountain in front of the house and old stone benches in the shade; swarms of bees droned like aeroplanes.

On the ground floor of the château, level with the lawn, in the high cupboards of the vast, empty rooms, the owners had stuffed away all the linens, silverware, and bedding—all the things they wanted to save in case the house in the village was blown up. The cupboards were crammed, and would only stay closed when they were locked. The kitchen, which also opened on to the lawn, was a mess: pots and pans on the floor, provisions, jars, faggots, and logs everywhere; you tripped over the long flex of the radio, which was plugged into a socket in the kitchen, while the radio itself talked and sang out on the lawn. They took their tea in front of the house, and ate bread spread with honey that ran down over their fingers and over the table, light and sticky as resin. The little girls wiped their fingers on their bare thighs. The boy made water in front of a tree, in full view of the family. They had left the light lorry in the park, where it smelled faintly of petrol, close to the tea table. Big Cousin Albert, scantily clad, carried the bundles, brought hot water, and ran errands on his bicycle. He had good teeth, a hint of down on his cheeks, and used his young strength only on command. What he really liked to do was make tarts; the baker, in whose house the first aid post had been installed, had taught him. When Cousin Albert kneaded the dough, he drew it out and back, like playing an accordion. The doctor's son-in-law ran errands too, when he was asked. He had cyclist's calves, and wore glasses.

They hadn't brought the children, because it would have made them too tired. This parachuting was a family affair. They left the château before eleven o'clock, some on foot, and others in the lorry. They must be there before eleven o'clock, even though *they* never came before 1 a.m. and sometimes not at all. A vast expanse of field, whose dim boundaries were invisible, uneven ground, stones, grass, trampled wheat that lashed the legs, shadows moving and talking.... There were about thirty people, unarmed.

They waited. Those who had had experience kept out of the way of the doctor, who was likely to force a flashlight into their hands and put them at one end of the field, from which they mustn't budge until after the 'planes had left. That was tiresome. It was cool and dark. Most of the parachutings took place at full moon, but not this one. People began to sit on the ground, on thorns and stones, leaning against each other. They talked about the landing in the South, which they waited for as eagerly as the first landing, and as they now waited for the 'planes. Who was that talkative fellow? He wasn't from this part of the country. He had a Southern accent.... Oh, he's a specialist sent from Marseilles. A specialist in parachutings! All they knew of this shadow in a basque beret was his voice, his orders.... With the morning, the man would vanish at cockcrow, and next night he'd reappear in another field in another corner of France. Strange

profession! Midnight, twelve-thirty, one o'clock, one-thirty.
. . . Waiting, waiting. . . .

A voice said, "Here's the field, but where are the
blighters?"

The "blighters" were here, waiting for something that didn't
come.

Then the droning started. Everybody up!

"Light!" shouted the doctor. The flashlight carriers at the
four corners of the field must send up their shafts of light into the
sky. But there were only three of them! Where on earth was the
fourth?

"Albert!" thundered the doctor in a terrific voice, without
regard for the silence of the night, or indeed for secrecy. "Albert,
light up! Albert! Damn that fellow!"

The droning deepened, like the sound a train makes crossing
a bridge. A single 'plane circled the field. There was someone down there directing it with a mysterious apparatus. The
miracle was about to happen: this 'plane, having left Algiers
in impenetrable darkness, was going to deliver here on this field,
on this minute point of France, our means for defending ourselves, and for attacking. . . . Wonder of human science! The
rumbling shadow of the 'plane glided above the dark, silent
field. In the sky, watched so passionately, shone a faint Milky
Way, and great, brilliant stars. Suddenly black spots appeared, like
the spots that float before your eyes when your liver is out of
order. But perhaps you've never had liver trouble, so let us say
that the objects floating up there were darker than the atmosphere. The 'plane was already far away and forgotten, and still
they floated there, lower and lower, closer and closer. They were
just overhead, they would fall on you! People who have been at
parachutings know that no matter what corner of the field you
are in you have the feeling that the containers are coming right
at you and are going to drop on your head. Slow and silent as black
cats, the objects passed the waiting people and disappeared into
the night.

The problem was to find them. The wheat-stalks lashed the
searchers' legs, pebbles scattered underfoot, the ground dipped
into ditches, high weeds and tangled undergrowth tripped
up the feet. A black velvet hedge indicated the edges of the field.

They ran hither and thither, until a pale, round, strange, immense, soft shape appeared on the ground. Found one? And this
—what's this white mass? A piece of wood? The skeleton of an
antediluvian beast? It has the curve of a huge spinal column, and
the stripes of gigantic ribs. . . . It's a huge, white, black-striped
parachute. Let's run right and left, and search. There's one,
there's another, more and more. . . . Lightly unfolded, like great
handkerchiefs fallen out of a pocket, like round spider's webs with
thin, solid threads supporting a dark, heavy cylinder, a veritable
strong-box. Twenty, twenty-three, twenty-five. . . . The women
darted about like gun-dogs, the men loaded the containers on to the
lorry. A small car carried away the fragile parcels. The driver was
a Lieutenant X., a very elegant young man, with a drawing-room
voice: "How are you, my dear lady?" The doctor's voice was not
a drawing-room voice. He thundered across the field: "Albert!
Where's Albert?"

Cousin Albert and the doctor's son-in-law were rolled up in a
blanket, asleep, in a far corner of the field which they should have
lighted up. They had seen nothing, heard nothing. They came
up in a daze, running into the containers.

The small car had left. The lorry puffed and stank. This
was its fourth trip, the last. This time it would take the
people back. Now it rolled along a narrow, winding road, as
dangerous as the Boches, or as the containers overhead. They
arrived at last, thank God!

A courtyard. The dark outline of a house. No, it's not the
château, don't expect an entrance on this side. Oh, I see. What
next? Come this way. The door didn't open immediately. Compared with the recent tumult, strange precautions were now taken.
You stumbled through a long, dark room that smelled of mildew.
through an opened door into a cavern.

Narrow, deep, vaulted, with dripping walls, just like a rob-
ber's den. The light was red and dim. Weapons lay on a blanket
on the ground. Right and left of the blanket a row of men, and
at the back, facing the door, the elegant lieutenant in command.
The weapons were passed from hand to hand to the rear,
filling up the shelves and recesses of the cellar. Then the
blanket was folded, and they went on to the next container,
which was rolled in like a barrel. They opened it, removed

the blanket in which the arms were wrapped, and spread it out like a rug. Each sub-machine gun was wrapped in a khaki shirt. The wrapping seemed to have been done by a careful woman, as she might have wrapped up her toilet flasks to keep them from breaking during a journey. The arms were passed back, sorted, and stacked. More containers arrived: hand grenades, various plastic objects. . . . Everything went very fast—necessarily, for day was near. They picked up the chocolate that was strewn among the weapons, and the khaki shirts. The doctor tried one on. It had big pockets, and looked like a jacket. The doctor, posing like a model, walked about the cellar. He looked like a bull with the head of an emperor.

Finished. All the containers were empty. The parachutes were stacked up one on top of the other. They looked strange in the light. You could see that they weren't all white: some of them were soft green, some pink. . . . They would make nice silk shirts and dresses, or good dish-cloths, if they were made of cotton. They, together with the chocolate and cigarettes, were the helpers' reward.

It was dawn outside. High time to return. After all, the country was still alive with Boches. The chirping birds, the virgin freshness of the air, the greenness of the trees, couldn't alter that fact. The bicycles rustled along the road. They soon reached the village. The eyes of the houses were still closed, but they saw everything. And tomorrow the empty street would tell what it had seen. Steps rang out, and the bicycles, pushed by hand, clattered over the bumps. The doors creaked. . .

Time to light the fire, prepare the breakfast coffee; already you could hear the seven-thirty news. Then to bed by day, to sleep uneasily, as if drugged, with the light on your eyelids and only a thin partition between the noises of the awakened village and the half-submerged consciousness.

How painful the awakening! How one would like to disbelieve those knocks at the door, that voice repeating: "The Germans are marching on the village in force. They're only two miles away . . ." "Oh, let me sleep! You can't fool me! Let me sleep! It's only nine o'clock." The friendly night was hardly over in our weary bodies and throbbing heads before we were confronted by this raw, cruel, implacable day, forced to believe in the hateful, insolent roar of 'planes grazing the roofs. Dreadful awakening! Machine-guns rattled. It was true. The Boches had come.

Masonry was shattering like glass. The 'planes dived very low, as though they meant to drive themselves like nails into the narrow streets. It was as though the villagers were already under-ground, exterminated; there was nobody, absolutely nobody in the streets and lanes. "We're still here! Give up hope!" the metallic voices vituperated from above. They dived upon the village, spat and righted themselves, circling back into the sky.

Oh, to get away while they're still up there, so they shan't have you except in death. To get away before their unclean hands strangle whatever is left to think and breathe and feel. To get out of their path, to preserve those hearts which beat to destroy them, hearts as precious as bullets. Don't waste your ammunition!

The bright, burning sun was implacable as they. There wasn't a shadow in the fields. Oh, to get underground, so they won't be able to see from above the small, running, crawling shadows! . . . The flying dragons dived towards the tiny shadows, pursuing those black ants scurrying off between the dropping bullets—the daily petty miracle of war. The sun; the speed; the thirst! A thirst unknown before, the thirst of the desert, a mortal thirst, the thirst of a whole lifetime, parching the very arms and legs, paralysing the tongue, stifling speech.

The little defile was steep. It led into the hills, far from the 'planes and the sun. There were cherry trees up there, cherries that would quench your thirst . . .

From up there you could see the village steeple, the 'planes circling round. . . . Farther, higher yet! Let's put miles between us and them! There were some cherries on a tree, half-eaten by the birds; black, warm, sweet, they seemed to revive you. Up, and up. . . .

In the little copse on the ridge there was some shade, and wild strawberries. The bright blue sky was clear and clean, the vast silence streaked with bursts of machine-gun fire, coming now from below. From there you could see the various slopes, the fields, farms and hollows, and the big poplar of the Chevalme farm. Here you could sleep a fragrant sleep, mottled with sun and shade. Or you could remain with open eyes, engulfed in imagined horror . . . the doctor, as he had been last night, prancing round the cavern in his American shirt, while they unpacked the weapons . . . and then as he may be now, the big corpse stretched out the way you see them on the screen, when the Boches show you the "Atrocities of Katyn", or the victims of a railway accident; a row of mutilated corpses, the big body of the doctor, and the bodies of the little girls with honey-sticky fingers. . . . "Light! Albert, damn that fellow!". . . Mutilated bodies lined up on the ground. . . . No, stop it! This is reality.

Help! They're playing their usual game. The men at the stake, with their arms in the air, are being flogged with wet ropes. The little wounded fellow at the baker's house lies in the garden, his legs slashed, his eyes torn out, his head crushed. They're drunk; they throw down the women, young, old, and little girls. They whistle through their fingers, and others come, ten of them to one. . . . Help! They pillage, sack, rape. . . .

They go up into the hills. They sack the farms, kill the cattle, throw the eggs against the walls, stuff their mouths with cheese, shoot the fugitives right and left, at random. . . . The edge of the little copse is littered with bullets, but the innocent, fragrant clump of trees has concealed the sleepers and their dreams. Just as the cavern has kept the secret of the arms parachuted by night, even though the deep wheel tracks in the farmyard lead straight there. They fire at a man leaving his house, who falls, understanding nothing, at the woman and children crossing the lawn in front of the château, who leap over the wall and run across the fields. . . . Towards evening their lorries, which arrived empty, leave the village loaded with furniture, bicycles, and radios. The fifteen hundred Boches move off, carrying hostages with them.

They left havoc behind them; yawning doors, windows smashed by rifle butts. Everyone suffered his share: those who liked the Boches and those who didn't, those who had "nothing to reproach themselves for", and those who had. The houses were all turned upside down, like this one abandoned so hastily only that morning, and which you now entered through a breach in the door. Ashes from the stove, scattered over the

floor, crunched underfoot. . . . Furniture overturned and broken,
empty wardrobes, drawers pulled out and turned upside down. A
strong odour of faded roses pervaded this house of crime. Their
petals were strewn on the floor, crushed amid the ashes, as though
flattened between the pages of a book. *They* had stripped them
from our gardens and dropped them here, and they enriched the
nightmare with their fragrance.

And this other dark house, in a dusky park. . . . The doctor
crossed the lawn, ringed with big trees, pushed open the door.
The shutters were closed; he tried to switch on the light, but it
didn't work. . . . He stumbled over furniture, stepped in spilt
wine, put his hands in the sticky honey that ran everywhere. On
the floor were mattresses, on the mattresses shapes. . . . What
were they? It couldn't possibly be. . . . No, it wasn't, God be
praised! More wreckage. The big cupboards were empty, the
mattresses on the floor disembowelled, everything broken and
turned upside down. . . . All the fragile things brought here from
the parachuting last night, the radio transmitter, the surgical
instruments, the foodstuffs, were gone. But where were his wife
and children? Where were they?

I cannot bear to answer. I cannot speak of that terrible discovery. . . .

The crushed, looted village had been unnerved by fear. It
had just enough strength left to curse. Those who liked the
Boches, those who thought they were safe because they "had
nothing to reproach themselves for", the collaborators, the
cowards, the cautious, those concerned only with preserving their
private lives undisturbed, all had to find a scapegoat, someone
they could hate without danger, someone in the family whom
they could take it out on without compunction—the already-
beaten, the disarmed, the barefooted, the so-called Dissidents,
Defaulters, Patriots, or simply the Boys. . . . The Resistance, that
mob of good-for-nothings, riff-raff, bandits—damn them all
to Hell!

In the village, which was now almost as empty as on the
dreadful day of the attack, where strangers roamed the streets
now defaced by their boarded-up windows, housewives who had
risen at dawn found leaflets under their doors. The Resistance,

hope riveted to their hearts, tenacious and obstinate, those under suspicion, were still speaking to those quite unsuspected.

Someone was awake, someone went about in the night, furtive and invisible, carrying from door to door the spirit of the Resistance; someone was still trying to convince and explain:

RESIST, YOU WHO HAVE SUFFERED!

CITIZENS tried by the terrorist raids of the Boches; citizens who have been looted, ruined, insulted and maltreated by the soldiers of the German Army, whose instincts are lower than the instincts of animals; citizens of the cities, villages, the countryside of France, try not to lose courage: this is the last stage before the liberation. It is the hardest stage, because, before he leaves, the usurper drops his mask, showing the face of a people who have let themselves be ruled by Hitler. . . . Four years of misery have proved to us that treason and cowardice do not pay, that to acquiesce and submit is futile. We have proof that the Germans do not keep their word, that they have not even respected the vile clauses of the armistice. Let no one tell us any longer that we should truckle to them! Let no one tell us that the Resistance is responsible for the terrorist raids of the Germans. *It is not the Resistance which has created oppression, it is oppression which has called forth the Resistance.*

We have been asked to fawn on them, and what have we gained? Hundreds of thousands of martyrs, prisoners, executions, deportations, and forced labour. Who still believes in the magnanimity of "our gracious conquerors"?

Do not work against the Resistance. To decry it is to undermine it. If blunders have been made in your town or village or on your farm, owing to youthfulness, inexperience, hasty organization, try to rectify them, and don't use them to hamper the action of the Patriots. Do not echo Dr. Goebbels' propaganda; you know that the Resistance, consisting of your sons, brothers, husbands, is not a horde of bandits but the young French Army. To condemn it is to condemn France, now ready to do what it was kept from doing in 1940, to defend and liberate itself. Woe to those who are always on the side of the strongest, who today treat the Resistance as riff-raff, but who will welcome them as heroes once the victory is won!

Remember: The German Army is now retreating on all fronts, its morale has been shaken, and the effective strength of the German Army in the French interior is by no means as great as they wish us to believe. The Boches can no longer be everywhere at once.

And now, when they wish to make a show of strength by terrorizing a village or a helpless town, they can only do so by seriously depleting neighbouring sectors, at times a whole department.

Then stop saying "We are too weak, we have no arms, we must submit to being exterminated." This is not true. The French Forces of the Interior already hold the invader in check at many points; help them to shorten the war. Non-resistance can only prolong it, intensify its horrors. Every one of you must aid the Resistance according to his means, however limited. It is no mean task; the patient labour of the ants will always, in the end, get rid of the carrion that seem about to crush the antheap.

Remember those sacred lines:

> *Entendez-vous dans nos campagnes*
> *Mugir ces féroces soldats?*
> *Ils viennent jusque dans nos bras*
> *Egorger nos fils, nos compagnes!*
> *Aux armes, citoyens! . . .*

Nothing has changed since the days which gave birth to the *Marseillaise*. Yet, if these lines seem to describe with striking accuracy the atrocities which we witness today, let us not forget that to their rhythm a people, thought incapable of defending themselves, having to improvise both their weapons and their leaders, ejected from French soil a "modern" army supposedly invincible, the Prussian army, routed at Valmy.

June, 1944.

True, the landing wasn't such a great thing after all; true, if they don't hurry up the *others* will do for us yet; but nevertheless here we are, weak against strong, and time will tell the tale.

Look at this town, a place where one would stop only to change trains. A town which is just a railway junction, a plain criss-crossed with tracks, a dumping ground for hundreds of scrapped locomotives, rusty and worn out. The tracks cross the town, skirt the main street, cleft by a menacing zigzag trench, a large timbered cinema, and shops filled with the most beautiful fruit in the world. The town is too flat, the streets are too wide, too badly paved, a Wild-West town, a mining town. The trees bordering the street, so small and meagre, look as though they have just been planted. The sham villas are built of boards, and grass sprouts in the wasteland of the public square.

A fair is in progress. Merry-go-rounds, swings, little motor-cars that chase each other and collide. A dense crowd, dressed uniformly in grey-green, saunter about as though they had a right to these innocent games. Last night these men were at the village. Individuals can be recognized. The assassins are having a good time. It's natural; it's astounding! You can go through the crowd and rub shoulders with a man who, last night, ransacked a home, destroyed the possessions of a lifetime, the bedding, and the bicycle; it was he who killed your husband, raped your daughter.

A black lorry charges down the street. Beneath the tarpaulin men are lying on their stomachs, men dressed in black, sinister and savage, pointing machine-guns and sub-machine-guns on to the road. The militia! Beware!

Homeless people roam the streets, finding no place to spend the brief night before they depart by train at dawn. Everything is full. The Boches have taken everything. The profiteering townspeople are renting their beds. The young butcher's wife rents her nuptial bedroom; she has beautiful breasts: as beautiful as the fruit in the shops. The bedroom is large, everything in it new, for she has just been married. In the middle there's a big, low, polished bed with a sky-blue quilted satin cover, flowered bedside rugs, mirrors, and on the marble mantelpiece a wedding picture of the butcher and his wife. Have you any weapons, ladies and gentlemen? The Germans search everywhere. If they find one they'll kill you on the spot, and me too. But above all, don't forget to close your shutters at night. No, not against the mosquitoes, but there's a blackout. The Germans shoot through the windows. . . . What an awful position, in the middle of the zigzag trench, and right by the tracks! If there should be an Alert, come down into the cellar with us, without switching on the light. . . . Remember—without switching on the light.

The complete silence of the night and the inhuman brightness of the searchlights enter through the window and the open shutters—but what can you do, it's so hot? In their abject fear of the *maquis* the Germans don't hesitate to light up the zigzag trench as brightly as possible. A long, leaden silence, not even the buzzing of a mosquito. . . . And then, out of the depth of the silence, from its very core, a piercing sound swells beyond endurance, desperate, the very voice of despair. . . . A siren! It sinks to take breath, the breath required for these interminable wails, going, coming, intertwining. It can't go on any longer. The cry dwindles and dies. Mortal silence. . . . Then voices, and heavy steps: it has awakened them! . . . But they're too busy to shoot into the windows, or to raid the houses: the bed of the butcher's wife is so alluring. . . .

Tonight this didn't happen here, but it must have happened somewhere else. When these things happen, the trains run behind schedule; six hours, ten hours.

At this period it was said in France that there were only two public services that functioned: railways and derailments. Here's an example: A certain station-master was asked by a traveller, "Is the X train late?" "Yes," replied the station-master, "my son has just left to derail it." It took all the courage and devotion of the railway men, all their skill and sense of duty, to help derail the German trains, and yet keep them rolling and arriving no more than eighteen hours late.

The trains are not very full, for the siren frightens passengers away, and it's likely to go off anywhere. Only the *Wehrmacht* and the Resistance are still travelling, except for a few diehards in search of food or black markets.

Here's a long train going at a walking pace. It dawdles along, starts, stops, starts again. . . . Everybody out! Time bombs have been discovered on the tracks. You must walk a few miles and take the train again on the other side of the danger point. The train starts rolling, slowly, grinding slowly, forwards. Dusk descends over the landscape; there's a town, or rather the remains of a town. A street formed of single, jagged walls, the framework of the windows, heaps of rubble. . . . The inhabitants, planted like trees along the road, stand motionless. They watch the crowd of travellers, the mass of field-grey soldiers plodding along like a routed army, and the few Frenchmen lost among them as though they were their prisoners (which they would have been had the others known!). They pass through the remnants of the town and vanish in the night.

2

Crumbling houses, derailed trains, blasted pylons, factories, bridges, men falling, hearts beating, weapons emerging from all the hideouts. . . .

In the midst of this infernal noise, which came from everywhere at once, from high and low, the country compacted itself for the final leap. Yet the roads were deserted; nobody was fool enough to walk out openly in the daytime. . . . There has never been anything like these empty roads of August, '44, unless it was the roads after the exodus of June, '40. Not a soul, nobody, except, as in 1940, German columns all moving in the same direction, the roads so blocked you can hardly pass. The agonizing France of 1940, realm of the sleeping beauty, everything remaining petrified wherever disaster had overtaken it, the trains motionless, the motor-cars in the garages, the people avoiding the smallest gesture, except to smoke the victor's cigarettes. France of 1944, exasperated, erect, scorching the soil, the better to warm the feet of the fugitive ex-victors in all their various vehicles, in removal vans, butcher carts, ice trucks, oxcarts, donkey carts, on bicycle, on foot, foolishly camouflaged in leafage that makes them all the more conspicuous. The cheering, heartening, dreadful spectacle of columns of field-grey prisoners on the roads, or billeted here and there, with faces the colour of their uniforms, their blue eyes pale with humiliation and panic, their shoulders bowed in resignation. They look like convicts brutalized by terror and ill-treatment, a look they couldn't have acquired in their few days of captivity, which they must have hidden all the time under their polished exteriors. How they march in step! How faultlessly they stand in formation! How they snap to attention before the Frenchmen. . . . The Frenchmen who escort them, the Boys, dressed and armed you can imagine how, sunburnt, boisterous and excited, at the peak of their courage, their self-devotion, living their own apotheosis; the Boys dissipate the torpor that envelops these lamentable men whom they have caught in the trap of France. For the Boches have spared us nothing, not even the terrible duty of humiliating other men, of trampling upon that for which, and because of which, we have suffered; human dignity. If only they could get to hell somewhere else!

On June 6 the message "A fine of two hundred francs for the first rip" announced the first landing.

On August 15 there was more damage . . . I've never been able to learn the cost of this one, for by that time the whole fabric was in tatters. In our impatience we had all begun tearing it apart.

Paris,
   November, 1944.

THE END

The first Virago Modern Classic was published in London in 1978, launching a list dedicated to the celebration of women writers and to the rediscovery and reprinting of their works. While the series is called "Modern Classics" it is not true that these works of fiction are universally and equally considered "great," although that is often the case. Published with new critical and biographical introductions, books appear in the series for different reasons: sometimes for their importance in literary history; sometimes because they illuminate particular aspects of women's lives, both personal and public. They may be classics of comedy or storytelling; their interest can be historical, feminist, political, or literary. In any case, in their variety and richness they promise to confuse forever the question of what women's fiction is about, while at the same time affirming a true female tradition in literature.

Initially, the Virago Modern Classics concentrated on English novels and short stories published in the early decades of the century. As the series has grown, it has broadened to include works of fiction from different centuries and from different countries, cultures, and literary traditions; there are books written by black women, by Catholic and Jewish women, by women of almost every English-speaking country, and there are several relevant novels by men.

Nearly 200 Virago Modern Classics will have been published in England by the end of 1985. During that same year, Penguin Books began to publish Virago Modern Classics in the United States, with the expectation of having some 40 titles from the series available by the end of 1986. Some of the earlier books in the series were published in the United States by The Dial Press.

Other PENGUIN/VIRAGO MODERN CLASSICS